A FAE DESTINY NOVEL

A KINGDOM OF DECEIT AND DESIRE

LESLIE O'SULLIVAN

A KINGDOM OF DECEIT AND DESIRE
Fae Destiny, Book 2

CITY OWL PRESS
www.cityowlpress.com

Cover Design by MiblArt. All stock photos licensed appropriately.

Page Edges by Painted Wings Publishing Services.

Edited by Lisa Green.

For information on subsidiary rights, please contact the publisher at info@cityowlpress.com.

Paperback Edition ISBN: 978-1-64898-501-0

Hardback Edition ISBN: 978-1-64898-502-7

Digital Edition ISBN: 978-1-64898-500-3

Printed in the United States of America

ALSO BY LESLIE O'SULLIVAN

Fae Destiny:

A Kingdom of Souls and Shadows

A Kingdom of Deceit and Desire

A Kingdom of Witches and Wanderers

***

Rockin Fairy Tales:

Pink Guitars and Falling Stars

Gilded Butterfly

Wild Azure Waves

Crimson Melodies

Emerald Spire

***

Behind the Scenes:

Hot Set

Press Release

Not to Scale

PRAISE FOR LESLIE O'SULLIVAN

"Romantic and magical, O'Sullivan whisks you away to an Ireland you could only dream of… Except it could very well be real." — *Evelyn Skye, New York Times Bestselling author of Damsel*

"O'Sullivan's writing is rich with metaphors. The story from reality to the secret Veil is so seamless, you believe it's truly possible. *A Kingdom of Souls and Shadows* is full of charming characters, intriguing Celtic folklore, and a delicious slow-burn romance. A perfect introduction to the romantasy genre." — *Dana Elmendorf, author of In the Hour of Crows, a GMA Buzz Pick*

"Full of surprises, lots of surprises, and secrets, lots of secrets that left me speechless. Everything Eala learns makes her question her life and who she really is. The book ends with a question which I can't wait to be answered in the next book in the series. I highly recommend. 5 Stars."— *Paranormal Romance Guild*

"*A Kingdom of Souls and Shadows* was a great read. I loved Eala and Sion both as individual characters and as a couple. They both felt very real and relatable (yes, the 200-year-old man felt relatable to a modern woman). O'Sullivan takes Irish folklore and moves it forward into the next century in a fun and exciting way." — *Cosmic Circus*

"*Pink Guitars and Falling Stars* is an interesting take on the story of Rapunzel…O'Sullivan has definitely nailed the initial animosity between Justin and Zeli. As they become closer, the relationship jumps off the page and morphs beautifully. There are awesome love scenes with a lot of description which pull the reader right in and keep a tight grip… A fascinating remix of a popular fairy tale with some very sexy differences. One to add to the e-reader and to be read list!" — *InD'tale*

"*Hot Set,* by Leslie O'Sullivan, is a contemporary love story that creatively infuses modern concerns with the nostalgia generated by a period television show. The Irish setting was fantastically romantic, and I thought the cast of characters was refreshingly practical for a group involved in show business." — *Reader's Favorite 5-star review*

"*Pink Guitars and Falling Stars* is a fast paced and very engaging read, with a constantly evolving main character and a colorful cast. The adventure wraps up nicely, and ends with a hint of what is next in the Rockin' Fairy Tales series. This is a great read if you are looking for an action-packed modern fairy tale with aspiring rock stars who fall from the sky." — *Paranormal Romance Guild*

"*Gilded Butterfly* is a unique and magical mashup of fairy tales, Shakespeare, and lore, unlike anything I've read before. At its heart, is a beautiful story about family, the destructive power of chasing fame and money, and the healing power of love. The twists, turns, and magic sprinkled throughout create an engaging story that brings a new kind of fairy tale to modern Hollywood." — *Megan Van Dyke, author of Second Star to the Left*

"Submerging readers into a fantastical world, *Wild Azure Waves* is a love story swimming with music, mysticism, and magic… Villains deliver with evil schemes and diabolical characteristics that readers will hear their sinister chuckle every time they are on the page. Leslie O'Sullivan's whimsical fantasy tale is an interesting take on sorrow, second chances, and soulmates." — *InD'tale*

"With wickedly clever wordplay, fresh and lovable characters, and an utterly unique take on a classic fairytale, *Pink Guitars and Falling Stars* is one of the swooniest romances I've ever read. You'll be cheering for B.A.S.E. jumper Justin to help Zeli escape her tower in the heart of Hollywood's twisted music industry and fall equally hard for their chosen family on the Boulevard. A romantic, heart-in-your-throat read!" — *Sarah Skilton, author of Fame Adjacent*

To Diane, Flo, and Laurie, the cherished sisters I always hoped for.

Finnbheara's Riddle

Passage sought to lands of mine.
Where wish and dream bide free.
Tales of old both true and told.
Will guide your quest to Sidhe.

To solve the task takes more than eyes.
Claim wit and guile your parlance.
The deadline comes when mortal moon.
Does lose its way and substance.

Face the ridge of grey and go.
When mortals fall to dream.
Upon the crest above fine lands.
A stone will wake with screams.

There is a number full complete.
Its quota ripe to fill.
A sharpened star shall be the proof.
Your path twists to my will.

Greed and haste may tempt your fate.
Be steadfast in restraint.
A thoughtless act is ruin's lure.
Your victories courting taint.

Discoveries bold you'll need to solve.
This ultimate conclusion:
What's all and each the selfsame piece.
Plain truth and no illusion?

A warning now. I must decry.
To launch our bargain true.
If failure be your end result.
My judgement is your due.

CHAPTER 1
THE KING'S RIDDLE

My curtsy before Finnbheara, the King of the Connacht Fae, sets my eyes inches from well-formed thighs, which his fitted silver and white metallic tunic do nothing to hide. I immediately lower my head to avoid the appearance of ogling the Faerie king. Impropriety is not a great start when I'm on the verge of bargaining with a mythical figure for the destiny I need to control.

Even though the air is cool and soothing, fear sends a rush of heat through me. My impulsive plan has to work. Everything that matters to me depends on not taking a single misstep.

My raging nerves are a bold contrast to the gentle strains of a violin and the barest hint of bells that permeate the transparent mist surrounding us. It's only been moments, but time flaunts its gift of endlessness as I wait for Finnbheara's response to my proposal.

What have I done?

I've asked this man, a Fae King, possibly the most powerful ruler of the *Tuath Dé Dannan*, the Irish Fae, to bargain with me. The Eala Duir I thought I was would never dream of being so bold.

Dream.

I wish I were dreaming. My current predicament mocks even the most outrageous of my dreams. This place, this reality, the Tír na nÓg where I stand, is the fodder of legends from stories my Irish grandmother, Máthair, told me as a child. Those same stories my soulmate, Sionnach, created as shadow plays in hearth flames. He spun fantastic tales for a girl who had no idea she wasn't a girl at all, but rather the concoction of a Fae King as a gift to his former human lover…my grandmother.

Out of the corner of my eye, I see Sion, the man I love, calling far too much attention to himself in the king's presence by frantically searching for a way out of here. The irony makes my head pound. A heartbeat ago, this was exactly the place we wished to be.

With a light touch, The Fae king lifts my chin until our gazes meet. "There's no need for posturing, dear Eala." Full, graceful lips curve into a sly smile as his hands take mine, helping me rise to my feet. It's as if his touch calms my fear.

The man is breathtaking. Pronounced cheekbones and a strong jaw enhance the beauty he radiates. "It is no secret I enjoy dealing in bargains." A deep melodious chuckle rumbles from his pretty Faerie lips as he tucks my hand through the crook of his elbow. "I expect no less than a well-crafted proposal from a child of my making."

Behind us, Sion unleashes his signature grunt that I pray the royal doesn't notice. I fight the urge not to pull my focus from Finnbheara to shoot Sionnach a warning look. Doesn't the stubborn man understand our future is dangling by a frayed thread? This is no damn time to spill distaste for the king all over the silver and green grass carpeting the threshold of Tír na nÓg.

Finnbheara whirls toward Sion, anger spiking. "Silence, spawn of Loho, or I'll add another fox to my menagerie."

I do seize this opportunity to widen my eyes at Sion with my own plea for his silence. I'm well aware that he and Finnbheara have history, and not a pretty one. My heartbeat stutters. I only exist because of that history. The king never would've created me if Sion didn't need help putting an end to the soulfall he was bound to. A parade of trapped souls would be forever banned from their chosen afterlives if together, we hadn't found the keys to open the gateway to their eternities. That shared purpose opened our hearts to one another.

The king tilts his head to one side, then the other, studying me with narrowed eyes. I swear his intensity forms ice crystals in my blood. "No," he says and runs a fingertip along the side of my face. "You are not a child. The beads of being I ignited into life successfully flourished into a woman of singular beauty." He closes his eyes and inhales deeply. "Ah, I sense bountiful talents lying within you. I have done well."

The crystals melt as warmth from his compliment soothes me.

Finnbheara pinches a lock of my flighty white-blonde hair and lets it fall strand by strand, seemingly mesmerized at the way each bit floats from his grasp. The admiration in his expression shifts as his eye color changes from lavender to peach, before settling into the smoldering deep orange shade of a banked fire ready to leap back to life. His gaze sweeps brazenly down my body, and I shiver. My shape is completely visible through the sheer, knee-length Fae tunic both Sion and I were clothed in once we shifted from fox and swan back into human form here in the Faerie realm. I suppose I should be grateful Finnbheara didn't leave us naked.

I fight the feeling of helplessness clutching at me. There's a clear imbalance of power between us that I can't discount.

The king's brazen, lustful stare deserves my disgust, but in truth, fascination and curiosity for this living myth give me pause. I've fallen into a bizarre firsthand research opportunity. It's a powerful draw for my scholar's brain.

Finnbheara's perpetual youth does add to his allure. The Fae looks to be close to my twenty-eight years, certainly not a day over thirty. His loveliness is difficult, no, impossible, to turn away from. An unexpected sense of pleasure courses through my body, shifting my offense at his prideful scrutiny into appreciation of his flattery. Lightheadedness threatens to overtake me as I'm drawn toward this elegant man.

Before our bodies touch, a hundred tiny pinpoints of heat prick my insides. The Veil sprites, internal magical flickers gifted to me when I first accepted the truth of Faeries, swim through my spirit. Their tiny stings prevent me from falling into the near-trance the king's attention invites.

Stay focused, Eala.

Finnbheara encircles my wrist with his fingers, extending my bare arm to study it. To my surprise, a faint river of golden light runs beneath my skin. It matches the odd color of the freckles covering my body. I've been able to feel but never witness the Veil sprites within me in any detail before.

Finnbheara smirks at the wandering glow. "Yes, you are a success indeed." He slowly circles his fingers up from my arm to my shoulder, his gaze never leaving mine. The royal contact summons my Veil sprites, and they cluster around his touch.

The tips of his fingers travel higher along the side of my neck, reigniting pleasant sensations. A swift movement off to my right steals my attention as well as the king's. Sion, with clenched fists and ruddy curls bobbing, charges in our direction.

I snap out of the Faerie's influence and raise my hand. "Everything is fine, Sion." I'm terrified of what may happen if he tries to lay a hand on the king.

Finnbheara looks bored as he flicks his wrist. Advancing out of the mist is a line of Fae soldiers. There are men and women among them, most statuesque and sculpted from the same lithe muscles as the king. A few echo Finnbheara's intimidating physique from his appearance as a colossus-sized warrior on the sea cliffs near Sion's cottage, albeit they assume more human dimensions. My mind twirls as it attempts to fit the passage of time into a logical frame. It seems as if only moments have passed since the king came to my aid when Olk was seconds from killing Sionnach and his parents.

Each soldier bears the youthfulness of the king with faces that exude a mix of cruel beauty similar to their monarch. The Faerie uniforms match the breastplate of white-gold armor the king wore when he answered my call in the mortal world. He's swapped it for his current garb of pale green trousers and a metallic tunic stamped with branches and leaves.

The woodsy pattern repeats across the soldiers' armor. A single embossed leaf the size of a hand rests on the space over every heart. Within the veins of each emblem is a thin line of bubbling liquid colored indigo or a radiant quicksilver, while others flow with an iridescence that doesn't settle on a single hue. I'm again distracted by my appetite for detail. What do the different colors mean?

The assortment of weapons, swords for some, and quivers and bows for others, are no joke. The presence of medieval weaponry sends a message that this may not be the magical realm of agelessness and peace from the stories. Irish histories, real or legend, filled with battles for power, territory, and even forbidden love, may be more on the nose for Tír na nÓg.

I press my fingernail into my palm. I must stay aware and on guard. Keeping our vulnerability at the forefront of my thoughts is survival.

A Faerie man and woman slide out of line to restrain Sion. Instead of exhibiting the potential for brutal power they surely possess, they are as graceful as wildflowers swaying in a lazy breeze. Their fluid movements are the opposite of my soulmate's full body clench.

"My patience wanes, fox," says the king, striding toward Sionnach. "You barrel your way into my kingdom without soulsong or invitation." When he wrenches Sion's chin up with a jerk devoid of the gentleness he showed me, my stomach cramps with fear. As strong as my soulmate is, Finnbheara could snap his neck in the space of a breath. "I granted your mother the gift of Eala to ensure your success with the soulfall. That task is finished. You are not welcome here. Go now to seek an alternate destiny or be banished to the Glade of Chimes with my former lover."

He nods to the guards, and they drag Sion, his feet not touching the ground, to a massive gate of white-gold metalwork that looks to be wrought of the same material as the soliders' armor. Its topmost curves swoop down, ending in flourishes reminiscent of the swan's wings I wore a heartbeat ago. Filling its frame are intricate twisting strands with their own ethereal glow. They create a meshwork strewn with a bough and leaf design also similar to the one woven into the king's tunic. The gate is indeed so bright, I can only stare at it for a moment before looking away.

How much longer do we have in this place before the king tires of us, and any chance to further our case is lost?

My heart batters my ribs as I rush to Sion's side. "Please, wait." The soldiers look to their king, who nods once. They drop my love unceremoniously on the ground but stay within striking distance.

As soon as I touch my *anamchara*, a charge runs between us. The battle not to be separated from Sion is one I intend to win. Before I jumped from the window of the soulfall tower after him, I feared I would lose him forever. We're together now, and I'll be damned if I'm going to say goodbye again. The ferocity brewing in his green glass eyes says the same. Courage rises within me. This is the man I made the choice to follow into eternity. He is my passion and my hope. I'm not going to stand by while a potentially vindictive Faerie king tries to strip him away from me.

As he stares at my fingers entwined with Sion's, Finnbheara's eyes flare pewter, a duller shade than the gleaming silver of the straight, long hair that flows from his head down to the center of his back. He stands, legs apart, arms crossed, not bothering to conceal his royal furor. The king is a spark poised to surge into an unforgiving flame. Moments ago, the air reminded me of a fresh spring morning from my academic life in New York, where apple trees burst with bright white blossoms destined to become fat, juicy fruit. Now, a hint of smoke winds through the mist.

I know in my gut I've only got one shot. The time has come to cobble together a Fae bargain to give Sion and me even a fool's chance of staying together. I help my love to his feet, keeping him close, then pool all my knowledge of this supposedly mythical, but very real king and begin.

"Your Majesty--" Finnbheara's ardent interest in me is unsettling given the preponderance of evidence in so many folktales about the Fae penchant for seducing mortals.

If I can still be considered mortal.

What power of attraction can Fae exert over other Fae? Internal warning bells blare. I must keep a clear head around the king.

I link arms with Sion. "Sionnach Loho is my *anamchara*, my soulmate. Separating us is to destroy us, to destroy me."

By his expression, I can tell voicing my deep connection to Sion is not what the Fae ruler wants to hear. I force a swallow, summoning my best professor lecture voice to give me confidence. I'll bust out every folktale and legend in my mental catalogue to present a convincing argument that will guarantee both Sion and I admittance to Finnbheara's kingdom.

With effort, I manage to breathe through my fear and find my voice. "It's well known from stories and songs you've allowed other non-Fae into Tír na nÓg at your own behest and that of others." I almost bring up Máthair but decide it's dangerous territory. "Some for lovers, others for your entertainment. Take Oisín, when he fell in love with Niamh. He was welcomed into your lands."

The king waves a dismissive hand. "Did my realm truly matter to Oisín, a fool incapable of resisting the lure of his past?" He levels a glare at Sion. "Shall I return you to your world as a pile of dust next to careless Oisín?"

I squeeze Sion's hand to keep him silent. I'm holding the king's attention for now. "If love holds no value for you, what of honor? This man faced your challenge and achieved a feat of grace and goodness by ending the soulfall. That alone should be evidence of his worth."

Finnbheara's face turns sour with a hint of menace. "None from the human realm are entitled to my kingdom as an eternal choice without my leave, even though many entertain such a notion. Your fool chose a road not open to him."

Ah, he's rising to my challenge. Good. I face the king with steel to match his. "He chose me." For a stalled second, we stare at one another before I continue. "Do you not delight in rules that twist and bend? Words with hidden traps and convoluted meanings?"

Finnbheara shakes a finger at me as a pleased smile brightens his face. "You do know me, my Eala." This man's moods shift as quickly as legends suggest, but he's still engaged. He taps a finger to his chin. "*Anamchara* or not, the spawn of Loho took two hundred years to end the soulfall in his keeping, and only after you appeared as his saving grace." He shakes his head, long silver locks shimmering with the movement. The tip of one ear, as sharp as a knife point, peeks through. "No. He is not a worthy match for one of my Fae."

So, the king does indeed consider me Fae. What category of Faerie does a person concocted from Finnbheara's magic and then born of humans fall into?

Questions for later. Right now, I'm in a fight not to lose Sionnach. He is the light of my soul. The heart that shares the hundred thousand heartbeats of a Celtic day with mine. If he is banished from this place into some dismal afterlife void, I will follow him.

The king's features mold into a mask of anger that frightens me. He reaches out a hand and the mighty sword he held as a colossus on the sea cliffs then drove into the ground beside us when we first landed in his kingdom, diminishes from the height of a building into one fitting the king's grip. He raises it above Sion's head. "Beyond that, the spawn of Loho deserves to be struck down for inciting the wrath of my rival, Aodh, the dark prince. The fox caused the destruction of Aodh's agent and stoked the god's vengeful nature. My blessed Veil was blighted with underworld poison in the pursuit of this--" He lowers the blade alongside Sion's neck. "Inconsequential mortal."

I stare at the place where steel meets my beloved's flesh, and my breathing grows heavy. A sense of dread that I may have pushed Finnbheara too far deepens in my gut. The mention of Aodh, the underworld prince sends a shudder through me. A picture of that Irish god in a book of myths I had as a child gave me nightmares for years. His dark eyes held fiery pupils in a too elongated face frozen in rage. That illustration of Aodh peered menacingly through a wall of blood red flames and seemed to look straight at me no matter how I angled the page.

By *his agent*, does Finnbheara mean Jeremy Olk, the corrupted priest who chased us through the Veil and burned its spectral walls? Olk claimed he was after Sion for retribution. On the night he nearly killed my fox, Olk spoke of a connection to a power other than Finnbheara.

I flash Sionnach a questioning look, but he only presses his lips into a tight line afraid to move. I'm sure he's taking the guilt Finnbheara hurls at him to heart. I wish I could offer him the reassurance of my touch, but that's impossible with a sword to his jugular.

Abruptly, Finnbheara lowers the sword to his side, and my shoulders slump in relief. The king marches a step closer toward Sion, hands coiled into fists, eyes pulsing the color of singed bronze. "I am eternally charged to protect this kingdom and its Folk. Any who challenge that certainty deserves my deepest ire."

My gaze sweeps across the warriors in their stoic line. If underworld gods and princes are in play, weapon-bearing Fae make sense. It's chilling to imagine Olk tied to a vengeful Fae god, and Finnbheara focusing his fervid displeasure for that association on Sion.

Stepping in front of my *anamchara*, I raise both hands to the king. "Will you hear my bargain?"

The mercurial king pauses for an instant, then his expression shifts into one of interest. "Ah yes, your bargain." He spears his blade back into the grass. I cringe at the crisp sound of metal slicing into soil. That could have been Sion's neck. Once again, the monarch claims my hand. In a leisurely stroll, Finnbheara leads me away from Sionnach. "Go on."

What in the holy hell do I have to bargain with? What does Finnbheara want that I can give? The answer is terrifying but true.

Me.

After his lusty scrutiny, I don't want to imagine what for. I try to remember Máthair's words in the Glade of Chimes about the king rarely using essences like those of swan and oak to create what would eventually become me. What's happened to the others he's tried to bring to life in the same way? Did Finnbheara's attempts to use his...what did he call them...*beads of being* fail before? Is that why he's so interested in me? I pray he's curious enough to not want me walking out the gates of Tír na nÓg with a banished Sionnach.

The king smiles. "Speak, and let us enjoy evidence of how my gifts have taken hold in you."

His gifts. No matter how many personas he may wear, Finnbheara is an arrogant ass.

I pull free of his grasp to face him. I send a wish to the universe for this to work. "Here is my bargain. Test me, test us with challenges estimable by the Fae. If we prove to be worthy of this kingdom on our merits instead of my..." I fight down the lump in my throat. How should I define my new existence? "...birthright. Then you will allow two souls, not just one, to enter your glorious kingdom."

I applaud myself for adding *glorious* as a bit of flattery a split second before the truth that I'm a careless idiot hits me. I've left the door open for Finnbheara to concoct a task to produce a freaking unicorn out of vapor or slay some horrible Fae beast. What was I thinking? Did I learn nothing from a lifetime of Faerie stories? Bargains have to be as airtight as a jar that keeps jam from spoiling.

I raise a finger. "And by estimable, I mean doable challenges you would bestow on any loyal subject such as myself—no capricious frivolities or impossibilities inherently doomed to fail."

My stomach drops when a look of unabashed delight flickers in the king's eyes. I've screwed something up. He's already found a glaring mistake in my bargain to guarantee him victory. It's not as if I had an opportunity to scan for loopholes.

Finnbheara actually claps before resting his hands on my shoulders and leaning in to drop a quick, very damp kiss on my lips. "There it is. Conditions to temper an otherwise easily won bargain. I applaud you, my treasure, Eala Duir."

The king clasps his hands behind him, pacing back and forth before his line of soldiers. Once or twice, he turns to speak, but then resumes his walk of consideration. I return to Sion's side and crush his hand with mine.

My *anamchara* brushes a kiss to my ear before whispering. "The bastard is cooking up trouble. I feel it in my bones."

"What else was I supposed to do?" Frustration starts to gnaw at my insides. "Finnbheara runs a dictatorship, not a democracy." The Veil sprites slide through me, attempting to douse my tension with their friendly warmth.

Sion looks at me with such adoration, it's all I can do to keep from melting against him. "You've done right, my Eala *bán*." He smooths a strand of hair off my face. "And I love you for it, no matter what Himself puts on us." Sion's arm slides around my back, holding me tight.

My smile fades when I realize the king is frowning at our obvious affection. He lifts his chiseled chin, aiming a piercing stare our way. "You accused me of not valuing love. I shall enlighten you. I esteem it highly indeed, but only when it is a just love, a right love." He feathers his fingers at us. "Not *your* fleeting indulgence."

I take a step forward. Standing up to Finnbheara is essential. I'm being challenged for my previous words. Backing down now is certain failure. I won't fail Sion, fail us. "Why is the judgement of love yours to make?"

In a blink, he's in front of me, grasping both my hands. "Because I've borne witness to eons of love assumed, love betrayed, and love celebrated. How much have you observed in your paltry mortal days?"

Is this part of the test, or is Finnbheara putting me in my place? My bones feel like soggy toast. It's a miracle I still have enough nerve to stand

and face the king. Honesty is my armor. "The quantity of my paltry days doesn't matter. I cherish a love that I believe transcends time and fate. A love worth forfeiting a life and a place in your kingdom. Does that satisfy you?"

When the king rests knuckles against his mouth, considering my question, I sneak a glance at the soldiers. They're as still as a copse of trees. Freakishly still. Expressionless. Is it a military thing or a Fae thing? Stories of Faerie revelry with music, dance, and drinking don't gel with this unbroken line of serious beings. The Fae will definitely take getting used to.

The mist around us begins to thicken. Delicate translucent ribbons with hints of emerald and silver twist through the air. For a moment, I worry that they will wrap themselves around Sion and me as shackles. The gates of Tír na nÓg loom above us, their brilliance shining through the fog.

Finnbheara closes in. "I shall offer you a riddle to solve as the entrance price of two souls into my kingdom."

Relief nearly turns me to mush. My thready gambit paid off. He's giving us a chance. The King of the Connacht Faeries is not willing to let me walk away.

Finnbheara's gaze is for me alone. "To earn your prize, I do insist on a caveat in addition to solving my riddle."

I draw my lips together. A caveat, singular. Maybe the deal I'm making won't be as insane as I fear. Who am I kidding? I'm entering a bargain with an ancient Fae king.

Before I answer, he continues. "You will allow the most trusted member of my court to conspire with you in the human realm. My kin will open your perceptions to the potential of what you may become once ensconced in my kingdom. Do you accept?"

A Fae tutor––I'd be an idiot to turn down his offer. The more I can learn about Finnbheara, his world, and its convoluted rules, the better for Sion and me. The folktales and stories I've taught for years only go so far to prepare me for landing smack dab in a very real Faerie situation.

Finnbheara's eyes go through more shades than a color wheel as his gaze bores into me, waiting for my answer. I wish I knew how each color reveals what's going on in his royal thoughts. Perhaps clues to his current mood? The downward turn of his mouth clearly indicates he's losing patience with our meeting.

"Thank you." Gratitude feels like the right play. "I would appreciate guidance with..." I open my arms wide. "...my place in all of this." As soon as my words are out, his countenance changes from the brink of frustration to satisfaction. I thought Sionnach's moods shifted with breakneck speed. They're subtle compared to the king's.

For a hot second after I answer, an ethereally lovely face breaks through the mist behind the king. It's gone before I can tell if it's a man, woman, or my imagination. Finnbheara makes no reference to the visitor, who I guess is the kin that will be my teacher, so I let it pass. Maybe fleeting visions are just a Tuesday in the Fae world.

The king circles us, stroking his chin as his eyes glow a disturbing obsidian. My psyche screams for an end to this psychological game. "I shall concoct a riddle that only a canny intellect may solve. It must hold a laudable challenge to balance your entitled desire." His scrutiny raises a hard knot in my belly. He wanders in and out of the mist as he considers. The colorful ribbons wave behind him like a cape.

I sneak Sion a hopeful look. When the king approaches, stress compresses my windpipe, and I gulp an inelegant breath. I wish Finnbheara would get on with it so we could leave this unforgiving doorstep of Tír na nÓg to dive into the task of reversing our current fortune.

In the space of a single blink, the Fae king's face is inches from mine. It takes all my willpower not to yelp in surprise. Instinct tells me not to show weakness. I need Finnbheara to keep his interest in me. If I give in to my old tendency to hide from life's challenges, he may decide I'm not worth his concern.

"Listen well, Eala Duir. This missive shall illustrate my offering." Finnbheara leans in, gently kissing me on the mouth, the tip of his tongue stealing a taste of my lips. Holding my breath is the only way to keep from panicking. I assumed he'd spit out a quick, snappy challenge or conjure Fae parchment scrawled with instructions. A kiss is not the delivery system I anticipated. I swear super-heated air wafts my way from Sion as the king's mouth lingers on mine.

Our lips still press together as Finnbheara begins to whisper his next words.

"Passage sought to lands of mine,
Where wish and dream bide free.
Tales of old both true and told,
Will guide your quest to Sidhe."

He cups my cheek in his warm palm as he drops more kisses on each of my closed lids.

"To solve this task, use more than eyes.
Claim wit and guile your parlance.
The deadline comes when mortal moon,
Does lose its way and substance."

The king's fingertips trail along my shoulder, finishing when he feels the pounding pulse point in my neck. My skin grows warmer with each of his touches. They are equal parts unnerving and soothing. I don't want to enjoy the contact, but it's hard to resist.

Finnbheara's breath carries a tempting hint of honeysuckle as he takes up his chant.

"Face the ridge of grey and go,
When mortals fall to dream.
Upon the crest above fine lands,
A stone will wake with screams."

Taking a step back, Finnbheara opens his palm. A chunky, white-gold necklace appears. It's a star with five blunted points and filigree detail in the center. The size and shape suggest a piece of jewelry more amulet or pendant than necklace. He spins me to fasten the piece around my neck.

"There is a number full complete,
Its quota ripe to fill.
A sharpened star shall be the proof,
Your path twists to my will."

His ever-changing eye color settles into the look of green glass with a golden ring around the iris. The same eyes both Sion and I share, those of a Veil wanderer, a *fánaí*, beings who use mystical pathways to travel through time and place. The king's gaze switches to Sion, his royal ire unmistakable.

"Greed and haste may tempt your fate,
Be steadfast in restraint.
A thoughtless act is ruin's lure,
Your victories courting taint."

Again, Finnbheara grips my shoulders, then rests his forehead to mine. His voice becomes a hurried whisper.

"Discoveries bold you'll need to solve,
This ultimate conclusion:
What's all and each the selfsame piece,
Plain truth and no illusion?"

The king takes two long strides away from us to stand with his hands on hips. Eyes shine as silver as the brilliant strands of his hair.

"A warning now, I must decry,
To launch our bargain true.
If failure be your end result,
My judgement is your due."

His expression softens as he stares into my eyes, as if we are the only two people in his kingdom. There's an odd desperation there I can't begin to comprehend. Even if we succeed, it may take eternity to truly understand the shifting winds of the Faerie king.

"This is no easy road you trod,
By royal riddle bound.
Prepare your hearts, the end you seek,
May end in sorrow, rift, and crown."

The king nods once, the period at the end of a last sentence. "I shall fetch you at my appointed hour to present your conclusion." Finnbheara raises both arms, muscles bunching as he tenses. There's no goodbye or warning before I'm sucked into a dense fog. I'm aware of Sion next to me in our midair tumble. Silence surrounds us until a great thundering sound announces the gates of Tír na nÓg closing behind us.

CHAPTER 2

THE RETURN

U p, down, sideways…who knows? With Eala sliding around me, we're tossed like salad at a church picnic in the blinding white soup surrounding us. I reach for her and thank all, I'm able to wrap my arms around her body. I'm afraid our landing promises to be a bad one, and I want to protect her.

"Veil." I call to her through our blanket of foggy dew to prepare her before squeezing my eyes shut to call the Veil to me. The otherworldly passageway that's been my companion for two hundred years while I traveled through time to reunite souls with their missing virtue has saved my sorry arse more times than I can count.

Not today.

Nothing happens.

My ears pop. Eala squeals as a rich, royal-blue sky splashes above us a breath before we roll down the side of a smallish hillock and thump into a ditch. Beneath our bums, fat green blades of grass poke through a shallow muddy puddle.

The impact of our tumble out of Tír na nÓg separates us as we roll. It seems Finnbheara chose the most undignified of his Faerie doors to send us back to our world. I suppose it's better than landing in the middle of a freezing *lough*. The base of a hawthorn tree or even a dank cave would have been preferable. If it was Eala alone, he woulda sent her sliding down a sunbeam. With me along for the ride, his high-minded majesty won't pass up any chance to humiliate or inconvenience.

Here's praying the shrubs surrounding us and oncoming dusk effectively hid our tumble through the sky.

"Sion," Eala cries, arms flailing to find me as her white-blonde locks cover her eyes.

"Here, love," I say, scooting close enough to catch her hands. I sit up and smooth the curtain of hair off her face.

She launches herself at me, settling her round bottom straight onto my lap and throwing her arms around my neck. Eala breathes against my skin. "You're still with me. We're together."

I try to pull back to meet her gaze, but her grasp tightens, nearly choking me.

"Don't let go," she gasps.

"Never, love. Never."

It takes her a while to stop panting and allow herself to put enough distance between us, so we are face-to-face again. I'm right rattled myself and appreciate the breather.

"Sion, oh Sion." She drops kisses across my cheeks. "I was terrified Finnbheara would take you hostage and make me do this alone."

I gather her to my chest, and her body trembles against mine. "I'd not let that Faerie bastard do such a thing."

"Neither will I." Her mouth crashes onto mine with the force of a train without brakes running downhill. We share breath to prove to one another we are indeed together. I part her lips with my tongue and give her the kissing of a lifetime.

This wonder in my arms was nearly lost to me. First, when I stepped out the soulfall tower window to meet my fate and had no notion of how to keep her by my side. Then at the feet of Finnbheara.

I pull away and cup her face in my hands. "My Eala *bán*." Tears stream down her face, and I kiss every last one of the buggers away as I coo to my darling. "We've done it, love. We're alive. It's a miracle we've managed."

Words fight their way through her sobs. "I, I thought he, the king, was going to hurt you." Her hands roam my body, checking for damage. "Did he? When you were still a fox, and he dropped you from so high--" A massive hiccup cuts off her words.

When her fingers prod a tender spot on my side, I grunt. Eala scrambles to lift my shirt and inspect the damage, but I catch her hand. Gently stroking her hair, I smile. "Whist. Whist. I'm no more than bruised." I take my turn to touch her, hoping she doesn't cry out from any injuries. "Are you fine?"

Eala crumples against me. "No, yes. Fuck."

She wiggles her glorious bum across the part of me that in any other circumstance would appreciate it. Her hands fist my shirt tightly enough to feel knuckles pressed against my chest. Eala's been the picture of bravery since she bested the hell demon Olk, leapt from the window of the soulfall tower after me, and faced down a Fae king. She's earned a bit of falling apart. I attempt to lighten the mood.

"With all this squirming against my bits, have no doubt, I'd like nothing more than to take you right here, love, but I think we'd best get our bearing first."

To my relief, a laugh escapes her pouty mouth, then her green glass eyes with the gold *fánaí* ring, the signs of a Veil traveler, stare into mine. "Promise me we will make love every damn chance we get, Sionnach Loho."

"That's an easy bargain to strike." I capture a handful of the feathery white-blonde hair near the nape of her neck and ease her head back, plunging my lips to ravage hers. Hot breath sings through our mouths as our tongues do their best to claim and claim and claim. If it weren't for the sloppy mess of ground beneath us, this might be a fine private place to fit in a quick bit of *gratitude for being alive* sex.

Eala eases her grip to press a palm to my heart, and I do the same. We spent a hundred thousand heartbeats each time we moved through the Veil during our allotted part of a Celtic day to travel, the length of a mortal night, to free the souls. How many will be doled out to us now?

I wrap her in my arms, doing my best to assure her I'll never let go. I mold her chest to mine, savoring every heartbeat answering my own. "I love you, my Eala *bán*, my white swan."

Her fingers press into the muscles of my back. "I more than love you, my fox." She gazes adoringly at me. "What's the word for that?"

With our faces nearly touching, we whisper the word together. "*Anamchara.*"

Soulmates.

Spirits who burst into light in the presence of one another.

Muddy water wicks through my trousers, sending an icy jolt up my arse. I'm thankful our stingy *leinte*, clearly designed to give the lecherous king a gander at Eala's body in Tír na nÓg, have swapped back to the clothes we wore before our fox and swan selves entered Finnbheara's lands. It might pose a bit of a challenge being dressed in peasant outfits from the late 1700s, my proper era. Our get ups may not be a match for where and when we've landed.

My body tenses with practiced alertness from two centuries of hurling through time. Year be damned, are we safe here? Eala follows my lead, and we scan our surroundings.

"Where we are?" She takes in a shaky breath. "Or *when* we are?"

"I'll wake my wee fox for a peek around." Absentmindedly, I scratch at my chest, imagining the unbearable itch that always comes with my transformation into the beastie.

"Don't leave me." Her fingers dig into my arm.

I give her a quick kiss. "I'll keep in your sight and only nose past those bushes."

Reluctantly, she lets go and nods. "No farther."

I close my eyes to drift into my foxy form. Not a tingle. Not an itch. I try to clear my mind to banish the tension of what we've endured into the shadows of my thoughts and relax. I wait to dissolve into the change, but nothing happens.

Heat rises from my chest to my face. I can't become a fox just like I couldn't call the Veil after Finnbheara gave us the boot. I'd hoped the Veil eluded me because the Celtic day wasn't yet upon us. A weight on my heart tells me the self-righteous king has stripped me of every gift he'd given me to service the soulfall. How am I going to be of any use to Eala and this damn riddle if I've got nothing extra to give?

My shoulders sag, and I open my eyes. Eala stares at me as I shake my head. "The change isn't coming, love."

Sympathy I'm not eager to digest settles across her lovely features. Before she speaks words that I'm not ready to hear, the rude air horn from a passing train breaks through the stillness of our grassy landing spot. The absence of a whistle spells more modern times. Following close on its heels, I hear the screech and blare of a car honking. Strike the eighteenth century then.

Eala cocks her head. "Train. Traffic."

I nod. "If I was a betting man, I'd say we're in the vicinity of your time."

She grips my chin, turning my face to hers. "Our time. I don't care what year it is. From now on, any time, every time, is our time."

How does this woman know exactly what my heart needs to hear? If my swan keeps saying such perfect things, I will have to take her right here in the mud bath. Traversing the years with no one but my sorry self to rely on is a weight on my soul I'm happy to shed. I'm not alone anymore. After centuries of waiting, I've joined the love of my life. I will do whatever it takes not to part from her.

I adore the way Eala pushes her lips out when she's thinking. It's not a kiss she's asking for, but I give her one anyway. Before we get down to serious kissing, my practical woman pulls away. Narrowed eyes tell me she's reclaimed a productive line of thought.

"Do you think Alfie followed us?"

It would be a boon if my own personal *fánaí*, Veil guide's tree, who I affectionately call Alfie as in *Al find your sorry arse, Sionnach*, that's followed me through hundreds of years is nearby. The botanical sweetheart always gave me a sense of feeling grounded wherever I went as well as keeping a sack of clothes from multiple timelines between her sloping trunks.

I stand up, boots squishing to get a better view of what's above us. The oncoming night makes searching a challenge, but sadly, there's no sign of my magical traveling companion, the white poplar with its pattern of green triangle markings on her trunk. Another cut to prove what was once given to me no longer exists.

"Sorry love, don't see my woody darling."

No Alfie, no change of clothes. I suppose if anyone questions our attire, we'll say we're kitted out for a local theater or Beltane hooley. If it is Beltane. We left this world as May Day was dawning, but I've got no notion how long Himself kept us in the Fae realm. I shiver from the wet britches cooling my skin. A fine festival bonfire would be appreciated as the sun dips below the horizon and the air cools.

"That makes sense. You didn't have time to call the Veil before Finnbheara kicked us out. Call it now and take us back to the hotel in Dublin. I'll get my stuff, then we'll decide on our next step." Eala chews her bottom lip. "Colleen will be insane with worry over where I've gone."

I'm a proud bugger and never one to advertise my weaknesses, but Eala deserves the truth. I reach a hand to help her to her feet. "*Anamchara*, I did call the Veil." I feel the stain of embarrassment crawl across my skin. "It didn't come to me."

Her face scrunches. "What do you mean?"

"As I said. When we were spat out of Finn's place, the Veil did not answer."

She grabs the front of my shirt, desperation in her voice. "Try now. Maybe Tír na nÓg affected your ability or sundown, the start of the Celtic day, wasn't close enough."

I wrap an arm around her waist, close my eyes, and picture the glassy prismatic walls of the Veil that have been my personal highway through time.

Nothing.

The sensation I've come to count as part of my very soul is lost to me. My voice is raw as I meet her concerned gaze. "I can't. No Veil, no fox, no *fánaí* tree. I'm useless."

She twines her fingers through mine. "Don't say that. You're essential to me." Eala shakes her body like she's preparing to take off running. "Let me try." Her eyes close, then pop open. "Maybe Dublin isn't the best idea. We don't know how long we've been gone. Colleen may not be there anymore, and God knows what she thinks happened to us." She shudders. "And how do we explain Jeremy?" Her voice catches on the fiend's name. "Where can we go?"

"Do you think you could find the way to my folks' cottage?"

Eala's face pales. "No. Not there."

Of course, she doesn't want to return to the place where the corrupted version of Jeremy Olk tried to hang my parents and nearly stabbed me to death. The same land where she called to Finnbheara, and he came to her aid in the form of a terrifying colossus. "No, my darling, not in their time. In this time. Our time now."

A crease forms between her brows. "You can't be sure the cottage is still standing or that someone else isn't living there. Maybe it's an Airbnb."

I kiss her worry lines away. "Sure as my arse is soaked in mud."

Shoulders bunched up nearly to her ears, relax. "I'm sorry. Not a big fan of the unknown."

I lay a hand on her lovely lips. "No sorries. You've a right to have a turbulent mind with what we've been through." My poor love. It's been no time at all since she discovered I was the last soul in the soulfall, we bested Olk, and had a riddle smacked on us by Finnbheara as our only hope of staying together.

She embraces me, studying the sky over my shoulder. "It's definitely twilight now. I'll try to call the Veil. Don't let go." As we clutch one another, Eala tenses. In our first stroke of luck, her iridescent, filmy impression of the Veil settles around us.

"You've done it, my brilliant love." I grip her tighter. The familiar tunneled pathway expands around us, shutting out the surroundings and plunging us into a place between times and realities.

"Help me picture it," whispers Eala.

I fill my mind with the image of my lands and the cottage as they stand today and whisper these details to her. Longing for the faint familiar tug of the Veil seizes me. I force myself to be thankful Eala and the Veil are still connected. Hand in hand, my love and I walk across the springy Veil carpet of glowing turquoise and violet spheres. We stop in front of a shimmering ring the size of a round doorway.

"What's this now?" I ask.

Eala shrugs. "I pictured a kind of giant porthole to allow us to see where we landed."

Evidence of why she's brilliant. It never occurred to me to refine my treks as a Veil guide to afford me a preview of what was to come. I just aimed and jumped.

Details through the opening shift from a blur into a clearer picture despite the deepening shadows of night. In the distance, past the stone wall Da and I put up so very long ago, settled between two yew trees, is the whitewashed cottage with a bright red door and matching window frames.

Home.

"You've done it, my girl." When I lean in to kiss her, my gaze catches a dark scorch mark over her shoulder along the wall of the Veil. On its edge is a purple blue smear, the color of the unearthly flames Olk had been using to damage this sacred route of *fánaí*, Veil travelers. Attempting to hide my shudder, we step into the world. The Veil dissipates around us.

Sion keeps me from stumbling as we step onto a road in front of the same wooden gate we left the night before. I glance behind to see the last wavering lights of the Veil melt away. My hand stretches toward our mystical portal.

"I'm afraid Finnbheara will take the Veil away from me too."

My fingers tingle as the familiar energy from the ethereal highway ignites the Veil sprites inside me. I feel reassurance in their steady thrum that the Veil will be there when I call. Less appealing thoughts follow. Does Finnbheara control my sprites? Does the king watch us?

"It's not gone, love. Only waiting," says Sion, giving my arm a pat. "Call it back now if it'll set your mind at ease."

There's a slight strain in his voice. He's the one who introduced the Veil and I to one another. It can't be easy for him to be separated from it.

"I need to. Just to prove I can."

He lays his arm on mine and together we point to where the Veil swirled moments before. I allow its gentle presence to seep into my mind. As soon as I do, the Veil sprites flare inside me. A faint circle of rainbow light distorts the air.

"There 'tis," says Sion in a gentle voice. "As I said, the Veil knows you, Eala Duir."

Relief washes through me. I blow the Veil a kiss, and it fades again. The sprites relax as well.

I always imagined the Veil as a curtain between the worlds of present and past, a thin barrier separating reality and the land of dreams and stories. It's so much more. A time tunnel, a transit from place to place with its own magical pockets like the enchanted Veil forest where Sion first revealed his truth to me, or where the soulfall tower loomed before the clouds. It's not a maze. When asked, the Veil sketches a direct line from where you are to where you wish to be. My mind reels trying to imagine how many roads must converge, diverge, and cross over within the Veil's system. I've always thought of a starry sky as infinite, but the magic of the Veil may be closer to a never-ending realm than the cosmos.

A drop of rain on my face shifts me out of the thoughts ribboning through my head back into reality. The light fades even more as the last vestiges of the setting sun sleep.

Sion opens his arms wide. "We could stand in the rain to wash the mud off or take a proper bath inside."

"A proper bath? As in a tub?"

His grin is a welcome sight after our travails of late. Sion holds out a hand to lead me through the gate and up the path toward the cottage. I take in the countryside with its muted greens shadowed by the gathering twilight clouds. It surprises me to see powerlines and other houses in the distance. It's a very different landscape from the one we left last night.

The lighthouse poised on the distant cliffs reveals no hint of Finnbheara's presence. I tip my head and inhale the fresh scent of rain on the breeze. This is indeed our calm before the storm.

Finnbheara's riddle is our tempest.

My moment of relaxation shatters.

The riddle.

How in the holy hell am I going to remember everything the king said? At the moment, I can't bring a single word to mind.

Sion stops in front of the door. A motion sensor light brightens the small stone porch. He reaches inside a fake rock tucked into the corner of a window box filled with bright purple geraniums.

I grab the front of his shirt in a panic as he retrieves a key. "Do you remember the riddle?" My fingers close around the star pendant Finnbheara placed around my neck, hoping the touch will bring back every rhyme. "How are we going to solve something that's totally wiped from our memories?" I release him to thread my fingers through the hair at the sides of my temples. "I'm so stupid. I should've insisted he give it to us in writing, or at least a guarantee we could access his words." Tears of frustration at my carelessness blur my vision. "I screwed up the bargain before we even started."

The fear on his face doesn't help. It's like experiencing a car crash, when the details of the trauma only begin to come back once you're safe. We are anything but safe. Finnbheara's riddle that holds the key to our forever has disintegrated into gobbledygook.

Sionnach fumbles with the key, his hand shaking so badly he drops it onto the porch.

I'm used to him being the steady one. It was me who refused to climb towers and venture willingly into historical predicaments until his confidence bolstered my own. If he falls apart, how the hell are we going to get through this?

I yelp when lightning rips across the distance sky. It's too reminiscent of the nightmare we last faced at the cottage. While Sion digs around the edges of the stones to retrieve the key, I gulp air to keep from hyperventilating. At the next lightning strike, I squeeze my eyes shut and cover the star pendant with my hand, cursing Finnbheara for playing us so mercilessly.

I hate you. I hate you.

As soon as I blank out the world, peace settles over me. There, behind my eyelids, is a pure white slate covered with an elegant script.

> *Passage sought to lands of mine,*
> *Where wish and dream bide free.*
> *Tales of old both true and told,*

Will guide your quest to Sidhe.

"There you are, you rawny bugger," grumbles Sion as he takes out his stress on the errant key.

I lay a hand on his arm. "I found it."

He looks at the key, confused. "I've got it just here."

"Not the key, the riddle." I cover my eyes with my hand and begin to recite Finnbheara's words.

I squeak when Sion lifts me into sturdy arms. "I've said it before, but I mean it every time. You're a wonder to me, Eala *bán*." The rain begins to fall in earnest when his lips claim mine in a robust kiss. He kicks the bright red door open. "You're very welcome to my home, love."

I gape as he carries me over the threshold of a very different Loho cottage than the one filled with nightmares. He nudges a switch with his elbow to illuminate the room. Gone is the trestle table, a cupboard with Máthair's collection of herbs and oils, and odors of straw and animals from a cordoned off area in the back. This is a cozy open plan space with an honest to goodness kitchen off to the side and an overstuffed couch facing a massive stone fireplace. Opposite the hearth is an archway leading to a bedroom nook with a door in the corner opening to a very modern-looking bathroom.

"How…what…?" I stammer.

"Didja think I'd offer you a tub and not carry through on my promise?" He grins as he sets me on my feet.

"You actually live here?"

"I do. Loho land never left the family."

I lean against the doorway to catch my balance. "Sion, how can this be?"

He reaches behind me to shut the door. "I never explained it all to you, love." He pauses, gathering his thoughts. "Out of spite, Finn showed up on Ma's doorstep to gloat when I, the son of the man she spurned him for, was dying young with shadows on my soul. That's when she struck the bargain with him to accept a place in the Glade of Chimes if the king would make me a Veil guide. Ma believed attaching me to a soulfall was my only chance at heaven."

"How did she know about soulfalls? I'd never heard of them."

Sion rubs his chin. "Ma learned much about such mysteries during her Faerie visit."

I shake my head as if the movement will help all of this make sense. "But if he banished her to the Glade of Chimes in the bargain, how was she able to raise me?"

"Her due to the king was collected at the end of her natural life, and she went to the glade." His gaze lights on the window where the rain now falls in sheets. He runs a finger down the condensation on the glass. "When the time came for my last go at ending the soulfall, Ma called on Finnbheara again to beg the royal shite to send help to me. That's when he allowed her to leave her duties in the glade to live a second mortal life and raise the child he created with his beads of being."

I tap a knuckle to my lips, trying to sort this out. "How did she know it was your last chance?"

"I happened on a wandering Fae in the same Veil forest where we met." Sion wears the dreamy look of recalling memories. "He asked if I'd share a fire with him. Never hurts to see what information you can get out of a willing Faerie, so I agreed. The man knew nothing to help me with the soulfall. To my surprise, when I prodded him about the Glade of Chimes, he told me his lover had been banished there by Finn. The Faerie vowed he'd never rest until he found a way into the glade to see his beloved. Veil traveling was the answer." He scoffs. "Isn't that the way of it? We bypass the simplest solution, yet it is the one that solves our problem." His expression shifts from memory to melancholy. "I'd sneak in to see Ma on Faerie feast days when I knew the king's eyes were lax. That's how she knew of my trials and failures."

I pinch the silver circle on his pinkie finger with the engraving *teacht orm*, find me, in Irish. It's the ring my grandmother left me when I thought she'd died, and then I gave Sion before he stepped out of the window in the soulfall tower. "When it was time, she sent me to Ireland to find you."

He slides the simple band off his pinkie and back onto the ring finger of my right hand. "This is where it belongs."

I twist the ring until the inscription faces me. "It's hard to fathom the complexity of it all."

Sion strips off his jacket. "Trying to make sense of Fae dealings is a waste of energy. Take 'em for what they are...mad."

The chill from my wet clothes can't rival the one in my heart. "So, when I thought she died, Máthair went back to the Glade of Chimes." My mind reels trying to overlay logic on Sion's unnatural lifespan, and my grandmother straddling so many different realities.

He nods. "Bound to the bargain she made with Finn to grant my soul a chance not to burn in the fires of hell."

My anger rises. "You were tortured and shot in the leg to give up the name of the priest you worked for. How is that a shadow on your soul or a sentence to hell?"

"I'd still done wrong no matter the cause. Her passion to save me drove her to deal with her former Faerie lover."

There's so much bitterness in his voice, my heart aches. "Your father came to me in New York. Where does he fit in this picture?"

"Finnbheara being the vindictive, jealous bastard he is, dangled Da's soul in and out of reach, not letting him pass on. Clever as she was and using some tricks learned in her time with the Faeries, Ma was able to communicate with Da."

"So, the Timothy Yew I met in New York was a ghost?"

Sion's expression is strained. "Ma knew you'd be able to see spirits. I don't know how she worked that out, but clearly, she did." The gold ring around his green glass irises flares. "I suspect Ma may have called on Finnbheara for more favors than she's let on. It grinds my guts to say it, but I think there was...is...unfinished business between the two of them."

I massage my temples with the heels of my hands. "I'm trying to fit this into the context of a story or folktale, but I'm getting the impression all the pieces won't quite mesh."

Sion toes off his boots. "Maybe you and Finn'll sit down to a cuppa one day, and he'll explain the fine details to you." He crosses the room to the hearth where peat bricks are already laid to start a fire. His hatred for the Fae king is palpable. Sion's mood is as dry and poised to spark into flame as the kindling he lights.

I rid myself of my own soggy cloth slippers and ease in behind him. Setting my hands on his shoulders, I press my cheek to his. "To be clear,

I'll never sit down to a friendly chat with the man who put you through hell for two hundred years."

His shoulders rise and fall as he takes a deep breath. "Truth be told, I don't know if I owe the man a debt or not. He granted my mother a kindness and if not for him…" The kindling smokes a little, and then a proper fire takes hold, filling the room with a pleasant peaty fragrance. Sion stands, bringing me up with him. His arms circle me, resting against the small of my back. "…my heart would have faced this cold life without you." He rubs his nose behind my ear. "And that would be no life at all."

I fit my body to his. A million questions about the evolution of his cottage flit through my mind. Is this where Sion was secluded except for the skimpy weeks between Éostre and Beltane when he was allowed in the world to save the soulfall? I always imagined him suspended in an enchanted sleep for the better part of each year.

He slumps against me. It's our bodies' turn to continue the conversation. "You promised to make love to me any chance we got, Sionnach Loho."

Sion perks up, wasting no time bringing his lips to mine. He smiles against my mouth. "I'll not be breaking any promises to you, woman."

His hands slide lower and grab my ass, lifting me against him. His hot mouth captures mine, and I wrap my legs around his waist. He walks us toward the rather large bed on the other side of the arch.

I break off the kiss. "Wait. We're covered in muck, and I plan on a nice, long mud-free sleep in your lovely bed." I feel a blush race up my cheeks. "If we get around to sleeping."

Holding me with the corded muscles of one strong arm, he manages to sneak his other hand under my homespun skirts to snap the waistband of my panties. "Then I suggest we rid ourselves of these sodden wrappers before I take you to bed." He takes my bottom lip between his teeth and growls.

A few strides later, we're in his bathroom. With a lusty squeeze of my ass, he sets me on my feet to click on a small radiator. There's a nice sized tub under a window with a tankless water heater on the wall above it. What a nice surprise my man doesn't spare any creature comforts when it comes to heat. At the moment, my internal temperature chases away any lingering chill from our wallow in the muddy grass.

I start to untie my apron, but Sion grabs my hand. "Wait. Read me Finn's riddle again."

"Now?" My word is breathy and a little desperate. I need Sion's hands on me without these damn period clothing.

"It'd be just like the fiend to set a petty limit to decode his madness." He cups my breast. "Can we take our time or get to it fast?"

I lay my hand over his, encouraging his touch as I close my eyes, reciting the riddle as Sion begins to knead one breast, then the other, making it harder for me to concentrate.

"Are you paying attention?" I say as he begins to get rougher.

He pauses. "Say that last bit again."

"To solve this task, use more than eyes.
Claim wit and guile your parlance.
The deadline comes when mortal moon,
Does lose its way and substance."

Sion drops his hands. My nipples strain against the cotton *leine*, eager for his attentions to continue.

His tone is thoughtful. "Mortal moon. Not the full moon of the Veil."

"Does lose its way and substance. When does the moon lose its substance?" I stare out the window, imagining a moonless sky when the truth hits me. "A new moon? No *visible* substance." I wish I had my cell so I could pinpoint its current phase. Hops through the Veil, where the moon is always full, threw me off track.

Sion drags a thumb across the copper stubble on his chin. "The night before you came to me at the wishing seat was as dark as a man without a conscience."

I blow out a long breath. "You're remembering a pre-moonrise sky not a new moon. It was waxing during the tour." I chew my lip and then slowly nod. "Looks like Finnbheara's giving us two weeks until the moon disappears again."

"How saintly generous of him," scoffs Sion.

The Veil sprites react to my distress by swarming like hornets around a threat to their nest. "It's less than half the days he gave you to work on the soulfall each year."

"You're his show pony in this race," says Sion with a very sour look. "He's set on claiming a swift victory."

I don't want tonight to devolve into a Finnbheara hate fest. Sion and I should be jigging and toasting with champagne we've ended up alive together in the same place at the same time. We deserve to jump each other like honeymooners. I try to ease the tension-tension and increase the sexual tension by unlacing my vest, freeing my breasts from the binding. I shimmy a little so they wobble under the *leine*. "Are you calling me a horse?"

His gaze falls to the string on the neckline of my shirt, replacing his gloomy expression with hooded eyes and slightly parted lips. Sion pinches the string between his fingers, and, with one slow pull, the fabric falls open to expose my bra.

I clasp my hands behind his neck. "Surely, we can be selfish enough to take one damn night, or at least part of it, for ourselves." I move my hands over his shoulders to the expanse of his solid chest and undo the buttons of the tan vest he still wears. The stock wrapped around his neck is next to go. When he tries to speed things up by roughly grabbing the back of his own *leine* to pull it over his head, I stop him. "Careful not to rip it. We may need these clothes. Don't get too hasty."

"Time's past for that." Sion presses my hand to the front of his loose britches to confirm a hard and hasty bulge.

After giving him an appraising fondle that sends a spike of heat straight to my own core, I work the tail of his long shirt over his head. "We can open with hasty, then move on to slow, naughty, and any other way you can think of."

Sion groans at my touch and then shivers as I drop his shirt to the floor. I run my hands across every swell and dip of his chest, pausing to twirl a finger through the tuft of soft fox-red hair between his pecs. We dedicate ourselves to shedding each other's clothing.

"That goes as well," says Sion, pointing to the star pendant Finnbheara fastened around my neck that currently hangs between my breasts. "I want no reminder of the royal ass touching you."

I reach around to unclasp the necklace, then hang it on the bathroom doorknob before moving back in front of Sion. We stand naked atop a puddle of fabric.

Sion takes my hands as his gaze lazily meanders from my lips to my taut nipples, that ache for his mouth, down past my stomach to the fluff of white-blonde hair between my thighs. "So very lovely."

I enjoy the landscape of his nakedness. His body is a stocky collection of muscles and scars built from decades—no centuries—of farming, climbing towers, and fighting. The small pink circle over his heart where Olk stabbed him in this very cottage makes my breath catch.

My wanderings stall at his arousal fully primed for what he so indelicately termed a *rut and burst* the first time we made love at the Leviathan telescope at Birr Castle.

"If you stare at my cock much longer, it's going to go off on its own."

I free my hands to pet his delightfully silky length from root to tip, then let my fingers trail over his hipbone as I slink behind him to get the full picture and admire his tight ass. When it's in full view, I bark a laugh and give one of his cheeks a good slap. "You weren't kidding. Your ass is frosted with mud."

He spins me so quickly; I nearly slip on the tile floor. Sion clamps his hands on my hips, carrying out his inspection. "Ah, I see your ample Amerrrrican bottom isn't without its own dusting as well."

I find my aforementioned Amerrrrican bottom pulled against his more than ready cock as he begins to grind against me. Sion whines when I untangle myself from his attentions and point to the tub. "There are places I'd rather not get muddy, especially when the remedy is right there."

Without warning, he scoops me over the edge until I'm standing in the middle of the tub before he joins me. In one quick swipe, he yanks the vinyl curtain around us. Reaching for the tankless water heater, he flicks a switch and then grabs the shower hose.

I back away and cross my arms over my breasts. "How long does it take that thing to heat up?"

"Not long," he says with a wicked grin on his face as he squirts a spray of water straight at my chest.

I screech at the cold blast, raising my hands as a shield. The icy water hardens my nipples even more. Before I can scold him, Sion drops the shower head so it sprays our feet. He cups my breasts and covers one of my cold peaks with his hot mouth for a nice long suck before warming the other. In the short time it takes him to get a good taste, the water is nearly roasting our ankles.

Sion crouches to rescue the nozzle. Instead of standing up, he starts at my feet and slowly runs the warm stream up my legs, following a path to one knee, then the other. His fingers work the tired muscles of my calves. It's surprisingly sexy. The anticipation of the water and his touch going higher has me gripping the windowsill.

Much to my disappointment, he skips my thighs to rinse and massage my shoulders and hair. "You're skipping the good parts," I manage to rasp out, dropping my head back as he gently caresses my throat.

What a glorious night alone in a cottage with the man so dear to me, my heart doesn't know how to contain the immensity of the feeling. Sion fills in the gaps I've wondered about myself, my parents, and why Máthair adopted me at her age. It's all led to this, baring my body, my soul to the person whose spirit sings the song to make me whole.

My fox's teeth graze the shell of my ear. "Far from it, love. I'm saving the best," he murmurs before moving to my breasts. The deliberate way he rinses and squeezes drives me close to coming apart. I grab his arm to pull him closer.

"Like this, do you?" He smiles against my wet chest, giving the underside of each breast a nip. The water travels lower and lower. Sion nudges my leg with his knee, and I widen my stance for him. His fingers lead the way as he opens me, allowing the force of the water to hit just the right spot. The orgasm blasts through me so quickly, I miss the final ramp up. My cry is a collection of half words and emotions strung together with one thought. I love this man.

Sion laughs. "That was one fine enthusiastic racket to say I love you."

"I do love you. I love you. I love you, Sionnach Loho."

"I won't ever tire of hearing those words, my Eala *bán*, but shall we try for a bit more volume the next go round?"

Sion moves the shower head closer to increase the pressure. I shudder as another wave builds as fast as wildfire through dry summer brush. Sion crouches and the water disappears, replaced by his eager mouth. Without raising his head, he lifts me onto the lip of the tub so my back is against the wall and splits my legs farther apart. With the flat of his tongue, he strokes the length of my slit, drenched and dripping courtesy of the hot water and my own need. He licks again and again, then after a hard suck that brings me to the very edge, he looks up from between my legs. "This'll teach you to grab my cock then move along."

With a wicked grin, he plunges a finger inside me, then pumps in and out while he feasts on my juicy nub. I thread my fingers through the mat of curls plastered to his head and pull him harder against me. When I come again against his busy tongue, I scream *I love you* loud enough to rattle windows. I collapse over his shoulder, gulping air. My fox slides down into the tub, easing my body onto his lap so I face him. He continues to run the stream of warm water over my back and sides in a soothing caress.

"I love you, Eala, my darling. In my long, often tedious life, there's never been the happiness or sense of peace you give me with every breath."

Our kiss begins with the most tender touch of lips brushing lips. In perfect sync, we open our mouths to let tongues taste and slide. It's as if every kiss with Sion is new; the steps of a dance being learned as we go.

I feel his cock give an impatient twitch where it's trapped between our bodies. As ready as he appeared after the loss of our clothing, I'm surprised he's held back. Leaning into him, I lift my hips and reach between us to guide him home. "Care to dance?"

His fingers dig into my ass. "With you, always."

I lower myself onto him, savoring every inch and shared moan. We gaze at each other with matching wonder. After all we've gone through, this casual moment is an unexpected respite from our usual frantic momentum.

When he's fully seated inside me, I reach for the shower head and let the water flow down his back to his nearly unmuddied bum, ridding him of the last tan flakes. We begin to rock together, slowly, gently as water fills the tub.

"Close your eyes," I whisper. As soon as he does, I run the hot stream through his hair, massaging his scalp. It's as if we're cleansing the horrors and trauma from our bodies with the simple act of water sliding across skin.

The act of joining with Sionnach goes beyond pleasure. It's a bond of belonging. One we will fight to keep through any Faerie bargain.

Our rhythm picks up speed. I imagine that every one of Sion's thrusts drives anything conspiring to separate us out of existence. His eyes are open now, inches from my own. There is no kiss, just reverence, as we relish mutual delirium.

If only the ever-present fear this might be the last time wasn't lingering in the corner of my mind.

CHAPTER 3
THE LOHO LAND

My life has been one sloppy helping of bizarre after another since I left New York and came to Ireland. Of Veil forests, Fae kings, and time travel, the most surreal of them all is lying here in bed with my soulmate to the sound of clothes thumping in his dryer.

Sion's hair tickles my cheek as I rest my head on his farmer-muscled chest. His hand idly plays with my fluffy locks. "So, after our last go, have we covered hasty, slow, and naughty?"

I kiss his Adam's apple. "Hmm? Well, I'd label the go with the shower head naughty." I nip the underside of his jaw. "Soaping each other in the tub before we got to the good bits fits into the slow category." I run a hand over his stomach, detouring to one of the V creases inside his hip bone to discover a half-hard cock waiting for me. "Plunging into me when I did nothing to encourage you but sit on the dryer naked ticks the hasty column."

"Sitting on the dryer with your lovely pout asking for a kiss, and your legs conveniently open."

I giggle. "You're very good at picking up signals."

Sion turns onto his side, effectively fitting his dick into my cupped fingers. "Go on…" he says, sliding his leg over my hip and yanking me flush against him, "…with your analysis of our pleasures."

I tap my swollen lips. "Well, walking through the living room with my legs wrapped around your waist while you were inside me before we even made it to the bed again is a bit of all three, I'd say."

"Aye, that was quite the achievement." His nose nuzzles my hair, teasing the soft skin behind my ear. "Which flavor shall I serve you next, love?

I grip his cock, delighted how eagerly it hardens at my touch. Sion is not my first lover, but he definitely wins in both the stamina and enthusiasm categories. This level of being wanted is very addicting.

I inhale deeply and assess if my rising exhaustion can withstand another round without a longer break. It was me who insisted Sion promise we'd make love at every opportunity. He's as good as his word. It's then I notice instead of the telltale musk of sweat and sex, the sweet fragrance of vanilla surrounds us. I sniff again. "What smells so nice because I'm guessing it isn't us?"

Sion pats the exceptionally soft mattress. "It's the lady's bedstraw."

I brace on an elbow. "You're kidding? The mattress is stuffed with a plant?"

He copies my position without removing his leg or the proximity of his substantial arousal in my palm. "Keeps the air fresh and the bugs away. I've got a nice bunch of it growing behind the cottage."

I shake my head. "You're probably the last holdout in the world using lady's bedstraw literally."

"Is it pleasing to you?"

Everything Sion has done tonight is pleasing to me. So pleasing, I won't be walking straight in the morning. "I'll let you know after a night's sleep."

He shifts me onto my back and slides on top of me. With tantalizing slowness, he strokes his hardness over my apparently insatiable dampening folds. "Shall I say goodnight to you, then, slow like?"

I lay a hand on his chest. "By the way, Mr. Loho, for someone who claims to have limited experience with sex, you are very creative."

"What I may lack in the doing, I make up for in the imagining." Sion flushes as red as the undertones in his nut-brown hair. "I've had the better part of every year to occupy myself. There are means to give a fella a bit of an education."

My gaze darts to the television in the other room. "Sionnach Loho. Are you telling me you watch porn?" His entire body heats as he squirms. It's adorable my question embarrasses him when he's spent the last few hours ravishing me in every way possible.

I kiss him sweetly. "Your sexual past doesn't bother me as long as mine doesn't bother you."

He covers my hand with his. "Truly?"

I run my toe up and down the soft hair on his leg. "Truly." Why should some long ago lass make me jealous? It's kind of gallant he wants to protect me from his history with other women. "You're it for me for the rest of all time, our time…whatever solving Finnbheara's riddle gives us."

The sheen of tears in his eyes surprises me. "And you for me, Eala. No one else will ever hold a claim on my heart or body."

We kiss, just kiss. Deep kisses. Light kisses. Kisses with teeth. Tongue tangling kisses. The sheer contentment of mingling breath with Sion is a wholly new experience for me. Kisses before were always a compatibility test or precursor to sex, never simply satisfying moments unto themselves. I suppose when you finally find the right person to kiss, you could kiss them forever without stopping.

I wrap my legs around him and pick up the sensuous slide of our bodies where he left off. As my heels dig into his ass, I breathe into his ear. "Slow. I want you slowly and completely."

"You have me, love. You have me."

At first, I think the rain wakes me. As I shift from numbness into awareness, I feel an intense rumble underscoring the steady beat of the downpour. Sion is curled on his side. My face nestles in the cozy space between his shoulder blades. His snores are the most wonderful, ordinary sound in the world. I ignore the music of the storm and snuggle closer to him, begging sleep to pull me back under.

A gust of wind rattles the window next to the red door with a violent *snap*. I sit up, fully awake. My eyes dart to the glass, half expecting it to wear spiderweb cracks. The steady drumming beneath the rain outside hasn't let up. In fact, it's grown louder. The *kerthump, kerthump* vibrates through my bones. Something is approaching the cottage.

Sion's earlier comment about a horse race comes to mind. The rising sound does remind me of galloping, but galloping what? My mouth goes dry as my mind files through tales of the *Sluagh Sidhe*, the Faerie Hunt. Has Finnbheara not even granted us one damn night before he sticks his Faerie fingers deeper into our business? Am I to be whisked away by the hunt for Faerie 101 already?

A different thought sends frigid tendrils through my blood. There is allegedly more than one Fae realm in myth and stories. What if Finnbheara isn't the one to send this hunt?

What if I'm actually losing my mind?

I ease out of bed and cover myself with a woolen blanket from the couch. Moving to the window, I squint through the coat of unrelenting rain streaming down the glass. It could be a trick of the far-off intermittent lighthouse beam playing tag with fat gray shifting storm clouds or just my imagination, but it looks like a substantial dark ball of shadow is tumbling toward the cottage along the road from the cliffs.

Stories of the Hunt usually mention a *Gaoithe Sidhe*, Faerie Wind, preceding the arrival of the Fae and their mounts. Part of my scholar brain is excited at the prospect of witnessing more legend made real. The not so fearless part of me is terrified to face whatever danger an actual Faerie Hunt might pose if that's what this turns out to be. I glance at my sleeping love. Would he be able to see the hunt, or will I be the only one with the *sight* for them.

"Get a hold of yourself, Eala," I hiss to myself. Loho land is so close to the sea, a phenomenon of a billowing cloud of fog is not impossible.

The way the thick gray clog churns up the road beneath it is.

My entire psyche jerks into high alert. Sion and I have been chased by a lethal shadow through the Veil. Finnbheara spoke of Aodh, another Fae god we might have pissed off. Sitting alone out here in the mortal world, are we fair game for any and all prickly Faerie royalty?

I'm not going to take any chances something unsavory trailed us from our Tír na nÓg exit to the cottage. I dash to the dryer and throw on my slightly damp *leine* to act as a nightshirt.

"Sion," I hiss quietly, as if the distant shadow might hear me. "Wake up."

His snoring hitches, but after a throaty fuss, he's out again. One more peek through the window to confirm I'm not going mental and then I'll shake his carcass awake if necessary.

I rub the window with my sleeve, which only clears a tiny bit of the blur. That tumbleweed of a shadow has reached the wooden gate at the end of the lane leading to the cottage. It clings low to the ground, unmoving and undisturbed by the rain. From the backlight glow of the lighthouse beam reflecting off the moist air, I swear I can make out shapes inside the mist. For a moment, the silhouettes remind me of animals on the Central Park carousel, but then they shuffle, becoming too indistinct to take on any definite form.

Despite this luxurious night tucked in the cottage with Sionnach, my fears hover too close to the surface. Just as I used to see shadow stories in the flames as a youth, am I imagining characters in the fog bank? Except, those flickering plays turned out to be real.

Dangers brew around us. The danger of Finnbheara's anger. The danger of not being able to translate his enigmatic riddle. The danger of Sion and me being torn apart.

I swipe the new layer of condensation off the window glass for another look and holler, "Sion, get up."

From the darkness outside, a face suddenly pops up on the other side of the window. Only one side of the head is lit by the beam of the motion sensor light, leaving its features in shadow. My scream jolts Sion out of bed and across the room to my side. Before I draw my next breath, the face is gone.

Sion throws his arms around me, drawing me tight to his bare chest. "Eala, what is it? You're shaking like the devil's on your tail."

I point to the window. "There was someone out there."

Sion surges around me to stare through the glass. He takes in every angle of the road and land before turning to me. "Where?"

"First by the gate––moving cloud, fog…I don't know. There were shapes inside it and then a face appeared in the window."

Sion, in all his naked glory, throws the front door wide open to get a better look. Over his shoulder, I have a clearer view of the yard and the path to the gate.

Nothing is there.

Not a wisp of mist or fog, just relentless rain. He closes the door then surveys our surroundings through every window of the cottage searching for a body to go with the face I swear I saw.

Concern etches lines across his ruddy face as he grips my shoulders. "Are you sure, love?"

I nod and rest the top of my head against his chest. "It looked like a man with longish light hair and a thin face."

Sion kisses my brow. "Sit down a bit, and I'll do a proper check." He grabs a heavy rain jacket from a hook on the wall and steps into a pair of wellies I hadn't noticed near the front door. To my horror, he pulls a mean-looking wooden club with nails pounded into the rounded end from the umbrella stand.

I run to him. "Don't go out."

"Better me clobbering the bastard in the yard before he tries to get inside."

My heart breaks for Sion. He's lived a life battered by failure and awful outcomes. From the moment I met him, he's been driven by desperation to beat a ticking clock. My bargain with Finnbheara lands him right back on a powder keg with an already lit fuse. I know he won't be able to settle until he can guarantee there's no stranger trying to break into the cottage.

"Sion, do you have a gun?"

His face is barely controlled rage. "No, but I'll consider getting ahold of one. Keep the lights off so you can see if he shows up again." He heaves the door open, then whips around to face me. "Lock it. Open it for no one but me." Purpose propels him into the rain as I turn the lock and start to pray the face I saw was nothing more than a distortion of my own reflection brought on by the stress injected into my exhausted brain.

I press my hands to the door. I've made nothing but bad decisions that bury us deeper and deeper in trouble since I jumped from the soulfall tower window after Sion. I'm shaking from the gravity of all we face and slide to the floor before my legs have a chance to give out. I've bargained for Sion's future with the King of the Connacht Fae, and now I've sent my dearest love into a storm with a cudgel to potentially chase shit knows what kind of monster. What if the Veil still harbors evil as horrifying as an Aodh hellish demon version of Olk?

What if Sion doesn't come back? What if I'm alone?

The pounding on the door elicits another scream from me.

"Eala, it's me. Open 'er up."

I walk my hands up the door until I'm on my feet and reach for the lock. After I wrench the door open, a rain-soaked Sion pours in. He hits the light switch.

"Didn't see a thing," he says, putting the disturbing club away and returning his coat to the peg. He shakes water from his hair. "It's pure wet out there." There's a *slurp* as he pulls off his boots. "Fuck," he growls, covering his privates with both hands then quickly removes them with a yelp. "My hands are as cold as my balls." He dives into bed.

I lock the red door. As Sion pulls blankets over his head, reclaiming the pocket of warmth we created beneath them, I strip off my erstwhile nightgown and drape it over one of the chairs at his kitchen table to finish drying.

His muffled voice sounds from his cocoon. "Bring your toasty arse back to bed."

I turn off the lights and take a final glance out the front window. Far off muffled by a cloud strewn sky, the moon's light leaks away a little more night by night. Once it cycles to new again, our fate will be sealed.

Sion plasters his body to mine. Damn, he is clammy. I grasp both his hands in mine and blow hot breath onto them. "Thank you for braving the elements to check. I guess I imagined a peeper."

He burrows his frosty nose where my neck meets my shoulder. "We've meddled in more than our fill lately. I'd not be surprised if a ghost or two snuck up on us."

"You think it was a ghost?"

"You've proven that you see 'em. Maybe something in you calls to 'em, Swan."

I burrow against him. "Well, I wish it wouldn't."

He chuckles. "We could cover the clocks and mirrors, so your visiting spirit doesn't get trapped in here with us."

"I don't think your superstition works if the ghost is on the outside trying to get in." I swallow hard. "Are we safe here?" A cottage far from its neighbors is fodder for a true crime documentary or isolated enough for Fae trouble that no one would discover for God knows how long.

Sion slings his leg over me, bending it to snug me closer. He frees one of his hands to stroke my back. "You'll always be safe with me, Eala *bán*. I swear it."

A bold statement from a man who's already dragged me through time with more variables than I can count. Not to mention the situations Finnbheara's riddle might plunk us into. I tip my chin until our lips nearly touch. "I'll hold you to that...Sionnach." The word *fox* is on the tip of my tongue, but I hold back. Given Sion's tendency to be in charge, losing his ability to shift added to the Veil snub are likely very sore subjects at present.

We sink into an exhausted kiss and then settle together with the vanilla fragrance of lady's bedstraw lulling us to sleep. As I drift off with Sion's fluttery snores tickling my cheek, a subtle rhythm, like the hoofbeats of horses galloping away, rumbles in my heart.

I jerk awake, sweat covering my naked body. I lay a hand to my mouth to stifle panting breaths so I don't wake Sion as my stare darts to the window.

The face isn't there, but a moment ago, in my dream, it was.

He was.

Certainty in my gut tells me the ghost or whatever vision I saw was definitely a man. I dreamed of him in more detail than what I could gather from his snoop at the window. The most unsettling part is I've seen him before. A jittery feeling tells me the man I saw at the window is the same as Finnbheara's guard who briefly poked through the mist in Tír na nÓg.

As a backdrop to the face in my dream, words in fancy script fell like black spidery raindrops. They looked similar in style to the lines of Finnbheara's poem that I saw behind my closed eyes, but I couldn't make them out.

With a racing mind coupled with the clot of dread in my stomach, there's no way I'll find sleep again. I hate my inability to embrace peace lying here with Sion. We promised each other one single night to revel in being together, and I can't even slow my thoughts enough to give him that.

Without worry lines threatening to take up permanent residence across his waking brow and the curly lock resting on his forehead, I can imagine him as a young man walking these fields with his father…before he left his family, before he became a spy, before he was shackled to the fate of the souls in the soulfall. I long to know a carefree Sion. Our truth is much more complicated. By the time morning comes, we have to devote everything to this riddle. It's more than our life and death. Solving it is the only way to ensure our *anamchara* connection will be in our hands and not the hands of Fae or fate.

Easing free of the arm slung across my hips, I slip out of bed. The banked fire warms the room a little, but not enough to strut around sans clothes. I groan at the thought of the itchy *leine* and eye a chest of drawers in the corner of the bedroom. The damn thing creaks like an irritated cat as I tug at the handle.

Thankfully, Sion doesn't budge. I'm envious of his deep sleep. If I can get a head start on teasing something from the riddle, maybe I'll relax enough to sneak back into bed before he stirs. It's hard to leave his side, even if it's only across the room.

Minimal rooting through his drawers produces a long-sleeved T-shirt with the emblem of an Irish football club on it and thick socks. Next, I retrieve the star pendant Finnbheara gave me from the bathroom doorknob and set it on the kitchen table. Luckily, my underwear awaits in the dryer to prevent the need to borrow a pair of Sion's boxer briefs. I stifle a snort. It would've been fun to experience the evolution of Sion's underwear through the decades. I'm sure he had definite opinions on trending styles and their comfort level.

Smudges of the dream linger in my waking mind. There's nothing to be had by fixating on the face that peered at me through the mist or at the cottage window. The most logical version is that he's a manifestation of my recent traumas and fears. The cascading letters are another matter. Are they related to the visitor or…

My professor brain kicks in, and I stare at the star pendant where I left it on the tabletop. For a split second, I swear it glows as if reflecting cool moonlight that isn't currently poking through the clouds on this stormy night. I drape the star around my neck and lower my lids. There, waiting for me as before, is Finnbheara's riddle.

The style of the script and words I saw when Finnbheara's riddle first appeared behind my eyelids is a near perfect match to the waterfall of letters in my dream. The man from the mists of Tír na nÓg and my window, the riddle, the dream, the pendant—disparate pieces that could all be connected. But how?

Next to the front door, I riffle through the contents of what looks like an antique rolltop desk missing the roll until I find a very modern pen, paper, and even sticky notes, not the parchment and quill I expected. There are books piled on top of the desk and on the floor next to it. I pick up a few to check the titles. Most are histories of Ireland, with several books of poetry among them. It must be a burden for Sion to ingest all that came before and then after his lifetime in case he needed the information to end the soulfall. Judging from his stationery supplies and the television next to the fireplace, he's keeping in touch with a changing world except for his lack of a cell phone, an impediment we now share.

If I have my way, we'll remedy that in the morning.

An oversized book near the bottom of the pile catches my attention. *Mythic Gods and Monsters.* With shaky hands, I wiggle it free. Flipping to the index, I find the name Aodh. Yep, he's got his own entry. Do I really want to revisit the face of a god that filled me with terror as a kid? "This is research, Eala," I whisper to myself and open to his page. The gaunt and decaying portrait of the Underworld god with his blazing eyes finds me again after all these years. I snap the book shut with a mix of horror and relief. It was not the face I saw at the window.

There are two chairs at the small, simple wooden table in the kitchen. One is wedged between the table and the wall, clearly never needed. It makes me sad to think of how many meals Sion ate alone. Carefully, I extract the trapped chair and place it next to its mate. No more lonely suppers for my love.

I settle in and close my eyes. Line by line, I scribble each stanza of the king's riddle on the paper. I double check to make sure I haven't altered any words. If we're not meticulous, the nuances hidden within his narrative could be our undoing.

By the time I finish, the rain has stopped. Dawn light blankets the rolling fields outside the cottage. In the midst of the tension ratcheting up every ounce of my being, I move to the window and marvel at the myriad colors of wildflowers dotting the landscape. Pastel purple lady's smock, fluffy white wild garlic, salmon-colored buttercups and others I can't name dust the ground like a delicate chalk drawing. Máthair would be able to identify every last bloom. She spent so much of her life, her first life, here in this very cottage. I've got a lot of emotions to sort through when it comes to my adoptive grandmother who plays the dual role as Sion's real mom. I stuff that particular task into the junk drawer of my mind to be dealt with later. Right now, this is a moment to treasure, the simplicity of being alone with Sion in his home, waiting for him to stir from sleep. Outside, spring flowers answer sunlight's call.

The ear-splitting wail from the bedroom puts a quick end to that.

CHAPTER 4
THE LAST CORRIGAN

E ala's gone.

I holler her name and reach for my *anamchara* as her face recedes into a shroud of fog rolling in from the sea. My darling swan is not just out of reach, she's never come to me. Eala is nothing more than the dream of a fool who'd fallen in love with the idea of finding his soulmate after two hundred years of walking the earth.

I have no one to love.

I am alone.

And then she's sitting on the edge of the bed, shaking my shoulders hard enough to rattle teeth. "I'm here, Sion."

I stare at her as the jumble of dreams and reality sort themselves out. She's not been in my bed for some time. The sheets are cold next to me, which is what probably brought on my desperate dream.

Eala's warm hand cups my face. "That must've been one helluva of a nightmare. Damn, you're loud."

I throw my arms around her, clutching more tightly than a typical good morning hug. "Up already, love? Not a good sleep for you either?"

She squeezes back, and I ease up.

"Nope," says Eala. "Guess it was too much to ask for one stress-free night. You just missed a spectacular dawn." She kisses my ear. "At least I was productive while you were snoring."

I love Eala in my clothes, in my house, in my bed. If besting Finnbheara's riddle gives us a chance to make such boons stick, I'm determined to get on with it.

"By raiding my drawers?"

She smiles, then her expression turns serious. "What scared you awake?"

You are nothing but the dream of a lost soul, and I'm a man alone.

I won't burden Eala with my irrational revisionist history. The truth is, we are together and facing enough trouble without unloading my weak bits. This is a woman who stood up to a king. Strength is what she deserves from me, not a confidence so damaged it's held together with rusted nails.

"A certain Amerrrrican woman missing from my bed gave me a fright."

I earn a quick kiss. She twists one of my curls around her finger, staring at me with a wistful expression. "There's so much we still have to learn about each other," she whispers. "How can you feel you know a person completely, yet not at all?" Her sigh sends warm breath across my neck. "Do you think fate or Finnbheara will give us the time to do it?"

"We're going to best him, Eala."

"Speaking of time, Mr. Loho, we'd best get to it." To my disappointment, she hops off the bed. "I think I've figured out a few things."

I groan, rolling onto my back and crossing both arms over my eyes.

"Put pants on. You're too distracting." Her gaze travels along my body, and she shakes her head. "Add a shirt too."

I prop myself on elbows. "Like what you see? Scars and all?" My body has seen its share of stabs, shots, and scrapes. It's nowhere near as perfect as her smooth, freckled self. Eala stares at the small round scar above my heart where Jeremy Olk's dagger tried to end me…Fuckin' hell, just a night ago.

She comes back to kiss that very spot. "Get up. I need your brain."

After tossing on tracksuit bottoms and a logo T-shirt from my mate, Robbo Corrigan's, pub, *A. Sidheóg*, I join Eala. My kitchen table is hidden under papers. Some are filled with writing and others are ripped into smaller squares and taped together. She's stolen my sticky notes as well.

"I know it looks like a crime scene map, but it makes sense to me," she says, arranging the snippets of paper. "You're out of tape."

Eala wrinkles her lips, pausing her detective work to look at me with curiosity. "I always imagined you anchored in the past, not the present. What was your life like when you weren't actively working on the soulfall?"

I fan a hand over the table. "Blathering about myself could kill this fine momentum."

She rolls her shoulders. "I need a mental break. Tell me."

I'm a fella who prefers to look forward not backward, but since I've dragged Eala into my life, she deserves to know all.

"Lonely. Desperate. Boring. All of it."

She lays a hand on my arm. "Were you awake?"

"'Twas a strange half-awake way of being, never truly living. I'd sleep for months after Beltane. It was a hard hit returning here after failing the soulfall again and again." I swallow down the catch in my voice. "You might say Finnbheara bound me here by shielding this land with a curtain of the Veil. I could putter about outside and never be seen."

There's a darling wrinkle between her brows. "How did you eat or navigate the world until Éostre came every year?"

I lean against her. "The short of it is, I got chummy with a Corrigan—" I tilt her chin up. "You remember Bobbo Corrigan, the authentic storyteller in Rowan Bend?"

"Bobbo? Do you mean Robbie Corrigan who let us crash in his flat after I passed out and nearly rolled down a hillside?"

I nod. "My association with the first Corrigan goes back a bit. Bobbo's five times *Daideo*, emmm, grandad to be exact. I'm on my fifth Bobbo in the fine Corrigan line. Using the name Bobbo between us is a code passed down, so each generation knows I'm him whom the family shares a bond with. Corrigans, bless 'em, put great store in dealings with the Good Folk. Once I let on that I'd got in a poxy state with the Folk all those years past, Corrigans have taken care of me. They left food, money, clothes, and such at the gate during those times they couldn't meet up with me, but knew I was here."

A gentle smile curls the corners of her lip as she rubs my arm. "Your guardian angels."

"Aye...emmm, I mean yes."

Eala threads her fingers through mine. "Don't modern up your language for me. Just be Sionnach Loho." The adoring expression on her face nearly brings tears to my eyes. I have a moment to enjoy it before she frowns. "I don't have your Corrigan backup."

"I can't count on it for much longer. The current Bobbo Corrigan prefers the company of men. He's happily married to a fine feller called Dale and has no desire to sire." There's a stitch in my chest imagining the end of the loyal, Fae believing, Corrigan line. "As undeserving as I am, the fool is leaving his pub and other assets to me when he passes in case I'm still around after." I kiss my fingertips and lay them over my heart. "That's a friend. He's vowed to make me learn online banking and ATM machines to break my habit of keeping my cash and coin, well..." I nod toward the floor next to the hearth where lifetimes of money hides under the floorboards.

"Did you tell him about the soulfall and me coming to help you end it?"

"No," I say a bit too brusquely. "I'd not burden him with all the unnatural specifics of my life." I wave my hands when Eala flinches. "Sorry. Not to say you're a burden. Keeping secrets has always been a millstone around my neck."

I tense when she drops her head onto her hands. Seeing Eala in distress pulls my strings tight.

"Sion, how am I going to get my driver's license, cell phone, and credit cards back? I've got no I.D. and no money." She whips her head, taking in the room. "I don't even know what day it is." Her breathing gets faster.

I grab a remote from the couch and click on the TV. A menu screen shows the current weather and other stats.

Eala looks skeptical. "A television but no cell phone?"

I shrug. "Who was I gonna call?"

She rolls her eyes. "The latest Bobbo Corrigan?"

I grab the knob and open the press nearest to the kitchen sink to reveal my phone and its tangled cord. "This does fine."

"Sion, why is your phone in a cupboard?" She shakes her head.

"It's useless when I'm in Finnbheara's bubble. Once I'm free each year, I Veil travel to see Bobbo man-to-man. He had the phone put in one year. I didn't ask for it."

She tilts her head and gives me quite a look. "Let me guess. You didn't ask for electricity or plumbing either."

I tap her Faerie kiss of a nose. "Those were my idea. I'm a very modern man."

Eala barks a laugh and follows up with an adorable squinch of a look. "And the Corrigans paid for all that?"

I've never had to account for my unconventional existence before. It's a bit of a cringe to do it now. "The Corrigans have always done well for themselves. I've had the luck of it to be in a will or two of their's."

Eala closes her eyes and taps her temple. "So—many—questions." She looks at me and sighs. "Back to the Fae riddle now—Sion questions later."

I love the way she gathers herself, getting down to business. My beautiful scholar. I look more closely at her work. She's taped small squares of ripped paper to each stanza of Finn's ranting with labels of *sources, deadline, place, task quota, warning, core question, power play,* and lastly *WTF.*

"We've already pegged our deadline, the next new moon." She points to the first four lines and reads. *"Passage sought to lands of mine, where wish and dream bide free.* That obviously refers to our admittance into Tír na nÓg aka *Sidhe."* Eala chews on the pen. "Okay, *Tales of old both true and told...*" She taps pen to paper where she's laid it all out. "...A statement that both stories and actual history are involved."

Eala groans when I lean over her shoulder to stare at her work. "He didn't skimp on the threats and warnings."

I drop into the other chair she's pulled out from the wall. "Himself makes no secret that he's cheering on our failure. He wants you with him and me gone."

Her eyes glisten with tears. "I hate him."

I take her hands. "On that, we agree." After kissing her knuckles, I give our hands a shake to keep us from falling into a fine wallow over our shit odds. "You've figured out more. Tell me."

Eala fingers the star pendant around her neck. Anger boils low in my gut remembering the king putting it on her and the way he touched her. The bastard even kissed her.

She puffs her cheeks, then blows a breath. "My hunch is the line about the sharpened star and a completed quota to fill are connected to this necklace. There are five points, so we have five tasks to figure out that'll help us answer the core question."

"Core question?"

She turns the paper to face me and points to a pair of lines. "Here's the only question posed in the whole thing. *What's all and each the selfsame piece, plain truth and no illusion?*"

I drop my forehead to the tabletop. "How do we know how to answer that bit of nonsense?"

"Sionnach."

Her tone is as sharp as a knife point. I look right up.

She pokes my sternum. "Don't you lose faith. We haven't even started."

The look of determination on her face puts some steel back in my spine.

She grips my bicep. "I need all of you. Mind, heart, and the belief we can do this." She removes her finger from my chest to stab two words on the page. "Your *wit* and *guile*."

No doubt my swan was capable of scaring the wits and guile out of any miscreant student of hers.

"So, boyo," she says, "turn them on. I'm stuck on this part, which sounds like he's giving us instructions to go somewhere, hopefully a starting point. Does it mean anything to you?"

I read the chunk she's tapping.

Face the ridge of grey to go,
When mortals fall to dream.
Upon the crest above fine lands,
A stone will wake with screams.

"There's only one stone I know of with a reputation for screaming; *Lia Fáil*, the Stone of Destiny, up on the Hill of Tara. Its squawk was said to confirm the next high kingly sort," I say.

Eala knocks her fists against her head. "Of course. How did I miss that?" She slams her hands on the riddle. "And the Hill of Tara was also called the grey ridge. The stone is on its crest."

I move behind her to massage her shoulders. "It's at least somewhere to start poking around."

She leans her head back against me. "Maybe once we're there, something will jump out to make the whole mess clearer." Eala grabs my hand and turns to face me. "Hey, do you think there's a possibility we could Veil travel during the day now?"

There's so much hope in those lovely eyes green glass eyes, I hate to dash it. "Doubt it. Himself already blasted the gifts he once gave me arseways and slapped us with an impossible deadline. Not a generous sort."

I hate the stress lines my comments raise across her forehead.

Rubbing her arm, I choose an answer without stinging nettles. "On the other hand, it can't hurt to give it a go."

"Okay." She slides her fingers between mine, then shuts her eyes. Her grip tightens and beads of sweat glisten on her upper lip, but there's no sign of the Veil.

"Shit," she says. "It's a no go. I guess traveling is still limited to half a Celtic day, our night, not our daytime."

I nuzzle her head. "We'll do our sleeping and other pleasant activities while our sun shines, then go where the Veil takes us when the moon's on duty."

Eala's attention flicks to the TV, and she growls a second. "Shit."

I whirl to look at the menu screen. Nothing up there looks shit provoking. "What's riled you?"

She's on her feet, pacing with enough enthusiasm to send papers flying off the table. "We left the soulfall tower on Beltane. Look at the date on the TV. It's May fourth. How could we have been in Tír na nÓg that long?"

I intercept her mad dashing about and gently grip her shoulders. "You know as well as I that the Fae tinker with time. Nothing to do but move on."

Eala lays her palms on my chest to push me away so she can keep moving. "You don't understand. It's the fourth. The Kennard Park University tour flies back to New York this afternoon." Her gaze flashes to the early morning light barging in through the windows. "We only have about eight hours."

Before I have a chance to comprehend the scope of her distress. She's back in front of me, squeezing my forearm in a death grip.

"When they go, so do my backpack, my suitcase, all my stuff. Colleen wouldn't leave it behind."

I peel her fingers free. "It's fine, love. We can replace it all."

Eala winds even tighter, a caged beastie circling the room. "We can't. If it goes, any proof of who I am disappears with it. We have to meet up with Colleen. Their flight leaves from Shannon Airport in the late afternoon."

"Call her, love."

Eala flushes. "Her contact is in my phone. I got lazy and stopped memorizing numbers."

The borrowed calm we stole during the night with sleep and sex drips away like the last of pooled rain off the eaves. As the gravity of our situation casts a gray pallor, guilt slices through me. We're in this desperate race for our future because of me. Eala was created by Finnbheara to help me end the soulfall. She's forfeited her human dreams for a man whose existence reads like a folktale. Worst of all, my precious love may have bargained away eternity in Tír na nÓg to stay with an *amadán*, a right fool, having nothing to offer but wit and loyalty. If only I'd not lost the Fae gifts that were once mine.

Lucky for me, a long life provided its own gifts. I open the press, lift the black handset of the phone, and tap out a number.

"Hey, Bobbo, it's Sionny. I'll be needing a favor."

CHAPTER 5
THE GARDA

Sion's pal, Bobbo Corrigan, turns off the narrow country highway into the town of Rowan Bend after retrieving us from the cottage. It's both unsettling and nostalgic to be back here. The postcard perfect Irish village was the Ireland I always pictured from my grandmother's stories. Its compact main street is lined with brightly painted buildings, only a hint of traffic, friendly people, enough pubs and stores to be interesting but not overwhelming.

This is where Sion and I began. Up the hill from here in a small wood, is where I first tumbled from my seat on a tilted standing stone into his arms and another world. It was the day my life as an adjunct professor hoping for a tenure track position slipped away. I fell for a time-traveling, fox-shifting, dear Irish boy.

As Sion chatters at Bobbo about our needs, my mind drifts, staring out the window at a rustic graveyard on the outskirts of Rowan Bend. Would I go back? Trade Fae-tinged insanity for my cozy life in a small upstate New York college town?

From the passenger seat, Sion laughs at something the last Corrigan, says. The sight of his smile and bobbing brown curls with their burnt melon undertones says it all. There is no going back. Sionnach Loho is every upward curve of my lips into a smile, every rush of joy. I lean my head against the seat. What I need to figure out is who Eala Duir is in my new Finnbheara-centric existence. The king says he was sending some sort of guide or teacher for me. Maybe they'll have answers to help me with this existential quandary.

Last night, when I thought the hunt was swooping in to carry me off to Faerie lessons, I dreaded the idea. In the morning light, with a mountain of questions rising higher and higher in my brain, I'm warming to the idea.

Bobbo pulls into a free spot in front of his pub, *A Sidheóg*. A travel backpack laden student group, the near copy of my tour from Kennard Park University, heads into the pub for their authentic Irish breakfast and storytelling morning. Down the street, I see a tour bus parked in a dirt lot. It could be the same one that ferried my grad students around Ireland. I feel a pang of loneliness for my bestie Colleen, who is probably mental, as Sion would say, over my disappearance.

The men spill out of the car. I join them in rolled up sweatpants, a borrowed T-shirt, and a dark green hoodie with a Guinness harp appliqué on the back from Sion's collection. The man likes his cotton products. When you're trapped at home for the better part of a year, comfort is king.

After a man-thump hug, Bobbo Corrigan says his goodbyes. He leaves to resume his pub proprietor duties. Sion dangles the keys in front of me. "We've got the use of Dale and Bobbo's rattletrap of a second car." He takes my hand and starts leading me down the street. "One quick stop and we'll be on our way back to County Clare and your suitcase." He tugs me toward a butter-yellow storefront with a sign announcing *Bend's Best*. "Two quick stops. You're going to go mad for Jess's boxty pancakes. She keeps cows and makes the sour cream herself."

After the miserly breakfast at Sion's of questionable hard cheese and stale bread, the prospect of hot food is appealing. "Can we get it to go?" My slip into an Americanism elicits a quizzical look on Sion's face. "I mean take-away?"

"We've got time for a sit down, love. It's only fifty kilometers to the airport and break days not long past."

I'll feel better if we stake out Shannon Airport long before the group is set to arrive. I don't remember the details of the flight number to New York to check if it's been changed. We can't miss Colleen.

My stomach growls. "There 'tis," says Sion. "Decision made." He grins, patting my grumbling belly. His touch sets off a craving that has nothing to do with food. For the love of Finnbheara's ass, the appetite I have for my *anamchara*, his body, his touch, hasn't dimmed despite our thorough attempts last night to satisfy it.

"What's our other stop?" I ask, hoping it will distract me from the pressure building in my body at very inconvenient locations.

"Emmm…" His face turns as deep red as his hidden garnet curls.

I stop walking to face him. "What's wrong?"

His smile is strained. "It's all grand." He puts a hand on the back of my neck and pulls me in for a confident kiss that does nothing to douse my simmering core. "Let's tick number two off before we tuck into breakfast."

We pass a tourist shop, then I nearly stumble in front of the plus sign marking a pharmacy. We lost three days, which means I've skipped my birth control pills during the time we've chalked up plenty of sex. They were in my backpack. Another reason not to miss Colleen. Did I technically miss biological days? Is it even possible for Sion and me to conceive a child? Neither of us can be considered your typical human.

Sion leads me toward a brick storefront with a navy-blue façade and white window trim called *Taste of the Past* that's set back from the street. Ivy trails around the windows and door, giving it a homey storybook cottage look.

I swing our joined hands. "I love the charming way ivy trails over the front of buildings. The look would totally work for your place."

He squeezes my hand. "I'll get to planting such."

The moment is bittersweet. My rush of happiness at the thought of making the Loho cottage our home dies as reality cuffs me on the head. Our goal is Tír na nÓg. It's likely we'll never see the cottage again if we solve Finnbheara's riddle. It's best to keep my focus on the present. I squint through the shadows cast by the trees in front of a *Taste of the Past*.

"Are you sure it's open this early?"

Sion slows his pace. "Not a worry, love."

The way he fidgets, and his cagey behavior, are typical for when he's keeping things from me. I stop walking a few feet before the shop door. "Okay, Mr. Loho, what's got your boxer briefs in a knot? No more secrets, remember?"

Sion starts to answer at the same time the door of the quaint shop flies open, and the poster girl for hot Irish lass launches herself at him. Flowing strawberry blonde hair frames a lovely heart-shaped face that's the cherry on top of a body with curves just this side of too-perfect.

"Sionny!" She cries. "Here you are. I haven't seen you in devil knows how long."

The Irish eye candy demotes me from Sion's arm candy to mere onlooker as she clutches him in a body-melding embrace. With her tongue in the lead, the woman crushes her mouth to his.

My simmering lust from moments before escalates into boiling jealousy.

To his credit, Sion immediately retreats from the kiss, bracing his hands on the beauty's matchstick thin arms to create distance between them. His gaze flashes to mine in a definite *help me* look. I return it with a *you're on your own* stare.

The woman tracks his gaze to me, and she visibly wilts.

Sion scrambles to my side. "Caity Byer meet Eala Duir."

"Tracked her down, didja?" says the local beauty. The corners of her lips curve south.

Sion takes my hand and kisses it. "Saints be praised, I did."

I feel foolish standing here, clueless as to what's going on. Not completely clueless. Clearly there's history here and not the buddy type like between Sion and his Corrigan.

Caity approaches, eyeing me. "Sionny's held a torch with your name on it for years. Please don't break his heart again."

Break his heart?

Again!

Sionny and I are going to have words.

Caity recovers her ebullience as she threads her arm through Sion's elbow and guides him to her shop. "I've stockpiled some grand stuff for you from the studio. Not your whole list, but most of it."

Sion slips her grasp yet again to affix himself to me. "Caity's sister works in wardrobe at studios in Dublin whipping up brilliant period clothes."

"We buy as much as we can after a shoot for the shop," says Caity. She appraises me head to toe. "I'd say we did a crackin' job matching your size, Eala. Did the clothes suit you?"

Here's one question answered. I'd wondered how the sack of historical garments Sion kept in Alfie, his *fánaí* wanderer tree, held an ample supply of women's wear. How many charming Caitys has he hooked up with over the years to pad his collection?

Sion holds the door for me, and we step into *Taste of the Past*. It's packed with a casual jumble of dress forms displaying costumes from Victorian bustled dresses and Regency ball gowns to chainmail with surcoats emblazoned with impressive family crests. Piles of folded leather and muslin garments adorn long tables marked with specific time periods. There's even a weapons rack along the back wall.

If this meeting wasn't awkward as hell, I'd love to poke around. "Yes, they fit as if they were made for me."

"Brilliant," says Caity, looking pleased.

Sweat beads along my hairline at the tension between us all. "Uh, thanks for taking the trouble." I hate how stiff and unfriendly I must be coming across, but after their hello kiss and Caity's warning about breaking Sion's heart, I'm not at my best.

She gives me a curt nod. "Anything for Sionny." Caity's expression turns wistful. "After more than a year, I had my doubts I'd ever see this one walking back through my door."

It's ridiculous how triumphant I feel to learn it's been a while since Sionnach enjoyed the company of Ms. Caity. How selfish am I? I certainly haven't led a celibate life. Why should Sion? I need to reframe my belief that his amorous entanglements are long dead.

The memory of our first-time making love is vivid in my thoughts. Sion didn't deny he'd had sex, but a sick feeling churns in my stomach imagining him showing anyone but me the tenderness and desire we've shared. Especially when he led me to believe he'd only had *scratch an itch* sex, not meaningful passions with someone he cared for.

Or is that just the way I chose to paint his past?

"I figured he'd got back with you, Eala, but a girl can hope." Caity locks her gaze at Sion long enough to raise my internal temperature a few more degrees.

Sion clears his throat, not for attention, but from nerves. "I'm happy to take what you've done up for us," he says, emphasizing *us*.

Caity finally seems resigned to her non-Sion fate as she flashes him one last doe-eyed goodbye and disappears behind a curtained doorway.

Sion slides his arm around me and lowers his voice. "Swear, she's nothing to me, love."

My body stiffens. "Don't dismiss her. She clearly was *something* to you besides your personal shopper."

"Eala, I—"

I hold up a hand. "Not here. Not now. I'm still adjusting to the reality of your very long..." My gaze darts to the curtain. "...And not so long past before you *tracked me down*. I'll deal with it."

Caity drags an overstuffed canvas bag from her storeroom. Sion scurries over to take possession and slings the sack over his shoulder.

Both Caity and I take note of the back muscles rippling through his T-shirt.

My soulmate's muscles.

Jealousy feels petty. Hell, didn't Sion deserve to enjoy physical comfort or passion in his life? How could Caity know the depth of our truth? She's only known Sion on his own in what sounds suspiciously like something he described as a jilted lover situation where I allegedly broke his heart. The man is a storyteller. There was bound to be some embellishment in his personal tale.

I approach her with a smile. "I really appreciate what you've done and what you're doing for us."

She's surprised and a bit confused. "Well, fine then."

I don't elaborate since I've no idea what reasoning Sion's given her as to why we need centuries' worth of clothing.

Sion covers the awkward moment. "Did Bobbo cover my bill?"

Caity nods. "Yeah. Thanks."

"We'll be off then." Sion gives her the look of someone who's leaving on a very long trip. "Best to you, Cait."

"And you Sionny." She forces herself to look at me. "Eala."

We don't even reach the end of the short path between the shop and the street before Sion blurts, "Once, and I shouldn't have. Too much whiskey and too little sense. It took a fine friendship where it never belonged."

I look at the shop where I see Caity fussing near the front window surreptitiously watching us. "She thought it belonged. You must've made an impression on her." What am I doing? Do I really want any more details than what he's offering?

With his free hand, Sion fiddles with his hair, making sure it covers his ears. His nervous tell makes me smile, remembering how many times I wondered if he was covering pointed Fae ears with his mop of hair.

"I was sloppy with her, far too quick, and not at all generous." His face is the color of the brick buildings. "I truly did not understand the difference between what I did with her and making love until you showed me what it could be."

I'm a terrible person for relishing the satisfaction his confession gives me. I rise on tiptoe to kiss him. "I haven't begun to show you what it can be."

His arousal arrives with gratifying speed. I'm not the only one with lust on the agenda. Sion's voice is low and gravelly. "Let's see about getting this bundle to Dale's car and then finding somewhere private off the road."

I hold his arm to keep him from walking away. "Are there any other members of the naked Sionnach Loho fan club we might run into?"

He makes a choking sound and looks chagrined. "To be fair, Caity didn't see me fully naked. Only the necessary bits."

My laugh is explosive and loud. I'm a little less jealous of whatever happened between them. I grab Sion's free hand. "Let's dump your costume haul in Dale's car, Fox, then grab boxty pancakes."

I don't miss the twitch of his fingers at the word *fox*.

Sion and I camp out on a bench in front of the main terminal of Shannon Airport. We've been here nearly two hours and there's still no sign of Colleen and company.

I blow on my hands, cold from the chilly spring day. I feel like a careless idiot for not memorizing Colleen's cell number so I could have called her on Sion's landline. For a hot second, I entertained calling the Celtic studies department at Kennard Park to get her number, but a niggling feeling told me not to involve them until after this meet up. Heaven knows what's gone on in the days since I vanished from the tour.

"I'll go hunt down coffee," says Sion.

I wrap both arms around one of his. "I don't want to get separated."

Sion kisses my cheek as a familiar bus rumbles toward the curb. The tour is here. "On we go, Swan."

The boxty pancakes revolt in my stomach. "You're clear on our Olk story?"

He traps my arm against his ribs. "Aye." Sion taps the side of his head. "Your practice drills from the car ride are burned in here."

I wish I could pull off Sion's easy-going confidence. We take a step to intercept the bus and comically screech to a stop. A pair of guards in windbreakers with *GARDA* across their backs stride out the glass doors of the terminal.

"Shit," says Sion, going completely still.

My pulse races as the guards board the bus. "Now what do we do?"

He eases us away from the curb and closer to the building, spinning me around so my back is to the bus. "Nothing much has changed from what we planned."

"Except for the cops," I say, stealing a glance over my shoulder.

"Surely, their business is about you and Olk going missing. Once you step in, half their job's done." He pulls me closer. "Or we walk away."

Boy, do I want to walk away, but I'll never forgive myself if I don't let Colleen know I'm okay. Hell, that I'm alive.

The grad students, led by Charlie, the most recent object of Colleen's affections, file off the bus. He tosses a worried look behind him before joining the others to retrieve their suitcases and travel backpacks from the luggage compartment. The group heads into the airport. Colleen and the guards are not among them.

Sion whispers in my ear. "I swear to you, Eala *bán*, you'll never fall when you're with me."

The promise he gave me and kept when I had to face my fear of heights gives me courage once again as we approach the bus. I nearly gasp when Colleen climbs down the steps to the curb. She looks seriously ill, skin devoid of color, dull eyes, auburn hair hanging in unwashed ropes.

It's my fault. I've done this to my best friend.

I rush forward. "Colleen."

Her head snaps up with more energy than she looks capable of. Our tears are immediate as I crash into her.

"Ellie," she cries, reverting to the name I carried all my life until Máthair's will christened me Eala Duir.

Her backpack thumps to the concrete as we clutch one another, weeping. "I thought...oh God...I thought you were—"

"I'm so so sorry, C. I never meant to—"

Colleen's body goes rigid and then she lets go and shoves past me. "You," she yells, and drives a fist into Sion's chest.

Sion takes the blow easily and captures Colleen's wrist. Before she can launch another assault, the guards who've left the bus gently ease a raging Colleen away from Sion.

"Whoa there," says the taller guard with close-cropped blond hair and a friendly face, who takes charge of Colleen. "Let's sort this out calmly, shall we?"

His counterpart, an olive-skinned wrestler-type with syrupy brown hair and matching eyes, gives Sion and me the once-over. "Eala Duir and Jeremy Olk?"

I start to nod when Colleen pipes up. "That is not Professor Olk. He's a local guide we *fired* from our tour." Her blood-shot eyes add fierceness to her glare.

Sion extends his hand to the guard. "I'm Sionnach Loho, sir."

After a brief hesitation, he takes it. "Ewan O'Rourke," He bobs his chin at the other guard who attempts to talk Colleen down from the shock of seeing us. "And there's Dan Clarke."

I will my hands to stop shaking. Sion, on the other hand, cranks up his easy charm. He addresses Colleen. "You've every right, Colleen, to be angry with us, especially me."

When the guards zero in on Sion, I jump in. "With both of us. I'm to blame. I totally screwed up. The tour was my responsibility. I walked away and left a mess with Colleen and Jeremy." If we hadn't lost three days with our trek into Tír na nÓg, my transgression of abandoning the group would've only been for one night. This mess with the Garda would never have come to pass.

Colleen stoops like she's been punched. Her fingers pinch the bridge of her nose. "You expect me to believe you blew off the tour and compromised your shot at a tenure track position to run off with *him*?"

Ewan O'Rourke snorts. "We've seen this before, eh Danny?"

"American falling hard, yeah." Dan's expression hardens. "No matter. What can you tell us about Jeremy Olk?"

I flash what I hope is a confused look at Colleen. "Jeremy?"

"He went missing the day you did," says Colleen. "I told them I assumed you'd run off together."

I hope no one else hears the muted rumble from Sion.

"I haven't seen Jeremy since I left Luttrellstown Castle to meet up with Sion at the old gatehouse," I tell the guards.

As rehearsed, Sion adds, "My last dealing with the professor was when he sacked me." He meets Colleen's acid gaze.

I pray our timeline of Sion disconnecting from the tour and our impulsive lover's leap jives with whatever big picture Colleen painted.

The guards do not look placated. I suppose popping back from oblivion to ambush Colleen at the airport isn't a great look for us. "When did you leave Dublin City?" asks Ewan.

"The same night. We've been at Sion's place in Clare since then," I say.

"Can you confirm that?" says Dan, jotting down notes.

"Call on Robbie Corrigan over at the Sidheóg in Rowan Bend. He'll tell you same as me," says Sion and gives the guard his friend's info.

"The three of you'll be around," asks Ewan.

Sion, Colleen, and I simultaneously say *yes*. The surprise on my face at her answer asks a question.

"I made plans to stay here until we found you and Jeremy," says Colleen. "My Shanna owns a vacation place near Ennis where I can stay."

Mixed feelings make my throat clench. On one hand, I'm happy Colleen isn't leaving so I can attempt to patch up what I've broken. Except now, I'll have to build another tower of lies about whatever Sion and I will be off doing to solve Finnbheara's riddle. She'll want to be in touch and won't exactly be tolerant of my relationship with Sion. Our already full plate cracks with the weight of making amends to Colleen heaped on top.

Sion's hand presses into the small of my back, keeping me on an even keel.

Charlie pokes his head out the door of the terminal. "We're cutting it close, Colleen."

He wears a hangdog look on his face. There's no evidence of the sizzle between them that ignited on the plane ride over and got brighter during the tour.

Colleen looks at the guards. "I need to go do a headcount before they go through security. Can you wait?"

Ewan waves her on. "We've got your contact. We'll be in touch."

Sion chats about hurling victories with the guards as I join Colleen. "You're still going to stay?"

It kills me how wiped out she looks. "No reason not to, and Jeremy's still a no show."

"What do you mean no reason not to?"

She stops at the door. "Kennard Park fired me. Two professors vanished into thin air from the tour on my watch."

Shit. "That's not your fault."

Colleen is drained. "Ruining the end of the tour was my fault. We never left Dublin for the itinerary stops in Northern Ireland. A cross country bus ride to the airport was not the finale the group signed on for. People were pissed, and they put in a call to Kennard Park University to complain when I dropped the ball and both team leads bailed."

"I am so sorry." I try to hug her, but she backs off. "This is all on me, Colleen. Well, not Jeremy, but the rest."

"Yes, it is." The breath she takes looks painful. "Sion? What the hell, Eala?"

"We'll wait while you deal with the tour and then drive you to Ennis. It'll give me time to explain."

Colleen holds up a hand. "No. I'm grateful—" She pauses. "Beyond grateful…" My good Catholic friend makes the sign of the cross. "…you turned up. I thought the worst." In her expression, I see the ties of our friendship still exist, however frayed. "Please, give me the chance to absorb everything. I'll call you when I'm ready to talk."

I'm about to confess my lack of cell phone when she says, "Oh, here." Colleen extracts my day pack from her larger travel backpack. "Charlie and I found it in the gatehouse at Luttrellstown."

I take it from her, stunned to get a piece of my life back so easily. I unzip the top and see my wallet, passport, and phone. "You didn't give it to the Garda?"

Her smile is flat and lifeless. "I wanted to believe you were so swept away with Jeremy that you accidentally left it behind. No one doubted, including me, you'd eventually show up at the hotel, so I didn't call anyone and kept your stuff with me."

The deafening whine of a plane taking off stalls our conversation. When it dies away, Colleen takes a deep breath and continues. "When the university got wind of student complaints and the fact that you and Jeremy had disappeared, they got the Garda involved. Another black mark in my column for not calling the police as soon as you two ditched the group." She gives me the saddest look I've ever seen on her usually energetic face. "I hoped you'd hooked up with Jeremy, so I stalled." Her laugh is bitter. "I think the cops who first questioned me in Dublin suspected I was keeping a shady secret about what happened to you two."

There's no explanation I can give her that sounds like anything but the Faerie story it is.

Her gaze flicks into the terminal where Charlie is waving his arms to flag her down. She looks pained when she turns back to me. "I can't wrap my head around what you did, Eala." She starts to say something else but stops and nods toward the bus. "I brought your travel backpack too."

Without a goodbye, she leaves. A thousand unspoken apologies burn my tongue. Sion is back at my side before the terminal door closes behind my friend. I point to the agitated bus driver who frowns at the last piece of luggage. "That's mine."

When Sion leaves me to grab it, on impulse, I turn on my cell and check my Kennard Park email, fully expecting a strongly worded reprimand over abandoning the group. Maybe there's something I can say or do to save Colleen's job.

Professor Duir, we are pleased to offer you a tenure track position in the Celtic studies department at Kennard Park University.

Hearing my cry, Sion rushes to my side, catching me before I hit the ground in a sobbing heap.

CHAPTER 6
THE HILL OF TARA

On our drive to the cottage, I try all my best stuff to pull Eala out of her mood: obscure folktales, off-color jokes I thought were gas, and some less than flattering occasions in my past when I acted the maggot. She sits, pretending to listen and doing a crap job of it.

Personally, I think the rendezvous with Colleen went as well as it could. At least we fed the Garda enough detail for them to bunk off a bit. The afternoon is flagging. We've got to get crackin' to the Hill of Tara as soon as she can call the Veil at dusk to test our theory on the hint in Finnbheara's damned riddle.

I slide my eyes her way. My swan is a piece of crumbled paper. I'm an ass to expect anything but distress from her. The message she got from her university would make the future she saw for herself come true. A dream dumped in the bin the day she took up with me.

I've no doubt Eala loves me, but my love for her was gifted the luxury to ripen and set down roots as I watched her become the brave yet tender soul she is. Her love for me is still a new thing. A precious thing, a fragile thing with no seasoning.

I grip the wheel. She's got every right to drive her fists into my breastbone harder than Colleen's go at me. Eala and I may be fated to be together thanks to Faerie influence, but it doesn't change the truth that I would choose her in any life, in any world, in any time. It also doesn't alter the fact I ripped her from the future she'd written for herself.

I hit my limit on patience for her silence. "If the ball of regret you're trying to swallow chokes you, love, talk to me."

She stares out her window. "I deserve to choke. I got Colleen fired. She looked sick and as pale as a ghost from worrying about me. I ruined her life."

"You had no way of knowing we'd lose multiple days."

Eala bangs her fist on the dash. "I should have known. It happens in practically every folktale where a human crosses into Fae realms. It was reckless not to tell her there was a possibility I wouldn't come back before I left the group to try and find you."

My volume is loud enough to startle her. "I'm an eejit for not considering the same before we blasted into the Veil for my purposes."

She looks at me then and continues in a quiet voice. "My regret is not about saving the souls, and I'd never regret you."

I'm so relieved to hear her say those words, I nearly piss myself.

Eala swivels to face me. "Colleen is a sister to me. It was hell thinking she was finished being part of my life. Knowing she believes I didn't care enough to say goodbye or even tell her I was leaving…" She presses both hands to her chest as if it'll stop her heart from cracking.

Pulling to the side of the road, I stop the car. Clicking off my safety belt, then Eala's, I gather her in my arms. "You're a rare soul, Eala. You'd put the rest of the world ahead of yourself."

She ducks her head against my collarbone, letting me soothe her. When her weeping seems to dry itself out, I pull back and gently run the uncalloused parts of my thumbs under her eyes. Eala grabs my wrists. "Sion, if I ever hurt you, swear you'll tell me."

I kiss her forehead. "I will. Now you swear the same to me."

Eala's gaze bores into mine. "I do." Her breath flutters and stutters as she draws it in. Concern digs a tiny crease between her brows as she peers out the windshield at the sky. "It's getting late."

We pop our safety belts back in place and head off again. Soon, the high hedges along the road give way to rolling fields. As the sun teases us by quickening its pace to the horizon, we hit Loho land. I pass the cottage gate to a break in the stone wall large enough for the car, then take a short, packed dirt drive until we're behind the house. I made this wee path after the first time I borrowed a car from Bobbo and Dale. Vehicles haven't done me much good for the type of traveling I do, but they're handy for grabbing other stuff like take-away from town or sticky notes. I smile, picturing Eala's detective map.

Eala trudges across uneven clumps of grass between the flowers I've let go wild. Ma kept a more orderly garden and Da the crops, but now I'm more inclined to see what the land serves up on its own. When she rounds the corner of the cottage, Eala makes a sound halfway between a shriek and a scream and takes off running.

I drop the bag of clothes I'm lugging to sprint and catch up to her. I'm thankful she's never one to run toward danger. "Eala, what is it?" I barely get the words out before I see what the ruckus is about.

There, with white curving trunks and a distinctive pattern of green triangles on her bark is Alfie, my *fánaí* tree, that's wandered with me in my traipses through time.

Eala pets the skinny trunks as she pops her head between them to check in Alfie's middle. "It's here," she calls out. "Your bag of smelly clothing." Then she reaches down to grab something she retrieves with a grunt. "Was this here before?"

I reach her side and gawk at the chainmail shirt she holds up. Running my hands over the interlocking metal rings, I shake my head. "No. New addition."

Eala smirks. "Alfie's been busy."

I get a better look at the green triangle pattern on the tree's white bark. There is a subtle difference in their position as well as a few added marks. "My sweetheart's got an extra bit of decoration." I point out the extended row of green triangles before grabbing up the familiar bag of clothes.

With an abrupt change in her demeanor, Eala drops the mail shirt and backs away as if the tree's about to pull her through time against her will.

"All is well. 'Tis my stash of clothes to be sure."

As I contemplate the sudden appearance of our woodsy visitor, Eala moves in behind me. "Sion, your tree is exactly where the man snooping in the window stood last night."

I look between her and the tree, then at the chainmail. "It's got to be Finnbheara's doing. The man can't keep his fingers out of our pie."

Eala approaches the tree again. "Maybe he's helping us? It's possible he realizes the riddle was too convoluted to give us a fair shot. My bargain did say it had to be a solvable task." She stares at the window now blocked by limbs and leaf.

A bitter laugh escapes. "Helping us? There's a manky notion."

Eala puts hands to hips and gives me her professor look. "Then what's your explanation?"

I slide my hands through the sideways V's she's made with her arms and pull her against me. "Dumb luck?"

She pinches my arse. "I think you should dial down your anti-Finnbheara propaganda."

"Do you now?"

She taps a finger to my chin. "We don't know how closely he's watching. You're already on his shit list. It's not wise to poke the beast any more than we already may have with our *we hate Finnbheara* rhetoric." Before I can unleash a comment that includes Finn and beast in the same breath, Eala slides her finger to my lips. "Remember, if I win, you win, and we know Finnbheara wants me to win."

"A fine point, Swan," I say, moving my mouth against her touch. "I bow to your wisdom as always."

"Good answer." Eala replaces her finger with her lips and kisses me soundly.

We end the kiss when the shadows take a steep dive, bringing twilight over the fields.

Eala rubs her arms. "Oooo, the Veil sprites just started a hurling match."

"Look at you, love, going Irish with your sports references. I'm so proud."

She laughs, and I study the darkening sky. "Looks like your bitty friends are telling us the onset of the Celtic day is still our cue to travel."

Eala wears her *deep-thinking* face. "The riddle clearly suggests traveling." She recites. "Tales of *old* both true and told." Peering at the mail shirt on the ground, she goes on. "We know to start at the Hill of Tara. Do you think this chainmail is a hint as to how we should dress?"

I jog to retrieve the latest bag of clothes from Caity and call over to Eala. "When in doubt, go native peasant. It's not failed me yet."

She's fingering the mail shirt, lost in thought. "The rings are flattish, but not what I'd call mesh." Eala frowns. "I can't get more specific than medieval."

"Irish peasant fallback it is," I say.

After stowing Eala's massive backpack in the cottage, we snag our traveling uniforms from the bags.

"Last chance to use indoor plumbing," I tease as Eala transforms from professor to peasant.

She tucks both hands under her chin. I slide in behind her, cuddling her to my chest and sinking my chin onto her shoulder. "You, okay?"

She turns in my arms, gripping my back so hard her fingernails bite through the muslin shirt. "I'm scared, Sion."

"That's not a bad thing, love." I kiss her forehead and lead her outside, locking the cottage behind us. We stand next to the Alfie upgrade with two bulging canvas bags within her sloping trunks. "On we go, yeah?"

Eala stretches out an arm and squeezes her eyes shut. A haze made of multicolored droplets surrounds us in a pattern reminiscent of intricately woven lace. "Hill of Tara. Hill of Tara," she whispers.

I clamp my teeth together to keep from mansplaining, a term I learned from her, that the Veil answers to the wishes resonating in your soul. Words aren't required to guide you along its pathways.

Hand in hand, we watch the mystical highway created to defy time and space unfold as the world behind us vanishes.

The familiarity of the Veil buoys my spirit. What I've lost the power to do, Eala replenishes with hers. The substance of my body is lost in swaths of glittering color as we travel. Next to me, Eala relaxes. Her face glows with wonder as she appreciates the magic of the Veil.

All too soon, the colors surrounding us bleed together until they become the night. We're standing on a deserted grassy hilltop under an ever-waning sliver of pearl moonlight. Before us is *Lia Fáil*, the stone of destiny.

Eala approaches the stone step by step, shoulders tense. She waits before moving forward, as if she's expecting something. Her head tilts as she pauses to listen.

I follow close behind her. "Is it the *sight, anamchara?*"

She takes the last step toward the stone that looks suspiciously like an erect cock. I suppose it's an apt metaphor for a giant rock that chooses a bugger manly enough to be a high king of Ireland.

Her voice is a whisper. "Should I touch it?"

"Wait," I say and grab her hand. "I'm not keen to have you lay hands on another fool's manhood."

"Sion!"

I grin. "What's the thing look like to you?"

She laughs. "A giant dick, but given our situation, mocking a sacred stone might not be the best way to go."

"I'd say we're offering up a compliment."

Eala guides my hand toward the stone. "Let's touch it together and see what happens."

"Touching another man's cock doesn't rank high with me."

She grumbles. "Focus, Sion."

"Sorry, I'm only coddin' ya to relieve the tension." I guide our hands the rest of the way to the rough surface of the stone, bracing for whatever comes. We wait and wait and wait. No luck.

Eala slaps palm to rock. "Thanks for nothing, dick stone."

A short distance away, someone loudly clears their throat.

I backpedal into Sion so fast it knocks both of us on our asses.

He wrestles me behind him. "Who's there then?"

When a tall figure steps from behind a nearby tree illuminated only by faint starlight, I scream.

Sion hisses into my ear to call the Veil, but the stranger raises both hands. He greets us in a gentle, melodic voice. "All is well. I'm a friend, Eala Duir."

At the sound of my name on his lips, the Veil sprites liquify and pour over my taut muscles, turning them into warm clay.

Sion does not experience a similar calm. "Not another step."

I can't take my eyes off our visitor. "Wait, Sion." The man slowly approaches, reaching a hand to us like he would for an agitated dog to sniff. "It was you," I say. "At the window last night." My memory of the fleeting image solidifies, as if the mere presence of this man fills in every vague detail. Both hands fly to my mouth. "And I saw you in Tír na nÓg, didn't I?"

The man slides toward us with fluid elegance, as if he's made of fluttering silk instead of muscle and bone. Only once in my life have I seen such a level of grace in someone's progress. He's tall, easily surpassing the six-foot mark. His hair and eyes seem to glow with a light of their own. The man wears a sleeveless tunic showing off corded biceps and forearms. His otherworldliness screams Fae.

"Finnbheara?" I ask, my tone rising with the question, suspicious this is one of the Fae king's disguises. Sion sucks in a breath, squinting through the dimness at our third wheel.

The Fae's laugh is hardy and loud enough to wake the dead buried in the Mound of Hostages beneath our feet. "Himself didn't mention your sense of humor, Eala Duir."

"Who the hell are you then?" says Sion, taking a step forward. "And what business do you have sticking your face in my window?"

If I expected Sionnach to don a new personality full of patience and rationality post-soulfall, I was sorely mistaken. He and the King of the Connacht Fae might be more alike than either care to acknowledge. "He's connected to Finnbheara. We need to hear him out," I whisper to Sion through gritted teeth.

"Robálaí Geal at your service," says the Fae, pouring into a regal bow. "I serve at King Finnbheara's pleasure."

He winks at me as he says *pleasure*.

Sion's hand wedged between us balls into a fist as he translates the Fae's name. "Well, Mister Bright Robber or Robber Bright, you're stealing time we don't have to spare. State your business and be off with you."

"Robber Bright. Robber Bright," chants the Fae, testing his title. A smile stretches across his preternaturally handsome face. Where Finnbheara's sharp cheekbones and pointed chin hid a thinly veiled malice, this Fae's are pronounced but rounded enough to give him the look of someone ready with a joke or jibe. A deep cleft punctuates the chin at the bottom of his long, narrow face. The scant moonlight reflects off dark aquamarine eyes, pinched at the corners but larger and rounder than the king's. They hold a gleeful twinkle that adds to his overall air of gaiety.

Shoulder-length hair flips up slightly at the ends and sways as he rocks his head to the rhythm of the sing-song chant of *Robber Bright, Robber Bright*. The color is hard to discern. First, I think it's silver like Finnbheara's, but then I detect strands of several shades of blond and yellow warming its glow. I'm curious to examine it closer, but when I take a step toward him, Sion takes hold of my arm, locking me in place.

The Fae gives a curt nod. "I shall be Robber Bright to you, Eala Duir." He offers me his hand. "Let's begin."

Sion mumbles something to the effect of *Fae foolery* before speaking outright. "As I said, we are in a bit of a hurry. What is it you're after, sir?"

Robber Bright cocks his head to the side, staring in confusion. "Why, to help Finnbheara's Treasure understand who she is."

Finnbheara's Treasure?

Máthair called me her treasure, *a stor*.

I do not appreciate that our visitor's connotation of *treasure* labels me as an acquisition or belonging of the king's.

"You're my teacher for all things Fae?"

Robber Bright bows again. "If you choose to term it thusly, yes."

I don't relish the idea of darting off with this odd Faerie. "Why are you called Robber?"

"Ah," he says, a sweeter smile brightening his face. "On the day I was born, my mother took her first look into my infant eyes and said, 'This boy has robbed me of my heart. It is forever his.'"

It would be a lovely story if my tutor were telling the truth, and with Faeries, that's a big if. A humorless chuckle tells me Sion's thinking along the same lines. He leans close to me, whispering out of the corner of his mouth. "More likely he's robbed many a lass of her virtue."

Given Robber Bright's hour of arrival, a new dread creeps through me. "Can you only come to me during the portion of the Celtic day we travel by, from sunset to sunrise?" We're screwed if this is the case, since it will interfere with our movement through time.

Robber Bright gives a long, low whistle. "No one would fix such a limitation upon the king's man."

Someone is very full of themselves. "Great. Since you obviously know where the cottage is, meet me there at midday tomorrow, and you can start teaching me about the Fae."

"I shall." He waves a hand to the tree line behind us. "I see you received my welcome gift."

There, front and center, is the new and improved Alfie.

"*You* sent the *fánaí* tree?"

Robber dips his head and smiles. "I convinced the king stripping this mortal—" he gestures to Sion, "of all his previous endowments was not in good form. Now the *fánaí* tree belongs to both of you trunk and bough."

Both of us? Ah, there's the reason for the change in her markings. The ole girl is decorated to reflect our dual partnership with her. Our first stroke of luck. The *fánaí* tree will find us as we move through the Veil acting as our personal travel trunk. Even though Sion never fully explained it, I have a sixth sense Alfie also acts as an anchor to the present.

"Thank you," I say. "We appreciate all the help we can get."

Sion glares at the Faerie. "And when you next show up at my place, give us the courtesy of a knock on the door, not a peek in the window."

Robber Bright's gaze bores into me. "Eala will sense my approach."

I don't need to look at Sion to know he's close to boiling over. "Robber—" I catch myself. "Should I call you Robber or Robber Bright?"

"Robber seems most fitting," says Sion.

The Fae stares at him without blinking. "You do not care for me as I do not care for you, but I have chosen civility. What do you choose, mortal?"

Sion puffs up like a damned rooster. "For Eala's sake, I can be as civil as the situation calls for."

I leap in with my own curiosity before their tête-à-tête has a chance to degrade any further. It can't be a coincidence he intercepted us here on the Hill of Tara. Robber Bright knew we'd be here.

"Since you helped with the *fánaí* tree, is there anything you can clarify for us in Finnbheara's riddle?"

The Fae clasps both hands behind his back and looks up at the night sky as if the stars will supply him with an answer. Slowly, he moves to an old hawthorn tree. A profusion of white blossoms gives it the appearance of a frosted pastry. Its gnarled branches are laden with trinkets and tokens tied between thorns. These items, dear to those who left them, are requests for Faerie help or favors.

At first, I think the faint silver glow around the base of the trunk is my imagination. Some latent instinct tells me to close my eyes. As soon as I do, the shimmer becomes streaks of brilliant silver light teeming with Veil sprites.

"The hawthorn is a Faerie door, isn't it?" I ask Robber.

He points a finger at me. "Ah, I see there are things I do not have to teach you, Eala Duir. Your connection to the *sight* is clear."

Has he been lurking on the other side of the Faerie door, just waiting to see if Sion and I would unearth this first stop on the Finnbheara Riddle Tour?

I tug Sion's sleeve as I rush to the tree. My own Veil sprites dance inside me. "Something about the hawthorn will help us fill the quota mentioned in the riddle, won't it?"

Robber smiles and shrugs but says no more.

Sion and I study the objects dangling from branches. There must be a hundred or more. How are we ever going to decipher which will help us? Then I see it. Embedded in the trunk itself are three rings of chainmail.

"There's something familiar." I point at the metal. "Chainmail links." I turn to him.

"Thought we were rid of those," says Sion.

I stare at what looks suspiciously like the artifact we returned to Strongbow's grave. "It doesn't make sense the same rings would show up here. Why?"

Sion's familiar grunt of derision joins us. "Why do the Fae do anything?" He taps his temple. "To mess with your reason."

I shake my head. "Reason tells me these links are connected to the chainmail shirt that inexplicably appeared in Alfie. I feel as if we're being led somewhere."

Robber leans a hand on the trunk and casually crosses one leg over the other. "If I were you…"

"Well, you're not," snaps Sion, reaching for the rings.

I try to stop him from yanking the metal from the bark. "Wait."

The moment our fingers touch the chainmail together, we're blasted backward through the air over the Hill of Tara.

CHAPTER 7

THE COURTEOUS LADY OF HIGH DEGREE

E ala is suspended before me, belly down as if she's flying in an elongated cocoon the size of a small train car. Our traveling chamber is surrounded by a tangle of thick branches covered in a layer of ashy black. Cracks along the charred bark allow me a view inside the limbs. A sizzle like a low burning fire leaks through as though the tree is burning from the inside out. In stark contrast is the shimmer of white gold beyond the boughs. I detest the sense of being captive within the limbs of a smoldering tree. One that appears to be flying with us trapped in its belly.

We're moving fast, too fast inside whatever's got hold of us. It accelerates, and my skin feels like it's stretching enough to fly off my bones. When I don't see any familiar signs or hear sustained notes of a violin or the soft bells I've come to expect after so many years of wandering through the Veil, my survival sense kicks in hard.

Ahead of me, Eala's white feathery hair flies furiously around her head as if she's caught in a gale. That same great wind blows us forward to who knows where. The three mail rings clenched in my fist heat up fast. If they keep at it, they'll scorch my palm.

"Eala," I holler, and see her trying to crane her neck to look back at me, but the relentless gusting currents surrounding us fight against her movement. We're like unfortunate birds caught in a vicious updraft.

"Think of home," I shout, hoping Eala can hear me since she's still able to call a version of our Veil. Taking my own advice, I summon a clear picture of the cottage in my mind. After my failure yesterday, I've thin hope the Veil hears me.

Eala's voice streams back my way, then passes without granting me the chance to understand her. I thrust my body forward as if I'm swimming against an unfriendly tide to get to her. No luck. Whatever moves us along makes all the decisions. A sick sensation rising in my gut suggests whatever thready luck I've had for the last two centuries is about to run out.

I stretch my arms forward, trying to grab onto Eala's feet. Just as my fingers reach the heel of her slipper, we're unceremoniously and none-too-gently dumped out of our charred, branchy compartment.

An unforgiving stone floor rises to meet us. We crash against one another in a heap. The familiar dank smell of wet stone and mildew spells castle. We're at the top of the stairs in an impressively large round room lit only by a few torches in brackets along the walls. This is no skinny turret. It's a more substantial fixture. Whoever laid the floor must have been properly pissed as it's uneven and somewhat treacherous. A particularly high bit of one of the stones scrapes the shit out of my arm. Blood already soaks my sleeve. Pain from the merciless landing shoots up and down my body. Beside me, thank the powers that still keep an eye on us, Eala and I are together.

"How bad off are you, love?" I ask, sitting up from my inelegant sprawl to reach for Eala.

"Sion," she says in a shaky voice, shoving closer to me. When her fingernails dig into the wound on my forearm, I yelp.

My cry echoes through the frigid air of the tower. Not as frigid as the boss-eyed expression on the pair of knights with notched arrows pointing directly at us. They've abandoned their nearby perch in an alcove that bears a plunging arrow loop.

One of the men growls an expletive from behind the steel nose guard of his helmet as he takes us in. "Don't be shrieking like a cat in heat."

They lower their bows. "Brought something to fill our aching bellies then?"

Luckily, our spill ended in such a place to look as if we've come from the stairs. I get to my feet, helping Eala to hers. "We've come to see if you've been brought up a bite."

The men are head to toe in mail with hauberks down to their knees, and helms that mean business. At my query, military shoulders collapse in unison.

Hungry then.

Manning the arrow loop.

What mess have we landed in? I grip the chainmail rings in my palm. They've cooled since our less than graceful plop into the past. Thunder rumbles from outside and through the opening in the wall, a flash of lightning brightens the night sky.

"The gate!" Someone calls in a commanding voice from a nearby niche. The archers surge back to their post. One aims low and fires while the other readies an arrow. They trade off shooting through the opening.

Eala tugs on my sleeve. "Stairs," she hisses, and we scurry like a pair of rats down a couple of steps until we're out of sight. We tuck in against the curved wall, panting. Eala touches her thumb to each finger in turn as she whispers, "Knights, medieval..." She stares at me. Fear clouds her eyes. "Siege?"

In answer, we hear a *thunk thunk* from the direction of our friendly neighbor knights in the niche. Likely it's the sound of arrows aiming for ramparts above and falling short of their mark. Suddenly, a *boom* rattles the whole damn tower. I can imagine the beast of a stone fired from a trebuchet impacting against the castle walls.

"Siege," I say, nodding.

Eala curses. "A medieval siege could be anywhere in Ireland."

"I think," I say, peering down the dark stairs. "The bigger question than where the fuck are we is how did we get here, and what are we supposed to do?"

"I didn't call the Veil," she says, shakily.

I flatten my palm to stare at the three rings. "Something went arseways when we touched these."

She chews her bottom lip. "Did you see burning branches in front of a bright metallic background when we travelled here?"

It hits me then, like one of the massive stones pelting the castle where I'd seen that particular white-gold shimmer before. "Aye. That background looked too close to the Faerie armor in Tír na nÓg for my liking."

She snatches the chainmail from my hand. "Maybe Finnbheara sent us here in his version of the Veil." Eala scrunches her nose. "But what's with the charred tree? Maybe a clue?" She lets the question fly off and focuses on the rings. "Do you think these are the same ones that belonged to Strongbow?"

I drop my head onto my hand. My mind's reeling so fast, there's no clear place to stop it. "I thought matching artifacts for the folks in the soulfall was mad. Having no clear connections to anything is as dicey as trying not to fall off a sea cliff when you're fog blinded."

Eala makes a series of quiet grunts like she's working something out. "Do you think that when we touch certain items on the hawthorn, Finnbheara sends us to a place and time where we're supposed to accomplish something or find a clue connected to the riddle?" She gently raises my head. "Maybe it's the reason you can't call the Veil. You don't need to."

We've swapped places. Eala's the one taking the lead while I turn into a flighty mess. I feel as useful as a cow stuck in a bog.

A rumble of voices rise in a heated argument below. Eala finds my hand. "Well, we know there's nothing for us up there, so we might as well go down." She sniffs and then sneezes loudly. "Mold," she says before slowly picking her way from step to step.

We perch on a curve of the stair above a large room filled with more mailed knights and a handful of lordly looking types crammed around a long wooden table. I've never found this sort to be worth the bluster they heat the air with. They're having words with one another until another boulder pelts the castle wall. The room falls silent for a beat as we slink lower for a better view.

There, at the end of the table, stands a woman who looks not much older than Eala. She wears a simple dark green dress with flowing sleeves but no under trappings to alter her natural shape. Around her waist is a wooden beaded belt with a cross dangling from it. Her hair is covered with a plain white cotton kerchief, trailing halfway down her back, held in place with a leather band spanning her forehead. Braids fall across her shoulders.

The woman is no docile maiden. There's iron in her gaze and the way she holds herself. Power. Every gaze in the room locks on her as if her next words will wipe away the siege and force the sun to shine through the depths of night.

When she strides the length of the table, talking and waving her hands, I see she's heavy with child.

Eala gasps my name. "Sionnach. I think that could be Isabel de Clare… Marshall, Strongbow's daughter." She tugs me up the stairs a bit.

"One glance tells you as much?"

She gives me a sour look. "One look and a PhD. Not to mention chainmail that looks identical to the rings we suspect are connected to Strongbow." She gestures to the round room. "The architecture of huge round towers could be Kilkenny Castle—her castle." Eala studies the woman closer. "I've always been fascinated by her. My specialty may be folklore, but there are pieces of Irish history that are grand enough to surpass mere footnotes and become legend. This woman is one of those. She's said to have commanded—" Eala gives a little huff and corrects herself. "Is commanding a siege while her husband William Marshall, probably the greatest knight ever, is off in England." Wonder fills her eyes. "While she's very pregnant."

A terrible thought curls inside me like too hot steam from a teapot. "Does she win?" I can't let my mind stray to an eventuality where this castle is overrun while we're in it or facing the terrors of a long siege such as starvation and the folks stuck inside turning on one another. I heard stories where those trapped in a besieged castle ate moss off the walls along with every rat and cat they could catch. In more gruesome tales, captured enemies became dinner. The desperate, hungry looks on the faces of the archers come back to me in a rush. I've got to save Eala from being subjected to such misery. God willing, Herself over there has rationed what food they have, if any's left.

Eala gazes with a look of adoration I've only seen on the faces of football fanatics for their favorite players. "She does."

But at what cost?

A huge thunderclap shakes the stone beneath us. Eala buries her head against my chest. She says her fear of heights ended when she climbed a tower for me, but I wonder if it's a transitory thing. Hopefully, her flight as a swan over Irish soil into Tír na nÓg contributed to knocking that worry off her plate.

I stroke her hair. "What in blazing hell does Finnbheara expect us to do here?"

"These rings plus the chainmail shirt we found in the *fánaí* tree…" Eala jostles the metal links in her hand. "I think we're meant to help her."

I don't mean to be insensitive, but a snort of disbelief escapes. "Been practicing with your bow behind my back, have you?"

"I'm dead serious, Sion. If I can talk to her, show her I've got a decent brain in my head, maybe she'll listen to me."

I take her face in my hands. "About what, love?"

She shrugs. "I don't know exactly. Give her confidence that victory is inevitable. Support her belief in herself?"

"No." I kiss her forehead. "If you act the prophet, you'd might as well announce yourself as a witch and climb onto a pile of kindling."

Her face tenses. "There is a reason we're here."

"No arguing that, but it would be best to be home safe before we try to puzzle this out." I pull her against my chest. "Try to call the Veil."

She frowns. "You're assuming the rules are the same for solving Finnbheara's riddle as they were for the soulfall. Hell, we don't even know how we got here. There's no guarantee we can return when we choose to." Eala clutches the star pendant around her neck. "If we leave now, we may fail before we've begun."

Her cool head to my hot one is the balance I've come to rely on.

"Then again," she continues, "we do know when and where to come back to, and I'm able to Veil travel." Eala locks gazes with me. "Do you think we should risk leaving?"

Another blow pummels the castle. We both duck and cover our heads as a shower of dust rains down on us. "I can't string one thought to the next with the possibility of being buried underneath a pile of stone, can you, Swan?"

Tears spill from her eyes. "This is horrible. All I care about is not dying."

I catch her tears with my thumb. "Right there with you, love."

Eala pulls her hands up under her chin and shuts her eyes. "Home," she whispers. The air around us warms for a heartbeat. She's going to do it. Get us out of here. But too soon, it cools again.

"I can't," she breathes, and in a voice so soft I barely hear her. "I can't even feel my Veil sprites." She stares at me with a look of total desolation. "We're trapped."

Anger heats my blood as a decision forms in my head. Fine. I cannot see or understand what purpose there is in us being here. Without being able to call the Veil or my wee fox self, I'm no more than extra baggage to Eala.

There is one action a man can take in any time for honor's sake. Maybe that's part of what ole Finn seeks, proof of my honor. If my actions show me to be worthy of his prized Eala, perhaps it'll go far in letting me stay with her.

I run my hands down Eala's trembling arms. "You might think me mad, but I believe the king is testing my mettle for a place in your future."

"What do you mean?"

I shake my head. "Hiding here on the stairs with you isn't moving us forward."

"Sion…" The beginning of a warning colors her voice. I have to remember Eala is a woman of the present not the past. I've lived many things she's only read about.

"I will offer the lady of the castle my loyalty. I will fight for Isabel Marshall."

Her skin grows pale. "No. You can't. It's too dangerous."

When I hold my hand out for the bitty links, she drops them onto my palm, and I stuff the chainmail in a pocket. "It's got to be me." I kiss her temple. "It's what a man does. Stay here." Before she can protest, I'm down the few stairs and into the great room. Separate conversations are brewing around the table, but the lady of the castle stands before a window made up of small leaded glass panes.

No one takes much notice of a servant crossing the room. When I reach Herself, I drop to one knee. The stone floor grinds against my bone, but I do not waver. "Milady, in this hour of great concern, I offer you my service."

She looks at me, startled at first, then with deeper scrutiny. "It seems you are already in my service, or you would not be within these castle walls, young sir."

"I mean to fight for you."

There is a snicker from one of the pouncy fools in her council as he approaches us. "Up, boy, and back to the empty kitchens. Don't be bothering the lady."

I silently curse my soft, youthful look. It's what made me a good spy in my own time, but here, my face works against me.

As Isabel waves him off, behind me, I hear more chuckles and comments about an unexpected laugh on a dark day. I burn inside as my gesture is taken as entertainment rather than earnest. Watching from his throne, Finnbheara's probably enjoying this loads more than these bastards.

Forcing myself not to be affected by their taunts, I remain steadfast in front of the lady. "I am a man grown, sincere, and decent with a blade," I tell her.

To my surprise, she reaches down with difficulty, given the size of her baby-filled belly, and takes my chin in her fingers. "Grown yet still clinging to youth. It's refreshing to see the curves of your apple cheeks and a spark in your eye when so many wear the gaunt faces of hunger and despair. Your offer is much valued, and I thank you for it. Now stand."

I do so, hoping my height and solid build add a few years to the age she assesses me to be. Would the lady christen me well-preserved if I told her I've walked the earth for two hundred years? I'd likely be tied to the stake next to Eala if we let even the smallest drab of our truth into the light.

"This is indeed a time of great danger and distress." She gazes out the window, hands resting on her belly. "There are those who would see the

Marshalls gone from Kilkenny." When she looks back at me, her eyes shine. "They will not get their wish while I have a breath left to spare."

I'm afraid she's going to dismiss me. Over her shoulder, I catch a glimpse of Eala in the shadow of the stairs. She hugs herself, holding in the grief I've surely caused her. "What will you have me do, Lady?"

"Live a life free of battle and enemies, but that is not the state of things." Her expression is inscrutable. I wrangle a brain full of arguments against her dismissing me. Finnbheara is a warrior king. He must see I will walk into battle to be a man worthy of Eala, Finnbheara's Treasure.

Isabel narrows her eyes. "Serve me as you do now and it is enough until the day you return before me, sword in hand, to pledge your loyalty. Even beginning training well past your boyhood, with a stout heart such as yours, you may still make a fine knight yet, young sir."

I bow and fade from her presence while knights, men, and the lady of great worth return to their siege.

Eala meets me a few steps from the stairs. Grabbing handfuls of my shirt, she hauls me back into the shadows with enough force to almost send us both stumbling down the curving stone steps.

"What have you done, Sionnach Loho, you impulsive, crazy man?"

I kiss her hard and fast before we're discovered. Eala's arms trap me with the unspoken understanding she wishes me to stay put and not pursue my insane notion. It's a desperate kiss. One colored with a dreadful feeling it could be our last. After what I'm setting in motion, it may be just that.

What I'd give to love Eala without the specter of our separation hanging over us like a reaper's scythe. If my hunch is right about Finn testing my worth, there'll be less chance for kissing and more invitations to put my neck on the block.

I break off before she's ready to let me go, but the pull of time has a hold of me. "Eala, I need a sword."

CHAPTER 8
THE GRAVE GOODS

I hear Sion's words, but it takes me a beat to process them. "A sword?"

He starts down the stairs. "There's an armory somewhere in this rock."

I grab the back of his shirt. "Are you out of your mind?"

Sion whirls. "Isabel said I could serve if I offer her my sword." He takes hold of my waist as we teeter on the steps. "Eala, I feel it in my gut this is why we've come. I'll enter the fight and show Finn what I'm about."

He is out of his mind. "Show him you're *about* getting yourself killed?" I want to slap him for diving into whatever he promised Isabel de Clare Marshall without bothering to discuss the specifics with me. "Shit, Sion. Aren't our lives close enough to the edge of death and danger for you?"

He fiddles with the curls covering his ears. "I'll say to you what I said to Herself. What else would you have me do, Lady?" He sucks in his cheeks. "There's no Veil to take us home, and an obvious job to be done here. It's simple really."

I open my mouth to breathe more fire at him, then shut it. Is it so simple? I wrack my brain for some other explanation or different task we're meant to fulfill, but nothing comes. We must be here to help with the siege. Sion's right. If I bust out modern speak, or act like I know the outcome, I'm a witch. He's the only one who can step up.

I hate accepting that truth. How much more is fate or Fae going to put us through before we can simply be together? The temptation to fall onto the step and sob is nearly impossible to stave off. I'm weary of being strong, but with no end in sight of solving Finnbheara's challenge, I have to be. For me…for Sion…for us, because we are worth fighting for.

It takes us a while to find the armory. Fat lot of good it does. When Sion sets the lighted torch into a bracket on the wall, it's not a pretty sight. Strewn around the room, is a sparse scattering of nasty looking weapons for maiming and killing. What's left is obviously not any fighter's first choice. Maces with missing spikes, rusty knives, and chipped daggers wait for their call to enter the battle. There are even what I take to be the disassembled parts of a siege engine, but no swords. The smell of rot is overpowering. Scuttling rats don't help my ever-growing freak out at our current situation.

"Fuck all," growls Sionnach. He picks up a long, very pointy knife covered in a layer of grime I'm loathed to identify. "I can't present something to the lady better suited to cutting meat than fighting."

I shudder. "How big is the piece of meat you're planning to cut?" An image of Sion thrusting the knife through an enemy's heart brings bile to my throat.

I tip forward, clutching my stomach. Sion lays a reassuring hand on my back. "I've had to fight before, Eala. I'm not a babe in arms when it comes to it."

"No details, please. What I'm already picturing is bad enough." Panic runs its rough hands over my soul. Here alone with Sion in the near dark, I dissolve and throw myself into his arms. "I can't deal with losing you. Please don't do this."

He strokes my hair and whispers, "Whist, whist."

His words of comfort are the same ones I've heard my whole life from Máthair. Of course, they're the ones he uses since he grew up with her soothing him in the same way. Leading us over to a wooden stool, he sits, gathering me onto his lap.

"When my mind's set, I can be a bit of an ass," he says, kissing my ear.

His confession brings an unexpected laugh from me. "Score points for self-awareness."

Sion strokes my back. "Let's sit with our fate for a few moments. I'll shut my gob, and maybe a different notion of what to do will come to us."

I snuggle against him and close my eyes. He rocks us, staying silent, allowing me this chance to think of an alternate plan. Even though my heart pounds with brutal beats, my racing thoughts settle enough to analyze our predicament.

What possible influence could we have at the siege of Kilkenny Castle? My knowledge gives us nothing but a shell to work with. I've no choice but to concede Sion's solution may be the right one. I'm not convinced his reasoning about Finnbheara testing him is on point, but there's no action I can take that doesn't put me in as much danger as Sion taking up arms. God-willing, just the act of him committing to walk into the fray will be enough for us to be whisked back to the Hill of Tara on whatever foul Faerie wind blew us here.

I inhale deeply and regret it when I get a nose full of musty stench. He thumps me between the shoulder blades as I cough.

"I think…you may be right," I say when I get my breath back. "Swear to me, you won't try to be a hero. Be as battle adjacent as you can without looking like you're faking it."

He chuckles. "Done and done, love."

Sion presses his lips to mine and moves against them in a desperate kiss. His tongue captures the tear trailing across my upper lip. He serves the droplet back to me, sliding it gently into my mouth. I suckle his tongue, savoring the warmth of our stolen intimacy here in the dank and disgusting armory.

"I love you, Sionnach Loho, and I plan to forever."

He nips my neck. The reminder his fox form is lost fills me with overwhelming sadness. "And I you, my Eala *bán*."

He reaches into his pocket and a look of panic crosses his face. "The mail rings? They were just here." Sion drops to his knees and starts patting the stone. "Och, here you are, you wee bastards." Getting back to his feet, he dangles them in front of me. "I've no explanation for keeping these close except that they're all we have connecting this place to the Hill of Tara. A warning in my heart says we've got to keep the rings safe."

The truth of his words resonates. These tiny pieces of metal are the only thing between the present we've left behind, and the future we're trying to secure. We're forced to function in a reality where the concept of time is woven and unwoven until it defies reason. I reach out to touch the literal links to our reality with a fingertip. The moment I make contact, the floor beneath us splits, and we tumble into blackness.

The terror I've lived with for as long as I can remember has finally come to claim me.

Falling.

Heights.

The very state I've strived to avoid traps me in its greedy jaws.

I've always wondered what goes through people's heads when they find themselves in a deadly fall. Are they at peace? Do they take the unchangeable seconds and try to reach for joy in their last moments? Is it a choice whether joy or horror fills one at the end?

There is no joy for me.

I can't see or hear Sion. Which of us will hit bottom first? I hope it's me. I can't bear to watch him break and die.

"Oof." The landing knocks the wind out of me. For a handful of daunting moments, I can't draw breath. When I do, the sensation is as painful as it is a relief.

I brush hair from my eyes and push to sitting. Beneath me is the mushy mound of grass that broke my fall next to a dirt path. I have a new appreciation for a fine patch of sodden Irish earth.

"Shit." Sion's curse from a short distance away is the most beautiful sound in the world. "Eala?"

I don't see him.

"Over here," I call, standing on the path to get my bearing. In front of me is what appears to be a collection of huge stones. At first glance, there's no rhyme or reason to them until I take a step closer. When I recognize what they are, I lose my wind a second time.

Sion appears from behind the stones, attempting to dust a layer of muck off his shirt and britches. "That wasn't grand." When I don't speak, he rushes to my side. I point at the rocky formation.

Two hefty vertical standing stones are braced by cube-shaped boulders at their backs. Behind them, on guard in a rough semi-circle, are more rocky sentinels. Each is a different width and height, all slightly leaning in as if protecting the massive front stones. Every craggy surface wears different smatterings of emerald moss and yellowish lichen, made visible from the glow of a very full moon.

A Veil moon.

We've been dropped somewhere in the realm of the Veil where the moon is always at its fullest and brightest.

Sion's gaze darts to where I point—a dark void between the standing stones not ten feet from us.

Still a bit breathless, I say, "This is a passage tomb, a burial site."

Sion leans forward, squinting at the opening. "Aye."

I follow his gaze but can't make out anything inside the smudge of black beyond the entrance. "How did we end up here?"

Sion moves the rings around his palm with a fingertip. "I think," he says carefully, "it's the rings blowing us about. We shared an intention to find a sword, then when we both touch 'em, off we go." A scowl and narrowed eyes punctuate his next words. "But it ain't us steering the ship." He closes his palm around the mail and stuffs them in his pocket.

"The tunnel with burnt branches that we traveled through to get to Kilkenny Castle didn't have the look of our Veil, no filmy rainbows or glass prisms." Suddenly, an idea prickles. "Sion, is it possible Robber Bright is trying to help us? Our visions of the Veil aren't identical. Maybe all Faeries all have their own impression of it, and that's his. We can't rule out that he's the one sending us where we need to go."

His face is skeptical. "In my experience, helping is not high on the Folk's list." Sion digs his teeth into his bottom lip. "Whether or not it's Robber Bright's version of the Veil, something's off about it."

I almost hold back my next words, but it's important to keep everything I'm thinking out in the open. Sion's been solving Faerie challenges for two centuries. He's bound to catch things I won't. "Maybe..." I hesitate, dreading his reaction. "Folk may not be helpful to mortals, but what if someone's connected to them...the way I am?"

The storm brewing in his eyes makes me want to take it back. I know he's cut up by his loss of Faerie benefits and Finnbheara's obvious dislike of him. Sion's ego will need to endure a little bruising if we're going to conquer this convoluted quest of ours.

"Helpful, is it? Plunking us in front of a tomb to have a go at—what?" He flings a hand at the stones. "What do you say, Eala? Shall we charge on in and pray an honor guard of bog body spirits isn't waiting to add us to the hoard inside?"

He's working himself into one of his pissy rants. Reminding myself we're both teetering on the edge of losing our shit, I resist the urge to retort with equal sarcasm. Instead, I lay both palms against his chest. My fingertips absorb the rhythm of his heartbeats as if they're the soft brush of a lover's lips.

Our collective tension abates at the contact. "Let's break down our situation before we do anything." The forest bordering the open space is so dense, its trees appear as charcoal sketches. With a glance, I take in the cool blush of the moon that dusts the tops of stones scattered across a grassy clearing the size of the Great Lawn in Central Park back in New York City. A wisp of sorrow that I'll never see the place I called home again floats through me.

"What did you call these places when you first explained the Veil to me? A pocket? An annex of the Veil? That's why…" I jerk my chin at the moon. "Full."

Grudgingly, he nods.

"We need to take advantage of this magical stasis and see if it matches any part of the challenge. Let me try something." I take a step toward the tomb and close my eyes. Finnbheara's riddle scrolls down the inside of my eyelids. When I found Strongbow's grave, Sion told me I have the *sight*, a kind of power of premonition or extra sensory awareness. If I concentrate and try to find a connection between this tomb and the riddle, maybe an image of something will come to me.

Sion's voice sounds far away. "Pwyll hung about such tombs."

Pwyll.

Pwyll, the Elemental, a druid spirit who helped Sion in the past. As if the name flips a switch, words stream through my mind…*druid, ceremonies, burial, treasures.*

There's a sound so high-pitched, the roots of my teeth throb.

My eyes snap open. "Did you hear that?"

Sion has moved next to the entrance, one hand leaning on a standing stone. The color drains from his face. "I did."

I hurry to join him. "I imagined Pwyll, then I heard the sound."

His face is grim. "I wish it were those dear ole bones, but the wail did not have the sound of him."

My heart beats faster. "Did you understand it?"

"Sorry, no. It caught me unawares." He hunches, taking his failure like a punch.

I rub fingertips up and down my forehead, trying to clear my mind. There are numerous tales of spirits who guard the grave goods in passage tombs and other burial sites. Since Sion and I are plugged in more than most to supernatural frequencies, especially where the Veil is involved, an ancient guard might very well be the entity we nudged by poking around. "We need to go inside the tomb."

He tugs me away from the opening. "I didn't open my mind to hear the words clearly, but the tone sounded more warning than invitation."

I dig in my heels. "Think about it. Passage tombs are where they buried people with belongings they'd need in the next life." I raise my palms to him. "Like…" When he doesn't finish my sentence, I do. "…weapons."

Realization adds color to his pale cheeks. "Swords."

"It's worth a look." I snuff my fear before it makes me change my mind, then charge into the rectangle of shadow leading into the tomb.

Sion mumbles behind me. "Grave goods, eh? I expect there's a good bit of digging in my future."

Once we pass through the stone threshold, it's a few steps forward and then a short downslope to find a low-ceiling chamber the size of Sion's bedroom. I'm pleasantly surprised an opening in the far corner of the roof lets in a weak beam of light from the full moon. We stand in silence, waiting for our eyes to adjust. When they do, my heart sinks.

My unrealistic imagination hoped the Veil would serve up something along the lines of a dust-covered, museum-worthy exhibit. We'd simply pluck a sword out of a case, touch the mail rings together, and finish with Isabel de Clare.

What we face is a low grass-covered mound littered with twigs and other debris blown in through the tomb's opening. The air is thick with the smell of loam and decomposing leaves.

"As I said—digging." Sion searches the ground. He finds a stone the shape and size of a clamshell, then drops to his knees. I scratch at the tomb floor with my toe, hoping to unearth my own neolithic shovel.

"Just like clearing a field of stone," Sion says. He stretches his arms and jabs the edge of his makeshift tool into the dirt.

Instantly, any trace of moonlight vanishes. The blackness surrounding us is so definitive we might as well be suspended in a vat of ink.

Terror explodes like dozens of lightning strikes inside my chest. I fumble in the dark for Sion. We manage to grab onto each other as an intense version of the sonic vibration we heard from outside fills the tomb. As the *voice* continues, somehow, I'm able to see shining rivulets of water blacker than the impossibly dark chamber spill down the walls. A coppery tang infuses the air. I grow rigid with fear as I imagine the tiny streams are blood flowing over stone since there's not enough light to show if they wear a crimson color.

Sion lets out a guttural gasp as if he's been stabbed, and then chokes as he intones strange notes I've heard once before when he was conversing with Pwyll, the druid ghost at Leap Castle.

Tugging roughly, I practically rip Sion's shirt. "Did you open your mind so you know what he's saying? Does he understand you?"

Sion doesn't answer as the vibrations get louder. My hair starts to float around my head with prickles of static electricity traveling the length of every strand.

"He gives the name Neit," Sion whispers.

I shudder hard enough to lose my balance and stumble against Sion. "The Neit?"

He tightens his hold on me. "Whatcha mean, *The* Neit?"

I whisper as if the presence in the tomb isn't able to hear everything I'm thinking or speaking. "Neit is the Irish god of war."

"Not a fella to piss off," Sion says in low tones. He makes his strange sounds. The vibrations around the tomb get stronger. Random bursts of silver light no larger than pinheads ignite, then die along the walls.

My head throbs as if two strong hands are slowly crushing my skull.

"Our host is named for him and pledged to him." Sion grunts. "He's none too pleased we're here."

I let go of Sion to press the heels of my hands against my temples to relieve the pressure. When I try to speak, only a whimper of pain comes out.

The intensity of the vibrations grows, and a high-pitched whine screeches through my mind. Stings like being poked with the end of a charged wire rise across my skin swiftly followed by horrible muscle constriction. I feel as if my entire body is in a garlic press.

"Sion, we…" Every word adds a new stab of pain. When I turn my head to try and find the entrance to the tomb, the vertebrae of my spine begin to crack one at a time.

Sion groans, suggesting he must be experiencing something equally unpleasant. "I'll…try…to…ask—" His words are cut off with a cry of pain.

I fall to my knees and start to crawl toward a slight movement in the air I pray is a breeze from the outside while Sion forces out strained sounds in druid to the namesake of the Irish God of War. Suddenly, there's a great clatter like metal hitting stone. The sound rings in my ears, then wave after wave of searing heat assaults my body from the crown of my head to my feet. The last thing I hear before succumbing to the internal flames stealing my awareness is scratching along the ground nearby.

The druid's attack is ferocious. If the bastard hadn't announced he was going to take my head off, I'd never have dropped to the ground in time to avoid the large and wicked piece of God knows what whizzling through the air above me. It hits the stone wall of the tomb with the *clank* of metal.

"Neit will splinter your bones, then feast on their marrow for plundering his trove."

I'm tempted to inform the surly spirit we're here to do no such thing, except it's fairly obvious that's exactly the situation. If this fellow is anything like Pwyll, he's no fool. Sweat streams down my face as I scrape my hands over the rough dirt floor searching for the projectile. I pray it's a shield to spare me from the fucker's next supernatural volley.

"Eala, stay low," I call out in a rush as I blindly paw around in the dark. "Get out of here."

She doesn't answer.

"Eala? Where are you?" God, I hope she's crawled out of this hell pit. "Eala," I holler louder, anxious to hear her voice from beyond the stones. Instead, my hand meets a too warm limp form on the ground.

"*There is no path but doom*," drones the druid. The temperature rises, and it feels like my skin and bones are liquifying.

Immediately, I throw my body over Eala's in case the spirit decides to fly at us. Laying my face next to hers, I check for breath. I take her single lone whimper as a good sign. I'm doing a fair amount of whimpering myself. Thank the saints, she's alive.

More sounds of metal hitting stone are followed by a shower of objects falling all around us and clouting me on the head and back. I shield Eala as best I can.

The druid unleashes a wail that pinches my brain mercilessly enough to blind if I could see anything in this place through the blackness. *Och*, the druid's sonic song continues to travel high up in a scale that my senses and body are not built to withstand. I imagine fissures webbing through muscle preparing to burst them open. I'd cradle my throbbing head in my hands, but I've got to get Eala out of this cursed nest of death's afterthought.

The fact our host isn't coming at us tells me that the druid might be restricted to a particular place in the tomb. Otherwise, he could have just thrust a sword through our middles. Maybe he was shackled to the wall as one of his master's prizes and died here to insure protection for the riches. Wherever he is, the old fellow is close enough to grab treasures and fling them at us.

Dragging her beneath me, I aim for the thin stream of cool air reaching into the tomb from the opposite direction from where the druid's voice rings from the grave mound. My knee bashes into the sharp and unforgiving edge of what could be steel or iron. It slices through my britches, biting into skin.

I pat the ground, not eager to grab the unfriendly end of a weapon or tug Eala over one. As I learn its shape, I discover this is some type of blade with a grip. It's definitely larger than a dagger.

That nasty sentinel of the grave goods heaved a sword our way.

Now, I'm even more grateful my head is still attached to my shoulders. This weapon'll be worth the bother if we can get out of here without becoming additions to the tomb's collection.

"*Coward. Coward,*" the druid taunts.

Aye, a coward who'd like to keep his head from splattering against the wall either by sound or blade. Inch by painful inch, I scoot Eala and the sword in the direction I'm betting is out of here. I'm rewarded when I feel the slope of the incline that I remember started just inside the entrance. I'd like to answer the druid curse for curse, but he doesn't need to be any more provoked.

I realize in my panic; I've closed off my mind to the druid's language. Using the strategy Pwyll taught me, I ease up and let the bugger's sounds wave through me instead of trying to fight them. The bone-crushing pain recedes slightly, but not the heat. Suddenly, a flash of fiery lightning like the surge of flame splashes across the wall, then swiftly decays into a glow reminiscent of the same crimson cast that surrounded the chainmail for a moment before we're once again drowned in darkness.

I don't pause for gratitude or the opportunity to see our tormentor but use the flare to confirm the way out of the tomb.

A muffled voice pierces my murky consciousness. "Eala, come back to me, love."

My mind yawns awake from the sleep of nothingness. The fire that melted my body has subsided, replaced with blissful coolness. Have my clothes burned away? Am I naked, laid out on the altar of death being kissed by the breath of a merciful breeze?

My head pounds, and it hurts to open my eyes.

When I do, Sion's face is inches from mine. "Hello, Swan."

I'm cradled in his arms on the ground. Sion's propped against one of the standing stones that forms the entrance to the passage tomb. Glancing inside, I see the slope leading to the main chamber. "Did I faint? Did we ever go in?" When I tried a seeing, did I knock myself out with the effort and collapse on a druid's doorstep?

Concern tightens his features. "Do you not remember?"

I sit up and my hair gives a little crackle. It's a matted mess around my head.

"Aye, we entered this sacred place, then a very bossy fella scolded us for doing so. I spoke the language Pwyll taught me." He snorts. "At least there's a talent ole Finn didn't take from me." Sion reaches for something on the ground next to him and raises a very real, and very ancient-looking sword. "Thanks to years of avoiding blows, I ducked in time or the old boy would have taken my head off with this."

My eyes widen, making the pulse in my temples throb. "He gave you a sword...from the mound?"

"I scrabbled in the dark for it after he chucked it at me." He circles a thumb over his temple. "I thought the druid bastard was going to squeeze my head like a grape."

"Me too." I sigh, able to remember more as my head clears. "What I'd give for a bottle of ibuprofen." I attempt to put my hair in order while checking my head for indentations from a druidic vise.

I gulp in a lungful of the fresh night air, then settle back against Sion. Drawing the pendant from beneath my *leine*, I tap the five rounded points of the star. "Whether you believe it or not, whoever sent us here is helping. They knew we'd be able to get you a sword from the tomb."

Sion nuzzles my head. "Managing five tasks such as these to answer Finnbheara's question will be a massive pain in my arse...and head." His warm breath is a balm against my scalp. "Now what, love?"

"We hope your hunch is right. Let's both touch the mail rings and pray whoever is shuffling us around sends us back to Kilkenny Castle to finish this."

Sion gets a good grip on the sword, then digs the chainmail out of his pocket. I wrap one arm around my *anamchara's* waist.

"Ready?" he asks.

"No," I say, and touch the rings.

CHAPTER 9

THE ROPE

E ala and I are greeted by a familiar mace and useless pikes with worn blades as we pick ourselves up off the filthy floor of the Kilkenny Castle armory. The torch I brought down has burned low, telling me we were gone for a bit but not more than a few hours. My hand cramps from clutching the druid's sword. Well, most likely not his personally, but a long past Irish noble of some wealth since he had fortune enough to be buried with his stuff.

"I don't even want to guess how many bruises I'll have before we get back home," says Eala, rubbing her bum.

I give a rueful smile since my earlier enthusiasm at the cottage will be responsible for her more intimate bruising.

"Lucky my tub'll be waiting for you." I'm going to play like I'm confident we will be seeing the inside of my home at the end of this. We can't leave Kilkenny Castle fast enough for my liking.

I examine the grimy sword and frown. "Not exactly fitting for battle."

Eala follows my gaze, and her disappointment joins my own. She begins to search the armory. "There must be something in here to clean it with."

We find an overused wire brush and tattered cloths. No oil to bring the thing up to snuff, but at least it loses the look of being dug out of centuries of dirt.

I raise the weapon to the guttering torchlight. "It'll have to do unless we find a scuttered knight sleeping it off and swap this blade for his."

Eala takes the sword from my hand. Her arm dips. "Damn, it's heavy." She hands it back to me, concern pinching her lovely face. "Are you sure you can fight with this?"

I swipe the blade through the air. "I'm no knight, but I can bash and slash with the best of 'em."

She stares at my face long enough to tell me she's got a fresh load of doubts. "Let's hope it doesn't come to that." Eala leans in for a quick kiss. "I've never kissed a knight before."

"Tick it off the list, madame." I return the favor with a kiss just as quick but far saucier before I gently tug my darling's delicate hand to lead her up the winding stone steps to the lady of Kilkenny Castle and my fate.

Isabel de Clare Marshall stands at the same window where we left her. She's as still as a statue of the Virgin Mary in a chapel. The candles on the long table in the center of the room have burned low. A servant replaces them one-by-one with taller ivory pillars. The brighter glow catches the tapestries on the walls, giving the room a less stark appearance.

We watch from the stairs until we're certain the great lady is mostly alone in the round chamber. The lords who attended her have left to sleep or kill. The storm downgraded to a steady rain. Neither thunder nor the onslaught of boulders against the castle walls interrupt the reverent calm. Judging from the light outside the window, dawn isn't close to knocking on night's door yet. This speck of peace calms my soul.

"She must be exhausted," Eala whispers.

"I wish respite from her mighty responsibility was something in our power to grant." I lean the side of my head against Eala's. "But it isn't."

"Who's there?" says Isabel in a voice that could bend if not break steel. We failed at keeping quiet enough in this echo chamber of a room. She's stepped away from the window and grips a long knife in her hand. Out of the corner of my eye, I see guards melting out of the shadows along the walls.

My love and I exchange a look, drawing courage from each other, then

I step into the candlelight and bow. "Lady, I have brought my sword and my service to lay at your feet." I make my way around the end of the table and kneel before her, head down, arms raised with the ancient sword.

Isabel sighs loudly. "I had hoped you would abandon your folly, young sir."

I raise my head, allowing her to read my sincerity. "It is not folly to pledge my loyalty to one such as you."

Instead of tired resignation and acceptance of troublesome me, Isabel's eyes open wide as she sucks in a breath. The lady of the castle takes a step back, clutching one hand to her round belly and the other to her heart. Faster than I imagined a woman so far along with child can move, she snatches a candle from the table and lowers it to the sword. The fear in her eyes is out of place in one with such stalwart courage.

"What have you done?" She backs away from me, fingering the cross hanging from the beaded belt around her waist.

The guards, all five of them, close in on me. Isabel recovers her poise and raises a hand to stop them. "All is well." She beckons me to stand. "Set your blade on the table and approach."

Her henchmen do not recede far as I draw closer. She pitches her voice for my ears only, never taking her gaze from the sword. "That is an ancient weapon. Tell me truth. Who gave you this?"

The wife of a knight knowing her weapons is something Eala and I should have taken into consideration. So much for our gamble. Good sense tells me not to admit I nicked it from a druid guardian spirit.

Isabel doesn't give me a chance to answer. "You do not need to say. I know. You raided the sacred place in the nearby wood." To my surprise, she grips my shoulders and shakes before letting go. "Do you not know such blades carry curses?"

I take a knee again, admitting my theft without saying it outright. "I did not think, Lady."

"It must be returned. I will show you my back and deny this meeting." She turns to the window, still grasping her wooden cross.

I've failed again. Failed Eala. Failed our future. I slowly rise, feeling unknightly tears threatening to bust free when Isabel suddenly whirls to face me again with a calculating look.

"How did you leave the castle?"

Bollocks. I'm losing my knack to think things through. How would anyone leave a castle under siege? Not by the front door.

I hear Eala's gasp from the stairs and raise a curse of my own that I didn't tell her to wait in the empty armory for me.

As if she would.

Isabel's head snaps from me to the sound. A guard is heading right for Eala. He roughly brings her toward the center of the room.

"'Tis my wife, Lady."

Eala drops into an acceptable curtsy. "Pardon. With death all around, I could not bear being parted any longer from my dear husband."

I stiffen. Eala's words are fine enough. I can't deny the thrill running though me at being claimed as her husband, but her American accent rings a slightly odd note. Isabel de Clare strikes me as savvy enough to pick up on the discrepancy.

"Not after suffering so when he left me to journey down a rope and back again from the far tower to retrieve a blade."

"Release the wife," says Isabel. "Come," she says, gesturing to Eala. "And get up," she says to me, impatience evident.

We follow her to the window as she waves the guards back to their posts. Her expression is grave. "Lad, were you not plagued by archers on your fool's errand?"

"I was naught but a shadow within shadows," I answer, hoping she buys it.

"You will do it again." She glares at the druid's sword on the table. "Remove that cursed blade from my castle. Go north in an unbroken line for a trio of hours. There, you'll find a force waiting for this signal." Isabel whispers in my ear. "*Maidin bheannaithe.*"

So, I'm to tell Herself's backup it's a *blessed morning* to come on and slaughter her besiegers. I swallow hard. Here it is. I feel it in my bones. This is the task we've been sent to accomplish.

She lays a hand on my shoulder. "Do this, and you'll be forgiven for bringing a portent of evil to lay at my feet."

What she's leaving out are the words *if you survive.*

Och, what a massive backfire it was stealing a sword from a passage tomb. Eala makes a low hum of despair next to me. I know from the sound, she's estimated the odds of me escaping a besieged castle on a rope and making it to Isabel's allies in one piece, much less returning here.

Isabel calls to one of her guards. "Wake all, there is a plan afoot." To another, she says, "Take this brave soul to the far tower and lower him on a fine, strong rope to our destiny." Then she turns to Eala. "You will wait with me for the return of your husband and our fortune."

Isabel is a savvy lass. She's keeping Eala close as a guarantee I'll follow through on my pledge and not slink off if this endeavor doesn't go well. If only the both of us could touch these bloody rings and travel to the Marshall reinforcements together. I hold back a huff. Praying the chainmail whisks us off to the right place is all well and good, but in the minds of these folk, vanishing is witchcraft no matter how it aids the lady with her siege. Such magic added to the cursed blade I brought into her presence would lead us straight to the stake.

Eala flings herself into my arms, and we hold tight. This can't be goodbye. I've not waited centuries to find my love only to lose her in storm and siege. If there is indeed a power lending us a helping hand, I pray it's watching.

Even if it's Fae.

"I love you, my Eala *bán*. You are my strength."

She captures my face in a painful grip and kisses me. Pointing to the stones beneath her feet, she says, "Here is where I'll be. Here is where you'll return."

I keep my steady gaze bound to hers. "You have my promise."

The tears wetting her eyes match the loveliness of the Veil's shimmer.

My pleas to accompany Sion to the far tower are denied. He's flanked by two soldiers as his last bobbing curl disappears into shadow. When I try to follow at least as far as the arch leading from the room, another guard blocks my way. Message received. Sion goes. I stay.

No one stops me as I lean against the wall next to a tapestry and begin to sob. I must appear a terrible weakling to Isabel de Clare as I weep.

Shoring myself up, I mentally prepare to be hauled away and locked in a room or—

My knees threaten to give out as I imagine overnighting in a medieval dungeon. It's a surprise to feel the great lady's hand lightly cup the side of my head.

"Fate tests women without mercy." She rubs her stomach. "We bring the children." Isabel gazes out the window. "We fight the battles when called to." I watch her shoulders rise and fall as she draws a deep breath. "We do these things alone."

I think of her husband William Marshall off in England while she's here defending their castle. Her courage is catching. If this woman can accomplish such feats of bravery, I can deal with showing some backbone while Sion risks our everything to fulfill what we believe to be Finnbheara's expectation.

Her gentleness with me is unexpected, but then I remember she is a mother. For a fleeting moment, I think of Máthair and long for her soothing comfort.

"Sit with me," says Isabel, sinking into one of the chairs at the long table. I didn't notice how fancy they were. Why wouldn't they be? William and Isabel Marshall are A-list celebrities. Very rich ones. I imagine feasts on fine precious metal platters adorning this table in times of peace.

Isabel doesn't come off as a privileged pup. Her dignity fills the room. She's heading up a siege in an era when women were generally not valued. Points to William Marshall for giving his exceptional wife her due with his trust. If he didn't, I wouldn't be sitting down with this amazing person in medieval Ireland while she commands an army.

"Talk to me of simple things," she says.

I freeze. It's vital to choose my words very carefully. Sion is much better at adjusting his speech to the past. I'll have to rely on the phrasing from the countless folktales and histories that painted my professorial life.

Doing my best to imitate Sion's accent, I say. "I am recently wed."

She smiles. "No babes then?"

I shake my head. I've never been with anyone long enough to consider having kids. An image of a freckle faced toddler with Sion's curls fades into my mind. How can such a thing ever be? There's no guarantee we're going to exist day to day. I don't even know how we'll age. If we ever earn our place in Tír na nÓg, will we grow old together or because he is fully human, will I watch the years change him even in the land of eternal youth? Speculation is a quick road to despair.

"May you be blessed with them." She cradles her belly. "They are your greatest pain and your greatest hope. Hope rising far above the pain." Isabel levels her gaze at me. "What is your name?"

"Eala, Lady."

She smiles, leaning forward to smooth a loose strand of hair off my face in a motherly gesture. "A swan indeed. Lovely name." Isabel settles into the chair. "What is your husband called?"

"Sionnach."

Isabel laughs. It lightens the burdens she carries in the lines of her face. "A fox and a swan. What an unlikely pairing." A noise across the room catches her attention. "Ah, they come."

I whip around to see what she's looking at.

Isabel notes my raised brows. "In my castle, I know all that goes on in both light and shadow." Her expression grows serious. "And there will be much shadow for those outside my gates. Leaders and their heirs alike will feel the ice of my dungeons. They will long for the sun, but I shall keep it forever from their grasp."

She's terrifying as she continues down a list of her plans for the prisoners she'll take once reinforcements arrive and break the siege. The room fills with her war council. Isabel stands, her efforts a bit awkward. Her hand goes to the small of her back as a wince betrays the discomfort she surely suffers from carrying both a baby and a siege.

The guards that escorted Sion away from me return. One remains by the arch and the other approaches Isabel with a bow. "It is done, Lady. The messenger is down the rope and into the wood."

She nods. "God go with…" Her gaze meets mine. "…your fox."

"Take your rest now, Eala." She tucks one of her own stray locks under her headpiece. "If you can find any." Her gaze sweeps the group of gathering men. Any sign of fatigue she let slip in front of me disappears. "I invite you to return at the expected hour to wait for your husband here on these very stones he pledged to return to."

Isabel shoots a look to the guard and fear lances through me as his hand touches my elbow. Oh God, is this the moment I'm carted away to some rat-laden cell? This great lady showed me sympathy, I hope she's got a little more to spare.

I choose words, attempting to sound period acceptable. "May I pass those hours at the place where my husband last touched your castle walls so that I may pray after him through the darkness?"

The daughter of Strongbow studies me with narrowed eyes. "I see no harm in that."

I curtsy and bow my head, genuinely grateful for a shot at a vermin-free night. "Thank you, Lady."

Without a word, the guard leads me from the room through a maze of stairs and freezing corridors. Fear for Sion, stress of the unending road of unknowns we face, and nervousness about pretending I belong in this time saps my energy. I wish I were here in a happier circumstance. It would be fantastic to ask others in the castle to share folk and fairy tales. What an unequaled opportunity to gather research from such authentic primary sources. The stoicism of my escort and lack of confidence in my ability to sustain correct medieval phrasing keep me silent.

As we continue to trudge through the castle, memories of Irish stories conjure new worries about my Fae bargain, and my already overtaxed brain grows even wearier. I should've been more specific with Finnbheara. Why didn't I include stipulations about Sion aging either alongside me or granting us both the immortality that comes with living in the Fae kingdom? I need to brainstorm with Sion every possible loophole and pit trap Finnbheara might have up his sleeve, especially for my fox. We will be better intellectually armed when we face the King of the Connacht Fae again.

Finally, after what feels like miles of hiking through the stale aroma of wet stone and filthy bodies, we climb a different round turret from the one Sion and I first landed in. The soldier sets his torch in a bracket, which doesn't do much to cut through the shadows. This tower boasts a square glassless opening overlooking a dense forest. On the stone floor next to the window, I can make out a pile of thick rope. I'm sure Sion used his natural charm to weave a convincing tale about shucking the coil he allegedly used to sneak out the first time to get another for a second descent.

There are no sounds of attack from the ground or archers on alert in the tower, giving me a sliver of hope that Sion didn't lower himself into a nest of besiegers when he repelled down the side of the castle. A darker thought punches me in the chest. I'm alone with a soldier whose exhaustion and hunger might very well knock any moral compass he has off of its true north. What the hell am I going to do if he decides I'm fair game for alleviating siege stress by assaulting me?

Trying not to look like spooked prey, I back toward an arrow loop. My guard gestures toward the window. "Your fool of a husband entered his folly from there." He grunts. "May you have God's ear for your prayers." With that, the man plucks a spent torch from another bracket and relights it from the one he brought in. He heads for the stairs, then turns back to me. In a voice that invites no argument, he says, "I'll return for you when my lady commands it. I advise you not to stray from this place."

With that, I'm alone with a single guttering torch. I press close to the window, staring out at storm clouds still crashing through one another as if to mimic the battle scene below. Checking to make sure I am indeed by myself in this lonely turret, I close my eyes and plead with the Veil not to abandon me.

It still does not answer. Whatever force is behind the chainmail rings that controls our travel, it's effectively shut out my ability to partner with my personal passageway through time.

Time.

I huff. What is time to me anymore? Does it pass the same here as it does on the Hill of Tara or do separate realities steal precious minutes or hours from us? How will we know when our part of a Celtic day is spent? After one hundred thousand heartbeats, will our lives be brushed away like crumbs off a table? I begin to break at the thought of dying here without Sionnach. Apart. Alone. Can he make it back to me before our last heartbeat?

The only certainty is that we have no control over time. Its dominion is divine, an untouchable power. We are its victims.

I clasp my hands and pray for Sion's safety. I beg anyone listening to help us survive this test, no matter who shackled us to it. Questions of fate weave a thorny vine through my soul as I lose myself to the hours.

My hands burn like the devil himself pissed on them. I've faced a bevy of challenges in two hundred years but sliding down a brawny rope in threadbare leather gloves from a sympathetic guard isn't one of them. If not for that last-minute kindness, I'd be dipping bloody rather than raw palms into the near-frozen stream. The cold burns at first, then settles into a bit of a balm for my aching hands. I'll be as useful as sheep dung in the upcoming fight if I can't even grip my filched sword without yowling in pain.

I'm so thoroughly coated in layers of sweat, dirt, and scratches from barreling through these woods for hours, I'd be tempted to wade in up to my neck if the water wasn't cock-shrinking cold. Where in the hell are the Marshall reinforcements? It's well past the time we should have met up. I fling icy water from my hands, growling like a beast over my senseless wandering. I'm fecking impotent without the ability to Veil travel.

Exhaustion quickly reforms my spike of anger and self-pity into the leading edge of despair. Raising my face to the moon, I implore the sky in a strangled voice. "I'm asking every last one of you stars in the heavens for help."

The damn ego I wear like armor convinced me the purpose of landing at Kilkenny is about me, not Eala. The chainmail rings are an unwelcome weight in my pocket. Why didn't I leave them with her? Surely as I'm standing here lost in the mud, my brilliant love would've figured a way to use them to get back home if I didn't return. I'm certain of it.

Splashing freezing water on my face prevents tears from falling. Truth is, Eala is so much more than a low-class fool like me deserves. Finnbheara knows it. He's doing all he can to shake me free of her like alder leaves in fall. I don't pretend to understand the connection between the king and my swan, but I have to believe if he doesn't care for her in some capacity, I'd already have faced the business end of a Faerie sword. That still doesn't change the fact that he's dead set on proving she's better off without me. If plowing through miles of wood, then fighting my way back to her side, is the way to show Finnbheara he's wrong about Sionnach Loho, I'll do it a hundred times.

I stare at the water, willing Eala's reflection to be the one looking back at me instead of my own weary face. Life was hollow before my love came into it. I need her to make sense of the world. She thinks she's not brave, but my *anamchara* shines with a quiet boldness to rival the most valiant warrior.

Eala does not give up. I've got to honor that and do the same. If I have to climb a tree and shout Isabel's password to the skies to summon every soldier in the fecking forest, I'll do it. For Eala. For us. I make a vow to the ripples in the stream. "I won't fail you, love. I swear it."

A cold blade bites against my throat as a massive leather-clad arm clamps around my ribs. "Failing, are you?" says a rough voice. If I even swallow, the sharp edge will cut skin and most likely vital veins. "And who is it you're failing?"

"*Maidin bheannaithe,*" I choke out the key phrase with as little movement of my windpipe as possible.

Blade and arm disappear instantly, and I collapse onto the ground.

"'Tis the sign," my ambusher whispers. His breath fans a thin mist into the chill air. Ignoring me, which is a far sight better than killing the messenger, he turns toward the wood and bellows. "The courteous lady of high degree calls for aid."

A roar rises from the shadows and in minutes, a hoard of metal and mail erupts from between trunks. Troops surge past me until a beefy hand pulls me up by the collar. I snatch the ancient tomb sword as my spent hide is hauled to my feet and swept along by their roiling wave of vengeance.

Raising my weapon, I call on my dwindling reserves of strength to join the march. After rewinding the hours I've just spent, we're back in sight of the castle. The order for the charge is given and the two great bulls, Isabel de Clare's reinforcements, and those holding Kilkenny under siege, collide. My druid's sword meets others whenever I'm not quick enough to dodge as I make my way along the outskirts of the battle. I've committed to this fight to show Finn what's what, but I'm more committed to living.

My sight locks on the nearest tower. I make my way round it where shadow lingers. In a desperate attempt to avoid blade and arrow, I reach for the last untried Fae gift Finnbheara had once given me. The ability to weaken solid substances was the trick I used to allow Eala and me to pass through a wall to find a lad thrown into the Leap castle oubliette.

As with the Veil and my fox, that skill is also lost to me. I cannot shift stone to plunge into the safety of Kilkenny Castle. My overtaxed sword arm doesn't react quickly enough as the harsh reflection of the rising sun off the flat of a blade blinds me.

A clamor coming up the tower stairs breaks me from my waking trance. I startle, hoping to see Sion slipping back in the window. Instead, archers now populate the niches with arrow loops. A few glances fall my way, but a disheveled peasant woman isn't a concern for the soldiers.

Sounds of battle grow louder from below. There is no bombardment from siege weapons, thank heavens. The dawning sun streams through the windows like a bright promise. I press a palm to my chest but don't feel the stress of labored heartbeats. Whatever time we've passed here must fit tidily into our allotted travelling half of a Celtic day.

Judging from the activity, Sion has done it. Reinforcements are here. The siege of Kilkenny Castle is about to be broken. Relief as sweet as the scent of blooming honeysuckle fills me.

The same soldier who brought me here in the dead of night returns to the tower. With a curt flick of his wrist, he beckons me to follow. Our pace is quicker this time as he leads me back through the arteries of the castle toward the war room. I try not to falter, but I've blown past exhaustion into stupor territory. His frustration with Eala duty is evident through his intermittent growls every time I slow to catch my breath. After what feels like a full day's hike, we pass through the archway to our destination, and he points to a place along the wall for me to stand.

Herself, as Sion calls Isabel, is caught in the maelstrom of issuing commands and answering questions. I cling to my position, attempting to go unnoticed. I don't want anyone ordering me away from here. I can't miss Sion's triumphant stroll back into this room without a cursed sword and with the favor of Isabel de Clare Marshall.

I ease farther along the stone to where I will see the exact place Sion vowed we'd be reunited. It's strange everyone gives that particular spot near the end of the table a wide berth.

One of the lords whispers something in Isabel's ear and then points at me. My gaze meets that of the lady of the castle to find deep sorrow in her expression. She summons me closer, then lowers her stare to the floor. I step farther into the room and approach, only to lose all my ability to move.

Lying as still as the stone beneath him on a dark green cloak is Sion, his shirt soaked in blood.

CHAPTER 10
THE FIRST LESSON

My wail momentarily silences the room. I fly across the chilled floor and drop to Sion's side. This lifeless form of my *anamchara* is not a reality I am capable of accepting. Certainly, a cataclysm would have resounded in my soul if Sionnach passed from the living world into spirit. My love can't be dead.

"Sionnach." I'm afraid to shake him in case it will make whatever wound he's incurred bleed more. His eyes are closed, his skin a hideous blue gray.

From somewhere above me, Isabel is speaking words of apology and praising Sion's bravery. I can't focus or respond to her. Gently, I lay my palm above his heart and close my eyes. A sensation trickles up from his chest to my lifeline. It's like the faintest ripple you feel at your feet when you stand in a pond fed by a gentle spring.

He's alive.

We have to get into the Veil. The Veil heals. The Veil will bring him back to me.

I thrust my hand into his pockets until I find the chainmail rings that brought us here. Taking his still, cold hand in mine, I can't consider what the people gathered around us will think about our *blink of an eye* disappearance. Closing my eyes, I try to call the Veil.

Colors streak behind my eyelids, but the sense of being immersed in the peace of the Veil doesn't come. When I open my eyes, Sion still lays bleeding on the cold stone floor.

The rings in my hand begin to warm. It might be crazy but given our suspicion they brought us here and to the passage tomb, they may be our only way back. Whatever force sent us here is tied to them. Wedging the metals links between my palm and Sion's, I press.

A closely woven net of smoldering charred branches settles around us. Beyond the boughs, I recognize the white-gold background and chill of this foreign portal that forced us to the siege of Kilkenny Castle. I want to take Sion in my arms and protect him from the battering of travel, but with the force of an unforgiving wind in this twisted version of the Veil, it's all I can manage to keep our hands clasped together. My feeling of helplessness is nearly as jarring as being thrust into a time where our purpose is nothing but a guess. I am a planner and lover of a checklist. Even though Finnbheara had a hand in my creation, Faerie caprice will never be a part of my so-called nature.

I was brought up Catholic, but I never fully embraced the deep faith my grandmother tried to instill in me. But as we're tossed like butterflies with broken wings through this passage, I pray harder than ever before. I pray to Catholic saints, Irish gods and goddesses, druids, and Fae kings. I pray for Sion's life because it is also my life, and I'm not ready to surrender either.

The air around us warms. We're gently poured rather than carelessly dumped onto the grassy Hill of Tara under the branches of the hawthorn tree. Night lingers over the land.

I crawl to where Sion lies motionless on the grass. I scream his name. I scream for help. I just scream while I lift his shirt to see the deep, nasty gash down his side running from the top of his ribcage to his hipbone. Whether from knife or sword I can't tell, but it's what I imagine a fatal battle wound looks like.

"As I tried to warn you...I wouldn't touch those," says Robber Bright, finishing his sentence of moments or eons before. While I press the fabric of my skirt to Sion's *leine* over his bloody wound and try to catch my breath, the Fae plucks the rings of mail out of the grass near us. He casually lobs them toward the tree where they fly and stick to the exact spot in the bark where we found them.

"Help us. Help Sion," I pant. "Save him or tell me how to do it." I rip the blood-soaked shirt off over his head to add more direct pressure, desperate to staunch the bleeding. Sion can't have much more blood to spare after what already poured out of his battered body onto the stone floor of Kilkenny Castle.

Robber tilts his head, studying Sion. "I'm not in the practice of healing mortals."

I aim a fiery glare at him. "I don't give a damn about your practices. Do something."

The Fae calmly nods at Sionnach. "The fox is your charge, but until you get him into the Veil, I suppose I can spare a little magic to set you on your way."

Another fear stands shoulder to shoulder with Sion's survival. "At Kilkenny Castle, the Veil wouldn't come to me."

Robber tilts his head, giving me a look as if he's questioning my intelligence. "As it would not since you traveled under the influence of another."

"Do you mean Finnbheara?" Tightness in my gut suggests Finnbheara is vindictive enough to have sent us into a siege to kill off Sion.

"I cannot say."

I glare at the Fae. "Cannot or will not?" A tick in his jaw muscle is the only indication my question got any consideration at all. Robber gives me no answer. There's no time to probe deeper when Sion's life is at stake. "Will the Veil come to me now?" I need to know if I'll be able to continue the healing this Faerie has promised to initiate.

He bobs his chin once, then whistles a short tune, followed by a trio of long blinks.

Sion's body trembles and a prolonged groan trickles from his lips. The blood covering my skirt and his skin flares bright scarlet, rising into the air a few inches. It twists and spins into one long thin red strand that snakes toward the wound, then dips inside ruined flesh. When the last of the bloody thread vanishes, the edges of the gash down Sion's chest appear to waver as if seeking one another.

"Tomorrow," Robber says, then studies the sky. "Rather, today." A glittering dark gray corona with streaks of silver shot through it outlines his body. I saw no such aura around Finnbheara or his Fae soldiers. "Midday."

"Wait," I call to him, an unanswered question still burning in my mind. "Did you send us to Kilkenny Castle?"

His voice grows fainter with every word. "Your touch allowed…"

He's gone before finishing the sentence. A certain Faerie has a lot to answer for when I see him next.

"Sion, can you hear me? Are you with me?" I lay a hand on the side of his neck, gratified to feel a weak but definite pulse. Whatever Robber Bright did was good, but not enough.

Black velvet sky is our canopy. Thank heavens, we're still in the window of the Celtic day when faith-willing, the Veil will answer my call. Our Veil, not the distorted version that ripped us away from this hill and back again with a detour to the passage tomb near Kilkenny Castle. Being careful not to disturb Sion's still open wound, I slide my arms under his back and visualize the delicate surface of a soap bubble on which the barest hint of light will awaken a rainbow. The scent of lemongrass and spearmint wafts around us as if it were hiding in the roots of the hawthorn, waiting to be called.

The sensation of drifting overtakes me. The Veil has arrived and holds us in its arms. I don't ask to be taken anywhere but rather to linger in the presence of this mystical passage that cares for those who believe in its magic.

Sion's body lolls on the surface of the soft orbs of the Veil floor. Every so often, I catch myself holding my breath and have to rediscover a steady in and out pace. If the Veil could cure the brutal stab to the chest Sion endured at Olk's hand, surely it will complete his healing now.

This is technically the second fatal wound Sion has suffered in as many days or possibly a few more, considering the time we lost while in Tír na nÓg. Still, a human body is a transient gift in the scheme of forever.

I lean my head back. Through the wavering prism of the Veil wall, I find the full moon. Maybe its celestial beauty is the source of healing for the *fánaí*, the Veil guides. Is that what we are still, or have we become nothing more than aimless wanderers entrapped by the cryptic riddle of a Fae king?

I stretch out next to Sion and trace circles above his heart. "Dream my love. Borrow the stories you've sent me of silver-horned stags, brave knights, and birds that sing your name. Let them sustain you under the splendor of a Veil moon until you return to me."

I watch and wish and hope, not allowing doubt or fear a place in my spirit. Like the yawn of a sleepy babe, the Veil sprites begin to glow gently within me. The Veil is their home. I'm but one soul allowed to visit here.

Sion breathes.

I breathe.

Slowly, a faint pink tinge spreads across his skin, chasing away the gray. I stare at, what by all rights, should be a killing wound to see it's knitted together into a ropy red welt. As I stroke ringlets from his face, tears fall from my eyes onto his cheeks, making them glisten. I lay my cheek against his.

His eyelashes sweep across my skin. I lift my head to see green glass eyes watching me.

He doesn't speak.

I'm afraid to. Afraid I'll say something to prompt his goodbye.

Sion opens his mouth then closes it, the effort too much. His eyes begin to flutter. I must speak now. It may be my last chance.

"Thank you for waiting all those years until I found you, Sionnach Loho. Our time together has been a life worth living." I kiss one corner of his lips and then the other before pressing a gentle kiss to his mouth.

The lazy smile I've come to love more than the most brilliant blooms in my grandmother's winter garden greets me. Sion's voice is a rough whisper. "Thanks for sticking with an *amadán* like me."

"You're no one's fool, you impulsive, brave, selfless man." I kiss him again.

With a shaky touch, he runs fingers through my hair. "What's a feller got to do around here to get a whiskey?"

We slide from the Veil, coming to rest a few yards from the front door of the Loho Cottage. I'm gratified to have managed my most subtle shift yet from Veil back to reality since Sion is in no shape to be overly jostled. I puzzle for a moment over why my Veil skills have become much smoother. Is it me or Finnbheara's doing? Maybe he's packed me in the Fae equivalent of bubble wrap, so I don't inadvertently damage the package he's hoping to claim when this is over.

Me being the package.

Bracing myself against Sion's undamaged side, I support him to stand and shuffle past the *fánaí* tree back in its place by the front window. It strikes me then, Alfie was nowhere to be found in our latest adventure, or rather, misadventure. I suppose it makes sense since neither Sion nor I were guiding our latest travels.

Once inside, I deposit Sion on the couch and peel off the remainder of his mud- and blood-stained clothing. Even though Robber returned blood to Sion's body, he couldn't possibly have given it all back. Did he have some Fae gauge of the minimum Sion would need to survive?

"Do you think you can shower?" I ask, pulling a twig from his hair.

He sighs deeply and then with effort, raises his eyebrows. "Will you be joining me?"

I purse my lips. "Seriously, Sion? Whiskey and sex, that's where your mind goes first?"

He chuckles, then winces. "Can't think of anything better after surviving the wicked end of a sword."

His obvious pain sets off a geyser of anger in me. Why didn't Robber Bright heal him completely? Did Finnbheara give his lackey a directive beyond teaching me Fae shit that includes making Sion's life a living hell?

Sion grunts as a shiver overtakes him. He crosses his arms and drops his head back onto the couch cushion. The poor man is sitting naked in a chilly room. "Come on, my valiant knight." I help him up and after checking that the water won't either freeze or scald, I steady him while he steps into the tub.

I rinse his body with the shower hose, being careful not to aim the stream directly at his mending skin. He hisses when the water sluices over it the first time, but then it doesn't hurt him much. I settle him against the end of the tub while I wash his hair. Even with leaf shreds and dirt, the brandied undertones of his curls are baby soft. I massage his scalp slowly and thoroughly as he relaxes beneath my touch.

"I'm no nurse, but I'm sure you're supposed to stay hydrated to heal," I say, helping him towel off. "Let's get you into bed, and then I'll get you some water."

The shower steals the last bit of energy from him. His chin falls to his chest before I get him onto the mattress. I force him into sweatpants and a T-shirt as he collapses on top of the comforter. Robber Bright is coming at midday, and I don't want a bare-assed Sion spread eagle on the bed in front of the Fae. He'd hate to be caught in so vulnerable a position.

I wake Sion to force a big glass of water down him before he flops back into dreamland. Maybe his Corrigan connection can hook us up with antibiotics in case the sword that cut him delivered more than just a slice. Laying a hand on Sion's forehead, I'm relieved there's no sign of fever. I kiss his cool skin and whisper, "Sleep, *a stór*, my treasure," the same endearment my grandmother aka Sion's mother, used for me...and probably him too.

Thankfully, Máthair always insisted on a fire in the hearth anytime the weather dropped below sixty degrees, so I know my way around a fireplace. I rouse a blaze to heat the cottage. After a shower to wash off medieval grime, I slip into jeans and a sweater from the rumpled clothes in my travel backpack. I'm actually looking forward to doing something mundane like laundry.

As tempting as it is to crawl into bed next to Sion, I can't spare the luxury. Poring over Finnbheara's riddle and my notes on the table, I munch on a hunk of cheese. How the hell do I confirm if helping Isabel de Clare end her siege got us any closer to answering the question: *What's all and each the selfsame piece, plain truth and no illusion?*

Is it bravery? Sion accepted the truth he had to offer himself to the Lady of Kilkenny Castle. I stifle a grumble. That only fits part of the question not the illusion reference.

I lean back in the kitchen chair with a huff and scan the riddle again. "Wait," I say too loudly and peek over to make sure I haven't disturbed Sion. The sputtering noises coming out of his mouth reassure me he's getting the sleep he needs.

A sharpened star shall be the proof...

I finger the star pendant on the table. It's five rounded triangles give nothing away. Not a point in sight. What will it take to sharpen the points? Will it be clear that they've become sharp and what we've accomplished to make that happen? How many days are we going to lose while Sion recovers? The mountain of frustrating unknowns is crushing.

A loud rap on the front door startles me. I don't know what I expected, but it wasn't Robber extending the courtesy of knocking that we asked of him. He strikes me as the type to materialize whenever and wherever he pleases.

I pad across the wood floor in socks. Our visitor is too close to the door for me to see them through the window. I debate whether I should call out or just open the damn door. Even though we've learned our peeping Tom was Robber Bright, I'm still nervous about safety here in this isolated cottage.

"Eala?" comes a familiar voice.

I fling the door open to find Colleen on the doorstep. "Hey, hi." The urge to hug her outweighs the fact she's probably still completely pissed at me. She's stiff at first and then softens, throwing her arms around me.

"I tried to call, but you didn't answer your cell. Since you gave me the address, I figured it was okay to show up."

I release her. "Yes, of course. You're always welcome here."

The initial awkwardness of the moment keeps humming along with the reality of Sion's snores bouncing around the cottage. Crap, I don't want her asking questions about the mess of Finnbheara's challenge strewn all over the table.

"Uh, Sion had a bad fall, probably bruised some ribs. He's sleeping it off." I open the door wider to give her a look inside to the bedroom alcove while I stick my feet in Sion's wellies. "Let me show you around the place, and we can talk."

She gives a curt nod and backs away to let me out. "I have things to say, Eala, but I need a minute first."

"Take as long as you need." We walk in silence down a path behind the house, heading toward the sea cliffs. I'm thankful for the patches of lavender with their soothing fragrance. It comes as no surprise Máthair was able to raise her beloved plant in a place where the ample rainfall should've discouraged its bloom. My step falters when a thought strikes me. Was Máthair's gift with growing things a boon she kept from her days in Tír na nÓg as Finnbheara's lover?

Halfway to the lighthouse, Colleen sits on a rounded cap of granite. She braces her elbows on her knees and drops her head. I give her space and stoop to pick a small, bright yellow buttercup.

I hold the flower to Colleen. "Do you remember Máthair used to tell us if you hold a buttercup under your chin and it makes a yellow reflection there, you'll always crave butter on bread?"

To my great relief, Colleen takes the bloom from me and sniffs it. "She always had the best stories." Her gaze meets mine, and she blows a long breath. "I'm trying to come to terms with what you did."

I crouch in front of her, striving to find words that will possibly begin to repair the damage between us. Carrying the burden of blame seems like a smart opener. "I'm so ashamed of what I put you through, Colleen." There are pieces of truth I can share. "You know I've never been impulsive, but as inexplicable as it is, I knew the inscription on Máthair's ring led me to Sion. *Find me* meant find him."

To my surprise, Colleen answers with a bitter laugh. "This thing with Sion and you isn't the only sucker punch I have to face." She lays a hand on her chest. "It's made me take a hard look at who I am. I've always been the flighty *act before thinking* one of us, not you." She stares deep into my eyes. "I cast you in the role as my anchor, so you were. The stable one. The focused one. I followed you to Kennard Park, knowing I'd be free from my parents, but still have someone to steady me if I stumbled."

"And I let you down." I drop my forehead to her knees. "You suffered the fallout for my actions."

She pats my head, and I look up. Her wistful gaze takes in the rolling land. "Do you know what my mom said to me when I told her I was not going to Kennard Park as a student? That I was done with school?"

I narrow my eyes.

Colleen copies her mom's New York accent. "*You're leaving to live a life of perpetual high school without anyone looking over your shoulder.*" She shrugs. "It's what I did. Got a job at the university to cover the bills and leave me with fun money."

"You underestimate yourself. You're excellent at your job, and you enjoy it. Right?"

"Come on, Eala. I'm a glorified amateur party planner." She rubs a hand over her mouth. "I totally botched the way I handled you and Jeremy disappearing." Colleen flails her arms. "Oh, they must just be having fun. Let me give it a minute." She knocks fists to her forehead. "I should've called right away when you didn't return on schedule because it was my responsibility. Even if the Garda called me nuts for worrying too soon, I should have tried. If I'd done my job, maybe we'd know where Jeremy is right now."

Her self-blame eats at my guilt. I wish there was something I could say. Maybe there is. It's not as if Jeremy Olk is going to turn up to discount my version of things. "Jeremy found Sion and me together."

Colleen's eyes go wide.

I decide to rewrite history for her. "He caught us in the old gate lodge in a…um…compromising position. It was ugly. There were pretty hot words thrown around. He said something to the effect of me not being worth it, and why would he ever take a position at a college that would hire me."

"Oh, shit."

"Yeah, and then Olk stormed out, saying there were plenty of places that would appreciate what he had to offer instead of an insignificant third-rate university." I can tell from the tingle my face is bright red, hopefully adding credence to the lies. Instant regret nips at me. Hopefully, Colleen won't share my fabrication with the Garda. My terribly thought-out confession could make Sion and me look like suspects in foul play.

Sion said his Corrigan buddy did all sorts of things for him. Some unorthodox like fake I.Ds. Maybe he can drum up Garda acceptable evidence Jeremy Olk bailed on the professorship at Kennard Park for greener pastures.

I watch Colleen process my fib. "That would explain why he refused to ride the bus back to the hotel with us."

Oh, thank God. There had been a last Jeremy Olk sighting that would save our asses in a Garda timeline.

She turns her focus back to me. "Does your life have to change so drastically, La? I don't suppose you and Sion would consider relocating to New York?" She raises a hand, reading my expression. "I didn't think so." Colleen looks nearly as exhausted as Sion did before I put him to bed. "Maybe fate intended this Ireland trip to present us both with different futures. You found your person, and I got a wake-up call." She presses her lips together. "I was ready to commit to Charlie because he was great fun and offered the perfect amount of Colleen worship. I nearly uprooted everything to move in with a guy I'd just met."

"Exactly what I've done with Sion."

She stands and paces. "But that's the thing. It's not the same. I was going to go all in with Charlie because it seemed like an adventure. You're changing your life because you are serious about Sion. You have with him what my Shanna would call a *deep knowing*." She meets my eyes. "Am I right?"

"Yes." Maybe before I slink into Tír na nÓg, Colleen will truly come to accept what Sion is to me.

She grinds the toe of her sneaker into the dirt. "I'm not going to pretend I totally understand your situation, but I do know I was playing at being serious with Charlie, the way I played at staying in a job to fuel my social life more than my life. I'm staying in Ireland not only to help in any way I can with finding Professor Olk, but to really get serious over where my life is going. What I want it to be in five or ten years."

"I hope I'm included." I regret the words as soon as they're out. I'm setting Colleen up for more hurt, more betrayal. Once the new moon comes, I may be gone forever this time.

She looks sad. "There's the reason I came to see you. I really want to get past you screwing me over, but I'm not there yet. I won't be able to deal with you calling me all the time to apologize." Colleen huffs. "Not that you did call, but I know you, La. Those messages would have come sooner or later because that's who you are."

Colleen is the longest relationship of my life besides Máthair. There's no Faerie magic to mend things between us. "You're asking me to leave you alone?"

She reaches to replace a loose strand of my hair behind my ear. "I'm asking you to let me figure this out on my own."

I grasp her hand. "You know where I am. Anytime. Every time." Pulling her close, I feel like the horrible person I am. I'm making impossible promises. I won't be here. If the day comes when she wants me back in her life, there will be no Eala Duir.

Maybe two betrayals will allow her to let me go for good. At least this is a goodbye of sorts. Her last memory of me will be one of open arms and sisterly hugs.

Colleen pulls away and shades her eyes, squinting at the distant hill. "What's that?"

Around us, fog has begun to sneak across the land. It's too early and too sunny for a natural mist to roll in off the Atlantic. Inside me, Veil sprites flare as if awakened by the disruption in the air. I'm not used to them showing up before dusk. A strange flutter beneath my skin that has nothing to do with Veil sprites starts gently, then becomes a steady pulse. The truth hits me. As Robber Bright promised, I sense his nearness.

This is a conjured haze.

Midday is here, and my Faerie visitor approaches.

My pulse races. I've got to get Colleen out of here.

"I really need to check on Sion. I'm supposed to wake him every hour. Concussion from the fall."

"You should," she says.

We don't speak as I set a brisk pace toward the cottage. Colleen parked her car off the road on the other side of the stone wall marking Loho land. She looks around with concern. "The fog is intense."

To my horror, rapidly approaching the cottage is a sight which I'll have no reasonable explanation to give her. The dense tumbleweed of fog I saw from the window the night of the storm is almost upon us. Beneath the soles of my boots, I feel a thundering rumble like an approaching train.

It's unnerving the way my heartbeat syncs with the sound as if it's calling to me.

"Come in the house for a while." I don't know where else to stash Colleen so she doesn't come face-to-face with the imminent arrival of Robber Bright.

"I can deal with a little fog. Goodbye, Eala."

It's then I understand that to her, this is ordinary fog, not a roiling ball of mist with oncoming vibrations that shake the earth.

A dreamy feeling seeps into my senses. Before it takes over completely, I've got to get my friend out of here. "Goodbye, Colleen."

She doesn't turn to go or blink or breathe or move.

A gust of wind blows me off balance as the leading edge of the rogue fog bank hits us, and I'm inside it with a non-moving Colleen next to me. We're surrounded by puffing and stamping from a source I cannot see. My first thought is of horses until barely perceptible growls and trills embedded in the sounds suggest a different story. Streaks of iridescent colored light break through the mist, some favoring dark red hues while others flash gold or clover green. There's an eerie thickness to the air. One I've only felt once before—in Tír na nÓg. This miasma blinds me to the world outside its boundaries.

Materializing like a shade spirit out of the swirling pewter vapor as he did back in Finnbheara's kingdom and at the cottage window is Robber Bright. It's midday. Whatever else he may be, the Faerie is punctual as hell.

He stalks toward Colleen. "Who have we here?"

"No one to concern you." I gesture at our stormy shell. "You've made sure she didn't see you coming. Please let her walk to her car and drive off."

The Fae slowly circles her and then sniffs as if shopping for fresh produce. "I smell sorrow, conflict, and the ambrosia of vulnerability." He winks. "Particular favorites of mine." He dips his face to the side of her neck and inhales deeply. "The sad ones are always the most appreciative." The Faerie smirks at me. "Although those who bite back are always a welcome challenge."

"Leave her alone." Prickles of worry break out across my chest. Isn't this what the Folk do? Seek candidates to snatch from my world for purpose or pleasure.

Robber runs his slightly curved nose that settles into a rounded point through Colleen's hair. "She is not like you or your consort who wear the skin of borrowed time."

"Stop, now. This is my friend, my mortal friend, and she was just leaving."

Robber positions himself behind Colleen. Before I can protest, he rests his chin between her neck and shoulder, sliding his hands down her arms before savoring the indent of her waist.

I pray her awareness is as frozen as her body so she'll have no memory of Robber's violation. His voice is a purr. "Yes, a ripe sugar plum to pluck for a lover. She pleases me."

I lunge at him, but he backs away just out of reach. "Take your hands off her."

He flashes me a wicked glance. Without breaking eye contact, he yanks Colleen against his chest. Long lean muscles tense in his arm, holding her in place while the fingers of his other hand trickle across her chin. Robber runs the tip of his pinkie along the inside of her lower lip. When he raises his finger, it glistens in the muted light from the moisture he stole from her mouth. He tastes, and his eyes brighten with a low burn. "Hot and sweet. Not a plum then, perhaps a peppered apple."

I wrench Colleen away from him.

Robber is nonplussed. "Did you not invite her as a gift for my service?"

"Absolutely not." I set myself between the Fae and my friend. "This is an unfortunate meeting."

He raises one eyebrow, studying me now instead of Colleen. "Interesting. I did not expect you to be so bold."

To my surprise, Colleen steps around me toward Robber. When I try to hold her back, she yanks out of my grasp.

He croons to her. "Come to me, friend of Fae."

I'm desperate to protect her from whatever charm he's clearly using. I follow her, trying to prevent disaster, and nearly fall when she pushes me off.

"Stop it, Robber. Colleen, please come here."

Robber gazes lustily down at her. If he lifted her into his arms, they could be models for the cover of a spicy romance novel, *The Fae Rogue and his Unsuspecting Bride.*

Robber Bright's sultry tone is right on point. "You would deny me one kiss?"

"I deny you anything that has to do with touching her." I try to take a step closer to them, but an invisible thickness in the air prevents me.

His expression is a challenge. "If you desire such, then tell me... plainly...clearly."

My mind races with folk stories and their advice on the proper way to talk to Fae and come out of it unscathed. I have to be precise. Leave him no wiggle room to twist my intention to his benefit.

Colleen's arms wind around Robber's neck. This cannot happen.

"Robber Bright, you may not kiss Colleen." Immediately, I realize I've blown it by using her name. This soldier of Finnbheara's or possibly the king himself could use that knowledge against me.

The Fae lays a finger on Colleen's lips, preventing the kiss, but flashes me a look of smug victory. "Colleen," he says as if he's just tasted a decadent dessert.

Colleen's mouth strains toward his. Robber's smile grows lazy and nonchalant. He's not going to stop her. It's up to me. I need words to snap my friend out of her Faerie daze. "Release my friend from the charm you hold over her now. Allow her to leave with no memory of you or your touch upon her."

With a hearty laugh, Robber spins her toward the gate, then lightly pats her on the head. "On your way, pet."

Without a backward glance, Colleen strides out of the fog bank. In moments, there's a car engine and the sound of tires bumping along the patchy road. I'm so relieved I drop my guard, and the Fae is upon me. Robber Bright gently presses a finger to the hollow of my throat.

"That was your first lesson. High marks, but not perfection." He lifts my chin until I'm forced to look up into his dark blue-green eyes.

It's hard to step away from him. The jerk is obviously sprinkling me with a charm or spell, attracting me to him. I visualize threads between my body and his, then slide a mental knife through them.

Robber's eyes widen when I'm able to put distance between us, but he doesn't remark on what I've just done.

"Okay, Mr. Faerie mentor, coach, or whatever your title, besides giving you my friend's name, which I admit was a screwup, what else do I need to improve on?"

By the time my brain registers that he's moved close to me again,

Robber has already begun to twirl a strand of my hair around his finger. "It was exceedingly kind of you to leave an open path for me."

I knock his hand away as dread, my new constant companion, compresses the air in my lungs. "Do not touch me without permission." Damn it. Another blunder. I didn't say whose permission. "And what do you mean by an open path?"

Robber Bright blows a kiss in the direction of where Colleen left the foggy shroud. "The fluid specificity in your command to release her *now*..." He stares at me with the contentment of a cream-sated cat. "... invites me to summon your dear peppered apple at my will."

Oh, hell. When Finnbheara whipped up his recipe for Eala Duir, he forgot to add even a pinch of Fae savvy. I vow not to speak again until I've run the words through every pitfall filter in my brain.

"We will waste no more time in this lesson on your careless verbiage." He rakes his gaze down my body. If he tries the same handsy moves he did with Colleen, he'll find a swift knee to his Fae balls.

Robber shrugs. "I suppose your present state of dress will do."

He gives me no time to be offended by his condescending statement.

"And now," says Robber, his arm slicing through the air in a sharp, sweeping gesture. "We ride." In a *whoosh* worthy of a wind tunnel, the gray soup around us dissipates to reveal a sight that stuns me into breathless silence.

Gathered in front of the Loho cottage is a vision more captivating than the most enchanting, vivid daydream I've ever experienced.

I'd heard the animalistic noises at Robber's arrival and sensed he was not alone. My trepidation over exposing Colleen to the Fae momentarily set aside any consideration as to the sheer number or what manner of companions might be in his company.

Robber Bright riding in on a fiery-eyed pooka or some other variety of curved-horned bad-tempered beast would not surprise me.

I never dreamed there'd be dragons.

CHAPTER II
THE BAD NEWS

"Welcome to my Faerie host," says Robber.

All around me are creatures of astounding magnificence. There must be at least twenty Fae atop beasts I've only glimpsed while deep diving into mythic tomes and legends.

"*Péist*," I murmur, the reference to dragons in old Irish popping into my head instead of the more modern *dragún*.

"*Péist síoda*," corrects Robber.

I continue to stare at the Faerie mounts. "Silk dragons?"

"The name is deceptive as you will soon learn," he says.

Slowly, I approach Robber's beast, stopping well out of its reach. As a child, I had a picture book with illustrations of legendary Irish dragons like an *oilliphéist*, the great serpentlike creature that comes to most people's minds when picturing dragons and the *murirdrís*, a more water-loving variation potential kin to the Loch Ness monster. What stands before me is wholly unique from anything I've seen referenced in my research.

My initial impression is that the Fae mounts are reminiscent of whimsical carousel animals, although they are half again as large as the ones I used to ride in Central Park. Their bodies favor an equine look with a thick neck holding a horsey head tapering into a snakelike snout.

Several ropey tongues flick out of each dragon's mouth, drawing intricate patterns in the air before retracting behind rows of pearly teeth so straight they could be a dental ad. One creature yawns, making the light trilling noise I heard in the fog. Inside the distended jaw, I notice concealed fangs lying in wait. When it closes its mouth with a loud *snap*, two puffs of mulberry-colored steam escape from slits on either side of its pointy muzzle. The scent of cherries fills the air. Not cherry flavored soda or candy, but the rich earthy smell of a bowl of fresh-picked fruit.

Robber speaks to his dragon in a language I don't recognize, and it draws near, head bowed. "This one's name is Aillil."

I offer my hand for the creature to sniff. "Hello, King Aillil." Sharing a name with a mighty ruler of Irish legend is an appropriate choice for an honest-to-god dragon.

Aillil tilts one eye, then the other, examining my hand. The dragon's eyes are orbs the size of grapefruits, resembling glass balls with light that swirls and flares inside them.

The Fae riders are not dressed in the garb of Finnbheara's soldiers. Today, belted tunics in an array of colors replace armor even though swords do hang at their sides. Each Fae, man or woman still wears an embossed leaf emblem over their hearts. As my gaze takes in this Faerie host, I notice the eye color of a dragon matches the indigo, quicksilver, or unsettled iridescence of the liquid bubbling through the veins in the leaf insignia on its rider's chest.

"What do the different colors in the…" I pat my chest. "…leaves mean?"

Robber shoots me a look as if it's the dumbest question he's ever been asked. "Why, rank and talents, of course." I make a note to dig deeper into specifics later.

Aillil's eyes are the same muddy amber of Robber Bright's leaf vein, a color uniquely his. The ancient king's namesake snuffles just before its trio of tongues weave around my hand. They're not slimy as I expect, but rather rough and dry. I wonder what, besides tasting, those are capable of. My instinct is to jump away and reclaim my hand, but I fight it. As if satisfied, the dragon withdraws, then shakes its head like a hunting dog shedding water after retrieving a downed game bird from a lake.

"Did I pass muster?" I ask Robber.

"You do still have your arm," he says with mischief in those aquamarine eyes.

I stare in relief at Aillil who balances on a pair of powerfully built front legs that end in hooflike shapes with unforgiving claws. There are no back legs to speak of. Instead, where the rump would be extends into a formidable tail that splits into double whips, each topped with a lethally pointed, three-sided spear. While the dragons are at rest, they swish their hindquarters and tails in a slow, hypnotizing rhythm. I marvel at the prowess with which they balance their mighty bodies on a single pair of legs, even though those substantial limbs do appear up to the task.

"Why are they called silk dragons?" I study the patterned skin of the beasts. They are made up of cascading teardrop shaped scales, each outlined with a band of hammered silver. At first glance, all the animals are the vibrant bright blue of a mountain lake. Upon closer inspection, I detect different color glazes on each animal, suggestive of the endless hues that make up the prismatic sheen of the Veil.

Robber snatches my hand, encouraging me to pet Aillil's haunch. As my palm trails along its hide, scales flutter. Where I expected them to feel like armor, the texture is as soft as a silken scarf.

The Faerie studies the sky. "We must go. Time is what we need, but time is not what has been granted us." He nods at Aillil. "Finnbheara's Treasure, you will ride with me until the day your own *péist síoda* is gifted to you by my king."

All the dragons wear metal saddles that look anything but comfortable. Bands of polished steel span their mighty chests, bearing rows of knives with menacing curved blades. Any lingering notion of Tír na nÓg being a kingdom of perpetual good times and lollipops fades from my mind.

Robber reaches for me, then raises his hands as if touching me will pain him. "Do you give me permission to lift you into the saddle?"

Well, look at that. Maybe I didn't botch the command not to touch me as badly as I thought. The smirk on his face suggests I probably did, and he's just humoring me for the sake of our ticking clock. I should go wake Sion and tell him I'm off to Faerie school, but he needs to recover for whatever might face us during tonight's Celtic day.

If he's even able to function.

"You may respectfully assist me." He takes hold of my waist and lifts me onto Aillil. I'm surprised when the metal beneath me is soft and easy to settle onto.

Robber mounts behind me, fitting his thighs to mine. He clamps an arm around my middle, easing me against him. His warm, solid body is unnervingly pleasant. The muscles of his chest ripple against my back as he lets out an ear-piercing whistle.

A muted buzz, like a far-off swarm of bees, fills the air. All around me, dragon bodies begin to shift and change. Extending from every scale, a fluttering strand half-a-meter long, with the look of opaline silk, glides free and begins to wave up and down, gaining speed until the movement creates a blur surrounding each dragon.

"Are those...wings?" I murmur.

"The very reason we are called The Host of A Thousand Wings," says Robber, looking pleased with himself.

Instead of my storybook image of batlike dragon wings, the *péist síoda* are encased within a nimbus, forming a sleek, glossy second body capable of lifting them skyward. We are the last to leave the ground. I glance below and notice not a single blade of grass has been disturbed by the host's ascent.

I'm enjoying the same lightheaded buzz a generous pour of red wine delivers when Robber Bright bellows behind me in a tone of definite command.

"Host to the waters."

We shoot forward with a jolt that would have snapped my neck if I wasn't flush against the body of a Fae hunk. I take in the group of riders and dragons around us. Multi-colored hides encased in winged shrouds shine like glitter as we slice through the air. It's as if we fly through jeweled rain. So lovely and smooth.

I could ride this dragon through countless sunrises and sunsets, never tiring of the thrill.

Robber's chest rumbles with laughter behind me. "When you join with your own beast, perhaps it will carry you on such an endless journey."

I slap a hand over my mouth, embarrassed to realize I spoke my feelings aloud. Or did I? It's miles past okay if Robber Bright can read my mind. I don't want anyone, Fae or otherwise, to be privy to my thoughts.

I practice a request over and over in my mind until it feels airtight. "Let my thoughts be my own, safe from intrusion until I choose to share them."

Robber's laugh is loud. He's clearly entertained by my request. His grip around me tightens as lips brush my ear. "Improving already, however unnecessary your wish. Not even our king can steal the mindscape of another."

I barely hear his words, delighting in the feel of his mouth against my skin. When I find one of my hands resting on his thigh, I snap back to reality.

"If you're pulling some Fae seduction trick on me, I do not appreciate it."

He whispers something that sounds suspiciously like *not yet*, just as a twinkling expanse of crystal blue water unfolds ahead of us. A medium-sized *lough* sits at the base of a substantial hill. I turn to look behind us, but all I see are rolling fields broken up by small stone walls. I can't find the cottage anywhere.

Robber slows Aillil, hovering on the shore to let the rest of the host pass by. Like a school of fish moving in perfect synchronicity, the company of dragons soars high above the water in a wide arc. I gasp when they turn downward and plummet through the surface of the *lough*.

My hands start trembling. "Where did they go?" Am I ever going to make it through one damn day without facing some supernatural terror? I twist to look Robber Bright in the eye. "I do not want to dive in there."

To my relief, Aillil slowly descends with balletic grace onto a clear circle of packed earth hidden among tall grasses that surround the *lough*. "There are many doors to Finnbheara's kingdom. This is but one." Mr. Touchy-Feely Fae strokes my hair as if setting it back in place after our swift ride. "You'd do well to remember it."

I lean forward in an attempt to put distance between us. "You'll have to draw me a map."

There's a light *thump* as Aillil touches down. Robber's dismount is as liquid as his dragon's flight. He reaches for me, but I clumsily slide to the ground on my own and maintain a healthy space between us. Not that it matters. The Faerie has already proven he can be on me in a heartbeat.

He spreads his arms wide. "On the private shores of this beloved *lough* we shall continue your education." Robber pats Aillil's rump. "Go feast, my beauty."

I expect the dragon to fly off and hunt for his *feast*. Again, I'm caught off guard when the creature's body compresses into a long serpentine form befitting its snaky snout. Spikey paddle tails slash behind as Aillil slithers off through the tall grasses.

"Aren't you worried someone will see him?" So much for St. Patrick's *no snakes in Ireland* promise.

Robber looks as if he doesn't have a care in the world. "He's Fae. We are only seen if we choose to be." He takes a step toward me. I counter with a backward one of my own.

"Give me a minute." I walk to the edge of the clearing, doing my damnedest to summon some clarity of thought after riding a Faerie silk dragon to the door of Tír na nÓg. Like it or not, I'm at Robber Bright's mercy and, by proxy, Finnbheara's as well. It's up to me to set ground rules for these lessons.

My gut tells me to show strength, not weakness. I wouldn't be here if there wasn't a part of me that's Fae. It means I do hold innate power even though I feel completely powerless. I wish Sion were here. His brazen stubbornness is a welcome example of a person who doesn't take shit from anyone.

I hope he's okay. I press my lips together and spin back to Robber Bright. He could have healed Sion with his Fae magic, and then I wouldn't be out here stressing about potential glitches in my soulmate's recovery.

"Why didn't you heal Sionnach completely?"

Robber swipes dust off the leaf emblem on his tunic. "Why do you assume I did not?"

"Because you only offered us a little bit of magic until I could get him into the Veil, not a full recovery."

He starts a leisurely stroll in my direction. "Oh, Eala. A *little bit* of Fae magic is all the healing a human requires." Reading my anger, he stops a handful of paces in front of me. "Next lesson: You must learn not to fall victim to mortal impatience."

My face feels hot enough to puff dragon steam. "Are you telling me he's healed?"

Robber looks as if I'm an imbecile. "Of course. When you return, you will find him most recovered. Now—"

I cross my arms. "Now nothing. First, we're going to set parameters." I could be delivering the first day lecture of a new term, setting clear objectives and expectations for the class. "I will participate in these lessons, but you must agree to a few things."

He just stares.

"You will never do anything to hurt Sion. I know your king—"

"Your king as well," he interrupts, studying my reaction closely.

"Finnbheara…has it in for Sion. If I sense even an inkling of Faerie bullshit in that direction, we're finished."

Robber's usually placid features tighten. "He is our king and therefore we are expected to deem him faultless." He begins to breathe heavily, another crack in his Faerie composure. "However…I have yet to witness a being that is all parts perfection. I do not follow blindly." The Fae grasps the hem of his tunic and tugs.

Before I can protest, he's exposed a sculpted chest and stomach even more beautiful than I imagined during our ride. Lovely, yet marred. Across his smooth muscled flesh that's lightly dusted with dark yellow hair is a long flat silver scar nearly four inches wide, running from his left shoulder to right hip. He pounds the side of his fist against the mark. "This is my reward for daring to contest the will of a king."

"Finnbheara hurt you?" Unaware I've stepped closer; I gape at the damage to his otherwise perfect torso. He nods. My fingers itch to trace its path. I shouldn't be surprised at the king's ruthlessness. Together with Finnbheara, I destroyed Olk, then watched the Fae monarch reduce him to sludge and dump the demon into the sea.

"Can't you heal it?"

Robber scoffs. "The punishment of a king, no matter how unjust, can only be undone by him. Finnbheara does not erase the lessons he teaches." Sensing my curiosity, he takes my hand and presses it to the scar. When I flinch at the contact, he guides my finger partway down the shiny center of his souvenir from Finnbheara's wrath. There's no warmth to the damaged skin, just a too smooth, too cold path of blighted flesh. The side of my finger brushes a portion of Robber's healthy heated skin. I yank my hand away, startled by the contrast in temperature.

His voice is soft. "Do you understand the lesson in this, Eala Duir?"

I meet his gaze. "Trust and Finnbheara are not a likely pair."

Robber gives me an admiring glance before retrieving his tunic. "You are an astute pupil."

I didn't expect praise. He seems like a taskmaster who would default to criticism. His cautionary tale in regard to Finnbheara helps me like Robber a little. I want to ask more about his crime and what he considers *unjust* punishment, but that might cut into my crucial learning time. There's still the matter of making sure I'm an active participant in what I need to gain from these lessons instead of allowing Robber to lead me unchecked through whatever paces he chooses.

The folktale, *The Wisdom of And*, comes to the forefront of my mind. In the story, Billy O'Gill comes upon a Faerie wanderer who takes a liking to the mortal. Ole Billy was given three minutes to ask for anything he desired from the Fae. He could stitch together boundless requests within the time limit as long as no more than two double pairs of the word *and* occurred in each compound sentence he spoke, plus an additional *and* to be used as the conjunction for a quota of 5 *ands* in all. I used the example:

I wish for gold and silver, diamonds and rubies, and I also wish for cows and chickens, sheep and goats.

Of course, as is the way of folk stories, there's always a catch. If Billy blundered the task, he'd lose everything and become a servant of the Faerie for a thousand years. In fact, the stress of a ticking clock coupled with the greedy desire to ask for as much as possible in the three minutes caused Billy to break the rule by inserting additional *ands* where commas should be. As is usually the case, the Fae won the day.

When I lectured on this particular tale, I'd ask for student volunteers to try the challenge with a goal of gaining at least twenty-five favors in three minutes. Most got flustered and blew it around the third sentence, but a few passed the test.

That was in a different lifetime, a lost life.

I don't know if the rule of *and* is a legit trap with Finnbheara's Fae, but I know wording is everything. What I need most from Robber Bright is information.

"Robber, for me to participate in these lessons Finnbheara insists upon, you will grant me a request at the start and finish of each lesson." I nearly make a request for him to answer questions, but I'm sure I'll have numerous inquiries during our time together. No sense in limiting myself. I want to keep my requests separate from questions for basic information.

"Agreed."

I'm momentarily thrown off by his easy acceptance, but forge on. "To begin, you will help Sion and me understand Finnbheara's riddle and guide us to the next step we need to take." Damn it. I should've said *solve* Finnbheara's riddle. At least I only used two *ands*.

He's amused as hell at the frustration that I'm crap at hiding. I wave a hand at him. "You know that I know I blew it, so don't gloat. Just..." A phrase that may work pops into my head. "Lend me your knowledge."

Robber cocks his head to one side and purses his lips. "I am not allowed to interfere directly, but if we are cautious, I may be able to lend some assistance."

I'm determined to skip right to the lessons geared to solving Finnbheara's riddle. If I need to learn to shoot a bow and arrow, or identify poisonous plants in Tír na nÓg, I can do those things once Sion and I are residents of the kingdom. The riddle is everything. Getting back to Sion is everything. Making sure we don't squander our limited time in a Celtic day is everything.

"Work with me Robber Bright. Do we need to return to the Hill of Tara?"

"Yes."

Again, I fumble it. "Why do we need to return to the Hill of Tara?"

He scans the tall grasses, then moves close enough to whisper in my ear. "Not here."

I set my hands on his shoulders to whisper back. "Will you meet us there tonight to answer the question?"

He rests his lips against my cheek. "With pleasure."

I pull away and note this guy will take advantage of any situation. I've got to be smart during my interactions with him. Sion and I will map out exactly how to ask for Robber Bright's help when he meets us tonight.

I should probe deeper about the riddle, but a different worry residing on the tip of my tongue spills out.

"Is it possible for me to bear a child?"

Robber's eyes sparkle. "Ah, an intriguing question." He lowers his chin, gazing at me through his lashes. "Are you requesting assistance for the endeavor?"

"Not from you." Again, I've botched a question. I take a breath. "Can I bear a child of Sion's?"

The Faerie looks as if he's smelled rotten fruit. "Why consider sullying yourself with a mortal's seed?"

"Please stick to the question." I treat him to an expression I've given many a student when disappointed with their efforts.

He gives a strange half-twist of his head, a sort of sideways nod. "It is fortunate for you no such fruit may ripen from a Fae and mortal coupling without first drinking elixir from the king's beads of being."

There's that term again, *beads of being*. Finnbheara spoke of them when referring to my origin. Robber Bright's answer is both a relief and a concern. At least I don't have to worry about getting pregnant now. As for the future...another complicated Faerie bridge to cross.

The next question burns in my mind. "Finnbheara took away Sionnach's ability to call the Veil. Is there a way you can give it back to him?"

Robber shakes his head. "Not I." There are flashes of light like the ones I saw in Aillil's eyes as he stares. "But you have such power."

Now he's playing with me. "Oh, please."

"Eala Duir, you deny the Fae gifts in your possession. As long as this is so, the dearth of your magic will lie dormant."

"Is that another lesson?"

"It is *the* lesson."

The sky dims as if a cloud has passed in front of the sun. When I glance up, I see the day is waning. Our journey here with the Host of a Thousand Wings once again altered my perception of time.

Robber follows my gaze. "There are many things that bring darkness to the sky," he says. "Heed them. This is yet another lesson."

Like the new moon. I assume he's alluding to the riddle with a riddle of his own. If this is his attempt at helping us, I'd best pay attention. "We figured out that part of the riddle. The new moon is our deadline to answer Finnbheara's question."

"You failed the lesson." He stares at me motionless, no blinking, no shifting of his weight. Robber Bright might as well be a Faerie statue.

Weariness from the weight of passing hours and my ignorance drive me to lean against one of the large rocks in the clearing. Robber Bright's lessons are certainly more circuitous and ambiguous than the ones I teach my students.

If a new moon is the wrong answer, then…darkness to the sky could be dusk, nightfall, a storm, even a cloud-packed day, but those are all vague markers of time's passage. Moon phases gave us a more solid frame. What am I not seeing?

Robber approaches me and bows. "May I have this dance?"

"Can we please stay on topic?"

He bows again. "If I promise an informative song will go with the dance, will that tempt you?"

Faeries and non sequiturs make perfect bedfellows. He's making fun of me. I start to decline his ridiculous suggestion until the seriousness in his expression doesn't waver. There's a veiled purpose in his request.

Not here.

Obviously, he suspects we're being monitored. Perhaps my tutor figures that a dance will douse suspicious eyes and ears sent by the king. I can't imagine Robber's previous treasonous lesson of not trusting Finnbheara will be well received, but that didn't stop him from blatantly delivering it. What could be more inflammatory than that? Unless he's afraid honoring my request to help us with the riddle his king doesn't want us to solve, would land him in a boiling Faerie cauldron?

A spin around the clearing in his arms may very well be construed by prying eyes as an example of teaching me to stave off Fae seduction. That's a vital lesson I must learn if I'm to navigate Tír na nÓg under no one's spell but my own. It also gives Robber an opportunity to share a secret.

I offer my hand. "I don't know Faerie dances." I grunt. "I don't know any formal dances."

He positions me, putting one hand on the small of my back and threading the fingers of his other through mine. "That is what lessons are for."

Even though I semi-expect it, Faerie music doesn't magically start playing as Robber guides me gracefully through the steps. Once he's led us to the center of the clearing, creating distance between us and the tall grasses where unwelcome Faerie spies may lurk, he leans so his mouth almost touches the side of my head and begins to sing.

"Stars above steal glimpses of,
Secrets, quests, and tears.
But errant glances slip away,
When the moon doth disappear."

I wait for a second verse or a chorus, but he just croons the same four lines over and over. It's peaceful here in his arms. The tension bubble I've been trapped in since we left Tír na nÓg eases. The questions flooding my mind caused by the urgency of unraveling Finnbheara's riddle pause their indecipherable deluge.

When the moon doth disappear.

My steps become more graceful as I allow myself to enjoy the dance.

When the moon doth disappear.

Goodbye, moon. Sleep tight, moon. See you soon, moon.

I giggle at the stream of nonsense this dance has unleashed. Is my Faerie brain opening itself to the frivolity of the Folk?

When the moon doth disappear.

The words lose their whimsy and begin to take on meaning.

When the moon doth disappear.

My steps falter, and we still. I tug at the Faeries's shoulder to bring his ear close to my lips and whisper. "Finnbheara's riddle isn't referring to a moon phase. The moon also *disappears* during an eclipse."

He takes my face in his hands. "Lesson accomplished."

This is a welcome revelation. The new moon is in two weeks, but an eclipse requires a full moon. I was to speak at the Kennard Park Observatory's lunar eclipse event, sharing Celtic folklore and beliefs about the phenomena. It was scheduled for a month after the end of my ill-fated study trip to Ireland.

I pat his hands and step away. "Thank you, Robber. This is a massive relief. A month is a much more reasonable time than two weeks to devote to Finnbheara's riddle."

The Faerie slowly shakes his head. "Take heed of lessons you have already learned. A reasonable king Finnbheara is not."

A slow leak begins to kill my elation. "Tell me."

Robber raises one finger to his lips, signaling the need for silence. His eyelids close as he cocks his head, listening. With the slight bend of a finger, he raises a wavering shield in front of a section of the tall grasses.

"We've only moments before our visitor notices the barrier." He waves his arm in an arc, summoning night to replace the daytime sky. The waning moon hangs above us. "Observe your mortal moon."

Our celestial ticking clock is nearly equally divided into its light and dark halves. "Yes, a third quarter moon."

"Beneath your lunar beacon dwells Finnbheara's moon."

My voice is breathy with apprehension. "Finnbheara's moon?"

Robber Bright flicks a single finger across the first moon as if he's turning the page of a book to reveal a different moon.

No, no, no.

My knees wobble. I lay palms flat against his chest to stay upright and stare into his eyes. "That second moon is waxing on the way to full."

"Finnbheara's moon, the one that bides in the skies over Tír na nÓg, is the gauge the king will use to judge you."

I recover my balance and back away even further, shaking my head as the true gravity of my Faerie task rumbles in my temples like a bass drum. We don't have the better part of a month to solve Finnbheara's riddle until the next full mortal moon.

Robber tilts his head, flashing me a pitying glance. "The Faerie moon will be at its fullest in nine days."

CHAPTER 12
THE BLUE TELL

The car is still here so I know Eala hasn't braved the country lanes and gone off on a mundane errand for washing powder. There's a bit of a sting knowing she left me alone after my run in with steel at Kilkenny Castle. I know in my bones it's got to do with Finn's underling, Robber Bright, and those damned Fae lessons. Just because they're part of the agreement for us to earn our way into Tír na nÓg doesn't mean I have to be happy about Eala going off with the smirky bastard.

I make my way to the gate and back for at least the tenth time. I'll carve a rut into the middle of the path if I keep at it. The sky turns the weak blue of paint with too much water. Late afternoon seriously considers taking leave of the fields to step aside for the gloaming, and still Eala hasn't returned.

Calling a halt to my endless march, I sit on the stump of a long-dead oak not far from the front door in the middle of what used to be Ma's herb garden. Luckily, I won't need to root for any of her long-neglected healing plants since my slash from one of the Lady of Kilkenny's enemies has whittled down to the width of a string.

I've no love of the Fae, but their Veil does possess a brilliant hand at healing.

"Where are you, my Eala *bán?*" I search the skies as if a great white swan will soar over a path of wildflowers and land at my feet. Its graceful neck will stretch, and with a ruffle of feathers, the lovely bird will transform into my *anamchara*. I long to take her back to my bed and count the golden freckles painted over her pale skin, dotting each with a claiming kiss.

The fading sky reminds me there will be no time to share our bodies before we're thrust back into insufferable Faerie business. This cruel task we had no option but to undertake feels designed for failure—a package of insurmountable confusion tied with frazzled string.

I pop to my feet and kick at a stone. Eala doesn't deserve my pessimism. I don't deserve it. Time to give myself a talking to. "Look forward, Sionnach. Expect the sun to rise on us as it's done before. We can best a Faerie king."

"We will, my love." Eala's hands slide over my shoulders.

I turn in her arms and deliver a possessive kiss before looking past her to the undulating rise and fall of the land for any sign of Faeries. Finding none, I rub my nose against the silky soft skin of her ear. "You've become brilliant at popping out of the Veil. Where were you off to?"

She pinches my chin between her fingers. "Kiss me again, and I'll tell you."

I trap her more firmly in my arms to capture her lips and the sugary sweetness of her tongue until a noisy flock of starlings overhead breaks the quiet of the late afternoon.

"I was with Robber Bright for my *How to be a Faerie* lesson."

I hold her at arm's length. "Did the fool behave? Are you well?"

She slides her hands to grasp mine, taking her turn inspecting me. "I'm fine. And speaking of well, you look in tiptop shape."

"The Veil's doctoring is up to snuff." I raise my T-shirt to show her the dwindling remains of my nasty slash. She stoops to kiss the center of my new scar, then gives me a squirmy kind of look. "What, love?"

"Robber Bright is actually the one responsible for healing you."

Her confession sits in my belly like a stone. I take in a breath to squelch the unkind words I'm tempted to spew and lower my shirt. "Och, another Faerie I'm not keen on owing a lick of gratitude."

She squints at the setting sun. "I've news."

Her tone suggests it's not of a variety I particularly want to hear. I return to the stump and pull Eala into my lap, bracing myself to hear about Faerie rubbish. "Give it to me straight, darling."

She strokes a finger through my hair, playing with one curl, then another. The stalling makes me edgy, but the touch is nice.

"We're kind of fucked."

My back stiffens.

She touches her forehead to mine. "We don't have until the new moon to answer the question in the riddle."

I lift her chin to read her expression better. "Robber Bright tell you that?"

She pouts her lips and assumes her thinking face. "I figured it out from a song he sang."

The idea of that *gum on the bottom of a shoe* Fae we're stuck with singing to Eala heats my blood. "Singing is part of your Faerie schooling, is it?" I say in a low grumble.

"Did you think any of it would be a straightforward lecture?" Eala tenses, and her already fair skin loses a shade or two. "Sion, our true deadline is the lunar eclipse."

"That's even grander. More time to scratch at Finn's misery." I nip her bottom lip. "And for other pleasures."

"No, it's the opposite of grand." The pinch in Eala's voice puts me on instant alert. "Have you ever heard of Finnbheara's moon?" She rushes to continue before I answer. "Apparently, the moon of Tír na nÓg doesn't match the phases of ours."

My heart sloshes into my gut. "We're dealing with two fecking moons?"

As if sensing her next words will set me off like dynamite blasting through rock, Eala slides off my lap to stand facing me. "Just one. Finnbheara's. And it's only nine days from being full."

I drive my fists into the sides of my head as if that will squeeze this latest blow of Fae trickery out of my mind. Rising rage heats my skin and sweat beads along my forehead. I focus on the fat weed at the base of the stump and wrap my fist around it. With more force than necessary, I yank it from the ground, spraying dirt over us both.

"Sion."

I smack the weed against the stump over and over until it's in shreds, then face the fields I used to work with Da. "Fucking Finnbheara. He's hellbent to twist our path until it's lost to us completely."

When my gale blows itself out, I hunch over, panting. "Load me up with everything now, so I only have to punch a wall once."

Eala lays hands on my shoulders. "It's not all bad news. Robber will help us. He's meeting us at the Hill of Tara…" Her gaze strays to the cliffs where the horizon has half swallowed the sun. "…soon."

"How do we know Robber Bright trying to earn your trust isn't another weapon Finnbheara will use to strike at us?"

"Think about it, Sion. Would Robber have shown us the second moon if that was the case?"

The question of trust here is mine. Do I follow where Eala's instincts lead?

Eala closes the star pendant in her hand. "We need to hear what he has to say at Tara. Unless you have a better idea of how to move forward."

I take my swan's hands in mine. The primary truth we've got to deal with is the new portion of time Finn stole from us. We need all the help we can get, even if it's from another Faerie. "No, love. I'm with you."

"Do you promise to keep your cynicism at bay until we can analyze Robber's input together?"

"I'll promise you my best effort."

She grunts.

I call over to Alfie. "Buck up, sweetheart, and step lively."

Eala tugs at my sleeve. "There is more."

The lovely and light expression on her beautiful face stalls another volley of my foul attitude. "You may be able to call the Veil again." Her words stop my heart as sure as overstaying my time traveling threatens to do. "Robber Bright said I hold the power to give it back to you."

I spread my arms wide. This news is worth suffering a battle wound at Kilkenny or an accelerated timeline. "Let's have it then."

Eala looks chagrined. "I don't know how to do it—yet."

Disappointment floods through the hollow of my bones, and I hunch like a man who's taken a blow.

She shakes me. "But I'll learn. I swear. I'll insist it's the next thing he teaches me." I want to give her a smile, but I'm not able to scare one up. I'm still playing the role of the ineffective fool in our partnership.

Eala slips her arm through my elbow. "Ready?" She hesitates. "If you still need rest, I'll go gather information on my own."

The last thing happening as long as I draw breath is Eala meeting Robber Bright alone under our waning or a Fae waxing moon on the Hill of Tara. I can't tolerate their time together being one second longer than it need be.

"I'm fine," I say more tersely than I intend. "Sorry, love." I kiss her plump lips with a promise not to be such a pain in her arse.

When we ease out of the kiss, Eala squeezes my cheeks so hard in one hand, they press against my teeth.

"Listen to me, Sionnach Loho. I don't like or trust Robber Bright any more than you do, but we need all the help we can get with Finnbheara's wickedly unfair riddle. So, play nice."

Eala in high spirits with a dash of bossy is one of my favorite Ealas. I capture her wrist, loosening her grasp enough to swivel my head and bite her finger. "Yes, Great Lady of the Loho Cottage." Our next Celtic day can't end fast enough so we can work on wearing out the lady's bedstraw filling my mattress.

Eala and I slip out of the Veil, that thankfully is once again at her beck and call, onto the very scene I imagine we left just before dawn. On the Hill of Tara, Robber Bright leans against the hawthorn tree with a self-satisfied expression on his Fae mug. I'd like to see that flouncy hair get stuck on a thorn.

"Ah, *mhuirnín*, the night is filled with grace at your arrival," says the Fae eejit who has the gall to reach his arms to Eala.

I wrap an arm around her waist. "She's no *darling* to you, Faerie."

He pushes off the tree and saunters the short distance between us. "And what is she to you, Mortal? Wife? Betrothed? Mistress?"

I shift Eala so her back is against my chest, fusing us together. "She is my *anamchara.*"

The damn Fae laughs as if I told the punch line of his favorite joke. "Why should I not be surprised you use the mortal construct of a soulmate? Such a term keeps a lady on a tether with flowery promises of eternal love until the man is finished with her."

Eala lays her hands on mine and glares at Robber Bright. "Not in our case. We love to the depths of our soul."

The Fae laughs harder. "You are indeed the treasure of Finnbheara speaking the same words he once used to defend his latest romantic caprice with a mortal." He wipes his eyes. "I've not enjoyed such tears of mirth for too long."

I itch to land a punch right between his glistening eyes.

Eala steps forward out of my arms. "We don't have time for this. You said you would help. So, get on with it."

Robber Bright composes himself and moves in front of Eala. He reaches to caress the side of her face with two fingers. "A treasure you may be, but not one the king deserves."

Eala has the look of one suspended by a Faerie charm. I'm about to intercede when she shoves Bright's arm to break contact. "I did not give you permission to touch me."

This is fine news. It seems my darling set boundaries for the crafty Fae. Gone is the frightened soul who quaked at the notion of climbing a tower.

I move alongside Eala and take her hand. Robber's gaze immediately falls to our twined fingers.

"I do not need her permission to touch." I may as well thump my chest like an ape and announce she's my woman. The Faerie fiend brings it out in me.

"It's not a competition, Sion," Eala says, the exasperation in her tone loud and clear.

Robber's lazy cat smile and the way he pins his gaze on Eala says he thinks otherwise.

Eala pulls me toward the hawthorn. "You claim you tried to warn us that touching the chainmail was dangerous. How did you know?"

He approaches the branch where the rings sit embedded in the bark. When he holds his hands inches from the links, they begin to glow a blood red so dark it's nearly black. "These hold the taint of one who wishes you harm." Robber withdraws his hand, and the glow disappears. "Consider yourselves lucky not to have paid for your folly with a life."

Eala squeezes my fingers. "Finnbheara is trying to hurt us?"

Robber shakes his head. "The king is most anxious for your return. He would not risk the life of his treasure."

I swallow the bile creeping up into my throat. "Finnbheara tried to get rid of me."

The Fae backs away from the tree. "That may be so, but it was not my king who commanded these rings to steal you away." His face takes on a stony quality except for the movement of his eyes from side to side. Robber Bright's voice becomes a thin whisper, flowing our way like a wisp of breeze no wider than a finger width. There's a slight charge to the air as his words buzz in my ear. I suspect he's using a bit of magic to keep whatever he's about to say between the three of us.

"I shall tell you now what I could not before. The thief was not of my king's Folk, but rather Aodh, the vindictive bearer of the crimson flame, who wishes to punish Finnbheara through you for revenge."

Eala's hand trembles in mine as she asks. "The god Aodh? You're certain we're dealing with Aodh of the Underworld?"

Robber is puzzled by her question. "As I said."

She digs fingernails into my palm. "Do you know if a man called Olk worked with Aodh?"

Robber shrugs in an attempt to assume an air of indifference to the topic. "I know nothing of the agents of Aodh." The tense set of his shoulders doesn't match the acting job.

Eala curses under her breath. "Finnbheara said Aodh was pissed at him for what we'd done. It has to mean destroying Olk." She stares at the rings. "You're telling us those were a trap."

"Obviously," says Robber, now convincingly bored.

I still smell the stench of deception and withheld information around the bastard.

Eala walks away, clenching and unclenching her fists. "Then the whole trip to Kilkenny—" She whirls around to face us. "Sion nearly getting killed." Her hand dips into her neckline to grasp the star pendant and holds it out to Robber. "Did nothing to help us answer Finnbheara's question?"

I'd like to close my hands around Robber Bright and this Aodh fella's neck. What fools we are to think we'd have any semblance of a clear path to solve the king's cruel riddle. I wouldn't be surprised if Finn and Aodh are sitting at their respective banquet tables laughing at our mortal stupidity. I clamp my teeth together. At least my mortal stupidity. I'm the idiot who grabbed the rings.

Eala marches straight up to Robber Bright. "Whose side are you on?"

He stands unnaturally still, gazing down at her. If I watch his eyes take on that dreamy look when he's close to Eala one more time, I'm going to clock him.

"I am the king's man; therefore, I am your man. Heed your lessons learned, Eala Duir."

Eala and Robber's gazes are glued tight to one another. There's something here I've been excluded from. First chance I get alone with Eala, I'm sure as hell going to discover what it is.

Eala jabs a finger at the tree. "If you are my man, tell me why being on the Hill of Tara will help us move forward with Finnbheara's damn riddle."

A struggle blares again in Robber Bright's dark blue-green eyes. It's another sign he isn't the hundred percent self-assured fool he presents himself as. In a flash, he molds himself to Eala's back, stretching her arm toward the chainmail in the tree trunk.

I lunge at the pair to prevent him from forcing her to touch the rings again, but I'm stopped halfway, trapped in an invisible Faerie cage. No matter which way I try to move, I'm rooted to the spot.

Robber holds Eala's hand inches from the chainmail. Again, the crimson glow radiates around the links. "Hover, but do not touch to see truth." Next, he guides her hand to a tattered bit of cloth tied in a knot around a branch. When her hand is close to it, no light shines. Farther along the same limb is what looks like an extremely large rope belt wrapped several times around the thick part of the branch nearest the trunk. Robber moves Eala's fingers until they almost touch it. A sapphire sheen flickers around the belt.

Eala turns her head to look to Robber. He nods once, releasing her and stepping back.

"We're looking for blue?" she says, seeking confirmation.

The Fae bastard just stares at her.

"She asked you a question," I growl, but neither of them appears to have heard me. I shove a shoulder against my Fae restraint. It gives way, landing me in a heap on the grass.

Eala studies Robber's face. "You can't say," she says matter-of-factly.

Without another word, the Fae takes a step back toward the shadows. Before moving off, he reaches out to pluck a fat, fancy looking gold ring off a jutting branch and clutches it in his palm. His hand gives off the faintest sheen of magenta, but there's no telling if the ring glows crimson or if I see the Fae's blood as it shines through the skin of his fingers from the light of the band. Did he snatch it to keep us from touching it? Or is he just a thieving prick?

Before we have the chance to question him, Robber Bright disappears.

We're alone on the Hill of Tara.

Questions burn in my gullet about Robber Bright, but I bury them for now. Eala is unwinding the belt from around the branch. The glittery blue glow surrounds her hands and the rope. She finishes quickly and steps away from the tree.

"Can you see the blue glow?" she asks me.

"Aye, and the red around the mail rings. Are we to assume blue means touch and red means hands off?"

Eala looks bone tired. "I don't know what else to think." She stares at me. "Before, when we both touched the chainmail, it forced us to travel."

"Are you ready?" I ask, stepping closer.

"I keep getting asked that question," she sighs. "The answer never changes. I'm not ready for any of this."

I put my arm around her shoulders, then reach for the rope belt. It's slightly warm to the touch, but nothing happens as we both hold it in our hands.

Eala drops her chin to her chest. "Dammit."

I rest my head against hers. "All those years I worked to end the soulfall, there was one thing that never failed me. Call the Veil, love."

She lifts her face but doesn't look at me. Her eyes take on the glaze of being elsewhere. All around us there's a shift in the air, a familiar energy. As Eala's eyes drift shut, her delicate wavering version of the Veil's prismatic drizzle flows across our skin, drawing us into its presence. Instead of the fragrance of soap bubbles I associate with the Veil, an aroma of lemongrass and spearmint as fresh as the scent of herbs growing wild across a springtime field surrounds us.

When Eala holds the rope belt in front of her, it slides out of her hand to bob in front of us. Slowly, it extends to its full length as if pointing the way, and we begin to float. The sweet familiar strains of a fiddle fill the air around us.

Being in the peaceful Veil fills my battered soul with renewed hope that we can conquer any obstacle the Fae designed to keep us apart. The Veil knows us. The Veil welcomes us. I even hate Robber Bright a little less since he gave Eala a push in the right direction. He certainly didn't do it for me.

Eala drapes her arms around my neck and touches her lips to mine. The first time we kissed was in the Veil. As if cementing its approval, the violin chirps a lively tune as our bodies press together. The carefree sense of my dearest's Veil is so lovely. If I ever regain my ability to summon the Veil, I won't think of it as solid glass prisms that enclose us *fánaí* as a box would. I will embrace Eala's Veil of brilliant beauty and choose patient travel over haste.

Her hands thread through my hair as the kiss deepens. I return the favor, easing my fingers through Eala's downy locks and gently tilt her head back to taste her long, elegant neck.

The sound of a whip crack startles us apart. The rope belt curls in on itself like an ouroboros, its blue radiance pulsing with renewed vibrance.

"Is that..." I point toward a spiraling circle of color forming a thin barrier between the end of the Veil and what appears to be a simple village beyond. There, barely within this threshold between magic and reality, sits a very familiar tree with a trio of sloping white trunks marked with a pattern of green triangles.

Eala's triumphant smile brightens the Veil itself. "Alfie."

I move in front of the tree and touch her bark. "The bugger is in the Veil with us." Poking my head between two of the slender trunks, I see the pair of canvas bags with our stash of clothing. "And she's brought the goods." I look at Eala. "Did you call her here?"

She joins me. "I imagined how convenient it would be if she came with us, and we didn't have to track her down wherever we land."

I fan a hand toward the transparent circle at the end of the tunnel. "Alfie and this picture window are sheer brilliance." Clutching Eala's hips, I pull her to me. "You are a treasure, Eala *bán*. My treasure." After a quick kiss, I squint at the filmy door of the Veil. "Now where in the devil are we?"

CHAPTER 13
THE GEAS

In my previous junkets through the Veil with Sion, we'd land blindly in the location his instincts desired. The accuracy was impressive. I'm shackled with the sole responsibility of travel now. It's a comfort that in my budding relationship with the Veil, it appears to be sensitive to my fear of surprises and unknowns. I prefer a preview of the situations we're destined to plow into, and *bam* the Veil has a front window.

I run a finger along Alfie's rough bark. I also wanted the *fánaí* tree close and here she is, trekking the trails of time alongside us within the Veil walls. I inspect the green triangles on her trunk. Sion's markings are intact with the slight flare of new ones near the lower portion. When I lay my palm across the additions, Veil sprites congregate at the point of contact. Their light shimmers on all three sides of each triangle. For the first time, I sense a tiny river made entirely of candleflame tips alive inside Alfie. The energy flows both up through trunk and limb as well as surging deep into the earth.

Celtic legend speaks of the tree of life, *Crann Bethadh*, and its connection to a river of harmony through natural forces. Is Alfie a tributary, a facilitator, of that mythic waterway? Am I?

Robber and Finnbheara both hinted at latent Faerie talents strumming their quiet notes beneath the mortal casing I cling to. Have I subconsciously loosened the leash on those powers?

Another question Robber Bright isn't likely to answer in a straightforward fashion.

Sion's nose almost touches the swirl of our Veil window as he studies the village beyond. "The place looks more recent than my time." He gestures at one of the whitewashed cottages sitting in a row along what looks to be a paved instead of dirt road. "Look at the roofs. More slate than thatch."

I join him. "I wish someone would walk by so we know how to dress."

Just then, a small group of people emerge from behind a small house toward the far end of the street.

Sion lets out a *humph.* "Your wishes have an interesting way of coming true."

A fuzzy feeling grips me. He's not wrong. Is someone helping us? Robber said Faeries can't read minds, but can they read intentions? What if wishes take tangible form when there's a connection between Fae like the ones I have with Finnbheara or Robber Bright? If that's a possibility, will I be able to read them as well?

An unhappy thought interrupts my musing. If there is some strange conduit between Faeries, could they decide to use my intentions and wishes against me? What part is my Faerie nature playing in all of this? I make a note to delve into this topic in my next lesson with Robber.

I study the people as they pass by. "A simple dress and a wool shawl will do," I say, digging into our clothes stash. "You grab a long-sleeved cotton shirt, vest, loose trousers, and boots. That'll give us a passable look."

Sion raises his brows.

"What? Don't you agree?"

He lifts a shoulder. "I do. Wasn't this side of a week that I was tossing proper clothes at you."

His tone is unreadable. He's not upset exactly, but not bubbling over either. We change quickly in silence.

I defer to Sion for our next step. "Do you think we should take the rope belt or leave it here?"

"Best take it. Don't know what we're looking for yet." He pauses. Concern sketches lines at the corners of his eyes. "Eala, it's not long past break day out there."

He's right. Whenever we've travelled during a Celtic day, traditionally mortal sundown to sundown, our destination has always shared the darkness of the night we left. We saw daylight at Kilkenny, but if I just consider the totality of hours we were there, that brief morning fits inside the timespan of our single Celtic traveling day or at least the half of it, sundown to sunrise, that we're allowed to move through time.

"Sion, I'm fairly certain our hundred-thousand heartbeat/Celtic day clock is synced to the place we left, not to where we go. It doesn't matter if it's day or night here, only that it's still mortal nighttime back home."

"'Tis true. As I served the soulfall, never did I choose to travel to daylight, as there are more opportunities not to be seen in darkness." Sion worries his lips. "Could this be a trap Robber Bright dug for us to fall into?"

I consider that for a moment, then think about the strange grudging loyalty my Fae tutor has to Finnbheara. There's no love lost between them, but I didn't get the sense Robber Bright was trying to betray us.

I frown, then shrug. "I wouldn't put it past Finnbheara to sow doubt about the way time translates between our Celtic day and the places we need to visit to solve his damn riddle. He's not going to make anything easy for us." My gaze falls to the belt. "I do believe the Veil brought us here for a reason, so we should give this a shot."

"Well, then…" He holds out a hand for me to take. We step around Alfie and leave the Veil.

Hurrying across the road, we duck behind the stone chimney of one of the houses out of sight of its square windows to get our bearing. The group we saw passing hasn't gone far. Their chatter is easy to pick up.

"No, Tom, it's been ten years since Mick's borne the burden."

"I say fifteen," answers the man who must be Tom.

"No, ten. Ole Mick and Betsy wed in 1919. Their first wee one a year later, then the two lassies four years past that. 'Twas then the business with the well started up. That's ten years."

"Judging from their figuring, I think we're in the early 1930s," Sion says quietly.

Since he's the one with zipping through time on his resume, I don't question his estimation. When I dare a glance around the chimney, I see a small crowd gathered at the end of the row of cottages. A *clip clop* like the sound of horse hooves and the creaking whine of wood rises from behind the house next to our hiding place. We crouch near a trailing vine of wild roses climbing the whitewashed wall where chimney meets house.

Walking past us on the road is a strange man with a body bearing the definite markings of supernatural mischief. He is extraordinarily large, but not the way of one with too much meat on his bones, as Máthair would say. He reminds me of the giant balloons in the New York Thanksgiving day parade. The poor guy looks...inflated. Instead of bobbing on a current of air, he's rooted to the ground. Every step a labor. Every breath a chore.

Sion's huff voices my thoughts. "I'd bet my father's Sunday suit there's Folk interference with that one."

The man is dressed in what I'd call a jumpsuit that billows over his extremely uncomfortable looking, Fae-tampered body. Crow-black wavy hair and bright blue eyes paint him as an attractive young man, maybe in his thirties. He moves as if gravity plays a cruel game with him. Sweat pours down the sides of his face as he bears the strain of effort and fatigue. This unlucky person is being tortured on the inside as a result of his unnatural frame.

Sion and I glance at the rope belt in my hands. Its length would be a fair match for the one this man wears.

As if a laborious hike to the center of town is not trying enough for the poor soul, he also leads a donkey strapped to a wooden cart. Sitting huddled in the small wagon is a slight woman who would be quite pretty without the deep stress lines at the corners of her mouth and across her forehead. Three children, a boy on the doorstep of adolescence and twin girls who share their father's shiny black hair, look as downtrodden as their mother.

Sion whispers. "I think this is the ole Mick we're meant to find."

I lay a finger on the belt from the hawthorn. "What do you think those people meant by business at the well? If Fae caused that poor guy into such a state, maybe there's something I can do to help him."

Sion's mouth is tight. "Aye."

"Not exactly the optimism I was hoping for."

He looks into the distance, not meeting my eyes. There's the strain of resentment in his voice. "If there's anything to be done. It must be done by you alone. I've no clout with Fae business."

I can't believe he's choosing this moment to feel sorry for himself or to pick a fight over my connection to the Fae when there's a chance whatever gifts I have could help an obviously suffering man. As much as I want to, now's not the time to dig into that topic. I stick a mental pin in it.

"Ho, Mick," calls a voice from down the street where the cart is headed.

A group of five boys in their teens appear from behind a house. "Come on, Ben. You don't want to miss the show at the stone well," says one, cuffing another on the back of the head.

Another small cluster of men and women approaches from farther down the road.

"Come on," says Sion, dragging me from our hiding place after they pass us. "Time to blend in. Leave the belt here."

When we catch up with the group, Sion hails them like he belongs here. "Good morning to you."

Instead of skeptical scrutiny for the strangers we are, a round of hellos welcomes us into the clutch.

"Come to see Mick Ryan and the bit at the well, have you?" asks a woman in a smart-looking skirt and blouse.

"Aye," says Sion. "Heard about it visiting my sister down the way. Seems a shame."

The man on her arm nods. "Every morning, we try to ease his burden, but nothing comes of it."

"The good Lord wouldn't want us to give up on the darling soul," says the woman. She shakes a finger at Sion. "He's not a glutton as people who don't know him accuse him of being. There's nothing he can do to stop the growing, even though we pray for relief of his burden. A curse isn't an easy thing to break. And so, it is."

Sion and I exchange a quick glance at the word *curse*. By now, we've reached the group of maybe twenty people clustered around what looks like a wishing well from a fairy tale. The cursed Mick Ryan stands at the edge of the curved stone with an oval pewter plate in his hands.

"Don't give into it, husband," begs the woman from the cart. Her scrawny arms are wrapped around Mick's bold one, as if she could shake the plate out of his hand.

Several of the men are doing their damnedest to haul Mick away from stony lip of the well, but they are useless against his bulk.

Tears stream down Mick Ryan's face. "God, help me," he cries. Despite the well-meaning aid of wife and friends, his body sags against the well. The plate falls from his hands into its depths. As if on cue, the crowd backs away. A low gurgle echoes from deep in the well. The weeping Mick leans on the post next to a hook that holds a well-worn galvanized steel bucket attached to a rope. The gurgle becomes a rumble and then a roar as if a flood is rising from the bottom of the well.

I cling to Sion. Taking our cue from the other onlookers, we step away.

Suddenly, the pewter plate launches into the sky. Close behind it, a profusion of food blasts from the well in a tight column. It rises above the heads of the crowd, then arcs through the air, aiming for Mick Ryan's wagon. Potatoes, carrots, all matter of greens, roasts and ham hocks, triple layer cakes and loaves of bread slam into the cart until the flying feast settles into a mound rising above its wooden sides.

"Fecking Fae," Sion hisses in my ear.

I agree with his sentiment. This has every earmark of a Faerie misdeed.

The villagers descend on the wagon in a wave. They reach into the pile of food, attempting to extract whatever they can get a hold of. Hands tug and tug, but not one piece comes free. There are tears from some and creative cursing from others, but no one can budge the bounty that sprung from the well.

With a round of apologies, pats on Mick's great arms, and sniffles, everyone, including his family, leave the suffering man behind with his cart full of food.

We are too dumbstruck to move.

"Off with you then," says Mick, waving a hand at us. "Leave me to my private hell." He turns his back on us, reaches into the bed of the wagon for a loaf of brown bread and starts eating it. The tortured man weeps as he eats.

"We're not here to give you grief, man," says Sion. "Obviously you're stuck deep in a holy show."

I slowly approach Mick, allowing my hand to hover near Mick's forearm. It's easily three widths of my hand. A faint crystal blue glow glimmers between us like the one that pointed us to his rope belt at the hawthorn tree. "We've come to try and help."

"I thank you for your concern, but there's no help to be had," says Mick, pulling away from me and starting in on one of the cakes.

Sion plants himself in Mick's eyeline. "Eala here has Fae gifts."

Mick's face flames the color of a red dawn. He backs away, waving a parsnip like a sword. "I should have guessed you strangers are Folk coming to gloat at my sorrow. I want nothing more to do with your kind."

At Mick's raised voice, the donkey twists its head, stamps a hoof, and tries to walk off. The weight of the cart holds him in place.

Sion stands his ground. "Eala may be kin to them, but she's wrought from a different mold. This woman leads with heart, not ill intent or foolery."

I welcome his words. He may be off put by my connection to Finnbheara's kingdom, but I'm grateful he understands I am still a person apart from it.

In my most soothing voice, I say, "I can't promise anything, but will you at least tell us what's happened to you?"

Sion stands shoulder to shoulder with me. "You've nothing to lose sharing your tale with us, man."

Mick lets loose a low sustained groan. "Have I your word you won't lay worse on me than the burden I already wear around my neck?"

Sion makes the sign of the cross. "I swear for the both of us no further harm will come to you."

Mick hangs his head. His voice is low and pained. "'Twas after my girls came. Times were bad, so very bad. I didn't have food enough to put on my table for five mouths." He side-eyes the well. "There were old stories this well was a door to the kingdom of the Fair Folk." He chuffs. "Fair never figured into the treatment of those who came here to ask favors. I didn't heed those tales as I should. Bringing our largest platter to the well, I threw it in and asked for it to be returned piled high with food."

I glance at the ridiculous amount of food in the cart.

Mick glares at the well. "'Twas then the voice of the spirit of the well came up from the water saying, 'Mick Ryan, do you swear to eat every bite we send you?'" He shrugs. "What else was I to say but yes?" A single tear meanders down Mick's face. "Then the voice said when I wake each day, I was to come to the well and throw down the plate. It would return with a generous bounty for me to eat. I agreed to the conditions and sealed my fate."

My heart pounds. I hear the mistake in Mick's request. He swore to eat all the food, not that the food would be provided to feed his starving family. What's worse, the simple act of waking compels him to bring the plate to the well. A horrible geas to be saddled with. The cruelty of some Fae is not just bad press.

Mick's eyes grow more watery. "I hear them, you know, the Folk. They spy in my windows at night with their mocking laughs about this." He fans his arms down the front of his body. "It's not natural, as you see. I eat the food, but it doesn't hit my belly or satisfy my appetite. It's as if I haven't swallowed a thing. I don't fill. After I finish the cursed food, every bit of skin stretches in one cruel pop." He hangs his head. "I'd rather be drowned in the well than suffer another day."

Sion motions me away from Mick's misery. "I smell the foul odor of a wicked geas."

I nod. "Agreed, but I have no idea how to undo it. It doesn't sound like there was any kind of end date in the bargain."

Sion rubs his chin. "And as long as the poor fool wakes, he's bound to the well."

I press fists to my cheeks. "The solution must be in the words. Let me think." I pace away from Sion. Reversing a geas is yet another topic I haven't broached with Robber Bright. If only there was some way to talk to the Fae who orchestrated the geas, maybe I could convince them to lift it. They've surely had enough of a laugh traumatizing poor Mick.

I think about the blue glow and how it seems to answer to my nearness. I wonder what will happen if I actually touch Mick.

My gaze falls on the well. Maybe it's not Mick I need to touch.

Without hesitation, I stalk up to the well and rest my palms on the cold stones. Faint sapphire light bleeds from my fingertips over the lip. When I peer in, I see lines of blue stretching down the slick stones to the water a few yards below. It begins to bubble and glow the same cool color.

An elongated face flickers on the surface, distorted by the uneasy water. Silvery-gray hair bobs in the bubbling current. When the figure meets my gaze, its bright eyes widen.

"What are you?" It asks.

Not who are you. The question disturbs me because I don't have an answer.

"If you won't tell me what you are, give me your name," says the well spirit.

If I've learned nothing else practical from all the folklore I teach, it's that you should never give your name unless you have absolute trust in the one asking it. Even then, it's best to stick to nicknames or titles. "Give me yours first." It's worth a try.

"You may call me the sprite of the well."

It's interesting Mick called this being the spirit of the well and not the sprite. One title rings of faith and the other mischief.

Since I have no title except for my name, I'm stumped until a wild idea comes to mind. Do I dare use the title Robber Bright has saddled me with?

"You may call me Finnbheara's Treasure." Veil sprites crawl inside my skin like insects decided where to sting, their creeping sensation a warning. When I ignore them, they smolder, not hurting me, but not masking their displeasure at my conversation with a very different variety of sprite.

The well sprite gives a fearful hiss at the sound of the king's name. Maybe I do have some clout here after all.

"What does Finnbheara's Treasure want with one he banished to the confines of this well?"

Here goes. I cross my fingers the sprite is indeed the one responsible for the tragedy playing out. "I want you to remove the geas on Mick Ryan."

The only reply is the muted slap of water against stone.

"What is your answer?" I dig my fingernails into the stony lip to keep from unleashing my anger on this sprite for his despicable way of taking a starving man's plea and turning it against him.

The creature's tone is as slimy as the moss-covered walls of the well. "What will you give me?"

I know I must guard every word. Be noncommittal. Don't leave myself open to the power of my adversary. "What do you want?"

"I want to be free of my dank, pathetic prison."

"I do not have that power."

A tittering laugh ricochets off damp stone. "I think you do. If you are Finnbheara's Treasure as you say, you have the ear of the king."

My mind darts in far too many directions. How many others in Finnbheara's domain know of me and my connection to the king? What about the bargain I made with their ruler? The sprite seems to think ole Finn, as Sion refers to him, and I are on chatting terms. I'll use his impression as ammunition.

"What if I do?"

"I would have you speak to him on my behalf to end my confinement in this miserable well. I fear the king purposefully forgets his promise to proclaim the hour in which my torment shall be fulfilled."

How many Faeries has Finnbheara dumped in wells, then forgotten them?

"I will only give my word to speak to the king if you withdraw the geas from Mick Ryan." It feels as if my Veil sprites titter against my bones. I picture them laughing at my cleverness. I've said I would speak to the king, not that I'd speak to him to plead the sprite's case. Maybe I'm getting better at Faerie talk after all.

The water churns as it rises. The Fae of the well rides its crest until he is just below the top of the stone, his face outlined in blue light. A rancid odor accompanies the sprite's nearness. "You vow to speak to Himself to end my torment?"

"When I see undisputable proof the geas is lifted, I will speak to the king at our next audience."

I hold my breath, waiting for the well sprite to correct the hole in my offer.

Either he is too eager or too downtrodden to catch my deception. "The bargain is set," he says. At his word, the water drops to the bottom of the well.

I've won.

"Eala. Eala. Talk to me." Sion has a death grip on my shoulders as he tries to pry me off the stones.

My forehead is mashed against the damp lip of the well. I fall back against Sion, utterly drained from my chat with the well sprite.

He traps me in his arms. "Your breath was as still as those stones. What happened?"

Just then, Mick lets out a thunderous wail and falls onto his back. Sion and I rush to him as he begins to pitch side to side. His donkey brays, twisting in the effort to get to its master.

"His head," I cry as Mick's skull bounces off the road. Sion whips off his vest and stuffs it between the man's thick wavy hair and the hard-packed ground.

Mick's convulsions grow stronger and then his whole body vibrates. Fear pounds in my chest. What has the well sprite done? Is he going to end the geas by killing Mick? My throat tightens. I said something wrong. I've done this.

There's a high-pitched whistle, and suddenly Mick starts to…deflate. There's no other word for it. His body pulls in on itself as smoothly as water pouring from a pitcher.

Sion and I watch open-mouthed at the transformation. Not more than a minute or two pass until there, lying next to the wheel of the cart, is the ruggedly built form of Mick Ryan. He sits up a bit dazed and looks around. When he catches sight of the well, he begins to scrabble away from it as if all the demons in hell are about to spill out and drag him into the water.

"Peace man," says Sion, crouching next to him and offering a hand up.

Mick stares down at his body, then pats himself all over.

The donkey takes a few tentative steps, pulling a now empty cart after him before stopping to look at Mick.

"How didja…" he stops himself. "I don't want to know anything except to ask if it is done for good?"

I bust out my friendliest smile but keep my distance. The guy will undoubtedly never want to speak to a person with Fae ties for the rest of his life. "Do you know what a geas is, Mick?"

He nods. "Aye. Faerie curses."

My professor self wants to explain the difference between a geas and a curse, but for all intents and purposes, what Mick has suffered could have been either.

"You fell victim to one when you bargained at the well. It's ended now." I reach into the cart and pull out the pewter plate. "This plate is nothing but a plate."

He looks skeptical until his gaze again takes in his body.

"Go home, man," says Sion. "There'll be those longing to see you."

Mick stares at me. "I suppose I owe you thanks."

I nod. "Just do me a favor and stay away from the well." As an afterthought, knowing the sprite isn't going anywhere, I add, "And tell everyone else to do the same."

"That I will." Mick takes up the donkey's lead. The animal bumps its head against him. With a still somewhat befuddled backward glance at us, Mick repeats. "That I will."

He doesn't go far before turning back to the well and saying, "*Slan.*"

Sion leans close. "Mick there's a good fella. I would have instructed the well to feck off."

We watch until he takes the turn in the road and is out of sight.

Sion sneaks an arm around my waist. "Home?"

I kiss his jaw, then lay my head on his shoulder. "Home."

I prepare to call the Veil, absently rubbing my thumb over the star pendant. There's a prick on my skin. As I pop my thumb into my mouth, I glance down at the star.

The top rounded point is sharp.

CHAPTER 14

THE MAGICIAN'S WIFE

Eala is unsteady on her legs as she waves a hand over the trinkets on the hawthorn within her reach. There's no knowing whether fatigue or nerves are the culprit since my love is silent and deep in her own mind as she searches every branch. Each time I approach her, she shoos me off. I feel as useful as dried mud in a boot tread.

The sky is long past the deepest part of night, already stretching toward dawn. At least that bastard Robber Bright isn't here laying his entitled Fae hands on Eala.

Her growl cuts through the air. "Nothing glows blue or red." She drops cross-legged onto the grass and stares at the necklace Finnbheara gave her. "I'm sure we were on to something after we followed the belt and helped Mick. That had to be what sharpened the star point."

She allows me to sit next to her. "Maybe the hawthorn knows it's too close to break day to chase after anything." I gesture at the tree. "This fine woody fella being atop a Faerie door stands to possess more sense than us about such things."

Eala pounds a fist on the grass. "If we at least had the next clue, we'd have a chance to research or make ourselves ready before the next Celtic day begins at dusk tomorrow." She drops her head into her hands. "We are in a mother of a time crunch." Her gaze darts back to the hawthorn. "What if the hawthorn only held one of the items to guide us through the Veil?"

I rub her arm. "As you say, Finn's riddle blathers on about a number complete. The star has five points, so theoretically, we only need four successful Celtic days at most to be done with it. We've got such and more before the Fae eclipse."

She turns her face toward me. "Even if we technically have eight Celtic days to travel, God knows how long it will take to sharpen all the star points and then answer Finnbheara's question." Eala scans the hill. "Robber said he'd help. Where the hell is he?"

"How much help do you think he's truly fixed on giving?" I chew at a rough thumbnail. "Besides Finnbheara, your teacher's also got eyes for you. Us failing to solve the riddle is a victory those two Fae asses would agree on since it knocks me clean out of the picture."

Eala slumps against me. "Don't talk like that. Don't even think like that. We can do this. What they want makes no difference. I'm not going to waltz into Tír na nÓg and leave you behind."

It's damn reassuring to hear those words from her. Even though we're committed to head into Finn's kingdom together, I can't shake a sense of foreboding that fecking Robber Bright will use Faerie influence to paint Eala a pretty picture of a future without me. I pray her own Fae abilities act as a shield against such persuasion.

"I know, love." I drape an arm over her shoulders. "We're both knackered. Let's go back to the cottage and start fresh after a snooze."

She bumps me. "I think my idea of a snooze and yours are two different things."

"It's what comes before the snooze that improves sleep." I nip her ear. "I'm beginning to suspect you put a geas on me to make love to you at every opportunity. A mere mortal can't fight such a thing."

I adore the way she plays with my ornery curls. It always gets me going. Her hand drops into her lap, and I miss her touch. "I'm frustrated that I can't figure out an answer to Finnbheara's riddle from the words alone. I have to accept this is a complex Faerie puzzle made up of pieces we've yet to collect."

I crook my arm through hers and help her stand. "We'll find 'em all, love."

Eala wraps her arms around my waist and snugs her head against the hollow of my throat. The Veil flitters around us like dragonfly wings, then gently lifts us into its arms.

We're as naked as the day we were born when a soft knock comes at the cottage door. Eala is sprawled across my chest as we lay on the thick hearth rug in front of the final gasp of a peat fire. Our pre-slumber athletics did the trick to grant us a fine sleep.

The sound doesn't wake her, so I ease her onto her side. She immediately curls up, and I toss the wool blanket we shucked off in the night over her.

Grabbing my pants from the back of the couch where I flung them, I make myself decent enough to tell our visitor to feck off. There's a chill in the room as I move away from the hearth and the delicious heat of Eala's body.

The knock comes again a bit louder. I crack the door, and bright sunlight hits me square in the face. Standing with her knuckles poised for another go at rousting us is Colleen.

A look at my wild hair and shirtless chest stains her cheeks a rosy pink.

"I tried to call first." Colleen sets her jaw and crosses her arms. "I probably should have waited longer to hear from Eala, but I'm still jumpy from her disappearing act."

"Fair point," I say. "Come in then. I'll wake Eala."

"I'm up," Eala calls from behind me. Colleen looks even more off put by seeing Eala wrapped in nothing but a blanket. "Give me a sec." My lovely lady scurries through the bedroom grabbing clothes, then disappears into the bathroom to dress.

Colleen reluctantly enters the cottage when I stand aside to open the door wider.

"Can I get you a cuppa? We've got coffee or tea."

Her eyes take in the space. "This is nice." She sounds surprised.

"Been in the family for generations. Now it's our home place."

She flinches at my last statement. Colleen may not like me much, but I won't pretend Eala isn't my everything.

"I'll take a coffee."

I almost guide her to the small round kitchen table until our paper trail of Finn's business catches my eye. Instead, I gesture to the couch. "Let me rouse the fire first to warm your bones."

Colleen nervously picks her way in my direction until she finally sits her arse down.

Eala bursts into the room, hair twisted and pinned to the back of her head. Stray wisps of white-blonde hair dance around her face as she moves. My swan's lovely feathers.

"I'm glad you've come back," she says to her friend. "Is everything all right?"

"I only came to let you know the Garda found Professor Olk," says Colleen in a flat tone.

I exchange a quick glance with Eala. How in the devil have they heard from the devil hisself?

"Apparently, Kennard Park got a hold of him to deal with his resignation. The guard that showed up with the news Jeremy'd been found gave me this." Colleen digs in her purse and retrieves a smooth oval stone the size of her hand. "During their investigation, it was found in the professor's hotel room in Dublin." She directs the next bit to Eala alone. "According to them, it had a note with it saying it belonged to you. I told them I'd bring it out here and let you know your former colleague is okay."

The tone in her last statement carries the stink of accusation. Not a subtle reminder that Colleen thought Eala was better off with Olk than me.

Eala starts to speak but thinks better of it and takes the rock from her friend.

"Thank you, Colleen." Eala sets the stone on the kitchen table, strategically turning some papers upside down in the process. She chews her bottom lip. Eala's eyes have the flitty quality they get when she's thinking hard. "A guard brought my stone all the way out here from Dublin?"

Colleen nods. "Yeah. Robin just transferred to County Clare from Dublin. Coincidentally, he lives close to my Shanna's place in Ennis."

"Robin?" she asks Colleen.

"Robin Bright."

Eala and I dart a sideways look at one another.

"He was very apologetic about the Garda insisting you and I stay in Ireland given Jeremy turned out to be fine." Her lips curve into a slight smile. "Robin's been helpful in showing me around. You know the best place to get groceries, good restaurants, and the cheapest price for gas." She waves a hand. "I mean petrol."

Eala's knuckles are white as she clutches the back of the chair. "So, you aren't going home now that everything's resolved?"

Eala's friend shoots her an exasperated look. "Nothing's changed. I mean, I'm relieved Jeremy is okay, but I'm staying here to figure out my life." She stands. "You know, I'm going to pass on the coffee." An uneasy Colleen heads for the door.

"Thank you for bringing the stone...and the news," Eala says, trailing after Colleen. "Maybe we can come try one of the restaurants you like out your way."

It's a blow to my heart to see how deeply the separation from Colleen affects my darling.

Eala opens the door, adding, "When you're ready, of course."

The two women lock eyes for a moment, and I hope for Eala's sake Colleen thaws enough to give her a fecking hug. No such luck. Our visitor bobs her chin with a tight smile and leaves the cottage.

Eala shuts the door but moves to the window to watch Colleen walk down the path to the gate. I hug her from behind, fitting my chin to the cozy place between her neck and shoulder. "She'll come 'round, love." I kiss her neck. "Anyone who knows you realizes their life is better with you in it."

She sags against me for less than a heartbeat before spinning to face me. Her fingernails dig into my arms. "We need to stop her. I'm sure

Robin Bright is Robber Bright. I have to warn her." Eala pushes off my chest and lunges for the door.

I catch her around her middle. "And what do you plan to tell her? That her new guard pal is really a Faerie sent by the King of the Connacht Fae to help you get in touch with your own Fae self?"

She literally folds in half over my arms. "Shit."

I lift her off the ground and carry her to the couch. We settle next to each other, and I take her hands. "Why in the name of all the saints is Robber Bright messing about with your Colleen?"

A guilty expression blooms across her face. "I haven't told you everything about my so-called lesson with Robber…and Colleen."

The sensation of steam rising from a boiling pot burns in my chest. Eala told me of a host of mystical dragons the likes of which I've never even heard stories of, Robber's proclivity to put his hands where they don't belong, the Fae's warnings concerning Finnbheara, and our new deadline, but not a squeak having to do with Colleen.

"When Robber and the host came for me, Colleen was still here."

This is so very bad. I've carried the weight of potentially failing the soulfall on my back for five lifetimes. I knew when Eala was sent to me, it would be a challenge to open her eyes to the Veil and worlds existing alongside those she knew. But Eala has Fae in her, a truth waiting to be awakened.

Colleen is pure mortal. There's no dormant Fae connection to rouse inside her. My shoulders ache with the phantom pain of bearing yet another weight.

"How did you explain Robber Bright to her?"

Eala's hand flies to her mouth to catch a sob. "I didn't. He…he…I don't know what else to call it but enchanted her. She was like a living puppet when he…"

The heat inside me roils hotter. "What did he do to her?"

Eala pulls up her knees and wraps arms around them, drawing herself into a ball. She doesn't look at me.

"He touched…fondled her. He made her want him."

A flood of curses and things I want to do to Robber Bright seethe like snakes climbing up my throat. I let her go on.

When Eala raises her head, tears wet her cheeks. "I told him her name. Robber made it clear he holds power over her if he chooses to act on it. Because of me, Colleen is leverage." Beautiful green glass eyes stare into mine, waiting for me to say how to make this right, how to break Robber Bright's hold on someone Eala holds dear.

I have no good answer.

My uselessness when it comes to Eala grows. I sucked her into my world. She's floundering, and the only help I can offer is going along for the ride.

I draw her close and gently rock us. She carries such burdens. My entire being screams to share them, take some off her, but I don't know how except to stay by her side through whatever shit lies in wait for us.

How can that be enough?

"Maybe Robber Bright or Robin Bright isn't being a right ass, love. Seems he wiped away the Gardaí business with Olk and cleared you from it."

If only I believed my own words.

Eala peers up at me from the vantage point where her tears soak my chest. "I didn't think about it that way." She starts to relax but then disentangles from my arms and pops to her feet. "The stone. Why did he send the stone?"

Eala is at the table grabbing the rock before I can speculate. She holds it in her palm and then gasps.

I spring across the room. "What is it?"

She pulls the stone out of reach. "Don't touch it." Her gaze meets mine. "Can you see it? The bluish corona?"

To me, it's nothing but a doorstop. "No."

"Oh." Eala's brow furrows.

I'm at full boil now. Has another Fae gift been stripped from me? Last night, I could see the glow around Mick Ryan's belt.

"Maybe it's too light in here." Eala cups her hands around the fucking rock, leaving a small opening. "Look now."

I peer in, but there's no telltale blue cast. I shake my head.

Eala studies the stone from every angle, then walks to the window where brighter light streams in. "There are faint scratches on it." She rubs a finger across its surface. "I think they might be *Ogham* marks or maybe neolithic symbols."

I stare at the thing as if it'll grow teeth and swallow us for breakfast. "Can we trust it's not another ticket to a situation as bad or worse than Kilkenny?"

Eala pats her lips with her fingers. "Robber showed us anything glowing blue like this stone helps…and he sent it to me." She meets my gaze. "Since it came via Colleen, you may be right about him not being a total ass. This could be a message of good faith that he's finished messing with her. A pair of positives wrapped in a single gesture." Eala looks perkier by the second. "I don't know if I want to kick Robber Bright or kiss him."

I stomp to meet her at the window. "Kiss him. Are you mad? You fell to pieces telling me what he did to Colleen."

She gives me a sour look. "It's just an expression. I have zero intention of kissing any Fae."

I cross my arms. "Let's keep it that way."

She ignores me, continuing to study her precious rock. "This could be a druid stone. There are some speculations druids used these stones like a calling card or advertisement for their services." Eala blows a puff of air, making strands of her hair flutter. "I wish the markings were clearer. Then I could try to translate them." She holds it out to me. "We should both touch it. See what happens."

I back away, remembering the hellscape of the siege, and the glint of sunlight off the blade that tried to slice me in two. "In the Veil you mean."

Eala licks her plump and perfect lips. I want to knock the stone from her hand and lower her onto the rug in front of the fire. Before Colleen showed up, I'd planned to slowly wake Eala with well-placed kisses inside her wrists, between her breasts, and down her thighs.

"It's glowing now, Sion. That could mean we can travel outside our half of the Celtic Day. Given our ridiculously truncated schedule, don't you think it's worth a try?" She pauses, drifting away from me to somewhere deep in thought. "What if…"

She wrestles with her next words.

"...this druid stone belonged to Pwyll, and it's a sign he'll help us again?"

Eala may as well have clouted the side of my head. The druid spirit, Pwyll, had been of great help to me until a bevy of Catholic priests had exorcised him from his centuries old haunt at Leap Castle. For a fleeting instant, back in the passage tomb, I'd hoped he was the druid spirit speaking to me. Is it possible the stone has come to us from Pwyll? Even though many associated druids with dark forces, maybe they are immune to exorcism. Did Pwyll simply move on from a place he clearly wasn't wanted?

Then again, the stone could belong to a druid spirit who's waiting to blow the brains out of our noggins with its otherworldly song.

"What if it doesn't?"

Eala makes a *pfft* sound and fusses with her detective work. Suddenly, she slams the stone on the stack of notes and whirls to face me. "Let's hear your ideas, Sion."

I sputter as her chest rises and falls with heavy breaths.

She pounds the sides of her fists onto the table. "My worlds are colliding. Colleen shouldn't be part of this, yet she is. Even if Robber means to help us, his pretending to be a guard who's going to squire her around town could be sending me..." She catches herself. "...us a message."

There it is. Eala knows herself to be in a world that doesn't include me. I need to step lightly here. My swan mustn't see us as anything but an irrevocable pair.

I take it slow. "I'm the most impulsive bugger who ever lived and look where it got us with the chainmail and Kilkenny. We know bringing a glowing thing such as Mick's belt into the Veil paid off. All I'm saying is what's the harm in sticking to a pattern that worked for *us*?" Without forethought, I emphasize the word *us*.

Eala reclaims the stone, shifting it from hand to hand. "I think we should try everything. If this is a druid stone, at least we know how to dress before we both touch it." Her eyes open wide as she stares at me. "Please, Sionnach. Will you take a gamble with me?"

Eala is the one with Fae gifts. She's the one with the ability to see what I cannot. The woman is half of my soul. There's nothing about her I do not trust. I can deny her nothing. "As long as you agree to first give the stone a go inside the Veil. At least we'd have its protection."

She gives a curt nod.

"Well then," I smile. "Let's go raid Alfie's stock."

Eala slowly rakes both hands down the sides of her face, pressing them in at her chin. "Thank you."

This long-sleeved knee length woven shirt and bulky shapeless skirt are the itchiest things I've ever pulled out of Sion's clothes bag.

"Potato sacks would be more comfortable," gripes Sion, already scratching under his wide-sleeved tunic of the same coarse material.

"The Internet says this is *de regur* in druidic times. Think of us as fashion forward since we're wearing shoes." What I wouldn't give for a nice satin slip to wear under my sacks.

"I prefer stuff from centuries with at least two digits," says Sion, attempting to pull his garment into some semblance of comfort.

He's been extra edgy since giving in to my wish to give the druid stone a go. We've basically swapped roles. Sion's turned cautious, and I'm taking the balls-out approach.

I get it. Each of us is trying to protect the other. Him by hanging back and me by barreling forward to do whatever I must to keep us together. Both driven by love. I suppose fate is taking a hand in keeping a cosmic balance between us. If we are both too careful or too rash, things could go seriously wrong.

Or maybe I'm justifying this potentially foolhardy risk when there is a safer alternative to not travel until the Celtic day begins.

Sion runs his hands over my body, stopping to give my breasts a squeeze. "Ah, you're still in there."

I return the favor, pretending not to be able to find his dick. "I'm not having the same luck."

He snatches my hand and sets it on the prize, which bobbles happily at my touch.

I give him a playful squeeze, then let go. "I promise to make up for lost time as soon as possible."

Sion nips at my lower lip, then kisses me with a loud *smack*. "Now there's the incentive I've been looking for."

I lift the stone from the tree stump in front of the cottage and study the sky. It's no later than mid-afternoon. Robber Bright didn't show for a noonish meetup. I suppose the message from Colleen and this stone are today's lesson. "Let me try to call the Veil."

Sion takes hold of my free hand. "Here's hoping."

I shut my eyes and concentrate on being bathed in gentle colors, willing the Veil sprites to flit to life inside me. The only thing I feel is a chill spring breeze and the smell of approaching rain in the air. I let my consciousness drift from the cottage to Sion then the fields surrounding us and picture a gray mist. When Robber Bright's face materializes in that imaginary mist, I open my eyes. Why can't I keep that man out of my mind?

Sion brings my hand to his lips and kisses it. "Don't try so hard, love. You're shaking like petals trying to cling to their stem." He rubs his cheek against my knuckles. "If it's not coming, it's not coming. I learned long ago the Veil is its own master." With a huff, he adds, "I'm not keen on the way the rules keep changing on us as we chase Finn's riddle."

"We need to keep an open mind." I shore up my nerve. "We tried it your way. Now let's give the other way a go."

Sion's growly grumble fizzles before he actually objects. I raise the stone between us. "Ready?"

Sion grins and throws my words back at me. "I keep getting asked that question. The answer never changes. I'm not ready for any of this."

I kiss his stubbly cheek. The morning was such a rush, he didn't have time to shave. Some saucy possibilities spring to mind about the intersection of my delicate parts and Sion's sprouting whiskers.

His hand hovers over the stone. "Should I count us down?"

"No." I shove the stone up to meet his palm.

My gaze locks on his as our hands clasp around the druid artifact. We're still standing in the field outside the cottage. No Veil. No traveling.

I only manage half a deep breath before everything changes with a *snap*.

The Veil skitters into view around us. We've been in this place before. It's the stretch where we were chased through a ravaged Veil. The usually vibrant colors before us look like diluted paint running down glass. Scorched slashes and gaping holes mar this usually lovely ethereal passageway. The edges of each blight wear signs of the purple/blue flames Jeremy Olk used to tear the walls apart. Through these gaps, grisly gray fog clings to the outside of the Veil. Through the soup, I can barely make out the blur of a full Veil moon.

Suddenly, through one of the damaged sections, I swear I see a distorted visage of Jeremy Olk as the spoiled shadow priest with burning eyes.

I scream a warning to Sion. "Olk."

Adrenaline threatens to drown me. My instinct is to run as the memory of being the prey of a determined predator seizes me.

Sion clamps my upper arms hard enough to bruise. "Eala, he's not here."

A moment later, Olk's face is wreathed in mist and shadow. For a split second, Robber Bright's image emerges from the ether. I point at the image. "Look. Can you see anyone now?"

"Nobody, love."

At his words, fog becomes just fog. Is this a Fae thing, my fears manifesting as the faces of enemies? Or are we being watched?

Behind us, a deep baritone speaks as if reciting an incantation. "I've been called much, but never nobody."

The scent of sage permeates the air. We whirl around to see a man who could be anywhere from twenty to eighty in a crouch next to the Veil wall. His mane of white hair escapes from under a loose hood to spill over shoulders and drapes all the way to his knees. A beard of the same color and just as long, joins the puddle of strands in his would-be lap. A staff of rough braided wood is held by spindly fingers tipped in long dirty nails. Several layers of forest green and gray robes cover his body, trailing across the turquoise and purple floor of the Veil beneath him.

The druid stone has found a druid.

An exasperated woman's voice rises behind us. "I deem you a worthless basket of festering bones, Cathbad."

Sion and I turn to see a fair-skinned woman, with yellow hair in countless braids woven together to form a version of a hood on her head. Leaves of every shade of green are twisted between the braids. She wears a dress the color of rich Irish soil with billowing sleeves and a leather belt whose clasp looks like the interlocking horns of a ram.

The stone also brought us a druidess.

The woman carries herself with the dignity of royalty as she scolds the crouching man. I'm transfixed by her otherness. Black tattoos shining with the slightest hint of indigo adorn her cheeks. On one side is etched two versions of the letter S, one vertical and the other horizontal, crossing at the center point of each. The opposite cheek bears the spiral symbol found on so many neolithic structures. There have been countless theories and speculations about that spiral. My blood hums with the need to ask the druidess to clarify its meaning.

Her irritation resonates through the Veil. "Sloth be thy name, Cathbad. Long here do you wait for others to do your work." She turns to us, fury in her eyes. "Do not fall into his trap. There is nothing feeble about him. Conchobar condemned this magician, my husband, to exile until all harm to the glorious Veil is renewed by his hand."

As Cathbad and Mrs. Cathbad quarrel, I tug Sion away to whisper in his ear. "I think he is *the* Cathbad, a druid superstar in the Ulster Cycle, and right hand of the legendary King Conchobar mac Nessa. Some stories even suggest he's Conchobar's father. If he's been sent to repair the Veil, this spirit or ghost is extremely powerful. Maybe the question in Finnbheara's riddle would be as simple to him as a knock-knock joke."

Amusement sparkles in Sion's eyes at my comparison, then he turns thoughtful. "Aye, I've told a few tales of the fella myself." He steals a glance at the druid. "Looks like he's seen better days."

Cathbad reaches a hand toward us. "*Fánaí*, does your presence presage succor to my impossible task?"

He sees us as wanderers who belong here. I stare at the stone in my hand, then take a step closer to the druid. "Do you know this talisman?"

Before I have a chance to pull it back, the magician's wife plucks the stone from my palm. She shakes it at Cathbad. "Slothful, duplicitous man. You've sent for others to complete your task."

The druid rises. He's easily eight feet. The air trembles as his commanding voice echoes around us. "You are wrong, wife, druidess most cherished of my heart. Such a powerful stone was stolen from me by those dark ones who would see the Veil unhealed. It holds the magic I have waited eons for in order to perform my sacred duty."

We back away as the power couple goes head-to-head. When we've put enough distance to see what they'll do, but hopefully not be overheard, I speak in a low tone. "Do you think Robber Bright is the dark one who stole the stone from Cathbad?"

Sion's eyes reflect the splash of color in the Veil wall. "I'd put nothing past the bastard."

I pinch the bridge of my nose as if it were a button that could dial this situation into greater focus. "The time crossovers don't make any sense. Olk just ripped up the Veil. How could Cathbad have been waiting eons to fix it? And at what point did Robber take the druid stone?"

Sion stands so still, for a moment I worry he's been enchanted by Cathbad or his wife. I'm relieved when he finally speaks.

"I told you I'd had a devil on my tail before I knew him to be Olk. The fiend was but an unknown shadow to me until the end." He continues to stare at the druids. "The Veil is ancient. Our personal evil can't be the first entity to threaten its sacred existence."

My eyes widen. "Do you think Aodh could be that evil? He's pretty damn dark and as ancient as they come as well as being potentially connected to Olk."

Cathbad begins to chant loudly in words unknown to me. I wrack my brain trying to remember what tongue was attributed to the druids. An ancient Celtic language, Welsh, antiquated Gaelic?

The druid touches the stone to the edge of the missing section of the Veil wall. A mist that appears to be made of multitudes of individual lights, like a star filled sky, curls out of the etched markings on the rock's surface. Each spark, the size of a pencil point, bears a unique color. Cathbad drones on, waving his hand in concentric circles across the void, guiding the vibrant trail until damaged edges quiver then drift toward one another. Tiny flicks of color mark paths, leaving brilliance in their wake that blend and merge to create innumerable tints and shades of primary, secondary, and tertiary hues.

A brushing sensation tickles me on the inside as my sprites mimic the strokes revitalizing the Veil. Spectral colors swirl and then settle as the brightness fades. My heart sings as this portion of the magical passage is fully healed.

Tears well in my eyes. My gratitude for what Cathbad accomplishes is beyond words. Sion asked me once if the Veil felt like home to me. At last, I truly understand the question. This mystical Faerie space weaving through time is part of me, and I part of it. Even though it doesn't fit any previous definition I have of home. It blesses me with a rich sense of belonging.

I understand Sion's devastation at losing his connection to the Veil on a deeper level than before. Despite his desperation, he shepherded my transition into this otherworldly life with kindness and love. I owe him the same as his reality endures its monumental shift. I can bring him into the arms of the Veil, but it's not the same as the synergy with magic he's counted on for two hundred years.

When I press a hand to my chest, I feel the pendant beneath my clothes. Quickly yanking it free, I check the star. A second point is sharp. Any doubts I had that we're onto the pattern leading us in a successful direction are gone. When an item with a blue glow leads the way, a task is revealed. Accomplish the task and sharpen the star. We freed Mick from the geas and restored the druid stone to its druid. The elation of a breakthrough removes one of the weights burdening my spirit.

Robber knew the druid stone would lead us here. Indirectly sending it through Colleen keeps his involvement shielded. It seems my tutor may indeed have decided to circumvent any edicts from Finnbheara not to help us with the riddle.

Keeping a tight grip on Sion's hand, I make my way back to Cathbad. The towering druid looks down at me before moving to the next spot requiring the stone's healing magic. I reach up to lay a hand on the sleeve of his robe. "Thank you, Cathbad."

Our gazes lock, and I see that he shares the green glass eyes with the gold banded irises of a Veil wanderer, a *fánaí*. He and I are kindred souls of the Veil along with Sion and Máthair. Many have passed through this tangible magic, yet so few meet.

The druidess clears her throat and bobs her head toward other nearby damaged portions of the Veil wall with the unvoiced command for her husband to get on with his important work. What she read as sloth was Cathbad biding his time until the return of his healing stone. I want to ask how he lost it in the first place. Was it stolen? Did he bargain it away? Is it the only stone that can fix the Veil? Is he the lone healer?

Darker wonderings intrude. We witnessed Olk wreck a small portion of the Veil. How many other scars exist, requiring Cathbad's magic? The safety I've always associated with the Veil may be the ignorant assumption of one still new to its mysteries. I must admit that I truly have no clear concept of the enormity of this Faerie creation. Will I ever grasp its intricacy or is that knowledge for Finnbheara alone?

The druid pinches the end of the stone to keep hold of it as he offers it to us. I can tell by the warning in his expression, he does not mean for us to take it. Cathbad knows we need the power of the stone to go home.

"Wait." I say, steering clear of the druid stone. "Cathbad, can you answer this question Finnbheara has posed to us: What's all and each the selfsame piece, plain truth and no illusion?"

He ponders my words, tilting his head one way, then another. "Shards of truth are what's needed to glean the answer. What shards have you?"

"A rope belt, a geas, a druid stone, a star pendant..." I babble. It sounds as crazy to me as it must to him.

Cathbad looks at me with pity. "Your disparate pieces conjure no clarity."

The magician's wife waves her hands and for a heart-stopping moment, I'm afraid she's going to fling a druid spell at us. "Your welcome has stretched far enough. Allow the stone to send you on and leave this slothful lout to his work."

I lay my palm over the back of Sion's hand, and together we touch the druid's stone.

CHAPTER 15

THE PROMISE OF LUST

Sion and I return exactly where we stood by the oak stump before we touched the stone. The sun hasn't moved, and the rain is still just a promise.

The exhilaration of success pulses through my body. I snatch the pendant from under the neckline of my sack dress and hold it up for Sion to see. "Two sharp points. Three to go." I fan my arm and twirl to take in the blue sky that's starting to gray over with clouds. "I hope we didn't lose time. The day looks identical to the way we left it."

Sion rubs knuckles across his chin. "We Veil traveled outside our bit of the Celtic day, but we weren't doing the steering. The stone carted us off to Cathbad, then home again. No doubt Robber Bright had a hand in the journey. I have no notion how this new travel piece fits the overall scheme of our time figuring."

"If we'd been able to keep the stone, the rules might have changed."

He shrugs. "If wishes were horses, we all would ride. So, on we go as usual." Sion yanks the tunic over his head. "In the name of Saint Patrick himself, I hope we have no more use of these bags of misery." He starts scratching his chest the way he used to after shedding his furry fox form.

It's the sexiest thing I've ever seen. I move in front of him to rake my fingers over his slightly ruddy, freckled flesh, pausing to give a ruthless yank to the forest of soft red hair between his pecs. Down every inch, my touch meets honestly earned muscle. Sionnach's sculpted himself into an exquisite piece of art.

"Are you ready for your next lesson on how to make love to a woman?" I'm so overwhelmed with the need for my hands to meet my *anamchara's* flesh, I barely get the words out.

His voice is breathy. "The answer to that question is always yes."

On impulse, I swirl my tongue over his nipples until they stiffen.

Sion's hands tangle in my hair. My name escapes his lips as a moan.

I continue with circling licks across his collarbone and up the front of his neck, before treating his lips to the same tease. When he tries to move in for a kiss, I back away. "Stand on the stump."

"I don't how much longer I can stand at all if this lesson gets any better," he growls back.

As I suspected, the low stump is the perfect height to bring his arousal in line with my mischievous mouth. Again, I dig a trail with my fingertips down his chest, along his sides, and continue over his stomach to the waistband of his black boxer briefs. I run my finger just inside the top. His body rocks slightly from panting breaths.

"Mr. Loho, this lesson is designed for you to admit there are benefits of not always being in charge."

Sion's rising frustration at feeling inferior on our current riddle quest has not escaped my notice. My *anamchara* definitely prefers to be the one steering the ship. It's partly a guy thing, but mostly a Sion thing. It's clear his loss of Fae gifts makes him feel demoted to sidekick instead of the boss.

I'm the one who struck the bargain with Finnbheara. Leading our current endeavor does fall to me like it or not. I need Sion, his knowledge and experience with living history and time travel as well as his catalog of folk and Faerie tales. There are definite gaps in my experience only he can fill.

It's his love I need and cherish most of all.

I hope by allowing me to give the orders in an activity that brings him pleasure, the chip on his shoulder will fall away.

Slowly, I ease the elastic of his briefs away from his body to allow his dick to spring free. I let go of the band. It snaps back with a *thwack* against his hard length. Sion groans low and guttural. Not pain or pleasure, but something in between. Wetness leaks between my thighs at the sound. When I do it a second time, his rough gasp and slight knee bend sets off even stronger quivers of want through my sex.

I work his briefs to his ankles, taking every opportunity to explore his thigh and calf muscles. He lifts one foot, then the other to shed his shorts. Once he's balanced again on the stump, I cage his cock between my fingertips, tickling a trail up and down his length with both hands, varying the pressure between subtle caresses and saucier pinches.

Adding the tip of my tongue to the explorations, I savor the new contours I've just begun to appreciate. Gazing at him through my lashes, I smile against his hot dick. He moans and strains to stay on his perch. I rub my nose through the patch of russet hair at his base, brushing my lips against his skin as I speak. "Oh, Sionnach, you can do better."

He's so engorged, his cock deepens in color. I marvel he hasn't let loose. His answer is a jumble of curses and pleas.

Taking him in my palm, I meet his gaze as I lick my lips, then paint them with his tip in a decadent wet slide. I taste the salty calm before the storm poised in the middle of his pliable crown. While continuing to circle his girth with my fingertips, I slide him inch by gloriously pulsing inch into my mouth, welcoming his length with an eager tongue.

My suction is relentless. I graze teeth along his smoldering shaft. I'm so turned on by his intense arousal, beads of hot desire drip down my skin. I take Sion deeper and deeper, pressing my lips like a vise against his thickness.

I brace my shoulders against him as he starts rocking into my mouth. Reaching one hand around to his ass, I pull him in tighter.

"I'm done forrrrrr," he bellows, sinking his fingers into my shoulders. I savor the shudder heralding his release. Just in time, I reach to stroke my pleading clit and moan long and deep around his cock as we peak in harmony.

My hot breath encourages him to empty himself completely before the violent trembling in his legs warns he's close to tumbling from his perch. I slide my lips off him. His head dips backwards, curls bunched against his back and hands fisted at his sides with the effort to stay where I put him.

I hold out a hand to help him off the stump. "You can get down now."

He steps onto the grass. Sion holds up one finger as if to say something, but then gives up and drops to the ground on top of his druid sack cloth, laughing and panting. "I don't know what inspired you, love, but that was brilliant." Sion slowly braces himself on his elbows. "Not much of a lesson for me except to appreciate your wicked mouth."

"And trusting me to be the boss." I smile at his pebbled skin, a sign of the cooling air. "Don't get too cozy. That was only act one."

He drops his head back. "I think I'm done for a bit."

"Are you?" The first raindrops fall.

Sion tries to get up, but I put my bare foot against his chest to push him back down. His eyes go wide. It doesn't take the sky long to go from drips to a light drizzle. It's not a chilling rain but rather a refreshing one since the sun has done its job warming air and earth. My top is quickly plastered against my breasts. I reach underneath the sack I wear to unhook my bra. Sliding the frilly piece free, I drop it onto his stomach. My bulky tunic is too thick to give him a good show of what's underneath, so I ease it higher and higher, exposing more skin as his gaze follows the path of the fleeing fabric. Finally, I fling it over my head into a cluster of dark pink blossoms.

Sion's stare is riveted on my enlarged nipples. I reach under the skirt to rid myself of my panties, which I toss to him. He catches them, bunching them against his nose and inhales deeply.

"Mmmm," he sighs and jolts to sitting so he can yank my unflattering skirt to the ground in one swift movement.

Water sluices down my back and between my breasts, dampening the hair between my thighs. Sion stares at me, eyes half-closed, breathing ragged. Raindrops stick in his smoky pumpkin-colored lashes like tiny beads of crystal. His rain-slicked chest shines with what sunlight can sneak past the clouds. He almost glows. I wonder if I look the same to him.

"Every time I see you or hear your voice, I want you," he says. Pulling me toward him, he buries his nose between my thighs and gives me a long, slow kiss. Looking up at me, his lips relax into a lazy smile. "You taste sweeter than the freshest raindrop."

Now it's my legs that threaten not to hold me up. I drop my knees to either side of his outstretched legs. He starts licking water off my breasts.

When my hand sneaks down between us, I find his hardening cock. "I thought you said you were done."

"Never with you."

He spreads my legs so I'm open to him, then runs a hand from my belly button, pausing to enjoy the depth of my slick cleft before he slips a finger inside me. The way he gently twirls and bends that talented finger takes my breath away.

"Would you like to go for a ride, my darling girl?" His finger slides free to be quickly replaced with two. I lean my sopping breasts against his chest, the star pendant bobbing between us. Lifting my body to settle more firmly over his hand, I take him up on his offer. I enjoy the slide of his fingers as they attend to my soaking core, rising and lowering myself in a steady rhythm. The pad of his thumb finds its way to my throbbing bundle of nerves and begins to circle.

He crushes his mouth to mine. Our tongues lash one another as rain trickles in between them. The taste of Sion and rain together bring me so close to falling, I begin to whimper. He increases the pressure of his touch in time with his thrusting fingers. I feel him everywhere on my heated skin, in my heart, in my soul.

I don't want this to end. Let lust kill me. My hands disappear into his rain-soaked curls, then I lose myself, screaming his name louder than the constant patter across the field.

Release does not bring relief. Our bodies are slippery as I slide down next to him and pull him on top of me. I wrap my legs around him and cry into his ear. "More."

His cock is stiff against me. I reach for him and stroke hard, hungry for his girth to reach its limits. He covers my hand with his. "Go a bit easier on me, love."

I whine, and he laughs. "I'll take you soon enough. I want to enjoy the way there."

He slowly slides his cock from root to tip against my aching need. Rain sluices off of him onto me. The sex is wet and raw and fucking amazing. I arch, and he takes my breast into his mouth, giving back the relentlessness I showed him earlier. I'll cherish every mark, every bruise he leaves on me. I fling my hands over my head and give him free rein to suckle and bite. The scratch of his stubble raises delicious friction against my skin.

I guide his shoulders lower, craving the sensation of his roughness against different parts. Reaching, I run my hands over his prickly cheeks and chin. "I want to enjoy this down there."

Sion's grin is so dirty, I clench. Then he treats me to the thorough experience of his unshaven face. I come as he purrs against me. His smooth tongue is a contrast to his rugged skin.

"Eala, my swan, my love," he murmurs.

I force words through the sounds of pleasure nearly choking me. "I love you, Sionnach."

His hand snakes under my bottom, lifting me. Atop our drenched makeshift blanket, as the sky blesses us with its tears, he enters me. We move together, clutching tight. Sion varies his pace and rhythm with each approach. Slowly sliding deep, then thrusting in a series of brutal strokes before pulling free, only to grind back in and out. Each insurgence favors different angles to uncover new points of pleasure within me.

I'm stretched and filled in a way I never imagined possible. My need winds into a merciless coil as I scream words of promise and unleash sounds of passion wholly new to me. We drown in lust and love, surrounded by the fragrance of the rosemary and mint plants beneath us.

Joined with my *anamchara,* I am alive.

Alive.

Alive.

We lie in the aftermath of our dripping sexual frenzy, catching our breath.

"Marry me, Eala."

The unexpected words clear a path through my lust haze.

I lay a hand on his cheek to find his expression filled with pure, steadfast love. My next words need to answer the intensity of his. "Does it get more married than wanting to join your soulmate in eternity? There's never going to be anyone else but you, Sionnach Loho."

The sky chooses that moment to truly open up, and the pleasant chill in the air grows teeth. Sion scoops me up in his arms and carries me to the cottage door.

Once inside, he doesn't set me down. We stare into each other's eyes. Sion's question still hangs between us. "Eala…"

"Please save the marriage talk." He looks devastated, so I kiss his jaw. "For now. If we're lucky enough, I want something that important and precious to have its own special place and time. Not wedged in between Fae imposed deadlines and everything else pulling us in a thousand directions." I rub my cheek against his. "Okay, my love?"

He answers with a kiss, begging me to change my answer. A shiver having nothing to do with passion starts with me and flows into him, ending the kiss.

Sion sighs. "Would you think me a villain if I say I need you again?"

Oh, thank goodness. I thought I was alone in my desperation. "Only if I'm a villain with you."

I sit on the edge of the tub in one of Sion's flannel shirts and my jeans, watching him shave with more than a little disappointment to see the stubble go.

He winks at me. "Don't give me such a sad look. It'll grow back soon enough." Sion shakes his mop of nutbrown curls with their hidden shades of rust and burnt orange. "This lot is getting a bit shaggy as well." He smirks. "Should I trust you with a pair of scissors?"

"Trust at your own peril. I'm not a hair person." I almost suggest we ask Colleen, who's a wiz at hair, to trim his curls before I remember that I promised to give her space.

Shirtless Sion is damn tempting. My urge to jump him one more time before our Fae riddle workday begins makes my mouth dry. A parched throat joins it when his marriage proposal comes back to me. Of course I want to marry him, and I wasn't lying when I said it felt like we are basically already married. An afterlife promise is pretty damn binding. My heart quickens with a guilty beat. It's only been a minute since I yearned for a future being married to a stable college professor. I shudder at the memory of casting Jeremy Olk in the role, no matter how briefly.

Sion is being a gentleman by not bringing up my basic dismissal of his proposal. I know him well enough to have no doubt the desire for us becoming Mr. and Mrs. Loho is set deep in his heart. Our connections with the fantastic awakened our soulmate bond. He's looking to double down with the mortal bond of marriage. Double the joy, also double the loss if we don't solve Finnbheara's riddle.

I've lived a fearful life. Since Sion, I feel the delicate shoots of becoming a braver person, but the fear of losing him will always be crippling.

A distant knell of my lapsed Catholic upbringing gives off a dull clank in my head. I know Sion loves me deeply, but was his proposal also prompted by a nagging sense of religious guilt at our situation that in his time would be considered immoral?

"Sion, do you think having sex with me is a sin?"

I can't tell if the sound he makes is a chortle of amusement or a grunt of derision, which he's extremely practiced at.

I tap my fingers against the tub. "Because that particular strike against morality has changed quite a bit since you were raised. For the record, making love with you isn't a sin to me."

He wrinkles his lips. "I've learned to drive a car, use a cell phone...use a regular phone come to that, appreciate electricity and indoor plumbing, but my moral plumbing hasn't changed much."

An unwelcome twinge of jealousy hits as I think about his tryst with Caity Byer, the vintage clothing supplier. Where did that fall on his moral compass? I try to banish the image. Sion's no priest, but he could have chosen to screw his way through centuries and hasn't.

I'm distracted by the prickles across my skin heralding the oncoming Celtic day and our need for next steps. Our traveling window is opening soon. We've been so consumed with each other, there hasn't been a moment to plan what to do next except return to the Hill of Tara.

Sion stretches his chin up to attend to his neck. "Lust is one of the big ones. It'd be disrespectful to ignore such, no matter how much lying with you…" He treats me to a brazen smile. "…or standing for you, feels like heaven. It's got a bit of a different reputation with the big man."

I've got no time or brain space to stress over personal sins. I fiddle idly with the star pendant, letting my mind drift to what the night might bring. Will Robber Bright be waiting for us against the hawthorn tree? Will the next item we need glow blue under my touch? What if neither happens? Then what?

My thumb stops stroking the pendant when I notice another rounded end wears a point. "Sion."

My tone stills his razor, and he turns to me. "What's wrong?"

"Not wrong." I lift the pendant. "Another piece of the star is sharp."

He looks as baffled as me. "But we didn't help anyone or do anything of note."

Except lustily jump each other's bones without restraint all day. What did Sion just finish saying?

Lust is one of the big ones.

I slide off the edge of the tub and rush to the kitchen. I look at the bright orange sticky notes along the side of the table that read *Isabel de Clare Marshall, Mick Ryan, and Cathbad the Druid.* Isabel's name is crossed off since our ill-fated visit there didn't affect the pendant. Could her star point have been delayed? Is there a time lapse for ends sharpening?

No, Robber Bright admitted our wasted trip to Kilkenny was because of an unfriendly meddler—most likely Finnbheara's adversary, Aodh. Unless Finnbheara is the meddler, and he intended to kill Sion, rendering the bargain unnecessary. I'm sure the king intends to win at any cost. Talk about mortal sins. Does the King of the Connacht Fae even entertain the concept?

Sin.

My inkling grows stronger. I call over my shoulder. "Sion, do you remember one of the villagers defended Mick Ryan by insisting the poor man's unnatural size was not a result of gluttony?"

"Aye," he says, coming out of the bathroom, wiping shaving cream off his face.

I write the word *gluttony* on Mick's sticky note.

The druidess accused Cathbad of being lazy, more specifically accused him of sloth. I scribble the term across his note.

Sion reads my chicken scratch. "Gluttony, sloth…" He raises his eyebrows as I write a new note with my fat black pen that says *Sion/Eala* and underneath it, the word *lust*.

After I stick it at the bottom of my clue column, I pull the pendant away from my throat. Touching each sharp star point in turn, I say, "Gluttony—sloth—lust. Three of the seven deadly sins." I snort. "For an all-powerful Fae king, he's not very original, is he? The soulfall was about restoring the seven virtues. Seems as if he's mocking us by dangling a hunt for the flip side of those."

I slide my finger under the lines of Finnbheara's riddle and read two of the stanzas aloud.

"There is a number full complete,
Its quota ripe to fill.
A sharpened star shall be the proof,
Your path twists to my will.

Greed and haste may tempt your fate,
Be steadfast in restraint.
A thoughtless act is ruin's lure,
Your victories courting taint."

I tap the pen against my bottom lip. "Okay, I'm going with the notion that sharp points mean we're on the right track. Let's presume our actions that caused the star to change are clues for the answer to Finnbheara's ultimate question."

Sion clears his throat a few times. When he speaks, he sounds like he's swallowed sand. "I think the second bit proves I fucked up." I shake my head, but he continues, "Haste, fate, a thoughtless act, those are all the fine qualities I brought to the table when I grabbed the chainmail without a second thought and sent us down the wrong road." Sarcasm drips off every word.

Not sarcasm, self-loathing.

I fan my fingers along the side of his neck. "Don't you dare blame yourself. I didn't believe the presence of those links was a coincidence either. They led us to success before, why wouldn't they do it again? If you hadn't grabbed them, I would have."

His weak smile is forced. I wish I knew what to say to convince him our mess will only be solved by this partnership no matter who takes the lead.

He swivels to kiss the inside of my wrist, lips lingering as my pulse beats against them.

I stare at his bowed head for a moment and then kiss the top of it. "I think we can assume the full complete quota he's referring to is the star."

Sion presses his knuckles against his lips, still swollen from over-exertion. "But it doesn't match up. The star has five points and there are seven deadlies—gluttony, sloth, lust, greed, envy, wrath, and pride."

I scrunch my nose. "Maybe we just have to uncover proof of five out of seven to solve the riddle. I did specify he couldn't make his challenge unsolvable. He agreed."

Sion plops onto the couch and drops his head back on the cushions. "Better he'd asked us to steal a golden bull or fight a three-headed sea beast. At least those tasks are straightforward."

I tuck in next to him, poking my head under his arm. "Now, where's the fun in that?"

He clamps me in a headlock and kisses me in a sweet but distracted manner. The lust fire we've been stoking all day has dwindled. Guess we did our part to point the star. Dotting my nose with a kiss, he rises from the couch and heads into the bedroom nook to finish dressing.

I return to staring at the riddle. How do the seven deadly sins answer the question: What's all and each the selfsame piece, plain truth and no illusion? A rope belt, a druid stone, and— What the hell object stands for lust? Sion's dick? My lady parts?

I hate feeling ignorant. Who's hasty and greedy for the answer now? Research is my obsession, but it usually travels in a straighter line. One nugget of information leads to another like steppingstones across a field. Finnbheara embodies the opposite of linear thinking. Do I even have the ability to reason in circles and treacherous backtracks like the Fae who made me?

I bury my insecurity...for now. Sion's already sinking into a troubling place with his feelings of inadequacy. I've got to be the one to keep our candle burning or we'll truly be in the dark.

My Veil sprites wake with a roar of urgency. I wish I could tell whether they're in an uproar over the nearness of the eclipse, reacting to my stress, or something even more troubling. What I do know, is my heartbeats are painfully out of control.

I press hands to my chest. "Sion, we need to get to Tara. Now."

CHAPTER 16
THE CHIEF OF THE NAME

I t ruffles my feathers when Eala stalls in front of the hawthorn tree, scanning the Hill of Tara like she's expecting a welcome guest. I've donned a new suit of possessive armor after our last go at lovemaking. The primal drive of a beast to tear the throat from any other male coming near his mate fires my blood.

Eala was convinced the ache in her chest was a summons from that Fae nuisance, Robber Bright, but he isn't here. Now, she's blaming Veil sprites for her galloping heart in their eagerness for the coming of the Celtic day. I hope that's the way of it, so she's got an answer that settles her. I worry the anxieties that rarely leave her will eventually diminish her fire.

I pat the hawthorn's trunk. "If he's not coming, I'm sure it's because you've got everything you need to move us on, love." It burns my bones to think Eala trusts anything Fae.

She looks troubled and paces off toward the stone church just down the hill, squinting into the dark. "Why would he stop helping us now?"

I hate to worry her more, but the answer is pretty plain to me. "I'm thinking maybe ole Finn got wind of him lending us a hand. The royal ass doesn't appreciate an underling poking his nose where it doesn't belong."

Eala crosses her arms. "Then why did *ole Finn* insist I learn about being Fae from Robber? The man he called *most trusted* and *kin*."

I push off the tree to join her. "Trust and kin to the Fae don't hold the same meaning to those folk as it does to us. Robber Bright most likely overstepped when he revealed the significance of the Fae moon, blue glow, or risked sending the druid stone." I squeeze her upper arm. "Never forget, *anamchara*, the king wants to best us. Anything or anyone stacking odds in our favor will grind his gut."

Eala runs a hand through her hair. "Why can't Finnbheara just mellow the hell out and let us into Tír na nÓg?"

I bark a laugh and kiss her forehead. "I don't think there's a single drop of mellow in the old bastard." I take her hands in mine. "He wants you for himself, Finnbheara's Treasure. Us being together will always be in his way."

She stares. "I can't even consider what he wants me for."

I shake our joined hands. "Neither do I, but the truth of it is, the king is not in the habit of being denied power or possession. We'd best keep such in mind."

Fingernails press into my skin. "I'm no one's possession."

It's a relief to see fight instead of fright in her. "Not even mine?"

She whacks my chest. "No one's."

"There's my Fae warrior. Now go wave your wee fingers at the tree."

She looks at me strangely. I've never called her Fae before, but I figure I'd better start getting used to the idea it's her truth, no matter how much I wish it not to be.

Eala cautiously approaches the hawthorn like it'll give her a sting instead of help. Given its roots are a Faerie door, that is a healthy concern. Raising a tentative hand, she works the length of one branch, then another. Nothing lights up.

My heart sinks a bit, but I encourage her. "Try around back."

She skirts the trunk, trailing her hand through the air as she goes. As soon as she's out of sight, fear tangles my ribs. I rush to the other side of the tree, half-expecting her to have vanished. Thanks to all the saints my sweet mother ever prayed to, Eala's there, hand hovering over a split in the trunk.

"What are you seeing, love?"

She practically sticks the round tip of her nose inside the slash. "I can't be sure, but I think something is wedged in there." Eala turns to me. "Something bluish."

I put an eye to what looks like the result of a lightning strike to the tree while Eala curls her fingers around the edge of the opening. Sure enough, a faint crystal blue glow is coming from inside. It's a relief to see it. After failing to notice the tint around the druid's stone, I thought I was done for as an enchanted object detective.

She nudges my bicep. "Stick your hand in. See if you can reach it."

I'm not keen to jab a hand into the guts of a Faerie tree. "I think we should peel some bark out of the way to see what we're up against."

Eala looks horrified and clutches her stomach. "Oof. No. The Veil sprites just informed me by practically blow torching my insides that's a very bad idea."

There's nothing for it but for me to potentially sacrifice one of my limbs to the tree. I reach my hand in as far as it will go, grabbing for whatever's raising the light. "Let me see if I can get a hold—hellfire!" Something wicked sharp digs into my palm. I yank my hand free. There's a shallow gash across the base of my thumb.

Eala seizes my hand. "What happened?"

"Nothing good," I say, reclaiming my hand to suck the line of blood welling across skin.

"Pull your sleeve down and press it on the cut."

I do as she says, using the cuff of my jacket to put pressure on the bleeding. "The thing isn't far inside the tree. I'll have another go." I huff. "I know where the pointy part is now so I can work the bastard free."

"Are there any tools at the cottage that could help you get to it?"

I examine my slice. I've a chance here to contribute, and I don't want to squander that. "I've nothing more than a wee scratch. Let me give this a go."

"Remind me to pack a first aid kit in Alfie," says Eala.

How many scars will I wear before the end? Better to suffer marks on my hide than Eala's.

More carefully, I slide my hand inside the scorched groove. Testing the shape of the thing with a finger, I find a thick bit to grasp. With not much wiggling, I loosen what feels like a hunk of something metal out of its nest. It takes strategic twisting and pulling, but finally, I free the hidden booty.

After dusting some bark shards off the thing, I hold it up. "Give it a pass with your magic hand, and let's see if this is our shiny fella." Sure enough, a silvery blue shimmer hangs in the air.

"Do you know what it is?" asks Eala, inspecting the thing.

Turning it over, I study the shape and heft. "It's cracked and part of it is sheared off, but if I'm not mistaken, this is a top piece of a pike or polearm."

Eala pushes her lips out. "Great, another battle."

I poke the air with the sharp end of the pike's head. "Guess we ought to add a portable armory to Alfie's stash as well."

She *humphs*. "Great idea. Let's go break into the weapons wing of the Dublin Museum and grab a few instruments of death and destruction from every century."

"Or we could just raid passage tombs as needed." I knock her shoulder with mine. "Brush up on my druid spirit conversational skills."

She bumps me back. "At least we can still laugh about it."

I almost say *but for how long*. For once, I keep my peace. Sliding an arm around her waist, I say, "Call the Veil, love."

Once inside our personal portal, the pointy bit guides us through the Veil to a tree line not far from a collection of cook fires. Peering out of Eala's brilliant window, we see an army all right. From the look of the robes, bulky tunics, and a slight smattering of armor, we've landed before the soldiering time in my natural life when Cornwallis terrorized the Irish.

"Let me guess," whispers Eala, "generic peasant?"

I draw her in deeper behind where Alfie stands at the churning circle of the Veil's round doorway. "For you, yes. I need to soldier up a bit." I riffle through the sacks and scrounge a padded tunic. From here, I can't see if legs or britches are bottom half attire in camp. I opt for britches. Anything between the point of a sword and my skin only works in my favor. I've been explaining my way out of not quite fitting in for long enough to know I can pull it off in a pinch.

"I can't tell if there are any women with them," says Eala with a slight tremor in her voice.

"Fair point. There most likely are, but I'll go and see what I can see before we risk you stepping out."

She clutches my sleeve. "What if you don't come back? Or get in trouble? You can't call the Veil."

Her words are a pike to my chest. Eala's right. I'm as vulnerable as she was when I first erased hundreds of years and took her to Leap Castle. Before she knew how to make the Veil answer to her.

I force confidence into my voice. "I won't go farther than the first fire. There aren't many lads there. My wits have served me over time and trial. They won't fail me now." I point down the tree line. "Look there. It's a sheltered spot closer to where I'm off to. Sounds carry in the night. Tread slow and lightly. Hear what you can, but Eala—" I set hands on her hips— "Keep the Veil close. Leave if you must. You've the pike head from the hawthorn so it can bring you back here to rescue my sorry arse if need be." I close my eyes to gather the will to speak my next words. "Bring Robber Bright with you if that's what it takes to dig me out of a bog."

Eala lunges forward to kiss me hard and quick. "I hate being separated from you."

I graze fingers across her cheek. "As do I, love." And leave her behind.

On the ground is a loose limb that will serve as a passable walking or whacking stick. At least I'm not parading into the lion's den empty handed. I can't deny I'm enjoying the fine feeling of performing a useful task.

A trio of men sit around the first fire. Rabbits dangle from spits over the flames. The soldiers pin me with stares as I approach. "Nothing in these woods to devil our night," I say, and then act surprised, looking at them each in turn. "Och, you're not my lads." I look back at the woods and then at the group around the fire. "Lost my bearing in the dark." Stretching my neck, I search the encampment, then shrug. "Mind if I sit with you to find my wind?"

The group relaxes. "You're very welcome to our fire," says a burly fella I wouldn't want to chafe. "We've not much food to go around." He speaks with the broad accent of a Scot. The massive claymore and metal helm at his side mark him as a gallowglass, one of the Scottish mercenaries often brought over to shore up an Irish army. This is no man to mess with.

I nod to him. "I thank you. Warming my bones is plenty."

I take a seat as the big man continues. "Eoghan here was just telling how it was when Red Hugh was made Chief of the Name at the Rock of Doon."

"Aye," says Eoghan, a well-built man who manages to look diminished next to the gallowglass. "'Twas a sight to see. He walked thrice sunwise 'round the peak and all the clans called out O'Donnell, O'Donnell, O'Donnell."

"A fine time it must have been," agrees the rock of man with a beard as bushy as his thick mane of hair, both shining nearly as cherry red as the firelight. His bulk seems to dent the very ground on which he sits. "May the O'Donnell call the fires of hell to rain on the Blackwater." He raises his wineskin and drinks deeply.

Eoghan points at the near giant. "We're in agreement that our fine leader, Red Hugh, is the flame to burn the English out of Ireland." He looks across the encampment. "He'll fire and maim until our land is wiped clean of 'em."

Ah. I'm in the presence of Red Hugh O'Donnell's men. I've read much of him. In fact, he was a hero to my Da for the chief's efforts to bolster the clans of Ireland when Queen Elizabeth the First would see them crushed beneath her boot. *A man with a heart raging as mighty as the wild Atlantic* my da would say of O'Donnell. From the looks of it, Eala and I landed in the gullet of the Nine Years War against the English. Da loved to regale me with tales of battles both won and lost, praising the days when our forebears fought with all they had for love of land and country.

The taxing question is why this place, this year?

Hopefully, if my new mates keep talking, proof of one of the seven deadlies will leap from the flames. I'll be able to bring back something of worth for Eala to add to her pile of scholar notes.

The Scottish giant grunts, his accent heavy and voice deep. "If mercy lies in Red Hugh's bones, now surely isn't the time for him to reveal it. If the English dare bait an Irish bear, they're to suffer its fury."

So much history streams through my head. The Scot's mention of Blackwater places us on the doorstep of the Battle of the Yellow Ford. These men will claim a significant victory here only to be decimated at the Battle of Kinsale further down the line. I pray somehow their souls will know of the contribution they make to those of us who come after them.

I glance at my three companions. Brave men. Men who paved the way for the loyalty forever stamped on every Loho heart. I would have passed such passion to my children, but the choices I've made will keep those innocent spirits from walking upon this earth. A blur at the edge of my vision moves between Eoghan and the silent youth by his side. When my gaze tries to make sense of it, the shadow slinks behind the soldiers. I swear on my Ma's eternity, in that half-second, I saw the repugnant countenance of Robber Bright.

As I scan the shadows of our fire, a loud snapping sounds from the trees behind me in exactly the spot I told Eala to creep up to so she could hear more clearly. My chest tightens so fast, I'd not be surprised if a portion of my heart will be forever wedged between ribs. Every man grabs for a weapon. I follow suit by lifting my meager walking stick. Flickers of orange reflect off leaves on the closest branches, burnishing them with tints of an oncoming autumn.

"You say you've just come from the woods, man?" asks Eoghan, suspicion pinching his face. "And naught was amiss?"

A dark form I know like I know my own breath passes between two trees.

Eala.

My swan ventured too close to the edge of her lookout. There'll be no hiding her now.

I rush forward to be first at her side. "I told you not to follow, wife," I say loud enough for the men behind me to hear. Taking her arm a bit roughly as a brutish husband is wont to do, I hiss in her ear. "I'm begging you not to speak except to bow your head and say sorry. These are not folks to be trifled with."

The soldiers are upon us just as I manage my warning.

Eala looks at the ground and mumbles with a fair stab at an Irish accent, "Sorry."

"We'll not trouble you further, friends. Come, wife. Let's be off to find our fire."

When I try to lead her away, they block my path. "Wife is it then," says Eoghan. He thrusts his face close to Eala's. "Or spy?"

Eala shakes her head so sharply, her hair comes loose from the cap she wears. Strands of white-blonde reflect the moonlight a bit too much, setting off an unnaturally bright shine around her head.

The gallowglass narrows his gaze at her. "Who comes out of a dark wood but a witch?"

I try for a convincing laugh and slap his arm. "Her patience with me has been known to blaze into a temper and rightly so, but there's been no spell work, I give you my word."

"Lad," says Eoghan to the slender youth, sharing their fire who's yet to speak. "Get word to the O'Donnell there are unsettling doings near the wood."

I raise a hand. "No need," I say.

"Do you not see the trouble you're in?" says the Scottish giant.

"Trouble?" I laugh. "I've been in far worse than this."

He crosses massive arms across his chest. "Have you now?"

Eala starts to get the dreamy look on her face before she calls the Veil. I give her a shake, and she glares at me. We're too close to these fellas. I fear they could be swept into the Veil with us. There's a heap of sorrow we don't need.

"Aye. Shall I tell you of it?" I say with a shade of mischief in my voice.

Eoghan and the big man shoot me wary glares, but I go on. I need to distract them long enough for Eala and me to create distance so the Veil will scoop us alone with no extra passengers.

Eoghan gestures us back to the fire. "I don't want my supper burning. Give us your story while we wait for those who would judge you better than us."

Our small group makes its way back to the fire. Eoghan and the gallowglass plant themselves on either side of us. One swipe of their swords is all it'll take, and we'll never move again.

"Let's strike a bargain," I say.

The big man snorts. "You're in no place for dealings."

"Let me have a go anyway. If my story proves I've been in a hotter kettle of fish than this, you'll give us leave to return to our own fire." At their squint-eyed looks, I fan a hand over the encampment. "Of course, you'll walk with us until our folk can prove we're as we say we are."

Eoghan turns the rabbits. The flames sputter as fat hits fire. "Give us a tale then...who are you?"

"Sionnach Loho at your service."

The Scot grunts, obviously his preferred manner of communicating. "A fox. Now there's a sure sign of your spying. Better we roast you over our fire, fox."

Long ago, there were suspicions the ancient Celt ancestors I share with the Scottish soldier were barbaric cannibals. One look at the gallowglass and his talk of cooking me don't make those rumors seem too far-fetched.

Eala's hand is twisted in my padded tunic. She's shaking and trying not to show it. If these fools notice, they'll take it as a sign of guilt.

I turn to her. "This one's a favorite of my wife's."

Eala plays her part and keeps her head down without answering.

I stretch out my legs, the picture of nonchalance, and fall into my best storytelling cadence. "You talk of witches. Well, I can tell you true they do share this world with us."

By the intensity of their stares, I know I've hooked the pair already. I've got to keep my language and tone as easy-going as possible, especially if I'm going to be spinning a long yarn. I don't want them any more on edge than they already are.

"'Twas on the banks of the Blackwater River nearby where the salmon were said to be the fattest and juiciest, where I sat with my wife, waiting to land a monster for our supper. Luck wasn't with me, and my hook was as empty as a crone's womb. The sun was falling fast, but I wasn't willing to give up. While Eala here dozed near the river's edge..."

I thought it was a nice touch using her name. More convincing than just labelling her *wife*.

"...I strayed a bit to the west, following the fading light with hope the evening's bugs might light on the water and call up the salmon."

Eoghan gives a slight nod, telling me he's used the same logic for his fishing.

"There was a tangle of tall grass near the bank. I pushed through and such a sight met me. There, with feet in the water, stood the shape of a woman, but instead of flesh, she was covered with yellow-gold blossoms of marigold and sunflower. I made a noise of surprise, causing her to turn, which roused a great gust that blew the blooms straight off her. She was of great height and had the look of strength about her."

If I remembered right, there were sturdy women who fought as soldiers among these Irish clans for my companions to use as a point of reference to my imaginary heroine.

"She didn't wear a stitch of clothes upon her body, but her skin was like nothing these eyes had ever seen. It was as if she were made of amber glass as it's being blown into shape, smooth and shiny, reflecting the sun's final gasp. The air around her wavered, raising a sheen the color of a yellow cat eye."

Cats, not having the best reputation in folktales, piqued my audience's interest even more.

"She was a beauty to be sure, and my eyes drank in the fine curve of her hips and plump breasts topped with peaks like glistening ruby crystals." I give my audience a knowing look. "My cock showed its appreciation, outdoing the lust in my eyes."

I add a lewd gesture to illustrate my point, drawing a grunt of approval from the Scot.

"The mighty woman turned fierce eyes on me then, saying, 'You've not the right to gaze upon the pure form of a wise woman without leave.'"

Eala presses harder against me.

"'Your lust is your doom', says the witch. 'I'll curse you to never take another woman to your bed for your crime.' And there she rose to a fearsome height, the light around her giving way to a dark mist as she pointed a finger straight at my cock."

Eoghan wriggles a bit, suddenly not comfortable with his position.

"'Twas then my darling, Eala, stepped through the reeds. She'd heard the curse about to be loosed on me and fell to her knees before the witch."

The gallowglass's eyes switch from me to Eala.

"'Sister,' said she. '''Tis true my husband is a weak man unable to battle the whims of his desire, but to steal his lust is to condemn me as well. For how will I ever bring forth a child if this man is plagued to keep from my bed? To curse him is to curse me.'"

I shift my voice back into that of a vengeful witch. "'To bring you woe is not my wish, dear sister,' says the wise woman. 'But his transgression must be punished.' My dear wife held her hands out like so." I stand and drop to my knees, putting a bit of distance between myself and the men. Clasping hands as if in prayer, I look to the skies. "And Eala said, 'Bless me to accept his seed, but allow him no pleasure in the act for a year and a day. If I should conceive during the time of his punishment, let the child be a daughter who I will pledge when she comes of age to be apprenticed to you, wise woman.'" I give the men a knowing look. "It is known to you how witches love to collect maidens for their covens."

My audience is transfixed. It's been too long since I've told a good tale. I'd forgotten the joy in it. The pause rankles the flame-haired giant.

"What of your cock, man?"

It takes all my restraint to hold in a laugh. Of course, he'd focus more on a limp cock than a child pledged to serve a witch.

I stand and grab my crotch. "Useless as a landed fish that's finished thrashing about." I'm gratified by their belly laughs. While they're enjoying themselves at my cock's expense, I shoot Eala a quick look and a nod to draw her to me.

She covers her face in her hands and turns away from the men as if embarrassed. It's probably the stench of their bodies on her modern sensibilities putting her off.

"Forgive me, wife. I've shamed you in front of these fine soldiers." I clasp her shoulder, pulling her from the fire. "Now," I hiss through gritted teeth, knowing there are only seconds before they herd us back into their grasp.

There's the sound of a whip cracking, then an electric sizzle makes all the hair on my body spring to attention. Eala and I are thrown onto the shining orbs of the Veil floor, flying so close to Alfie, one of her branches scratches my cheek.

I reach for Eala, expecting her to be a mess. She surprises me by slapping a hand to my chest with gusto. "You were freaking brilliant." Her tempting lips push out. "Whatever we gain tonight is no thanks to me."

I yank a lock of her hair. "Och, catch yourself on, love. Your intentions were right, just not your forest skulking skills." I relish the feeling I've accomplished something significant in our mad journey to best Finnbheara. It's much more satisfying to be a partner to Eala instead of her second fiddle.

"I'd rather catch this." Eala's hand snakes between us to fondle the lead player in the tale I wove for the soldiers. Her fingers give a naughty pinch to the base of my growing arousal as she flashes me a saucy smile. "Please tell me you haven't suffered the same fate as the hero of your tale."

My pleased grunt is all the answer she needs. I hope Alfie isn't paying much attention to how we occupy ourselves the rest of the way home.

Sion and I straighten our clothes as we step out of the Veil onto the path in front of the cottage. The sky has already begun to fade to the cool lavender of predawn. We've yet to test the hundred thousand heartbeats rule, but this is cutting it close.

"So, love. Do I get proper marks for telling the best dick joke of its day back at Eoghan's fire?"

"Sorry, dude." I say, looking pointedly at said dick. "Shakespeare was ripping them off left and right around the same time."

"Once again bested by an English whoreson."

"Extra credit for using era appropriate vernacular." I reach for the star pendant and hold it out for Sion to see. "Something worked. You earned us the fourth star point."

"For all the good it does us?" says Sion.

I slide my fingers through his and swing our joined hands as we approach the house. "No pessimism please. Four out of five star points is eighty percent. We're a significant step closer to cracking this nut." I stop to look him in the eye. "You were brilliant back there. Own that."

I'm housing enough fear of failure behind my breastbone without taking on Sion's as well. I can't bring myself to tell him eighty percent is a B minus on the precipice of a C. We need to be in A plus territory.

When he smiles, one of the virtual stones weighing me down rolls away. "It did feel fine spinning a tale." His expression grows wistful. "Like a part of me lying dormant finally gave a stretch and a yawn."

I tug him toward the cottage. "So, my spicy storyteller, what sin do we credit with that lovely encounter?"

Sion gives his britches a shake. "Which sin is connected with nearly soiling trousers when facing a gallowglass?"

"Excellent question. Sin aside, how does Red Hugh O'Donnell or his army help us with the riddle?"

Sion rubs his lips together. "Maybe it was the gallowglass or that fine sword of his, rabbits over the fire, the eve of a battle—" He grunts. "Burn it all to hell. Maybe it was the branch you stepped on to crack the quiet of the night. How will we know?"

I stare at the distant lighthouse. "I do believe we're on to something using the seven deadly sins as our template. Once we've decided on at least five to match the star, there's a chance more pieces will fall into place." Neither of us says there's just as strong a possibility nothing we find will help us solve Finnbheara's riddle.

Sion's voice is barely above a whisper. "We could run."

I forget to breathe for a moment. "What do you mean run?"

"Finn's got enemies. Maybe one of them would help us wiggle out of this. Find a different place we could be together."

"You mean Aodh?" I grow cold saying the god of the underworld's name. "No way. I'm not going to make a Faustian bargain with a dicey myth. Let's stick with the devil we know."

Sion's grip is painful on my chilled fingers. "I'm walking a path with shadows of desperation on one side and despair on the other, Eala. You can't blame a man for entertaining other possibilities."

The prospect of Sion losing faith in our success to answer Finnbheara's question is more terrifying than any time travel. I wrap my arms around him. As he pulls me closer, tendrils of his desperation and despair pierce the shell of confidence I'm trying so hard to keep from shattering. They find my own doubts and twine together, forming larger knots of dread in my breast.

Running is tempting.

Maybe instead of aligning ourselves with some enemy of Finnbheara, Robber Bright might know of a different solution for Sion and me to stay together instead of betting our eternity on one high-stakes bargain. There's no way in hell I'll share my thoughts of entertaining such a possibility with Sion unless my Fae mentor does offer a viable alternative out of our dilemma.

"Believe me, I know how hard it is not to feel that way, Sionnach, but promise me you'll keep moving forward on the path between your shadows with me."

He digs his chin into my shoulder. "I promised you once you'll never fall with me, Eala *bán*. I swear to you now, I'll never let myself fall either."

Our kiss is deeper than lust or wanting. It's a kiss to say my eternity is yours.

If only a kiss could be a guarantee.

We continue hand in hand to the door until the sight of a flapping silver ribbon tied to the knob catches my eye. "Sion, is it common for people to decorate doors in the neighborhood?"

"No." He increases his pace to the cottage and slides the swath off the handle. When he stretches it between his hands to examine it, the storm on his face is darker than the one brewing over the sea cliffs. "Yours," is his only word, before he thrusts the ribbon at me and stalks down the road toward the gate.

The ribbon looks like hammered silver, but it's as thin as tissue and as light as duckling down. The script is flowy and written in midnight blue ink. Fae stationery? Three words gently bob on the ribbon, flower petals floating on the surface of a barely disturbed pond.

Midday, my darling.

As soon as I read Robber's summons, a morning onshore breeze steals it from my hand. The ribbon soars upwards until it shatters, sprinkling the underside of the clouds with a shower of silver glitter.

Frustration corkscrews through my middle. It's more essential to devote my time to unspool the connection between the seven deadly sins and Finnbheara's godforsaken riddle instead of wasting time caught up in the random syllabus of Robber Bright's Faerie lessons.

I blink to clear a speck of glitter that sticks on my eyelash, then hurry to catch Sion with sins and silver on my mind.

CHAPTER 17

THE FAERIE FOREST

E ven with the limp Sion was saddled with after a run-in with a musket ball during his natural lifetime, he's so fast, I have to jog to catch up with him.

"Sion, stop. Let's talk about this."

He pauses but doesn't turn. "I fear I'll regret whatever slips out of my gob at the moment."

I lay the flat of my hand against the center of his back. "I'm sorry we have to deal with Robber Bright."

Sion's muscles bunch as he drops his head. I move my hands to his shoulders and work my thumbs against his granite neck muscles. He reaches back to stop my movement, still not facing me. "I'm burning, Eala. Just let me be for a spell. Walking along the cliffs with the Atlantic roaring at me will be a balm for my weary soul."

I don't consider myself naïve, but clearly when it comes to intense relationships that's exactly what I am. My belief that Sion and I were past withholding our feelings from one another was misguided. I'm blindsided by his reaction or in my opinion *overreaction* to the ribbon message. I don't know how to shake Sionnach free of his snit over Robber Bright's unavoidable role in our lives.

My fleeting irritation melts as the distance between us grows. Sion

Loho is as dedicated to protecting me as I am to him. He knows there's shit he can do against Robber or Finnbheara's Faerie powers. The desperation Sion endures faced with that reality must be brutal.

Sion's current mood bleeds into my own feelings, darkening them alongside his. When his hunched form follows a curve in the road, I lose sight of him. His pain is a bruise on my own heart. "Be safe, *anamchara*," I say, even though I know the wind carries my words in the opposite direction.

I don't begrudge him the space, but I worry he's internalizing very counterproductive thoughts we should address together. Sion makes no bones about his hatred of the Fae. When you've endured two centuries of your fate beholden to anything, it's bound to color the fragile relationship we all have with sanity.

I open the gate and trudge up the path to the cottage, pondering the journey that brought me to this point. A man called me his soulmate when I barely knew him. That's who Sion is. Don't hold back. Don't self-edit. He is so far from the life script I wrote for myself. Even though *old Eala* chatter occasionally pops into my head, the truth is, no matter how irrational, there is no hope or dream for me without him in it. My love for Sion exists beyond the visceral. We're connected on a metaphysical level where the ether of soulfire sears two into one.

I'm incapable of turning away from such a miracle.

The sun clicks to its zenith, the hour of Robber Bright. After changing into my own clothing, I sit on the small porch of the cottage. The brandied melon-colored scarf matching the hidden color of Sion's curls that Máthair made me is wrapped around my neck.

Low thunder from the approach of the Faerie host rolls through my senses. A turbulent cloud of mist tumbles in from the direction of the glacial *lough* at the base of the hills. Why does Robber travel with an entourage? Probably to feed his ego. I release an unladylike snort, unbecoming to someone labeled Finnbheara's Treasure. It's not as if he needs bodyguards.

Or does he?

A chilly spike precedes the host's progress—the faerie wind. Now that

I'm aware a thousand tiny silken wings create the enchanted storm, I can identify the bluish tinge underlying the gray cloud.

Robber rides out ahead of the Fae windstorm alone. Not quite alone. He's holding the lead of a silk dragon three-quarters the size of Aillil. The smaller dragon is gorgeous. Its lavender, pastel mulberry, and watery blue scales tipped in silver blend together, reminding me of the multicolored hues of hydrangeas Máthair grew in our greenhouse garden. They were my favorite flowers. Even the wallpaper in my childhood New York bedroom bore pictures of their blooms.

I notice the pattern of scales on this new dragon are chevron tessellations unlike Aillil's that carry a V motif. Both dragons' hides remind me of M.C. Escher drawings. I'm curious to examine other dragon scale patterns in the company.

I get my wish as the ball of fog dissipates to reveal Robber's faerie host and their mounts. They gather in front of one of the large yew trees at the back corners of the cottage. The gauzy cerulean blur of dragons in flight fades as wings lay flat against their now masked multi-hued scales.

The host appears as if they're on alert. Riders don the somber colors of earth, night, and darkest green leaf. I catch the gleam of armor beneath a few cloaks. Dragons hiss as triple tongues sample the chill air. There's a collective low-level growl emanating from the pack while puffs of steam in countless shades of reddish-purple rise from nostrils. The ripe cherry scent of dragon breath now carries an acrid edge that wasn't there before.

My desire to study their scales as art pieces vanishes as waves of tension twist around me.

The smaller beast with Robber and Aillil keeps craning its neck to look at its fellows, reluctant to leave the Fae's side. My tutor pivots on dragonback to address his company. "Move off," he says, waving a hand toward the hill and lake. "The little one is picking up on your unease."

"Is that wise, Commander?" asks a strongly built woman with rich brown skin, wearing intricate braids of multi-hued earth tones. She holds a spear with a point that makes the one we dug out of the hawthorn look like a sewing needle.

Robber Bright meets her unrelenting glare. "Yes, Acacia. Just far enough to dilute the battle-ready scent coming off the beasts." He darts a glance over the fields. "Yet close enough to act."

Battle-ready scent? To act on what? I was hoping to get answers from Robber at this lesson, but now I have an urge to be far away from him and his warriors. What new supernatural shitstorm did the Host of a Thousand Wings bring to the doorstep of Loho cottage?

"We shall join you momentarily once these ladies are acquainted enough to ride," says Robber Bright, flashing me a smile.

I press a hand to the base of my throat as I croak, "The scent of what battle?" I've hit my limit with potentially violent situations after Kilkenny Castle and Red Hugh O'Donnell's encampment. "As in, someone is planning to attack?" I scan the rolling land between the cottage and the lighthouse, hoping to see Sion heading this way.

Robber slides off Aillil as smoothly as his ribbon disappeared into the sky. "First lesson of the day, Eala Duir. Within the Sidhe dwell many powers and territories. Finnbheara's dominion is not without its challengers." He peruses the fields again. "Leaving Tír na nÓg is never without its dangers. Fae and beings of darker intention prowl beneath your mortal sky."

My mind slips to Finnbheara's heavily armed backup that Sion and I encountered when we entered the gates of the Faerie kingdom. The monarch made no bones about Aodh being an adversary. Is he the current concern of the host and their dragons? The creature that was Jeremy Olk's true form also alluded to other dark forces. Who or what else lurks at the fleeting edge of mortal vision?

Robber takes hold of my arm. "Are you well?"

I look up at him. "I was before your battle-ready scent and danger talk."

He gives my shoulder a reassuring squeeze. "No harm will come to you when you're with me, Eala Duir."

Robber Bright's words echo Sionnach promises of safety. My faith in the Fae's vow pales in comparison to my belief in Sion's.

A howl like a torrent of wind on a stormy night fills the air as the host takes flight. In a blink, they've shifted back into a tumbling mist. Aillil releases a slurping whine as they leave but settles when Robber coos in his mount's ear. The words also soothe the smaller dragon who's plastered against her kin's side.

Robber strokes the space between her eyes to coax the timid creature away from her protector. "Eala, I'm pleased to present Nuala, your Faerie mount."

"Hello, Nuala," I say, carefully approaching her. She may be smaller than Aillil, but she's still a few heads taller than me and anything but frail with solid flanks and a thick neck. If I had encountered her roaming the forests of Tír na nÓg, she'd have made my heart stutter.

"Interesting name," I say. "Named for Finnbheara's wife, I assume."

Robber stares at me intently. It's unnerving how long Fae can stare without blinking. I wonder if that's just how they're made, or if it's an intimidation tactic.

"A wife, indeed."

I'm tempted to wave my hand in front of those eyes. As I stare back, I discover the Fae's eyelashes have as many shades of honey, yellow-gold, and blond as his hair, although his brows are as black as the ash after a Beltane bonfire.

"Names carry messages, Eala Duir. Yours marks you as possessing qualities of swan with its connection to Tír na nÓg and oak, granting you coveted breadth of vision." His gaze drifts off me to patches of flowers. "Nuala is a gift from the king. He bred her to be your royal mount. Make of that what you will."

My patience for the quixotic Robber Bright is wearing thin. I need a Faerie Rosetta Stone to decipher what message is being sent. Is this a warning to be wary of Queen Nuala? She can't be too happy her husband is calling me his *treasure*. But according to Robber, the creature is a long-planned gift to me from Finnbheara. The implications of that leave me reeling.

The king always knew I'd come to him eventually.

Could he intend Nuala, the *péist síoda*, to be a royal mount for a different potential queen?

I rub my forehead as if that will wipe away these unnerving thoughts. "I don't suppose you'd deign to clue me in on the meaning behind the name."

"I would have called her Medb, an exquisite name for an exquisite creature." Robber pats the dragon's neck.

Medb. I know of the legendary queen, although famously unfaithful, to the equally legendary king, Aillil mac Máta, from the Ulster Cycle of Irish mythology. It's unsettling that Finnbheara and Robber both connect a queenly name to my dragon.

I swallow the very creepy and unwelcome notion either of these men have designs on me as a queen or otherwise. Do all Faeries bide their eternity by skipping from conquest to conquest?

I reflect on the near insatiable lust I feel for Sionnach, and a buzz rises in my chest. Is that appetite a byproduct of getting in touch with my Fae side? I don't want to consider I'd be as sexually voracious for anyone but my soulmate.

"Hello, Your Majesty," I say to the dragon.

Nuala wraps her tongues around my wrist, one of them slithering inside my sleeve up to the elbow. I force myself not to act skittish. She tilts her head so her giant eyes are on the same level as mine. The dragon sounds a sustained hiss, and I simultaneously inhale as our gazes lock on one another. I may not have a leaf emblem plastered on my chest with liquid to match Nuala's eyes, but her bulging spheres echo my own green glass color complete with a thin outline of gold.

Delicate energy pulses from Nuala's tongues against my skin, then probes deeper. Pleasant beads of warmth bob through the blood coursing in my veins. When I stroke her side, she nuzzles into my touch. I slide the arm still held in the grip of her tongues up the side of her neck. Nuala lets out a gravelly trill and settles her body against mine, nearly knocking me over. The rest of the world falls out of focus. My dragon and I exist in our own symbiotic bubble, her powerful heartbeats syncing to my insignificant human ones.

The lovely moment is stolen when static in the air prickles my skin. Nuala's tongues retract into her jaw with a crackling slurp as she feels the disturbance as well. Robber's languid posture snaps to attention like malleable clay suddenly hardened by a kiln fire. His head turns so far from side to side, I half expect it to complete the illusion of an owl-worthy revolution. Without permission, he clutches my waist and heaves me up onto Nuala's saddle, thrusting her reins into my hands.

"We must be off." A moment later, he's on Aillil's back.

I grip the reins in one hand and the pommel of the saddle with the other. I'd throw my arms around Nuala's neck if it wasn't as thick as the trunk of one of the yew trees near the cottage. "The closest I've ever been to riding anything is a carousel horse. I don't know what to do."

A look of frustration crosses Robber Bright's face. "Yes, you do. Riding a *péist síoda*, especially one bred to bond with you, is inherent to our kind."

"But I'm not one hundred percent *your kind*."

He silences my protest. "Nuala will teach you. Trust her."

This poor dragon has her work cut out for her. I've gotten better at not succumbing to a panic attack at heights but sitting here on dragonback with nothing resembling a seat belt triggers familiar wooziness. Add in Robber's unease, and I'm headed toward a spiral. I whip my head side to side, searching for any hint of what has the Faerie on edge. My rudimentary Fae gifts give up nothing.

"Robber, if something here worries you, we have to warn Sion."

He settles into Aillil's saddle. "The fox is not of interest."

"He is to me." Visions of Veil shadows and dark underworld gods batter my nerves. I should stay, but my bargain with Finnbheara binds me to these lessons with Robber Bright. "Can you promise whatever danger you're freaking out about will not hurt Sionnach?"

He looks baffled. "I've just said as much."

God forbid a Fae should ever speak with anything resembling clarity.

Robber gives a sharp command and both dragons shift from stationary mode to flight prep. Blue silken feathers like elongated butterfly wings stab from hiding and begin to whirl. In seconds, we're airborne. My thighs grip Nuala so tightly, I cry out from a cramp above my knee. As much as I'm not comfortable getting too close with Robber Bright, I'd feel safer sharing a saddle with him about now.

The Fae slows until Nuala is side-by-side with Aillil. "Your mortal lover is in no danger." After the much-appreciated reassurance, he immediately regains the lead, all-business.

We soar toward the distant hills. Oddly enough, once I know Sion isn't being left behind as a snack for some nasty Fae entity, I allow myself to try and settle into the saddle. To my surprise and relief, my body adjusts, seeming to know instinctively how to sway and lean in harmony with Nuala's movements. She looses a perky cry of approval when I find my seat.

Once on a blind date Colleen set up for me, I forced myself to leave my comfort zone and ride on the back of the guy's motorcycle. It was terrifying. The entire time, I imagined flying off and kissing pavement.

When we first took off, I was afraid dragon riding would be like that, but this is intimate, not frightening. I grow a deeper understanding of the stories praising the affection and camaraderie between knights and their steeds. Mounted on a silk dragon, my silk dragon, I begin to understand the synergy of two living beings existing in tandem with a singleness of purpose. As mind-blowing as the idea of a Faerie king breeding a specific dragon to bond with me is, I find myself accepting the truth of it as we cut through the air.

No fantastical dream flash, the waking visions I've had my whole life, equals the magic of this reality. A carousel animal has indeed awakened here in the fields of County Clare, Ireland. Nuala's magnificence surpasses every imagining of a girl with a love of stories.

My dear dragon is a good soldier, staying just to the right of Aillil's flank. I gradually embrace the mystical experience of riding a non-imaginary silk dragon, a *péist síoda*, bestowed on me by the King of the Connacht Fae. Part of me still expects to wake from this Ozian dream under a red maple in Kennard Park University's grassy quad.

As the cottage disappears behind us, so does the teeth-throbbing static that gripped the air. Robber Bright's hand strays off the sword strapped to the side of his saddle. Nuala isn't kitted out with weaponry like the other dragons in the Fae retinue. I don't appreciate the feeling of helplessness it gives me. Not that I'd have the faintest notion of what to do with a knife or sword.

Up ahead, I see the open space surrounded by hedges and tall grass where we stopped before. As much as I genuinely enjoy the ride, I'm anxious to get on with the lesson and return to Sion.

We don't stop at the lake. Instead, we surge over the water. Nuala falls in line behind Aillil and to my horror, we repeat the arc the Fae host took last time before they vanished into the lake.

"Robber," I cry, but my voice is lost to the high-pitched whistle of the wind as we careen toward the glittering surface—

And break through it.

My shriek isn't silenced by a mouthful of water. It's absorbed into the thrill humming through my body. We're not sinking into glacial depths, instead, Robber, the dragons, and I are suspended inside a giant crystal. Light refracts in a thousand crisscrossing beams around us, stretching up so high, I can't tell where the ceiling above us ends. Color within the bright streaks is only visible at the corners of my vision. Looking directly at them yields the pure vibrancy of unbroken white light. A gentle shush like water lapping the shore fills the chamber. Before I have a chance to truly appreciate this luminous cathedral, Robber speaks in a language tonally reminiscent of Irish but different from the modern language I'm used to.

A giant oval in the curved wall in front of us thins. It reminds me of the sheen marking the entrance portal between my Veil and what lies beyond. Here, instead of a familiar landscape past the barrier, swirls of jewel tone light punctuated with flickers like fireflies appear to float through the air. As we pass through the surreal door, all sensation stills.

Robber's hand squeezing my knee awakens me from the trancelike state the passage caused. By not protesting, I tacitly allow his touch and teeter unsteadily off Nuala's back into his arms. After guiding my feet to the ground, he gathers me to his broad chest. Heat and a gentle bubbling from the leaf emblem on his tunic seep through my sweater. It's a heady feeling being in his embrace. Not at all unpleasant. He gently caresses my arms. A warning voice buried deep in my thoughts whispers not to enjoy this, but I can't imagine why not. Something so soothing can't possibly be wrong.

"One's first trip through the crystal gate can be disorienting." Robber transfers me to his side, but leaves one arm crooked around my back, facilitating my view of the scene. "Welcome to the Gem Kissed Forest."

Nuala stamps and blows a wispy cloud of mulberry steam from her nostrils. Her long snout slides over my shoulder until we are cheek to scale, my dragon's welcome to this enchanting realm she calls home. I reach up and stroke the velvety space between my new friend's eyes.

Friend, yes. That's what this creature is to me. Not a gift or pet or possession, a friend. *My* friend. The Veil sprites flicker inside me, then blossom into a blazing flower of confidence. They are awake here no matter the hour of the Celtic Day clock in my real time.

I don't like the implications that Nuala's queenly name supports Finnbheara's belief he has a claim on me, so I will simply give her a new name. Names carry undefined and changeable power with the Fae. By taking charge of my dragon's name, I'm exerting my own power. She is my friend so friend will be what I call her, *Cara*, the Irish word for friend.

"*A chara*, my friend," I say, and turn to dot a kiss on the dragon's neck. "*Cara*, that is the name I give you." A rumbling purr of satisfaction sounds deep in her broad chest.

Robber raises an eyebrow. "Friend? Am I not the same to you as well?"

I lift my own brows in answer. "That remains to be seen."

With whinnies and hisses, the two silk dragons curl into roiling spirals until they're the size of my hand. I laugh as they playfully dart up the trunks of trees covered with thick velvet moss in shades of neon green and fuchsia to disappear among branches decked out in the same vibrant palette.

I'm overwhelmed by the beauty surrounding me as I attempt to take it all in. All my life I've short-changed the possibility of other realities. I was content to be rooted in the single dimension in which I existed. When he brought me into the Veil, Sion introduced me to a new truth about the complexity of being alive and the vastness of a world only glimpsed in imagination. We may have lingered on the doorstep of Tír na nÓg, but this place, the Gem Kissed Forest, is story come to life. How much more is there to discover about the multiple realities and places brushing up against the ones I know? Instead of fear, I'm hungry to learn about them.

The contour of the forest floor undulates around and between a grove of rowan, yew, and white poplars like Alfie. Robin's egg blue and berry-colored boulders, polished to a brilliant shine, peek here and there through rolling grasses.

Scattered at the base of trees are glass perfume bottles as large as gallon jugs with stoppers in the shape of mushroom caps. Each one is filled with different amounts of glowing liquid in shades of electric aquas, red grape, limoncello, and countless others. Beams of light escape each bottle, spilling in dazzling lines over velvety moss and grasses. Streaks combine and create yet unnamed colors where luminous pathways cross.

I waver within my own casement of wonder, taking in a deep whiff of the slight breeze infused with the fragrance of lemongrass and spearmint. "The Veil and this lovely place..." My senses delight in the magical ambiance of the forest. "...have the same scent."

Robber lifts a loose strand of my hair and inhales. "Ah, the tang of citrus and the coolness of mint. Your Veil signature carries a contrast to match your essence, Eala."

"Veil signature?"

He lets my hair slowly glide over his fingers, sighing when it leaves his touch. "It's the connection that thrives between you and the passage between time and worlds. Think of it as a sign the Veil gives permission for you to enter."

Sion's Veil smells like soap bubbles. I'm not surprised his essence is clean and pure like his true heart. The one that dedicated his existence to saving the spirits in the soulfall. What is Robber Bright's Veil signature? Knowing that may be a window into whether his arrogant wrapper is indeed the truth of his nature.

The quiet harmony of birdsong devoid of a single shrill note floats through treetops. A fizzle from one of the oversized perfume bottles catches my attention. I watch as a deep tamarind liquid bubbles up until it refills the glass all the way to the mushroom cap, then settles.

Fanning an arm around the collection of bottles, I ask, "What's the liquid in these for?"

With a loud pop, Robber pulls the top off the nearest one that's filled with midnight indigo liquid. He dabs his pinkie to the bottom of the stopper, then touches the tip of his tongue, smacking his lips. "Dragon speak. It gives the gift of the *péist síoda* language."

I walk up to the bottle. Peering into its contents, I poise a finger above the rim. "That would be handy. How much do I need?"

Robber grabs my wrist before I can dip my finger into the dark liquid and shoves the cap back into place. "Not yet. Your human mind still resists the entirety of your Fae gifts. If you aren't ready, instead of synthesis with your essence, these potions have the potential to cause…misfortune." His hand slides up my arm. "I would not have that happen."

Here in this place, the warring halves of my brain call a truce. The desire to fully embrace my connection, my right, to belong in these enchanting surroundings pecks at me. Why do I resist? Truth fizzles through me like the bubbles in the Faerie bottles. Until I understand what I might lose by sliding fully into my Fae skin, there will be pushback from my human side. Maybe with more knowledge, I will be able to dare the transition. Most importantly, I need to know how my change will affect Sion.

"Are we in Tír na nÓg?"

Robber presses his lips to my hair. "One small corner of the kingdom, my darling."

My darling

The ribbon

Sionnach

Truth breaks whatever charm has me captive, and I free myself from Robber. "Don't do that."

One side of his lip curls, belying his attempt at wide-eyed innocence. "Enlighten me."

I set hands to hips. "I think you're enlightened. The rule is no touching without permission, and you tried to…" I wiggle fingers in front of my face. "…spell me. Enchant me."

The other side of his lip curls to join the first. "Perhaps, but you continually shed my influence with scant effort. Another of your natural abilities. I am curious how many talents you cast aside without examination."

I hate the way he studies me as if I'm a specimen. "My request for this lesson is for you to keep your *influence* to yourself."

"Agreed. I shall not exert external influence on you." There's an annoying twinkle in his eye. "Here's a truth for you to learn, especially once you dwell here among your kind." He taps a finger to his chin. "Without the seeds of desire already within you, my suggestion or *influence* as you deem it, would melt like a snowflake on a warm stone." Robber Bright levels a stare at me. "Do you desire me, Eala Duir?"

I back away from him. "I do not." Guilt prickles over my skin from the enjoyment I did feel in Robber's arms. "Sionnach Loho is the only one I desire for now and all time."

The damn Fae looks at me with the condescension of a master to a belligerent apprentice.

"Let's get to the lesson. Teach me how to return the abilities Finnbheara took away from Sion."

Robber Bright looks genuinely baffled. "But what of your untapped magic? Defense against a foe? Are not these things more vital?"

I rub my scalp. Will the boundless unknown of my Fae side ever stop overwhelming me? "Let's cut a deal. Show me how to restore Sion's gifts and then you can decide what we do next." As soon as the words are out, nausea rises in my stomach. That was far too open-ended.

Robber considers and then bobs his chin in a nod, hunger blazing in his aquamarine eyes. "Agreed."

Yep, I'm screwed.

"To grant a human those gifts natural to us, you must meld your essence to theirs. Come, and I will demonstrate."

Meld with their essence better not be code for Faerie sex.

"Talk me through it first."

He chuckles. "You will ignite what humans call consciousness within your spirit, then seek the same in the one you wish to commune with. Once an alliance is struck, promises and gifts may be offered and accepted."

My fleeting hope he could simply explain the steps to help Sion dissolves. First rule of teaching, model first, then the learner can take the new knowledge out for a spin. I detest putting myself in a vulnerable position when it comes to Robber Bright, but what other choice do I have? "Okay, show me without *influencing* me. No tricks."

I do not trust the sparkle in his eye that rivals the first star announcing itself in a clear night sky. "For the lesson, we must indulge in physical contact. Is this acceptable to you?"

To be able to help Sionnach, I must comply. "Only whatever is necessary—for the lesson."

Without further preamble, Robber pulls my back flush to his all too familiar chest.

The leaf emblem on his tunic presses between my shoulder blades. His arms wind around me, hands clasped beneath my breasts. The Fae whispers against the shell of my ear. "Close your eyes. Ignite your spirit, then picture mine as radiance flowing from my body into yours. Call me without words."

I visualize my spirit as a radiant mist filled with flickering Veil sprites. As soon as I do, a similar lustrous cloud of tumbling wisps of aquamarine and citron rises in the air above Robber. Imagining the flow of a hearth fire's heat that first seeps into skin before warming to the bone, I pull Robber's spirit into mine.

The sensation is overpowering. We're embroiled in an ethereal waltz, gliding effortlessly through the trees with twirls and spins. His spirit wraps around and through mine. We are not separate, but a new concoction of esoteric brilliance. Robber fills me with joy and belonging. The Fae within me recognizes and welcomes a kindred essence.

Instead of words, wonderings waft into me from Robber.

What will you have of me?

I answer him in kind.

How do I grant the gift of the Veil and transformation to a mortal?

Our waltz slows as images of the Veil blast through my mind.

Push these visions into my spirit, dear Eala.

I do as Robber asks. Like a spool unrolling its thread, my sense of the Veil streams from my spirit into his.

Perfection, my darling.

Next, I summon memories of Sion turning into a fox: the wispy cloud that surrounds his transformation and him scratching with complaints about the itch. Like blowing the fluff from a flower, I send everything to Robber Bright.

Your gifts for the fox are as wondrous as you, Eala Duir. Now, what will you give me?

This time, delicate energy switches direction, and honeyed words pour into my mind.

What blaze shall be roused by a first kiss? Does the heart quiver? The breath stall? Oh, blessed heat. Fire ignited from briefest contact. Not flames to destroy but enliven. Not to burn but consume with sensual hunger. Desire be awakened by one forbidden touch.

Desire does indeed flood my veins. My breasts become heavy, yearning to feel Robber Bright's hands upon them.

This fervid tongue yearns to savor the ambrosia of your pleasure.

A single bead of liquid heat escapes the corner of my lips, trickling down my neck, then between aching breasts, and over my belly until it seats itself between my thighs. There the drop pulses, growing larger and larger with each beat, its heat stroking my pussy like a lover's burning tongue. The force of my need coaxes slick juices to spill across my skin.

With urgent rapture, my flesh shall worship the pathways of your passion 'til those who were two become one.

Robber's spirt begins to shift from wisp to something more substantial as it streams around me. My essence feels naked, every inch of my body sparking with desperation for his touch. An impressive arousal searches for an eager seat. I open my legs, guiding his hands to my wanting breasts. I moan when the ring on his finger scrapes across the tender flesh of my nipples. Hungry for pleasure, I bend forward and fit my ass to his length, encouraging his gossamer form to take me hard and fast.

Your desire is also mine, my darling.

My darling.

The term of endearment screams through my mind, instantly shattering my lust blindness. I am not Robber Bright's *darling*.

Like a rubber band pulled too far until it snaps, I'm fully back in my body. To my dismay, there is a very real dick pressing against my thankfully clothed ass. I spin and smack Robber across the face. I'm relieved to see he's still covered in tunic and britches.

"You bastard." My face burns with the anger and embarrassment that I was susceptible to his unscrupulous advance. He twisted my desire to understand Fae powers into desire for him. I didn't armor myself enough with words when we agreed on a lesson. Robber Bright isn't morally gray, he's moral sludge. If he's the rule and not the exception, I have serious doubts I can handle Tír na nÓg.

There's some satisfaction that instead of his usual smugness, Robber Bright is discomfited. "I did nothing but allow my spirit to answer your desire. There is no shame in wanting. It is the fulfillment of a sacred trust."

I'm breathing hard enough to hurt. "My desire. Bullshit. You acted on *your* desire. You've been putting moves on me since you showed up on my doorstep." I stab a finger at him. "Let me make this abundantly clear, Robber Bright. I do not desire you. Whatever tricks you're using to manipulate me, they stop now."

"Not desire me?" He has the audacity to look amused. "Lies told to oneself are often the most powerful."

Fury chokes my words. "If you continue to disrespect me and my wishes, our lessons are finished." I must choose my words to convey strength in our obvious imbalance of power. The fact remains that Robber Bright holds answers to many burning questions about my Faerie self. As much as I'm inclined to fire him as my tutor, I agreed to these lessons as a caveat in my bargain with Finnbheara. If I break the rules of our deal, then so can he. That is a gamble I will not risk.

When Robber's grin widens, I change tactics. "I'm certain the king will be eager for every detail of our lessons. Especially your overstepping." My threat may be empty since the Fae monarch's recognition of physical boundaries may be as fluid as Robber Bright's.

His expression becomes more circumspect. Good. The ass didn't consider I'd rat him out to the boss. "How will the king react, I wonder, when he learns you tried to stick your dick in his *treasure*?"

Robber clenches his teeth enough to cause a tick in his jaw. I've hit a nerve. Hopefully one sensitive enough for him to keep his hands off me.

"Not favorably."

"Exactly," I say, forcing confidence I don't feel into my voice. What the hell is up with these Faeries and their apparent lust for me? Is lust Finnbheara's intention behind calling me his treasure and the reason he gifted me a dragon with the name of a Faerie queen? Is Robber Bright trying to screw me to screw the king?

One thing I am damn sure of is I need to get away from here and back to Sion.

"Cara," I call, praying she comes. To my delight and relief, my currently tiny *péist síoda* flutters down from the treetops and unfurls to her horsey size. I climb a low boulder and maneuver into the saddle without help. I'm enchanted anew by the foreign texture of her scales and hidden wings.

Pulling the reins to the side like I've seen in movies, I angle her to face Robber Bright. "How do I tell her to take me home?"

"This is your home," he argues. "You are safest within our king's domain."

I flash on the distress the Host of a Thousand Wings demonstrated at the cottage but push past it. "Not without Sionnach."

Robber steps up to Cara and takes hold of the strap around her chest. His eyes hold wildness I haven't seen before. Instead of muddy amber, they glow like a yellow moon. "Here is a truth you must hear, Eala. You are most safe with me, my darling, not the king nor the fox. It's time for you to accept this path. Your spirit tells you so. Why do you deny it?"

I glare at him. "I do not deny this is all a game, a sport to you." I picture the scar across his torso from Finnbheara. "Pretending you're helping me with the riddle to spite your king is just part of your deception. My spirit doesn't give a damn about you. You're nothing but Finnbheara's servant assigned to me. Help us or don't, but don't kid yourself into thinking I'll ever give into your delusion."

My resistance rattles the Faerie. His Adam's apple bobs. Per our bargain to participate in his lessons, I can request help from him. There is so much I need to know, but at the moment, all I want to do is get away from him. Even though it's tempting to jump down and take a sip of the dragon speak potion, I decide to heed Robber's warning about my readiness to ingest Faerie spells. I rephrase my earlier question into a clear direction. "I request you tell me what to say to Cara to take me home."

Slowly, he removes his grasp on my dragon and speaks in the strange language he used earlier. I mimic the phrase, and her wings sprout and spin. When I drink in a stuttering breath, she cranes her head around to rub my leg with her snout in a reassuring stroke. After a loud dragon's cry to warn the clouds of our approach, we rise for a brief moment before Cara surges forward.

As Robber Bright stands alone in the center of the Gem Kissed Forest, Cara and I fly.

CHAPTER 18
THE SILVER SHIP

My fecking hair is plastered to my neck from the sea spray. In this walk to the cliffs, I've ventured farther from my cottage than I intended. My wretched bad leg is aching something fierce. Eejit me hoped after being free of the soulfall, the old wound would magic away. I suppose the past is always with you no matter how far and fast you try to run from it.

A particularly ornery finger of wind circles me like a beast scenting prey just before a gust knocks me off the path. My temples throb from the overabundance of noise in my head about fucking Faeries and the task Eala and me have been put to. Is there an alternative for Eala to grasp her Fae reality without being swept off by Robber Bright whenever he has an itch to scratch? I don't trust that Faerie fool. Granted, my experience with women is limited, but anyone with at least one good eye can see the fiend has designs on Eala.

As much as I'd love to run from Robber and Finn, Eala is right. The only way forward is to kick open any yellowjacket's nest before us and pray we can manage the stings. Eala learning about her Fae side is a necessary part of the journey. I make a mental promise to stop being a belligerent ballbag about the obligatory time with Robber Bright.

Out of nowhere, static spikes through the fog. The charge slaps me in the face, running down my neck and arms. Spice against skin. It tingles with a bit of a burn, but no pain to speak of. There's a strange red peppery reflection bouncing off me. A slash of ruby in an oncoming sunset would be a logical source of the color, but it's early in the day. Only a drab sky with tinges of slate and blue-gray rise over the sea.

As quick as it came, the odd buzz is gone, leaving me feeling like I've gone a few rounds with the village bully. I lean against a long-neglected fence post to catch my breath. In the field beyond, none of the sheep show distress or any sign of a strange happening. The dimwitted flock has no intention of wandering away from their supper.

Darker suspicions bite me in the arse. If this jolt is Robber Bright having a go at me, Fae or not, we're going to exchange more than words. I plow forward. Anger is effective fuel even when you're sloppy wet, and your weary bones prefer you jump off the cliff rather than walk another mile.

As soon as I'm through my gate, which could use a new coat of paint if I'm ever granted leisure to work my place again, I see my darling. Eala sits with her back against the door to the cottage, knees pulled to her chin, staring over the fields. Something's off about the way she's wound up in a knot. I'll kill Robber Bright if he's harmed her body or soul.

The gate gets away from me and bangs like a gunshot against its post. Eala's on her feet and running at me before I can say a prayer. Five steps and she slams into me.

"I was half a second from searching the cliffs for you." She dots my damp face with kisses.

If I could suspend time and just hold this woman in my arms, I'd be gloriously happy. Fate has decided not to offer us such simplicity.

I hold her at arm's length. "Are you grand? Has the foul Fae upset you?"

Eala presses her face into my shoulder and starts to sob. I'll roast Robber Bright's bollocks if he's harmed her. I hurry her into the cottage as a brilliant lashing takes over the sky.

Once inside, she leans against the door and sets her hands on my shoulders. Her gaze bores into me. "You know that body, soul, and spirit, I love you, Sionnach."

I run my hands along her arms until my hands rest on her shoulders.

"It's the same for me, Eala, and it always will be no matter what future's coming for us."

She touches her forehead to mine. "When you stormed off, I was afraid you'd finally hit your limit with the entire boatload of shit that comes with whatever part of me is Fae."

I rub my nose against hers, disturbing the raindrop lingering there. "It doesn't matter to me if you're Fae or a fecking mermaid, I love every bit of you."

I softly brush my lips against hers and whisper against them. "*Anamchara*. My darling *anamchara*." Twining a hunk of her wet swan feather hair around my hand, I tilt her head back and part her lips with mine. As if we've no care about eclipses or hawthorn trees, I swipe my tongue over her teeth, then visit every bit of her mouth. She purrs against my attention and returns the favor. I don't care if this is our twentieth kiss or our hundredth, it's as sweet and delicious as the first. Every kiss with Eala deepens the connection between us.

"My jeans are soaked," she murmurs.

I don't know if she's referring to the dousing from the rain or the rise of her desire. Either way, I peel off her clothes and then mine. She jumps up into my arms and wraps her legs around my middle. Despite weariness from my clifftop trek, I hold her flush against me and walk us to the bed.

We make love with slow generosity, taking turns gifting each other with velvet kisses. Mouths brush flesh, pausing wherever a beating heart presses against lips. I draw fingertips across her creamy skin. My touch dabs each golden freckle, enjoying every inch of this beautiful woman especially places that in my haste, I've not taken the time to know well.

As we climb toward the peak of pleasure, our bodies feel alight with the radiance of wanting as if we've been painted by a brush dipped in firelight. When I enter her, we linger in the blissful state of becoming a single entity, fate-to-fate, love-to-love. We each soar and crash in our own time and then melt into the arms of a well-earned slumber.

Eala braces her head on a bent arm as she stares at me.

"How long have you been watching?" I say, squeezing her leg between mine.

"Never long enough," she says with a lazy smile before dropping onto her pillow.

I nuzzle her neck. "Why didn't you wake me? We're off soon, yeah?"

Her focus strays to the window. "We've still got a few hours before dark, and six days left to finish our noble quest."

I run my hand over her belly to her hip. "Good." It's these rare intimate moments I wish could stretch into days, weeks, a lifetime.

She lays her hand on mine. "Sionnach, which afterlife did you plan to choose…before I came to you?"

I pull back to look at her. "There's a bit of a tough question. Heaven, I suppose."

"But after the soulfall, you followed me to Tír na nÓg."

I heave a chest-lifting sigh. "And here I am, doing everything in my power to do it again. It's the way of things, love. Where you go, I go."

Her fingers trickle across my chest, stopping to twirl through the mat of hair she claims to be fond of.

"You've watched me since I was born." She *humphs*. "Which is never not going to be unsettling. But when did you actually fall in love with me? Was it before I came to Ireland?"

This is a tricky thing. "Truth be told, I don't know when it began. I watched you grow in wit and smarts, but the way you care for folks, that's the heart that captured mine, love."

She slaps my chest. "You were a real jerk when we finally met."

I capture her hand and kiss it. "Aye. I was fighting my feelings for you and letting doubt win the day." I sit up against the headboard and pull Eala to me. "I was scared to the bone I wasn't gonna be what you wanted. My heart sang for you no matter what I did. There was always the chance yours wouldn't hear the song."

"Sion…" I don't like the serious edge to her voice. "You talked about running. I want you to know you do have that option. The deeper I'm entangled with the Faeries, the less I trust them when it comes to your safety. If Heaven is truly where you believe your soul will find peace, go to the Glade of Chimes and play your soulsong. I'll find a way to bargain with Finnbheara and give Máthair the same chance."

"That right there—you putting me first. It's your heart song to me. Soul songs have their place to be sure, but this music between us, *anamchara*, is the sweet sound I'll always choose whatever road it sends us down."

"No matter what the Fae throw at us?"

I raise my fists poised for a fight. "See, I'm ready for 'em."

She laughs and then returns to serious. "I have something for you then…" Eala guides me to turn onto my side away from her, then fits her body to mine. She strokes my hair. "…gifts you thought were lost. Do you trust me to give them back to you, no matter how strange the process feels?"

Heat rises quickly where our bodies touch. "Emmm…aye."

"Close your eyes. Find the place in your mind where you used to call the Veil and wait for me there."

Sensing my tension, Eala continues to run her fingers through my tangle of curls until I relax. My mind expands, reaching for the Veil. What I find instead is Eala encased in a shroud of flickering light. She drifts closer until the shimmer of her spirit flows into mine. It's a bit of a jolt at first, but then it feels as natural as the stretch of a muscle after a long sleep.

Eala whispers assurances that the Veil will answer to me. She raises my arm and asks me to call it. Sure enough, the glassy walls of the blessed passageway rise around us. The familiar feeling of connection awakens in every blazing cell.

My darling has done it. The Veil and I are joined once again. If spirits weep, mine does so with blinding joy.

Next, my mind fills with the image of my fox. I feel the haze of transformation fall over me like a net made from stardust. I see the world through the eyes of my other self, low to the ground and as keen as the slice of well-sharpened knife. A surge of confidence that what was lost is restored makes my spirit grow brighter.

Eala's melodic voice floats in the air around our spirits. "These gifts I have given you. No one, human or Fae, is granted power to alter them."

Her words continue as a song. Here, as our spirits comingle, my body loses substance, yet energy and awareness course through my senses. In this indefinable plane, Eala exists as a collection of minuscule points of golden light as if her endless freckles create their own luminescence. It's the Veil sprites dwelling within her that I'm seeing. I've witnessed these bright flickers flitting through the boughs of Faerie forests, but never so clearly within my love's glorious being.

She doesn't speak another word as her song shifts into the slow rhythm of slumber's deep breath. I work to match my breathing to hers. A great wave of diaphanous twilight studded with the spark of newborn stars crashes over us. It washes away the twining of our spirits until I am once again a man apart.

Flurries of warm dewdrops dance across my cheeks and press the underside of my lashes until I open my eyes. The world sloshes from side to side like the water in a bowl being roughly carried. A jolt of fear replaces the nauseating movement.

Half my body is cantilevered over the edge of the sea cliff where my feet recently trod. Quickly, I roll away from the edge. My heart feels set on bursting as if its daily allotment of hundred-thousand heartbeats has been squandered in a mere moment. I clutch my chest and bob my mouth open and shut, straining to breathe. Did the act of Eala's giving kill me?

I force out the stale breath stalled inside my lungs and then greedily inhale through my nose. The action jars my panic loose. I claw at the rough scrabble of the path, bracing myself to stand. Neither day nor night surrounds me, but a gloaming lighter than a true twilight splashes over cliffs and the stretch of sand at their base.

I stare across the sea at the delicate mist lingering above unsettled waters. Instead of watching the sun retreat in the west as it should, brightening clouds pile in layers on the horizon. These out of place harbingers of dawn wear the pale pink of a maid's first blush. Inside each are subtle golden streaks of infant lightning, biding time until their strength builds enough to sear a waiting sky. There's a cloying sweetness to the haze wafting from the sea as if the air is sewn with sugar.

Turning where I stand; I struggle to understand the world. East is where the sun bows to night. Dawn has no place here on the western shores. Once again, the day blows off its dependable sequence. A twilight washed over Eala and I as she held my spirit in her arms. Now that same twilight shifts backwards to gloaming heading into a misplaced dawn. I am alone, the solo witness to earth's altered rhythm and sway.

I've spent many years splitting my days between reality and the fantastic. I recognize this as a place leaning toward the latter. A whispered hiss breaks the silence. Below on the beach, a circle of sand shudders, then rotates into a slow-moving tawny whirlpool stained a rose color from the false dawn. Rising from its center is a woman.

Not a mortal woman.

Her body glimmers with faint otherworldly light. This is a goddess with the notes of a lament on her lips. Even though the distance from cliff to shore is vast and shouldn't allow me to see more than the vaguest outline, I clearly make out her form. Long slender fingers strum a lyre made with wood of a polished honey color. The sadness in its strings competes with the singer's voice.

From the tone of her melody, I expect a funeral procession to rise from the sands after her. This song is surely a lamentation for the lost. The goddess remains alone as the shifting sands beneath her still. The simple shift of sheer daffodil fabric she wears shines with a brilliance I can only bear to examine for a moment before having to shift my gaze. Ropes of delicate green glass gems drip down the front and back of her gown. Strands of the goddess's pearlescent hair are swept up in competing waves from nape and sides until they join at the crown of her head. When she turns as if called by the lighthouse's beacon, I see wisps of short, fine hairs dance around her face like a lacey veil from the sea breeze. The beauty of what are surely her exquisite features are shrouded from my sight.

A warning from many a tale comes to me.

Mortals do only look upon gods at their own peril.

Slowly, the goddess's attention is drawn to the sea. Her body flows toward the water as if she is part of the receding tide. She strums the same trio of notes three times and then heaves the lyre in an unnaturally high arc above the sea. It scrapes the underside of the clouds, tearing a gash in the gray. The instrument plummets into the water, leaving nothing behind but a foamy spray as pure white as a smiling star. The goddess stands before the waves, arms outstretched.

Through the rip she tore in the sky, a single beam of light breaks through, illuminating a circle like the yellow glow of candle flame on the water. As the goddess had risen from beneath the sands, the mast of a ship emerges from the ocean's depths at the bright spot touched by the goddess's lyre. Sails, deck, and hull swiftly follow, until a magnificent vessel made entirely of polished silver seats itself atop becalmed currents.

I shake my head to clear it, but the sight before me doesn't change. As clearly as I saw the goddess, I see every detail of the ship. Its masts are carved in the shape of mighty oaks, their bark and hollows crafted of purest silver. Everything about the craft is precious metal from the spun silver cloth of the sails to the planes of its hull overlayed with a lighter shade of silver-white fillagree in a design of leaves and flowers.

Awe flows through my blood.

The bow is decorated with the masterful copy of the hawthorn tree from the Hill of Tara, every bough brandished with silver leaf to set it shining even brighter than the rest of the glistening ship. This descendent of a Viking longship is encased within a corona as brilliant as that of the goddess. The vessel is an elegant sculpture better enshrined inside a glass bottle than claiming a berth on the sea.

The happenings are theatrics played out before me. The sand a stage. The sea a painted curtain being lowered to set the scene. A dream? A vision?

Whatever is unfolding, I'm its captive.

Manned with oarsman dressed in all white, a smaller boat from the silver ship rows toward the goddess. Prow cuts through the waterline, leaving a frothy wake as it approaches. Standing at the front of the ship, gaze locked on the goddess, is a man dressed, no surprise, in a silver-white tunic. He's tall with formidable muscles. His features are a blur, but waves of silvery hair stream down his back, tamed only by a circlet of thin woven metallic branches across his brow. I've no doubt he's Fae.

Finnbheara is my first thought. Who else would sail to the Connacht shores on a ship of such splendor? Anger at the sight of the Faerie king sloughs off the daze holding me in its grip.

But is it the king? Without seeing his face, I cannot be sure. Many of Finn's warriors are hewn in his likeness. Why not a captain of the king's ship?

The Fae captain leaps from the boat onto the shore and drops to a knee before the goddess. Their actions and words are as clear as if I stand on the shore beside them although neither acknowledges me.

"Why do you call upon me, Lady?" says the impressive fella in a voice as rich as dark ale.

She holds out a hand for him to kiss. "I was destined to bear a child to rule kingdoms, but I angered the gods. They cursed my womb to wither instead of thrive."

The man stands and cups the side of the goddess's face. "Foolish gods." He leans in to press a kiss to her lips.

Or where I suppose her lips to be. Their faces are still unclear.

"Most gracious lady, for what crime were you shunned?"

I expect a tale of curses and murder. Irish gods, Roman gods, Greek gods are all a bloody bunch.

The goddess rests her hand on his. "I have loved a mortal."

Now this is news. Couplings between humans and gods or Fae are on many a story menu. It's not usually the gods or goddesses who pay the price.

The Fae captain draws his lips across the goddess's forehead. "We will defy the gods and lie together on these sands this dawn. I shall give you a daughter." The captain removes one of his rings. Their gazes lock as he holds the goddess's hand in his and slides the golden circle onto her finger. He kisses the shining band, never taking his eyes off the face of the goddess. "When the girl tastes the first fruits of womanhood, put this ring on her finger to tell me she is ours. You will send her to me, and I will take her to wife. Together we shall rule."

Och, now we're getting to it. A bit of myth, a bit of incest, and you've got a tale. Which particular story being played out here doesn't come readily to mind.

The captain produces a gleaming white bedsheet edged in silver stitching that catches the rays of the sun now rising in the west. The fabric billows as he shakes it, settling it onto the sand. The goddess waves a hand. Every green glass jewel adorning her body collects into a delicate stream of green mist that flows around their impromptu bed. Once there, it transforms into a border of shining emeralds.

The Fae nods once to acknowledge the goddess's bejeweled acceptance of his offer. Stepping close to the goddess, he pulls the ties at the shoulders of her gown. The blazing daffodil shift puddles at her feet. She stands naked before him. He draws her into a kiss while lowering her onto the gemstone lined bedsheet.

I've no inkling to watch these fine folks take their pleasures, so I turn away.

The deep voice of the captain rolls up the cliffside to me. "Do not turn from your truth, Fox."

Fox.

Damn, I am known to these players.

Invisible hands grip the sides of my head and even though I fight it, they turn me toward the lovers.

It's then the face of the goddess becomes clear.

Eala.

The body of the man making love to her gives off a faint blood red sheen. As he raises his face to meet my gaze, the crimson cast disappears. His features swim and shift, taking no definite form for the length of a heartbeat until it's Finnbheara's face I see.

"Eala," I shout with all the wind in my lungs.

The goddess Eala, my Eala, tilts her head to where I stand on the sea cliffs, a beatific smile lighting her face. Her expression rips the guts from me. I raise a fist at the king with a promise of murder, but it isn't Finnbheara who meets my glare. The body now wears a sapphire shimmer, and Robber Bright sneers up at me while his body undulates like a serpent, seating himself deep into my *anamchara*.

"I'll tear the skin from your bones," I bellow, then my voice and body are consumed by the sands.

Instead of the beach and the cliffs, I've twisted my bedsheets into a tourniquet around my waist.

Eala seizes my shoulders and shakes. "Sion. Sionnach."

With fists clenched, I whip my head wildly from side to side to take in the room. Heart pounding, salt from sweat stings my eyes. I growl as if to scare off a demon.

Eala smacks me across the face. We both freeze, staring at one another. I'm in my own bed with my love beside me.

Between panting breaths, I manage to eke out, "You gave me back the Veil and the fox, but then there was…"

I grasp her upper arms. "Did you send the silver ship to me? The goddess? The man?"

"No, my love. After I returned your gifts, we slept."

I grab the edge of the sheet to wipe the sweat from my face and chest. "You slept. I had the worst sleeping terror of my two hundred years."

"I'm so sorry, love," says Eala in a tone to calm my raging mood. She rests her hand on my chest. My heart beats mightily enough to rattle her fingers. I look down to where her palm touches my skin and rip her hand away.

There, on her ring finger, is the captain's band of gold.

CHAPTER 19
THE VIKING

S ion pulls the ring off with such force I'm afraid my finger will go
with it.

"Where the hell did you get this?" He pinches it between his
thumb and pointer finger, holding it at arm's length like it's going to bite.

"You didn't put it there?" I stare at the beautiful ring. When I woke to
find the band of gold with delicate etchings of waves and flowers covering
it, I thought Sion had slipped it on my finger as part of his campaign for
me to marry him.

It would have worked.

After what we shared last night, and our ridiculously nebulous future,
my objections over becoming his wife feel as thin as a paper kite in a
storm. He is my soulmate. Adding the title of husband is another precious
layer of devotion between us, not a thing to worry about losing. I'm angry
that once again I let fear instead of joy take the lead when he proposed.

"I sure as shite did not." He untangles himself from the covers to cross
the room and slap the ring on the table. The blow is hard enough to make
my notes jump. As much as I admire the rear view of his ass and stocky,
muscled body, it's clear from his mood something is seriously wrong. He
hasn't been in such a furor since the night Pwyll was exorcised from Leap
Castle.

Sion pounds the floor back to the bedroom to grab clothes. He's puffing hard with curses strung between each breath as he sits on the edge of the bed to pull on boxer briefs and jeans.

I reach out to touch him but think better of it until he deescalates. "Are you going to tell me what the hell is going on with you?"

He leaps to his feet and jabs a finger toward the window where we can see the lighthouse in the distance. "I saw that Fae fucker, no two Fae—" He runs a hand through his hair. "Possibly three, taking you on the beach."

I narrow my eyes at him. "As in kidnapped? You saw me being taken by Fae?"

He furiously tugs at the curls covering his ears and strives to find his breath. "Not that kind of taken." He knocks a knuckle against his temple. "In the nightmare, I saw a glowing red bastard, Finnbheara, and Robber Bright fuck you on the sands below the cliffs."

I pull the covers to my chin. Disgust rockets through me at his coarse description, especially after Robber Bright's attempts in our last lesson. I think of the vivid daydreams I had growing up and understand whatever Sion dreamed would have every sensation of reality.

"Sion, I promise you it did not happen." This vision coupled with Robber's actions and accusation that I desire him weave an ominous warning through my mind. I considered telling Sion about Robber's indiscretion, but his current state ends any wavering inclination I have to share. It would be thoughtless to add to my love's distress.

His face flames, hands gesturing crazily. "Aye, but it's a clear message some Fae fucker wants it to happen." He pinches his own ring finger. "How else would the fancy band I saw as clear as day in the dream end up on your finger?" He rushes back to the table, slapping the surface so hard, half the papers flutter to the floor. "When I find out which one of them—" His hands grip the edge of a chairback as he drops his head. He's panting hard as if he'd run here from the sea cliffs. "Thinking of them touching you makes me burn to throw you down on this table and prove you're mine."

I slip out of bed, tossing on Sion's T-shirt that I've appropriated as a robe. "I'm coming behind you. Don't swing at me."

He huffs as I slide my hands over his shoulders and rest my head against his bare back.

"I would never...do you hear me...never sleep with Finnbheara or Robber Bright." I gently turn him to face me. "You are the last and only man I'll ever take to my bed. If you need to pound me in the kitchen as proof, have at it."

He deflates, dropping chin to chest. "My waking self knows you're mine alone, love." His body still thrums with anger as he lifts his head. "I'll not dishonor you by taking you when I've got such blazing anger on me."

I kiss the skin between his shoulder blades. "I appreciate that."

We stand in silence for long minutes. The stony tension in his body eases up.

"Eala, could it be that you returning the gifts that Finn took from me opened a road for he and his kind to drive me mad?"

I drop hard enough onto the wooden kitchen chair to sting my bottom. Never did I imagine that sharing my Faerie essence with Sion would expose him to other Fae. I'm afraid he's dead right to assume there was insidious motivation behind Robber's intrusion. What have I given the Faerie power to do?

Sion crouches in front of me, saying my name. It takes me a beat to parse out my suspicions and speculations to focus on him. At least my distress takes his down a couple notches.

"Did Finnbheara ever try to influence you in dreams or visions while you were involved with the soulfall?"

Sion shakes his head, curls wobbling.

I suck my bottom lip into my mouth and think aloud. "Maybe that's because he didn't have a stake in the game before." Lines across his brow deepen as I continue. "It does make sense the king would want to plant distractions in your mind. If you're drowning in jealousy, you aren't focusing on the riddle."

Sion grunts, considering my idea. He retrieves the fallen papers from the floor and sits in the chair next to me.

"Sending you a vision of me being with another man is the perfect way." I huff. "Believe me, I know." The images of Sion making love to Caity Byer in Rowan Bend are an unwelcome distraction in my head.

He leans on his forearm, peering at me. "Did he do the same to you?"

I fool with my hair. "Uh, no. It's just that after you told me about being intimate with Caity…"

Sion's hands curl into fists. His face flames, making his green glass eyes almost glow in contrast. "There's no comparison. I had to watch the men I hate more than the devil hisself, driving into your body like beasts while you wore a Christmas morning smile."

The combination of heat rolling off him, along with the disgusting picture he paints, has me sprinting for the bathroom to vomit. When I finish, Sion is next to me, one hand on my lower back. He fills a glass of water and after I drink, helps me sit on the edge of the mattress.

I take both his hands in mine. "We've certainly hit the low point whoever sent the dream and the ring intended." I kiss his knuckles. "Screw them. Let's show Finnbheara and Robber Bright their nasty little tricks are not going to take us down."

Sion's smile is weak, but at least it's there. He nods at my bare legs. "A challenge better met with your pants on."

I quickly shower before dressing in jeans and my last clean cable-knit sweater, a *heading to the hawthorn tree* uniform. Sion leans over the kitchen table, staring at the jumble of notes. To my relief, he's subdued but not depressed. He picks up the ring. "I can't believe I'm going to say this, but since you're convinced Robber Bright's actions were meant to help us—" He grunts. "In his twisted way, maybe the ring is not a malicious message but represents information we need."

"I prefer that theory, but I'm surprised he'd help at all after I pissed him off by cutting our last lesson short."

Sion grimaces. "Maybe Faeries have a conscience buried deep after all."

I snort. It seems Sion and I have traded places in our opinion of Robber Bright. If he knew why I ended our last lesson, my *anamchara's* focus would be on physical damage to the Faerie instead of accepting his help. "I'll need more conclusive evidence before I believe they acknowledge the word *remorse* exists."

Sion bounces the gold band in his palm. "I've told a lot of tales in my day, and rings play parts in many of them."

I stare at the golden ring. "Very true. Ring symbolism runs through folktales, myths, and legends."

"Look here," says Sion, pointing at a pair of lines in Finn's riddle. He watches me as I read.

Tales of old both true and told,
Will guide your quest to Sidhe.

"And here." He taps on another part of our enigmatic treasure map.

Prepare your hearts, the end you seek,
May end in sorrow, rift, and crown.

I look up at him. "What are you thinking?"

He breathes heavily. "The first bit, both true and told...I think we've been chasing history like I did for the soulfall, but we're not leaning hard enough into tales, fictions, stories connected to the items on the hawthorn. We should at least try to find any folktales with connections to the history no matter how slim they may be. It'd be just like the Fae to hide things in plain sight."

He circles his hands. "Ole Mick Ryan was more about the well and the geas, not the time in which it was happening. The lesson of the tale with accusations of gluttony was the purpose calling to us."

I rub thumbs over my fingertips, considering this. "So, we lucked out with our timing on his trip to the well?"

"Maybe, or maybe Robber Bright does have a stake in our success."

The scar across Robber's chest inflicted by Finnbheara springs to mind. "Robber Bright swears he's loyal to the king, but he did allude to unfortunate history between them."

Sion raises his eyebrows. "There it is. A Fae grudge. Powerful stuff. Something to keep in mind, especially with what gives me a sour gut about this next part." He pauses.

I can tell he's grinding his teeth. "Out with it, you curly headed bastard," I say in my best Sion accent imitation.

Thank goodness it pops his tension bubble enough for him to go on. "It's the crown bit."

"Yeah, Finnbheara flaunting his power."

Sion grimaces. "No, love. Not his crown, yours. The dread seeping through my bones tells me Finn sees a Faerie crown on your wondrous feathery head."

I recoil at the thought.

"Finnbheara's Treasure, Eala. We need to face the possibility he desires to make you his queen."

Robber Bright's warnings about the king come rushing back along with the fact my gifted dragon bore the name of a queen. I want to argue how preposterous Sion's notion is, but I can no longer ignore the festering fear. We are dealing with a mercurial narcissist. "Unless you want me to be sick again, let's not talk about this because it's never going to happen." Visions of being flung into a Faerie dungeon until I accept the king's hand leave an ugly stain on my thoughts. "Let's get to the hawthorn."

Even though we're already getting a late start on our Celtic day, Sion makes me eat a ham and cheese sandwich before we travel. By force of habit, I prepare to call the Veil but then stop. "Will you do the honors, my love?"

Sion looks like he swallowed his gum. "Nah, you go on."

"I promise it'll come to you." Worry lines blossom at the corners of his mouth and between his brows. I rest my back against his chest and pull his arms around me. "Let's go *fánaí*."

His breath pushes against my spine as the smell of soap bubbles wafts through the air. He's doing it. Sion's calling the Veil. His signature scent overpowers my own familiar lemongrass and spearmint awareness of our portal. The glass walls of his version of the Veil flicker in and out around us until, with a mighty slam, they trap us inside. Time and space flow around us like the wind off a late afternoon sea. Happiness fills me as Sion's thundering heartbeats play against my back. I did it. I restored the magic Finnbheara heartlessly stripped from him.

I spin in his arms to see his face. The smile I find there is so full of awe there's no force in this world or any other than could stop me from kissing it.

Sion whispers against my lips. "Thank you, *anamchara*. Thank you."

The Veil is part of us both again, our ally, our personal magic. There's a bump as we land next to the *Lia Fáil*, Stone of Destiny, on the Hill of Tara.

Sion's grip on my hand telegraphs nervous anticipation. He's searching for Robber Bright. After Sion's sexmare, I'm prepared to throw myself between the two. Luckily, we are alone on the hill. I cast a glance at the base of the hawthorn, half-expecting Robber to step through the Faerie door from Sidhe to our side.

"Let's get on with it before company comes," says Sion, jutting his chin toward the tree.

"Amen to that," I say and start to wave my hand near every branch I can reach. Nothing glows blue. A sinking feeling creeps over me. "If Finnbheara discovered Robber was making the clues we need glow blue, he might have killed the light."

Sion breathes loudly out his nose. "That thinking does us no good. We found the poleaxe well enough."

I fill my cheeks with air and pop my lips to let it out before starting in again on a branch I swear I've gone over thoroughly. This time, when I reach its thinnest end, the faintest glow of crimson rings the branch.

"Oof," I grunt when Sion throws himself hard against my body, knocking me out of the way. We roll onto the grass.

"Shit, Sion. I wasn't going to touch it."

He pulls me into his arms, showering my face with apology kisses between words. "I'm sorry, love. I saw the fecking red shine and lost my reason."

I cradle his face in my hands. "Next time, a 'look out' will do." I dot a kiss on his lips and stand, pulling him up with me. Returning to the branch where the circle of light shone, I search for a lingering glow. There's none.

Sion's grumble has sharp edges. "Could be Finn's pal Aodh is trying to fuck with us again since I grabbed up his chainmail rings fast enough."

I wave my hand near the branch, careful not to make contact to see if I can get the crimson circle to reappear.

Sion gently yet deliberately tugs me toward the other side of the trunk. "Please, love, let that bit of the tree alone unless you want my heart to burst from my chest."

"We need to know how far Aodh's influence stretches. If he's the one who screwed with the Veil and took us to Kilkenny, can he get to us..." My mind flashes back to Sion's description of his nightmare and the red glow around one of the men he saw me with. "...outside of dreams?"

He rakes a hand through his hair. "I've no answer."

"Before I left with Robber Bright for the last lesson, he and his host were edgy. I was stressed they were on alert over a threat that might be a danger to you."

Sion scowls. "And I'll bet your *teacher* didn't bother to explain the nature of his concern." He spits out the word *teacher* as if he's bitten into a rotten piece of fruit.

I try to ignore his souring mood while I attempt to find some clarity. "What if they could sense the presence of an enemy...like Aodh?" I meet his stormy gaze head on. "Maybe I can feel that too if I tune in better." I drop my chin to my chest. "I just don't know how." My lessons with Robber Bright are on hold for now as far as I'm concerned, but there are volumes filled with nothing but Faerie question marks I fear I'll never find the answers to.

Sionnach squints at the sky. "My darling, I don't want to brush aside your worries, but we'd best get on with our friend here. Keep faith what's worked will keep working." He nods at the hawthorn and holds his arms out to me. "Up you come. I'll lift you to reach higher."

With minimal effort, Sion heaves me up to ride on his shoulders.

"Mind the thorns, love," he reminds me as I thrust my hands between the ropy branches. Sion maneuvers on the uneven ground as I stretch as high as I can. We cover the entire side of the tree opposite the recent red circle with no results.

"Anything?" he asks.

"Not yet," I say, trying to mask the worry in my voice. "Do you need a break?"

He shakes his head. The swivel of his neck causes a tasty friction between my thighs. It successfully distracts me for a moment from my rising feeling of failure.

In the crook between the trunk and the beginning of a higher branch, I catch sight of a round object the size of a cantaloupe. The light of a waning, mortal moon backlights the sphere. There's no sapphire sheen, but I'm powerfully drawn to it. I say a silent prayer that it doesn't glow red when my touch nears.

I pinch the top of Sion's ear. "I need to get a little higher."

He grunts and then presses his hands under my feet. "Stand on my hands and brace yourself against the trunk. I'll raise you."

Out of nowhere, the fuzzy feeling of vertigo starts to rise. Sion feels my hesitation.

"It's no tower, love. There'll be no falling on my watch." He squeezes my calf.

His reassurance is all it takes to chase the fear away. Well, most of it. I lay my palms against the trunk, and he hoists me into the heart of the hawthorn. Sure enough, when the orb is almost in my grasp, a blue shimmer surrounds it. I snatch it from the branch without fanfare.

"Got it."

"Hold tight to it."

I squeal as Sion tosses me, his arms circling my body. An instant later, he guides my descent back to solid ground. I smack his shoulder. "I'm getting better with heights, but let's not push it, Fox."

I love that I can call him Fox again.

A curious look drifts across his features. In the next instant, a light fog surrounds him, and Sionnach becomes a *sionnach* once again. I swear the little red fox smiles before bracing his front paws on my leg to nip at my fingers.

The man returns a moment later, furiously scratching at his chest. "Wanted to give switching a go before time came to count on my wee beastie."

When I use my free hand to slide under his shirt to assist with the itches, Sion indulges in a slight moan of pleasure. "Do I tell you enough how grand it is to feel your hand against my skin, Swan?"

I lightly draw my nails down his chest once more before temptation sets in.

"What do you have there, my beauty?"

Another surge of happy relief warms me at Sion's much improved mood. I weigh the heft of the sphere in my hand. It's lighter than I expected. I knock on it. "I'm not sure. It sounds hollow." I hold it up to the moonlight. Its milky surface shines. "It looks like a giant pearl."

Sion takes it from me, examining its surface. "It could be the top of a scepter?"

"Do you think we might be hitting the history road again for some royal doings? Or maybe another magician?"

"Dunno. Could just as well be your giant pearl is part of a folktale. Any come to mind?"

I squint at the possible pearl. "None that feel like a lead. There's the one about two men collecting seaweed who happened to glimpse the Queen o' the Sea covered in her pearls. It was bad luck, and they both met untimely deaths."

He nods. "Aye. And there's a superstition pearls worn at a wedding symbolize tears and the sign of an unhappy marriage."

I run a finger over our pearl's smooth surface. "Let's hope we're both wrong." I gesture toward empty air where in moments we'll jump into the Veil and this pearl will soon whisk us off to God knows where. "After you. Don't forget Alfie."

Instead of affording us a view through a portal, Sion's Veil dumps us on the rocky shore of a *lough* with Alfie poised at the top of the sloped bank. I'll have to share my tricks of a Veil window and the *fánaí* tree's first-class seat instead of strapping the poor woody dear to a celestial roof rack. There's a collection of boulders near the water suitable for hiding behind, which we do. Although, what should we avoid—water or land?

"Any ideas?" I ask Sion.

His lips press together as he scans the *lough*. "Look," he points. "There's an island not far off. Maybe that's where we're meant to be." Just then, the rounded top of a full moon breaks over the horizon, and I know we're in a Veil pocket with its perpetually full moon.

Since I met Sion, my reality accepts two moons, one mortal and one in the Veil, neutral keepers of passing time. It's the third moon, Finnbheara's Faerie moon, that sings its dreaded song of our defeat.

The moon above us rises with unnatural speed. When it's halfway to its zenith, its vermeil glow splashes over the *lough*, and I muffle a cry. Beneath the waters of the *lough*, a thousand pearls the size of the one I hold in my hands come alive in a silvery light. The entire lake bottom appears to be covered in them.

"This is Lough Geal," Sion says in an ominous tone.

I move closer to him. "What's wrong with Lough Geal?"

Robálaí Geal.

"Please tell me you're not upset because in Irish, *Geal* is part of Robber Bright's name."

"No denying any mention of the eejit doesn't bring a smile to my face, but no, that's not why there's a stirring in my bones. The *lough* is called Bright Lake due to its bevy of precious pearls."

"They are stunning."

Suddenly, something casts a sinuous shadow over a swath of the pearly highway. It's as long as a freaking bus and just as thick. The way it whips and switches through the water is pure serpent.

My voice quavers. "Ireland's not supposed to have snakes, not even water ones."

"Not our Ireland, love. But the Ireland of myths had plenty. If my calculatin' is right and this is Lough Geal, that fella's the Carrabuncle of legend. It's said to lay eggs of pearl. They fall to the silt and give the *lough* its shiny floor." He winds a hand around my back. "You're looking at a serpent's clutch, love."

"Wow. There's a story to add to my collection." I hold our pearl against my chest. "Do we throw it back?"

Before he answers, the great head of the serpent bursts from the water. "Where is my child?" It hisses.

"Is it talking to us?" I whisper to Sion.

He shakes his head and bobs his chin at the shore. Standing at the water's edge is a massive man. The giant towers close to seven feet. Fae soldiers are little boys in comparison. His hair shines coppery in the moonlight. It flows down his back and over superhero-sized broad shoulders. A beard containing a pair of braids on either side trails to the middle of his chest. Even his nose is so long and sharp, he could use it as a knife. The man is clad in a pastiche of leather, metal, and fur. By his side, on the rocky shore, lay a maroon and teal shield with a definite Nordic design in its center, an ornately carved metal helm, and an axe begging for a head to separate from a body.

This fellow is Viking with a capital V. Instead of growling threats at the Carrabuncle, which I assume he's shown up to slay or conquer or some other form of Viking violence, the mighty man is wailing.

He drops to his hands and knees, bowing before the serpent. "I've no treasure to restore to you, my lord."

Sion and I both stare at the pearl and then each other.

The mournful keen of a woman rises from the island. "Husband, oh husband. Free me from my peril."

Her cries are drowned by the malevolent hiss of the water snake.

The Viking rises. Fists nearly the size of basketballs punch the sky. His voice roars across the water. "When I sail to you, the beast crushes my ship to splinters. When I try to swim to you, its teeth ravage my flesh until the outpouring of blood weakens me. When I swing my axe, the monster's hot breath melts blade and turns wood to ash."

"There is but one way to spare your wife from spending the rest of her days as my hostage," says the Carrabuncle, every word dripping with malice. "Return the child you have stolen."

"I have striven to do so, great one, to undo my crime, but the pearl is lost to me. Bid me perform any other task, I beg you."

The Viking stares across the *lough*, and his voice softens. "My wife is the blood coursing through my veins. She is the only bud of gentleness that blooms in the sorrowing garden of my violent life. Her loss is my death."

His words fragment my soul. The love I have for Sionnach is echoed in the man's utter devotion to his wife. Their separation is the very tragedy we long to prevent from happening to us.

"We have to give this to him, Sion."

I look to see tears running down his cheeks. He's heard it too, the devastation of a love torn apart by an insurmountable force.

He snuffles and wipes his nose with a sleeve. "We can't just walk up to that guy. He'll be swinging his axe the moment he sees the pearl." With as much stealth as possible, we slink over to Alfie. "Call your Veil with the nice screen door so we can do our figuring without an audience."

I summon the Veil. Once we're safely tucked inside, we don medieval peasant chic and stare out at the Viking. The Carrabuncle has stopped taunting him, but the man remains on the shore, weeping as he stares across to the island. The Viking's wife stands with her feet covered by the ripples of Lough Geal, long yellow hair whipping in the wind. Her keening rises to meet her husband's halfway across the expanse of water between them.

I'm not as enchanted with this pearl knowing it's the snake egg of a ruthless sea monster. "What are we going to do, Sion?"

He paces the narrow width of our cozy Veil tunnel then stops. "We've got to fool the poor fool."

"What? Roll the pearl over to him and hope it doesn't smash into a scrambled Carrabuncle egg before it gets there?"

"It's a bit of a daft idea, but here 'tis." He takes a deep breath as if he's about to break out in song.

For a moment, I drift back to Charleville Castle and the memory of Sion's beautiful singing voice. I yearn to hear the richness of that voice wrap me in a love song.

"Can you fire up your Veil sprites to give yourself a bit of a glow?"

I've grown so used to my internal lights; I barely notice them unless they're sending me warning stings. They ebb and flow like a constant current of warm melted butter through my body. I concentrate and give my passengers a little poke. Their smooth flutters skip a beat and then they flare hotter, setting my skin aglow.

"Aye," says Sion with a sigh.

"How do you know anyone outside the Veil can see them?"

He nods his head to the lake. "The Veil's out there too. Not our personal highway, but one of its special places held in time. Your magic should be fine."

My magic. I still don't think of my Fae tendencies as magic, but I suppose that's exactly what they are in mortal context. I can deny it all I want, but I am a Fae spirit within human form akin to Finnbheara and his like.

A muscle ticks in Sion's jaw. He's going to grind his teeth to nubs. "I saw you as a goddess in that bloody dream. I'm hoping the big man out there may see you as such." His gaze lands on Alfie. "We must refine a few details first. Off with those clothes."

"Are you nuts? Gods and goddesses may have no qualms about flaunting their ethereal bodies, but I'm not going to approach our friendly neighborhood Viking in the nude."

Sion digs into our stash of garments and selects a wad of white fabric. When he flaps it into shape, I see a watermarked satin shift dress with deep purple trim around the neck. It has a Greek or Roman vibe. A thin rope belt of the same deep hue as the trim with threads of gold running through it is tied around the middle.

"As much as I'm sure our berserker would enjoy such an eyeful, this frock is better suited to your entrance."

I shed my skirts, *leine*, and vest but keep my underthings on. "Why are there ancient dresses in your stash? No one in the soulfall went that far back."

He makes a few throat clearing rumbles. "New addition."

An ego-stinging image of Caity and him playing toga dress up scratches through my mind. I force down the little geyser of jealousy and let Sion ease the shift over my head. I wiggle into it, then stare at the cloth slippers on my feet. "Unless you have some kicky gladiator sandals in your new acquisitions, I think barefoot is the way to go."

"Aye," he says, frowning at me.

"What? I'm not goddess material?"

His frown deepens. "Too much so. You may be such to me, but it pains me to offer you up looking as heart-bursting beautiful as this to any other man."

Resting my hands on either side of his neck, I brush my lips against his ear. "Yours is the only heart that matters to me."

The desperation in his answering kiss frightens me. "We're going to succeed, Sionnach, and solve the riddle. Once we've collected all the pieces, I know that together we will best Finnbheara."

He nods but says nothing. I wish I could do or say something to ease the doubt festering in him.

"Do I just show up, glow, and hand him the snake egg?" It feels too simple and dangerous. I need to play the part of a poised goddess, but I feel like a kid who wants to hide under the bed.

"We need to convince Mr. V. that he's having a vision." He scratches at his curls.

I think of the dream flashes I had for so many years. There was always a strange gauzy feeling that preceded those moments and the faraway sound of a sustained note.

"I...I think I need to hum or sing to get his attention."

Sion's expression brightens. "Brilliant. And when you do speak, turn the words into a song. Adding that bit of a shine from your wee sprites should help enchant our fine Viking as well."

"What should I say or sing?"

He gives me a lopsided smile. "You speak the language of story, Eala bán. Use your gift to dazzle him."

The way my insides writhe, I feel like I swallowed the damn Carrabuncle. "If it doesn't work, and he comes at me with that wicked-looking axe..."

Sion takes both my hands. "The Veil and I will be ready to pull you free of yon broken soul."

I may loathe Robber Bright, but I am grateful for his help in giving Sion back his bits of magic.

He hesitates as his gaze locks on the weeping Viking. "Losing his love shattered the brute from stone into a drooping willow branch. There go I if we are ever parted. I pity and fear his pain."

I rub my thumbs across his cheekbones. "Then I'll sing the best damn fake goddess song that's ever been heard." Bringing his hands to my lips, I kiss them, then retrieve the serpent's pearl from the ground.

Sion and I leave the Veil. We are poised between great tree roots trailing onto the powdery dirt of the lough's shore. He kisses my cheek and ducks behind a tree.

I wrack my brain for a song with a pearl. There was one Máthair would sing, but it eludes me. It was about a forgiven thief and pearl restored. I'll just have to wing it. But first, the Veil sprites.

I sink my nails into the bark of the tree to hold myself to the spot, watching Eala. I am the fool, not the weeping giant on the shore, for sending half my heart within the reach of the water snake. My fingertips tingle as I begin to call the Veil and reclaim Eala before the Viking and Carrabuncle become aware of her.

The single sound of a breaking heart stops me. Across the *lough* on the island covered with rocks and roots, the Viking's wife calls her husband's name. In her cry, I hear the bond between them, a life bond, an eternal bond. The beast gloats at their separation, but they are not apart. In life or in death, they are one.

That is a bond I know well for Eala and I share it.

If we can give the gift of reconciliation to the Viking and his wife, I know in my soul it will carry Eala and me within sight of our victory.

So, I embrace stillness, my gaze locked on my *anamchara*.

Within the shadow cast by trees upon the shore, there is the faintest hint of light. As it grows in intensity, breath is stolen from my lungs. Across her face, neck, arms, and legs, Eala wears a lacework of golden brilliance. Patterns of triskeles, Celtic knots, and myriad symbols lost to time cover her pale skin like tattoos of candleflame. Even the air around Eala softly flickers with her incandescence.

My goddess indeed.

The pearl in her hands brightens in concert with its brethren beneath the waters of the *lough*. The Viking has not yet seen her. Eala's step falters, and I know she's afraid. Once I thought her a weakling, but in truth, what I saw was only a shell of fear primed to crack and allow the birth of one of the bravest souls to walk the earth.

My love will see this done.

As soft as the night breeze, Eala begins her song. Its first note meanders up and down the scale like a chant.

In one forceful swipe, the Viking lifts his axe to face this intrusion on his solitary misery.

Eala doesn't hesitate, but her progress is cautious, keeping distance enough for a rescue. I wait for the words of a story to join the notes, but there is no story. She sings a poem.

"Fasten your hair with a golden pin,
And bind up every wandering tress.
I bade my heart build these poor rhymes:
It worked at them, day out, day in,
Building a sorrowful loveliness
Out of the battles of old time.
You need but life a pearl-pale hand,
And bind up your long hair and sigh;
And all men's hearts must burn and beat;
And candle-like foam on dim sand,
And stars climbing the dew-dropping sky,
Live but to light your passing feet."

It's the perfect choice. These words of W.B. Yeats connect with the pearl in her hand and the night to vanquish a beast. Her visage and song mesmerize the Viking. Eala waits for him to speak, but he's struck dumb.

Eala continues in her singsong voice. "The steadfastness of your love has undone the crime of your theft. I return to you that which another mourns. Give back what you have taken, and you shall be rewarded in kind."

Damn, she's good. The woman should be writing poetry, not just speaking it.

With tentative steps, Eala approaches the Viking. She offers him the pearl.

Reverently, he accepts it. "Humbly do I take this from you, Lady."

Eala nods, every bit the goddess. "Reclaim your lover from the beast before you." I swear she's floating on a cushion of air as she begins to back away from the Viking. He watches her, reeling slightly from his supernatural encounter.

Behind him, the lake begins to boil. Rearing to the height of the tallest tree on the shore, the Carrabuncle roars as it arches out of the water. A fire within its gullet makes its fangs glow orange. It's a massive terror.

The scream of the Viking's wife slices through the night as the beast coils, preparing to retrieve its egg.

"Eala," I holler, but she's frozen on the shore deadly close to the ugly that's set to explode on Lough Geal.

The Viking spins so quickly, the pearl egg falls from his hands and shatters on the rocky ground.

We are thoroughly fucked now.

"My child!" The Carrabuncle's bellow shakes the ground. Its thrashing body sends wave after wave, drenching the silty shore.

I tear down the bank to Eala. Panic clouds my focus, and the Veil wobbles out of my reach. It must be a trick of my fear, but it looks like Eala is moving toward the water not away from it.

"Eala, no." My words might as well be swallowed into the belly of the beast for no one pays me any mind.

The massive water snake prepares to strike. Eala is so close behind the Viking, she's sure to be swallowed with him. This can't be the way things end. We were here to right a wrong, not get sucked into the fate of another.

The Carrabuncle's long neck moves whiplike, launching its attack on the Viking. Its dripping necklace of lakeweed flares beneath its jaws. Thank the heavens, Eala stops a handful of paces behind the big man as he slings back an arm, preparing to throw his axe at the beast.

As the weapon leaves his hands, Eala flings her arms toward it, crying out, "*Scian a shá i gcroí beithíoch.*"

At her words, the axe catches flame, blazing through the night sky until it plunges straight into the heart of the Carrabuncle as Eala commanded. The dying wail of the beast batters my eardrums, and I drop to my knees. Ahead of me, Eala is crumpled on the ground. I crawl the last few feet to gather her in my arms.

The body of the dying serpent slaps the surface of the water, covering the island with a brutal wave. I watch the Viking's wife cling to the roots of a tree to avoid being washed into the *lough.*

With a final shudder, the beast finally stills. The lakeweed that adorned its thick neck floats to the surface and is carried away by decreasing ripples. In the same moment, every pearl covering the bottom of the *lough* flares once, sending up radiant blue beams to meet the full moon until their light is no more.

The Carrabuncle and her children are gone.

The Viking whirls toward Eala, palms pressed together in thanks. When he finds her limp in my arms, murderous eyes stretch wide. The man's blood is up. He thinks I've killed the goddess who changed his fortune.

Just then, his wife's call beckons to the Viking across the water. I seize the moment of distraction to find my wits and call the Veil to us. The last thing I see before walls like the inside of a crystal blink into shape around us is the Viking diving into Lough Geal to reunite with his *anamchara*.

Once in the Veil, Eala's eyes flutter open as I hold her. The lacey patterns of light she wears across her skin fade. Wild-eyed, my dear one sinks her nails into my arms and frantically takes in her surroundings.

"Whist, love. We're in the Veil. You're safe."

She sits up. "Did the Viking save his wife?"

I kiss her brow. "That honor, my darling goddess, belongs to you."

Eala yanks out the star pendant. Sure enough, the fifth point has sharpened. She holds it to her lips and kisses it, then lays it against mine so I do the same. "We're almost finished." Her body slumps back against mine.

"Are we going to talk about the flaming axe in the room?" I say, rocking her gently.

"Let's go home first." She brushes her feet to rid them of pebbles. "I need fuzzy socks and a whiskey."

I brush a strand of hair behind her ear. "One stop before then, love."

CHAPTER 20
THE SOMETIMES BEACH

Thank Saint anyone for jeans and hearty Irish wool sweaters. After my stint as a goddess, I'm chilled to the bone despite the Veil's pleasant temperature. It's grounding for me when Sion and I reset to the modern clothes I'm used to. Although, I'd be lying not to admit he is rather dashing in period costume.

After teaching Sion how to let Alfie ride along with us, we linger inside Sion's Veil next to the *fánaí* tree as we pull on sneakers. My feet could use a good wash and soak after the rocky shore of Lough Geal. It's worth this discomfort to have all five star points as sharp as the gorse spine I inadvertently touched behind the cottage. I can't wait to get home and write up sticky notes to finally sort out an answer for Finnbheara's Fae forsaken riddle.

I pull my hair free of my collar and try to finger comb it into some semblance of anything but the fluffy white mass of its natural state.

Dispelling any hope we're heading somewhere warm and toasty, Sionnach tosses me the puffer vest I've appropriated from his wardrobe, while he shrugs into the bulky peacock jacket he wore when I first met him in the Blarney Castle Rock Close. I'd love to be in one of his T-shirts after sharing a sexy shower with him doing something boringly normal like making scrambled eggs with sweet onion and cheese. I do have to admit, it is a luxury being able to change outfits inside the Veil instead of behind bushes in the cold spring air.

We tuck our cache of clothes between Alfie's trunks. Sion opens his arms to me, and I gratefully sink against his deliciously defined chest. We embrace and enjoy the simple act of breathing without a legendary beast or ill-intentioned Faerie on our tail. It's a lovely peace.

Sion brushes his lips to my temple. "Did I mention how brilliant you were with our burly berserker? The poem, your voice...pure goddess."

I snuggle under his chin, grateful my Viking-saving goddess self seems to have replaced the promiscuous Eala goddess from his nightmare. "Did I mention it was my turn to nearly soil myself when that stinky water snake was set to enjoy us for supper?"

"The ole gal did have a reek of the devil about her." Sion stays quiet for a longer stretch than he's usually capable of as he gently rocks us. The quietude, the feel of the man I love, is bliss. I send a wish to the stars for this to be the norm in our forever instead of desperately clawing at fate to not rip us apart.

"I must ask, love. Did you call on ole Finn to send the fiery axe into the Carrabuncle's chest?" His voice is calm, but his rapid heartbeat gives away the fear behind the question. Sion's never said it aloud, but I know he worries about how my Faerie self will affect us.

Truth hits me like a flaming Viking axe. I've been holding back on truly delving into my Fae essence because of Sion's hatred of the Fae. I'm afraid he'll think differently of me.

"I did not." Pulling back, I gaze up at him. "But Sionnach, there's a nature lying within my spirit that will always be Fae. There are...abilities I sense, biding their time until I embrace them."

I swallow hard and continue. "I dug for the same feeling of power I felt when Finnbheara vanquished Olk." I lay a hand on my chest. "It came to me as the words I needed to slay the *lough* monster." I cup his cheek. "Are you okay with that?"

I'm more frightened than I was facing the Carrabuncle. Sion kisses my palm and smiles against it. "You'll know the answer soon enough."

Fantastic. He's going to make me stew over his opinion of my panic-induced display of Faerie power at Lough Geal. The tenderness in his voice and touch soothes me. There are enough things to stress me out in our situation. Sionnach's constancy doesn't belong on that list.

The Veil fades around us. Dawn splatters wisps of tangerine clouds across the sky as the sun waits offstage for its cue. Another of our Celtic days has come and gone. As soon as we finish with Sion's agenda, I'll need to confirm my calculation that Finn's eclipse is three of our mortal nights from now.

A blast of icy cold wind sets off a full body shiver. Sion rubs my arms as he turns me to face the sea. "You're very welcome to Ashleam Bay."

We're halfway up a cliff path overlooking the sea. The sight below is striking. A band of water outlining the curved bay is as green and clear as an emerald. Ireland gets its name *The Emerald Isle* from its rolling green land, but anyone witnessing this vibrancy would swear the bay is responsible for the title. Beyond the verdant swath, the water turns to a deep teal, a bright contrast to the blue-gray Atlantic further out.

"The color of the water is magical."

Sion takes my hand and leads me down the steep path toward the beach. "As it should be. The beach before us is a living myth."

I navigate a particularly slippery stretch of the path. "Tell me its story, Sionnach."

"Patience, love. We're almost there."

Yearning for scrambled eggs aside, the thought of snuggling with Sion in front of this beautiful bay while he whispers, or even better, sings a story in my ear is a tempting respite. Within the ruthlessness of Finnbheara's deadline, we've managed time for sex, which I thoroughly appreciate, but precious moments of actual romance have been sparse.

Hand in hand, we stroll along the white sands of Ashleam Bay. I swivel and wave a hand along the path we've made. "Look. Our footprints are the first of the day."

He twirls me under his arm. "Aye. And these sands may not see any others for seven years."

I glance around. "What do you mean? Should we not be here? Are we trespassing in a wildlife preserve?"

Sion guides me to a massive rock just off the water boasting the perfect scoop for a seat. He plants himself on it and pulls me onto his lap. "This beach here on Achill Island is a bit of a wonder. It only comes back once every seven years for a short time and then vanishes."

"What do you mean, vanishes?"

He shrugs. "There's no dry sand. Seaweed covers a stretch of muck. The sand once disappeared for twelve years, and some older stories say it's gone away for even longer." Sion breathes deeply. "It's a special place. Smell the tang of salt skipping along through the pure air."

I lean against him and close my eyes, taking in the briny scent and crisp kiss of the breeze.

"The Atlantic has always connected us. Me in Ireland and you over there in New York. I often wondered if drops of water I touched on these shores made it to where you once put your wee toes in the tide." He presses his cheek against mine, creating a tiny bead of heat where our cold skin meets. "I figure this beach is a marvel like us, Eala. Here one moment and gone the next. All three of us are visitors betwixt worlds."

I slip my hands into his cuffs. "True enough."

"So, we should take advantage of every moment it's here and we're here. Not waste a single breath."

I close my fingers around his wrists, savoring the steady beat of his pulse. "You're very philosophical this morning."

He eases me around to face him. "I'm very much in love this morning. I also believe since the beach is not a fixed point in time and space, an impermanent reality, ole Finn doesn't have eyes on us where we sit. I'd bet his Fae attention span pays no mind to someplace that's neither here nor there for long."

I chuckle. "You're saying the beach at Ashleam Bay is not a shiny enough object for a Fae king?"

"Aye," he says, his gaze lingering on mine. I take a moment to enjoy the brightness of his green glass eyes and the ever-constant circle of gold around the irises marking him as something special in the world. To me, it's the heart of this man that shines brightest. When I move in for a kiss, he meets me. Frosty lips are warmed by our tongues' sweet caresses. We breathe our warmth into each other as our kiss lazily stretches like the foamy caps washing across the shore.

When we finally part to greedily inhale more of the bay's morning ambrosia, I lay my ear against Sionnach's chest. I'll never tire of hearing his heartbeat.

"Sion?"

He rubs his nose and lips through my hair.

"Why are we hiding from Finnbheara?"

His heart ratchets up so quickly, I lift my head to look at him. His skin is flushed, and the dawn light sets the red undertones in his hair aflame. He's beautiful, my dear Irish boy.

"I asked you something before, but I didn't do it properly." Sion swaps to sit me where he sat on the rock, then drops to one knee before me.

Now my heart takes off like a shot. "Eala Duir, our love didn't follow a common course, but I know with every bit of my heart it's one that will never end. This sandy shore and our strange reality may be transient, but not us. Our love is strong enough to anchor a star."

I know what's coming, and this time I'm not afraid.

He takes my hands in his. "In addition to being my *anamchara* and forever love, will you accept this humble farmer's hand in marriage?"

I slide off the rock into his arms and pepper his stubbly cheeks with kisses. "In my heart, it was always yes, my darling fox." I draw my thumbs gently across his brows. "Married or not, losing you is something I will not do. I'm sorry I hesitated before."

We kiss with passion and promise, breathing not only heat but surety into each other. A kestrel pipes a series of short sharp notes, interrupting as it hovers in the sky above us. I stare up at the hooked beak and contrasting colors of its inner and outer wings. Apparently, we're a distraction from its dawn foraging, and it's not shy to let us know.

We both laugh as the bird glares at us in the way of imperious winged critters. Sion turns serious and shakes a finger at the bird. "If you're a crony of ole Finn's, fly to the fool and tell him to feck off."

The kestrel loses interest after the scolding and flies away.

Sion flings an arm at the bird, and then looks at me with a very mushy expression that's rapidly becoming my new favorite.

"Now back to business." I lean in to resume *shiftin'* with Sion, which he's informed me is Irish slang for making out.

"Soon enough, love." He reaches for my right hand and slips off my grandmother's silver ring that sent me on a journey to Ireland. *"Teacht orm,"* he says, reading the inscription and then slides it onto my left ring finger.

"Find me," I whisper, repeating the words in English.

"Find me," he answers, kissing the ring.

Sion pulls me to my feet, and we press our bodies together. "My da gave Ma this very ring when he asked her to be his wife."

"Then why does it say *find me?*"

He strokes my hair. "Oh, their's was not a smooth road. Ma's family was leaving County Clare for Dublin and city living. Da's roots were too deep to leave his home place to follow her, and her da didn't much like the Lohos so he'd never agree to the marriage. The two of them had what you might call a grand scheme to come together once she could make her way back to County Clare."

I lean into his touch. "A real Romeo and Juliet situation."

"Romeo, Juliet, and a Fae bastard. 'Twas in their time apart that she caught Finnbheara's eye." Sion grunts. "Let's not waste anymore wind on him today."

"Agreed."

A dog barks in the distance. It hustles off the path to the beach followed by a couple with two young kids.

Sion tucks my arm into his. "Come on, someday wife."

Wife.

Sion's called me his wife out of necessity on several of our jaunts, but now the word is filled with the richness of a destiny that was never on my radar. I planned to marry a steady, reliable, intellectual college professor. Instead, my husband is going to be a somewhat volatile, unpredictable time traveler. Laughter rolls out of me. It's the kind that catches you unawares and escalates without warning. I pat my chest and do my damnedest to squeeze in a breath or two.

Sion cocks his head, staring at me in confusion. "Funny, am I?"

"No," I manage between giggles. "I'm the funny one." I lean my head against his shoulder, still laughing like an idiot. "I was such a timid, focused person, yet here I am engaged to a stubborn, two-hundred-year-old man I haven't even known a month...who turns into a fox." A snort chimes in between my wheezes. "And I've never been surer of anything in my whole life."

My goofiness is contagious, and Sion begins to chuckle. "And I'm taking a woman to wife who, until recently, was afraid of climbing her front porch step and as close-minded as a churchman in a brothel."

We lean on each other, sharing tremors of jollity. "Which means..." I say, recovering a modicum of sanity. "...we're perfect for each other."

Sion catches his breath and holds my face in his hands. "Aye, Swan. That we are."

I love the little shock as his cold lips touch mine. Our kiss is brief, but indulgent none the less. Sion slings an arm over my shoulders. "We've a bit of a trip ahead of us."

"Where are we exactly?"

"North of Galway above Clew Bay. Since the Veil's off the clock, it's time to bus it home."

I squeeze his arm to stop. "Clew Bay, the hangout of Granuaile O'Malley, the pirate queen." I puff my cheeks. "If only we could spare a few hours to poke around here."

Sion pats my arm. "That time'll come, love."

I relish his confidence.

We reach the couple and their kids. "Mornin' to you," says the man.

"To you as well," says Sion as I say, "Hi."

"Came down to show the kids the beach before it's off again," says the woman.

The man smiles as he looks over the bay. "Who knows how long it'll bless us on this visit, eh?" He gestures to his children. "Wanted these 'uns to set eyes on it while they still believe in magic."

"Let's hope magic never leaves them," says Sion.

"That'd be grand," says the woman.

With mutual smiles, we part. For a woman who's just gotten engaged to the man of her literal dreams, my heart is heavy. I can picture Sionnach with our kids snuggled around him in front of the fireplace while he tells story after story from his repertoire. I'd add my own to the mix. We'd make a family of story lovers and storytellers.

After Robber Bright's news about us needing whatever the hell *beads of being* are to potentially have kids, a family is a magic I'm afraid Sion and I may never enjoy. Maybe when we're past riddles and threats, fate will give us the chance to find out.

Climbing the inhospitable path up to the green blanket of grass covering the cliff tops isn't conducive to talking. Once we catch our breath, Sionnach winds his arm around my back. "When do you want to wed love?"

I push my lips out, considering the answer, and Sion steals a kiss. "You're making it hard to concentrate, Fox."

He treats me to a full-blown smirk.

"Do we have to go the priest route?" His face answers the question even though I can tell he's trying to stay neutral. "Okay, that's a yes."

"I think Ma, Máthair to you, would want such."

"Lapsed Catholic guilt strikes again." I sigh. "Do you know a local priest near the cottage?"

"I think we can drum one up."

We head for the road. Sion's limp makes the going slow.

"Good because I want to get married before the eclipse."

He slows. "We're talking days then?"

I smile. "Hours would be better."

His arms reach around to grab my ass. He yanks me against his body. "Afraid I'll change my mind?"

I return the favor and give his solid bum a squeeze. "What I'm thinking is that our speculation about Finnbheara and his designs on me wearing any sort of Faerie crown could be null and void if we're married."

Sion's shoulders slump. "If only it were that easy, love. Our sacraments mean nil to the Fae."

"Well, they mean everything to me."

He nuzzles my neck. "Me too, Amerrrrican gal."

Watching him limp kills me. "You know, Fox. I've got quite a nest egg, as do you under your floorboards. Since Veil travel isn't possible during the day, what do you say we splurge, skip the bus, and hire a driver to take us home?"

There's a beat of hesitation but then his exhaustion wins. "I think my bed is speaking louder than my thriftiness."

I take the cell from my pocket to call for a car, hoping our jaunt through the Veil hasn't destroyed my chance to raise enough bars. Thank goodness there's a signal. I make a note to change my cellular plan to Ireland once I become Mrs. Loho before shaking my head. I doubt there's cell reception in Tír na nÓg.

Sion is snoring as soon as we cross the bridge from Achill Island to the mainland. Before I give over to sleep, I scroll on my phone to peek at our eclipse clock. My stomach drops.

We've lost time again. Shit. We never wasted a single Celtic day's travel. I press my knuckles to my forehead, except for our first night at the cottage and the ill-fated jaunt to Kilkenny Castle.

I can't beat myself up. Both those detours were before Robber showed me Finn's moon and our righteously unfair deadline.

No matter how hard I wish it were more, there's only one Celtic day left—tonight, a single mortal night, standing between now and the mortal night of Finn's eclipse.

Out the window, the Atlantic's ceiling of clouds can't decide if they're popcorn or marshmallows. If only I could read their message the way Máthair used to read the sky.

What the hell screwed with our one-to-one Celtic day to mortal night ratio? My lessons with Robber Bright, the Faerie king's whimsy, or…

Revulsion twists my gut. Is spiteful Finnbheara stealing time when Sion and I make love? That would quantify him as an insufferable voyeur.

Seriously, Eala.

As if the King of the Connacht Fae has nothing better to do than watch us for his salacious pleasure? Finnbheara notoriously has an endless supply of visitors to his royal bed, fulfilling every lascivious inclination.

The king must sense Sion and I are close to answering his riddle. Why did I ever trust that Robber Bright wasn't reporting every iota of his aid to us to Finnbheara?

One certainty wraps tight bands around my heart: The king will act as he pleases to thwart our success.

I kick myself for not paying closer attention. I've been counting down by Celtic days, never checking mortal dates. Where is Eala the over-organized, queen of spreadsheets, check boxes, and color coding?

I've been meticulous in my devotion to solving the riddle but not careful. It's vital for my sanity and any hope we have left to stay concentrated on what we still have.

Thank my grandmother's soda bread cookies, every point on Finnbheara's cursed star is sharp. Time's cut short for us to connect the dots on my detective board and answer the riddle, but it hasn't run out.

A need to share my panicked revelation has me leaning into Sion, but I stop myself. At my core, I am a logical person. That Eala reminds me there is absolutely nothing I can do to reclaim lost time.

I drop my head back against the seat and turn to stare at my fiancé. There are so few guaranteed moments of happiness left to me, I'd be a fool to squander a single one.

Sion's dimples deepen when he snores. It's damn adorable. I'm engaged to this amazing dimpled *fánaí*. My frisson of joy may be silly considering Sion and I were already eternally bound, but it's still a big deal.

News I always imagined sharing with my best friend.

Screw our vow of silence. Colleen would never forgive me if I got engaged and possibly married without telling her. At least I hope she still cares enough for this to matter. With a shaky finger, I hit her contact and hold the phone to my ear. It goes to message.

"Hey, Colleen. It's Eala. I wouldn't renege on my promise to give you space if it wasn't important. I've got great news. Sion and I just got engaged. I know you're still dealing with accepting us, but C, he is my person. I love him and the prospect of spending our lives together. We've decided on a quick wedding, which I hope you'll want to be a part of, but…" The tears come on fast and furious. It's hard to force out words. "… if you can't. I respect that. Love you."

To the sounds of Sion's heavy rattling breaths. I cry myself to sleep.

I jolt awake as the car bumps over the uneven lane, leading to the Loho cottage. Sion still sleeps like the dead. I shake him awake as we pull up to the wooden gate. After giving the driver a nice tip, we trudge along the wildflower bordered lane in our sleep-drunk state.

We're within spitting distance of the cottage when I clutch Sion's arm. Sitting on the tiny porch thigh to thigh, his arm around her shoulders, are Robber Bright and Colleen.

CHAPTER 21
THE PERIL

S ion stumbles at the sight of the unlikely pair. "What's the bastard up to now?" he growls quietly.

My thoughts mirror his. I can barely process Robber Bright sitting there in jeans and a navy blue, waffle-weave Henley unbuttoned to show a little triangle of dark blond chest hair. His long tresses are gathered into a sloppy man bun.

Colleen catches sight of us and leaps to her feet.

She closes the distance between us and smothers me in a hug. "I got your message. Congratulations." I'm crushed in her arms as she rocks us. "After so long, I was starting to think this was never going to happen."

Glaring at Robber Bright, Sion looks as ready to strike as the Carrabuncle.

Colleen releases me and transfers her full body slam to Sion. "A year ago, I would've been talking Eala out of her decision. I'm grateful I ended up staying in Ireland since then and got to know you, Sion." She steps back and beams at both of us.

Sion slides a *what the hell* glance my way. I meet it with equal confusion. "Lovely stuff, Colleen," he says. "Doesn't feel like a whole year."

She wobbles her head. "Technically, a little over a year since La and I landed here right before last Beltane."

I'm startled at Colleen's timeline. It's then I meet Robber Bright's triumphant gaze, and a sick realization washes over me. He's rewritten Colleen's life. I was naïve and downright stupid to believe if I crossed him, he wouldn't retaliate in some way. The scar across his chest proves the form Finnbheara's displeasure takes, but Robber's is more subtle. Of course, he wouldn't provoke the king by harming me outright. Instead, he's delivered an indirect blow that slices through me just as viciously by taking advantage of Colleen.

"I feel terrible for all those months I wasted being angry at you, Eala. I'm glad to be stronger and more together now." She gives me a crinkled smile. "It took being on my own to finally grow the hell up." She extends a hand to Robber Bright, who takes it, playing his role. "Thanks to Robin and his patience, I understand what a real partnership is."

Colleen wags a finger at us. "You two happened so fast, I never believed you were more than the *fast burn then kick them to the curb* flings I was addicted to. I'm glad to have been given the time to know you and Sion as a couple and be proved wrong."

I want to shake her out of this Robber Bright induced fantasy. Maybe I can meet her on a spirit level like I did with Sion and rip her away from the Fae's influence.

Robber Bright offers his hand to Sion. "It's grand to celebrate you."

He's replaced his formal Fae speech with a regular guy Irish accent. I want to call him out, but I'm scared of what it might do to Colleen. I grab his hand to shake since I can tell Sion has no intention of touching him unless it's to pop him in the jaw.

The moment our skin touches, I see flashes of silk dragons and the Gem Kissed Forest. I try to pull away, but his grip on my hand is firm. "It's lovely that Colleen enjoys such a good friend in you, Eala." I burn to scratch the self-satisfied grin off his face, especially when he extends his hand to Sion again.

My red-faced fiancé backs off. "I'll not be shaking your hand, Mr. Bright. Have a bit of a bug." He fakes a cough and glances at Colleen. "Sorry, I didn't stop you from hugging before. Hope you don't catch anything." He turns angry eyes on Robber.

Every time I think my life can't get any more bizarre, it manages to do just that. Colleen hooks her arm around my waist. "Shall we go inside and talk wedding? You said it's happening fast so we'd better get on it." My friend dots a kiss to my cheek. "Isn't it great we've both found our person, Eala?"

"Uh, now?" I stammer. "I mean..." I'm interrupted by a loud bleating cry from around the side of the house.

"Oh," says Colleen, giggling. "We brought you a goat. Engagement present." She turns to Sion. "Remember you said you were thinking of buying one or two to help trim the weeds?"

Sion is as flabbergasted as me by the extent of the Fae fabricated history. Robber takes the opportunity to smack him on the back. "Aye, our gift of a poor man's cow will make short work of your thistles."

The Fae deftly steps back when Sion whirls toward him with a murderous look. I quickly thread my arm through my fox's and clamp him to my side.

Robber aka Robin flashes a smile so loving at Colleen, I want to vomit. "Remember, we said this was a pop-in, love. I'm on duty soon, and we've been sitting here a bum-bruising long time waiting for the happy couple."

So, he's still playing the role of an upstanding member of the Garda.

Fake Robin continues. "And don't you have a girl's night with Acacia and the gang at the pub?"

Acacia, holy damn. She's in his Host of a Thousand Wings. How deeply mired is Colleen with the Fae?

My friend waves her hands. "Right, right. I'm just over the moon for you, La."

This is torture. Authentic Colleen should be off on her mission of self-discovery, instead, mind-addled Colleen is convinced she's the girlfriend of a deceitful Faerie.

It's my fault; therefore, my responsibility to fix things and get her away from him. How can I turn back time without damaging her mind? I send up a quick prayer to my old pal St. Augustine that today is a one-off and Colleen will still be Colleen once Robber's made his point by shocking us with his time-bending antics.

Sion, to his credit, isn't saying anything to escalate a bad situation. At least he's growing a healthy respect for the shitstorm the Fae can rain down on a whim.

"Wait for me in car, love." Robber leans in to give Colleen an anything but casual kiss.

It's unbearable to watch. I clench my fists, imagining other more salacious advantages he's taken with her.

Like a good little Fae puppet, she starts to walk toward the road where there definitely isn't a car parked.

As soon as Colleen is out of earshot. Sion rounds on Robber Bright. "What have you done to Eala's girl, you Fae villain?"

Robber Bright fades into his tunic and Fae speech. The leaf emblem on his chest is covered by an odd blur that reminds me of the annoying fuzzy patch that lingered in the corner of Máthair's clunker of a television screen before it gave out completely. "Not half as much as I'm tempted to enjoy." His grin holds all the trappings of repulsive ideas.

I join Sion for a two-pronged assault. "You un-do everything you've done to her, then back the hell off."

Robber Bright tilts his head. "I think not. She is dear to you, my darling; therefore, she is dear to me also."

"In a massively twisted way," says Sion raising his fists.

I push his hands down. "What do you want, Robber?"

His gaze bores into mine. "That is a lesson you've already learned, my darling." The Fae zeroes in on Sionnach. "As have you, fox. I taught you both." In a flash, he grabs my hands and frowns. "This is not the ring I gifted you."

With a feral roar, Sion lunges at Robber, who steps aside, pulling me with him. The lingering damage from the musket ball coupled with Sionnach's enraged momentum sends him sprawling onto the ground.

I shove my elbow into Robber's solarplexis then use my body to block Sion from the Faerie, terrified of what he might do to my soulmate. If my rudimentary skills set an axe on fire to kill a serpent, heaven knows what a soldier of Finnbheara has in his arsenal.

The turbulent, blue-tinted storm cloud carrying The Host of A Thousand Wings surges toward the cottage with mind-numbing speed. A fierce wind precedes them, whipping my hair violently enough to blind me. Dropping to the ground, I grope for Sion and brace myself against him.

In moments, we're surrounded by a hoard of agitated silk dragons, puffing balls of mulberry and orchid-colored smoke from their nostrils as they clack their teeth. Cara is not among them. Instead of the mishmash of clothing they wore last time, the company is now clothed in battle gear. Spears, swords, and bows stand at the ready, every sharp point aimed at us. Their armor is not the white gold of Finnbheara's guard, but a dark crimson.

The eyes of the *péist síoda,* Aillil, standing at the ready for his rider, are changed as well. They now shine charcoal with forked streaks of blood-red lightning flashing within.

More disturbing are the breastplates of the host. They no longer wear the leaf emblem of Finnbheara. A crest in the shape of a trio of flames on a shield of black now covers their armor. The high flame in the center bears a two-pronged curved tip. The shorter licks of fire on either side sport single tops as sharp as dagger points. Crimson liquid roils up through the center of each to set all three pinnacles aglow. The color matches the dark red sheen surrounding the chainmail rings as well as the deep smolder within the charred branches of the strange Veil tunnel that stole us to Kilkenny Castle.

The presence of fire has been circling us. Sion watched a blood red flare surround the captain in his dream before the man wore the faces of Robber and Finnbheara.

Fearful thoughts weave dark threads in my mind. Would Robber Bright kill to get at Finnbheara?

It seems the answer to the last question might be undeniably yes until Robber raises an arm decorated with a wide, black hammered metal band. The warriors stand down, but keep their stares pinned on us.

I grip Sion's arm. He's already stunned to silence by the scene around him. I hiss, "Don't say anything," in his ear. There's no doubt every one of these Faeries would jump on any excuse to kill Sion.

Robber Bright prowls around us with leonine strides, the emblem of flame blazing on his now clearly visible breastplate. The Fae's teeth gleam in the sun, as does the long dagger in his belt.

I stood up to the King of the Connacht Fae, I can stand up to this villain.

Robber shakes his head. Strands of hair fly free from his temporary bun to light upon his shoulders. "I still have many lessons to teach you, Eala Duir." His gaze locks on mine. "Such as how the price of time is paid by mortal sleep."

Fury pounds in my chest. He's so flippant, I'm tempted to punch him myself. Dammit, all we had to do was sleep for this robber to steal time.

Sion coils beside me. "What are you about, Faerie?"

Robber flashes an oily smile. "Has your lover not shared news of squandered days?"

Sion turns a cherry red face to me. "Eala?"

"We lost days again. I just figured it out in the car."

He sputters, switching a crazed stare between Robber and me.

"I'll explain as soon as he leaves," I say under my breath. "We still have time."

Robber Bright opens his arms to me. "I shan't be gone for long, dear Eala. When I return, our next lessons will take on a different...hue." He thumps a fist to the flame emblem on his chest.

I stand tall and wear the coldest expression I can muster. "You can't take me against my will for any more lessons."

He gives me his unnatural frozen stare, as if he's suspended in time. Finally, he speaks. "No, I cannot, but a will is a malleable thing, my darling. Motivated by so many different incentives." Robber flicks his wrist.

There's a yelp behind me. The host laughs with amusement at their leader's stroke of malice as a familiar red fox cowers at my feet. Robber Bright speaks in tones of sinister delight.

"We are The Hunt, Eala Duir."

Sionnach grunts as Robber rips him back into human form.

"Our prey is as varied as the flowers in a Faerie glade."

Within a shower of sparks, Colleen appears at Robber's side, looking up at him adoringly. A moment later, she's gone.

I hold my ground, forcing myself to look formidable when inside, I'm crumbling like a brittle flower pressed within the pages of a diary. "I will not go with you."

"Not yet, my darling," says Robber. "But soon enough. Thanks to my guidance, you will solve Finnbheara's riddle and enter the Fae realm." He stretches his arms wide to include his companions as he speaks. "Once there, our roads will converge when Eala Duir comes to *us*."

At the sound of Finnbheara's name, the host lets out a collective murmur of disgust.

My deceitful tutor flashes me a lascivious grin. "Of course, if you wish to bypass your king's circuitous requirements to enter the domain of Folk, there is always the golden ring I placed upon your finger, my goddess. It is your key to my door."

The flame emblems, Robber's hints about the ring, and his threats lead to one conclusion. This traitorous Faerie broke with the King of the Connacht Fae.

I don't miss his use of *us*. Is he claiming royalty now, or does the *us* mean the host? A knot forms between my ribs. Is the new sigil Robber's alone or do the flames coupled with *us* signify his allegiance to a different master? This Fae is the one who revealed to me that Finnbheara's kingdom is not the only realm in play.

Crimson flames

The horrifying picture of Aodh, prince of the underworld, that haunted me from my childhood storybook is as clear in my mind as the first time it chilled me to the depths of my soul. Could Robber be so consumed with revenge for Finnbheara's treatment of him that he'd turn to the king's enemy?

In a graceful arc, Robber Bright swings into Aillil's saddle. "When next we meet, our true lessons will begin, Eala darling."

His aquamarine eyes glow with an unnerving internal light. He leads the dragon until rider and mount are poised in front of me. Sion stumbles to his feet and plants himself at my back.

Robber sneers and flicks his wrist twice more. Sion transforms back into a fox, then within moments, he's once again a man. My soulmate's moans of anguish raise a look of satisfaction across his tormentor's face.

I expect the Fae and his treasonous host to sweep away after one last parting taunt or jab. Instead, Robber Bright leans over Aillil's neck to skewer me with a warning stare as he drones,

"Kingdom's strong may fall to shade,
Purged from light with bow and blade.
Misalliance takes its measure,
When this Robber steals the treasure."

He cackles with the hubris of a man who's just shared the cleverest words ever uttered.

The dragons unfurl their legion of wings as a deafening buzz assails our eardrums. They kick up dirt and pebbles as well as their usual cloud of mist. The music of dragon wings shifts into the receding thunder of a malevolent host.

Sion and I hide our eyes against each other's shoulders, then to my horror, he goes limp and collapses at my feet.

CHAPTER 22
THE NUMBER COMPLETE

No wicked itch rages across my skin. Instead, the aftermath of those merciless swaps between man and fox at the hands of Robber Bright thrusts me into blinding agony as if he's carved up every one of my muscles to serve to his dragons. Chaotic thoughts whirl through my head like a child's pinwheel caught in too strong a wind. I'm vaguely aware of Eala dragging my feeble frame through the cottage door. I struggle to speak words of reassurance to her, only to blather nonsensical syllables or mews of pain.

She wrestles my plagued bag of bones to the couch. Her touch, which in any other circumstance I'd crave, is excruciating. I attempt to nudge her away.

My love forces words through sobs. "What's happening to you? Sion, I don't know what to do."

I want to tell her a kindness would be to stab me through the heart. At least that'd be a faster death than being peeled apart from the inside.

My swan deserves a final kiss before I leave her to the mercy of her Fae destiny, but the darkness is coming for me too quickly. Her voice fades farther and farther away until I dissolve into a scalding well, deaf and blind. There is no Sionnach Loho. There is only the disintegration of what I once was.

Something filmy and cool glides over my skin. It wraps around me like a delicate robe of frost. Feather light touches brush my legs, back, chest, then caress my face. I'm afraid if I open my eyes, I'll be alone in the Glade of Chimes to choose the notes of my soulsong. As long as I do not give over to this sensation, Eala and I are not parted.

An insistent presence flows through me. Fear rides on my back that I'm being taken over by a force I have no strength to combat. With the next beat of my heart, familiarity chases off alarm. This gentle company is one I know. One I've felt before.

One I love.

I welcome Eala's essence within me. The beauty of the Veil permeates my closed lids with colors as vibrant as the first bloom of a yellow iris, the mellow green in a shallow pond, and every bewitching indigo shade claimed by a moonless sky. Faraway notes of a violin voice a promise of oncoming peace. My *anamchara* soothes my spirit. Barely perceptible vibrations trickle through the pain, chasing it from my battered body.

A jolt sends a shockwave through me, and I am the fox. He's still tormented from the brutal wrenching between forms. His whimpers differ from the moans of a man but are filled with the same misery.

Eala's healing spirit pours sweetly through my fox. Like the lacy tides on the beach where I asked her to be my wife, the pain recedes. The sensation of drifting through the Veil melts away as the notes of its healing melody fade.

I ache, but it's the weariness of muscles pushed to the limit, not ripped and beaten. The eyes of a fox take in the room. I'm home, held like a babe in the arms of my love. She gently strokes my ears, back, and even my tail, kissing the top of my furry head so very carefully.

"I think it'll be okay now if you want to try the change. If it's too painful, I'll take you straight into the Veil."

My fox climbs back into the skin of the man. I lie on the couch with my head in Eala's lap. She continues to run fingers lightly through my hair, making soft noises I recognize as a song my ma used to sing to me.

"Too-ra-loo-ra-loo-ral…"

When I absentmindedly raise my hands to scratch my chest, she laughs, then her expression crinkles.

"How bad is it, my love?" she croons.

I sit up, giving my neck a good scratch and test my arms and legs. For once, I wish the change from fox robbed the clothes from my bones to downgrade the itch where fabric touches skin. Since skipping between fox and man is nothing but Faerie illusion, I keep all my bits of clothes when hopping from one to the other. Only Fae cruelty such as Robber Bright's could inflict harm in both forms. "Nothing a hot soak in the tub and whiskey won't fix."

I wish I believed that. It'll help my body, but not my soul. Here I am again, even with the return of my own Fae gifts, a liability to Eala. She needs strength, and I'm no more than a bowling pin in Faerie sport.

She runs the back of her hand along the side of my face. "Fair warning. I didn't do it on purpose, but there's barely any brown left in your hair."

"Have I gone silver then?" I wouldn't be surprised if this latest ordeal added a few decades to my hide. When I stretch a curly strand until it's straight, I see it's the russet color I imagine my fox fur to be, like the hair across my chest.

Fatigue wrings me out. Dropping my head onto fists, I speak to the floor. "I'm sorry you had to put me back together…again." I sit up and take her hands. "It's me meant to protect you."

Eala gives my hands a shake. "Toss your ego outside, Sionnach Loho. You protect me in every way that matters. You believe in me. You keep me going when I want to hide under a toadstool. You write stories when I see nothing but white space on the page."

She threads her fingers into the hair behind my ears and pulls so hard it stings my scalp. Eala raises her voice to a scold. "We are parts of the same whole, dammit. Who the hell cares who is protecting who or how?"

I ease her hands free before I'm bald around the ears. "Are you yelling at a fella who just had his guts pulled apart?"

She falls against me, releasing bottled tears. Hiccups punctuate her sobs. "I didn't know if I could heal you. What if I'd made you worse?"

It's my turn to comfort her. I fold her onto my lap, wrapping my arms around her in a silent promise to never let go. "You were brilliant, love. Those instincts of yours are gold. You've every reason to trust the magic tossing about inside you." I kiss the shining tear that's decided to go no further than her cheek, then immediately dab my tongue for another taste to test my senses. The tiny bead has traded salt for sugar.

There's no time to temper my look of surprise before Eala catches it.

"What's wrong, Sion?"

I think of the sugary fog from the dream of the silver ship. Both the vision and now Eala's tears are infused with sweetness. Could it be this odd flavor swap is another part of her pretty Faerie package.

I catch another tear on the tip of my pinkie and hold it to her lips. "Tell me what you taste."

The oddness of my request distracts her from the weeping. She narrows her gaze, but curiosity gets the better of her. The point of her luscious pink tongue licks my finger. The contact against my skin distracts me massively from whatever's still aching. I'm confident the attentions of that tongue on other places would be a grand way to speed up my healing.

Eala smacks her pouty lips around the tear. "I taste a little salt." She tips her head against my shoulder to look me eye-to-eye. "Why? What did you taste?"

I'm not keen to delve into any comparison to that cursed dream, so I stick to the present. "Sweetness." I kiss her nose. "My icing sugar swan."

The way she squirms on my lap as she gets to her feet incites a flash of eagerness to explore the sugar index on other sweet parts of my fiancée.

I catch her arm when she heads for the kitchen table. "Give it to me with no soft landing, love, how many Celtic days do we have until Finn's fecking eclipse deadline?"

"Tonight is our last Celtic day to travel." Her voice catches. "The Faerie full moon is tomorrow night."

I sit with that for a moment while Eala goes about rewriting and rearranging notes. What's to say? We're at the mercy of Faeries.

My spine creaks as I stand, not letting me forget I've been to hell and back courtesy of Robber Bright. My swan's written each of the seven deadly sins on its own orange sticky note and lines them up in a column. Next, come notes with *Mick, Cathbad, Us, Red Hugh O'Donnell,* and *Viking.*

Eala chews on the pen and slowly faces me. "Can you forgive me for not keeping an eye on our days?"

I clutch her arms and force my seething rage deep in my belly; it won't help Eala any. "There's nothing to forgive. We don't know when the Faerie bastards stole our days. You coulda been tracking 'em like a storm off the sea, and they still might have changed as soon as you turned your back."

She drops her head on my shoulder. "I keep relearning the lesson of how *other* the Fae are."

I stroke her hair. "Beings of and not of this earth, love." Lifting her chin, I turn her to face the table. "No more talk of *them*. On we go." I won't be satisfied until I drive my fist between the eyes of Robber Bright or Finn hisself.

"Okay." Eala sucks in a breath and knocks on the table. She's far from okay, but to stop moving forward is to give up. Neither of us can do that. "Let's match these up. We agree Mick goes next to gluttony, Cathbad to sloth, us to lust."

I squint at the notes. "Why did you write Red Hugh? Maybe it was Eoghan or the gallowglass we were supposed to pay attention to."

There's a dot of ink on her bottom lip where she chewed the pen. "Hmmm. Do you think the three could have a sin in common?"

I lay fingers on two of the sins. "Could be pride in their cause or wrath in their hearts for the enemy."

"The head of the poleaxe we dug out of the hawthorn's trunk took us to a war camp. To me, that points a finger at wrath."

I clap my hands together. "Wrath it is."

Eala huffs as she hovers over her detective work. "Maybe it doesn't matter. We sharpened five star points with five sins."

"How about our egg-stealing Viking?"

We look at each other and say in unison, "Greed."

I waggle a finger at the Viking note. "Aye. I'm guessing he stole the Carrabuncle's pearly egg as plunder. That certainly backfired on the ole boyo." The pen's back in Eala's mouth as she ponders the notes. I gently pull it away and dab the ink with my pinkie. "Not your color, love."

We both stare at the notes. Even with all we've gathered, they make no sense to me at all.

Eala moves the paper squares that say, *belt, druid stone, axe head,* and *pearl* to the person they're attached to. Still, nothing comes into relevant focus. I dive into the volumes of folk and faerie stories living in my head, but they don't add up to anything that comes close to answering Finnbheara's obtuse question.

> *What's all and each the selfsame piece,*
> *Plain truth and no illusion?*

"This is everything we know." Eala walks over to the front door and knocks her head gently against it.

I've not my swan's scholarly brain, but even hers isn't serving her well today.

"What are we missing?" she grumbles. "Every point on the pendant is sharp." She stares out the window. "These elements don't fit a single story, history, myth, or legend I've ever heard."

I take up the pen and write on a square of paper. I'm as heavy as stone as I join her at the window and hand her the note with its two words.

Eala crown

She makes a strangled sound like someone's got their hands around her neck as she rips it in two. "I can't even think about that."

"I hate it as much as you do, but what else could Finnbheara's Treasure mean? Even Robber Bright warned you off the king. We have to consider where it might fit, love." I gently turn her shoulders to face me.

Eala punches her fists into my chest, sending me stumbling backwards.

Her eyes are wild with fury as she screams with the blood rage of a warrior. "I will not let Finnbheara touch me. He has no right." She pursues me as I back away. "I don't care what claim he thinks he holds over me." Eala grabs the collar of my T-shirt with such force, she rips it down the middle. Her palms slap my chest with a loud *smack*. I'm ready for her and brace against the blow.

She lets loose a throat-ripping howl. "This is what I *claim*, Finnbheara." Eala slams her body against mine and snatches handfuls of my hair to pull my lips to hers. We crash together with bruising force. Our teeth and tongues go to battle with growls as fierce as Red Hugh's gallowglass or the ferocity of wolves defending their mates.

Eala's lips find their way to my ear. "Take your crown and shove it up your ass, Finnbheara."

Leaving me wanting with bones the consistency of wet sand, she returns to her clue map. If only winning came with the option of murdering Finnbheara and that geebag, Robber Bright.

I shuck the remains of my shirt, then step next to her and catch her left hand to give her a bit of a distraction from the cliff she's sending herself over. "I've no ring for you besides this one. Do you want a better bauble for your wedding, Swan?"

Eala twists the silver band on her finger. "Absolutely not. It's a symbol of the family we've both come from. It should be part of our new family."

I know she means the two of us as a true family. I can't help the pretty picture flashing through my head of a chubby lad with my curls, poor bugger, and Eala's pouty lips next to a slip of a girl with her nose in a book. Visions of a life that will never be.

In this life, I will be content with Eala alone as *my* treasure.

"I'm the one with no ring for y—" She abruptly cuts off her statement. Rushing to the table, she searches through the papers. "Where's the ring from your dream?" Her voice wears an edge of panic. She spies the etched gold band on the floor under the table and retrieves it.

Seeing the ring Robber Bright put on her finger causes a storm to break inside me. Surging forward, I close my fist around the band and tear it from her grasp. "The cursed thing is going in the fire."

Eala's on me before I can cock my arm back to chuck the Faerie bane into the flames.

"Stop, Sionnach." Our gazes lock onto one another with equal turbulence. "It might be important." She snatches it back.

"As what? Another sign Finnbheara or Robber Bright want you in their beds?" I throw a series of punches at the air, aching to hit something, but careful not to swing anywhere near Eala. "Damned thieving, arrogant, prideful, remorseless, conceited, covetous villains, the lot of them."

I expect a scolding for my temper, but Eala stares at my strutting around with a vacant expression. A sure sign those wheels in her brilliant mind are spinning fast. She returns to the table, her focus riveted on the bright orange notes each with a sin written in bold black letters. Slowly, she raises her hand and sets the ring on *pride.* Then my beautiful scholar grabs the pen and scribbles *Fae* on a paper square, which she settles next to its sin.

Her gaze slides back to me. "This could represent a sixth deadly sin. Robber Bright took a ring from the hawthorn the first night we met up with him. This could be the same ring."

Hatred turns my blood black. "It fits." The cursed ring and dream are blazing examples of all the faults I just spouted off about the Fae. "He knew you'd need it for the riddle, but the bastard delivered it to you in a way that forced me to watch him steal your body in the dream."

Eala shivers. "No more talk of the horrible dream."

"We are in total agreement there," I say.

"What I don't understand…is why there are only five points on the star if we're after seven deadly sins." Dipping her fingers into her collar, she fishes out the star. "Sion…" Eala's voice quavers as she holds the necklace for me to see. "Look."

In the middle of the star is a tiny etching of two fanciful triangles, bases meeting so their tops each face opposite sides. One of them wears a pointed angle, the other a rounded one.

Her voice is low and a bit on the shaky side. "Máthair believed the points of a Celtic star stand for the five senses we know, but the center of a star honors the Sidhe."

"That wily bastard," I growl. Of course, Finnbheara would add trickery to something as plain as a star. "He was setting us up to stop after five clues."

She clutches the pendant. "I know you don't want to hear it, but I believe Robber sent the ring to help us beat Finnbheara."

Dead to rights I don't want to hear it, but by all appearances, Robber Bright has split from Finnbheara. Also, the Fae as much as admitted that he'd set us up to best his king.

"I'd love to cut him out of our lives, but…" Eala's eyes glisten with tears. "…We don't know what Robber Bright's plans are for Colleen."

I'd like to think the Fae fiend is only using Colleen to rattle Eala, but his duplicitous nature points to darker intentions.

"Oh, shit," says Eala and grabs the sheet of paper with the riddle and reads.

"There is a number full complete,
Its quota ripe to fill."

"Sion, the number he's talking about is seven, not five. More proof the star was supposed to throw us off track." She shoves a strand of hair out of her eyes. "In folklore and many religions, the number seven means completeness in some cultures and in others it represents hidden knowledge." Her gaze locks on the ring. "If Robber hadn't gotten this ring to us to sharpen the sixth point, we'd never have tracked down enough information to solve the riddle."

I continue to glare at the shiny band. "The ring's been with us since before the Viking and his wife. Why did it not sharpen a point of the star when it first came to us?"

Eala stares at nothing, then her eyes flare. "The only logical explanation is that we never considered this ring as part of the answer we're looking for until now."

I firmly grab her by the shoulders. "It doesn't mean we trust Robber Bright. Don't go soft on me."

She flashes me a mirthless grin. "Believe me, if I've learned anything from this twisted challenge, it's to never trust a Fae."

I attempt to lighten the darkening path. "Are you giving me a message I shouldn't trust you, my Faerie beauty?"

Eala looks startled for a moment, but then meets my gaze dead on. "Oh, no," she says, draping her hands over my shoulders. "Because I'm not your typical Faerie beauty." There's mischief in her eye. "I'm something else entirely."

I'm treated to a kiss with the trappings of triumph in its enthusiasm.

An indignant bleat near the front door of the cottage interrupts us. I drop my head to Eala's shoulder and growl. "The damn Fae could have at least taken the fecking goat with him." I head for the landline that now sits on the kitchen counter. "Robbo and Dale keep a few goats. I'll call 'em to come pick this fella up. Hopefully, he won't devil the ones they already have."

At the mention of devils and goats, unpleasant imagery from my religious past rears its head. Goats were herded down to hell while sheep got golden tickets to heaven. Is there subtext in Robber Bright's engagement gift or was he playing on mortal superstitions to be an ass?

I finish my call with an appreciative Corrigan. The gift of goat sits well with him.

Coming up behind Eala, I trap her in my arms. With an eye to the fading light of the afternoon, I ask. "Well then, Professor Duir, what's next?"

She pats my hands before turning to meet my gaze with one of stalwart determination. "We dive deeper into sin."

CHAPTER 23
THE MONK

S ion keeps a steady grasp on my arm. Even though I'm on solid
ground, rising panic bubbles in my chest. I understand why people
mistake surges of anxiety for heart attacks. No matter how many
deep breaths I take, I can't seem to tame the unforgiving pace of my
heartbeats.

My love forces me to sit in the grass in front of the hawthorn tree as he
attempts to knead some of the tension from my shoulders and neck. If
only we had time for him to croon a calming song.

I twist to face him. "We need to have another go at the tree. It's our last
Celtic day to travel. There's got to be something we missed hanging on
the branches or hiding inside the trunk."

Sionnach kisses my temple and picks at a snag on my sleeve, the result
of a failed attempt to dodge thorns. Despite his stab at calm, telltale
ripples of his stress heat the air around us. The man definitely runs hot.

We combed every inch of the hawthorn's dangling offerings as well as
the grass around its root diameter and trunk. It'd be in keeping with
Finnbheara's love of trickery to bury a necessary clue inside a tangle of
roots. With Sion's help, I even scrambled up a few of the larger spiky
branches, loosing white blossoms in my wake like a shower of tiny
meringue cookies.

Our results are as fruitless as a child digging to the center of the earth with a plastic spoon. Not a single blue glow shows itself. I suppose I should be grateful no crimson glare appears either.

The statue of St. Patrick near the church a short distance from the tree seems to be giving us a knowing look. I can imagine his judgy inner monologue.

Consort with Faeries, embrace frustration.

To add to my now pounding head, a bossy crow or raven, I've never paid much attention to the difference, continues to rattle and caw at us from its perch near the top of the hawthorn.

"We've no loose chips for you to steal, eejit bird." Sion digs around in the grass for something to heave at our annoying visitor.

"Don't crows sleep?" I groan. The lyrics to the Beatles hit about a blackbird's song disturbing the dead of night answers that question.

A blended cocktail of frustration and despair churns through me. Thick clouds clog the sky, preventing even weak moonlight from breaking through to lift our spirits. I've always considered the moon a friend who watches over us from its starry bower. Its recent shift from benevolent overseer to time-thieving enemy inspires a couplet of sadness I'd add to the personal philosophies I used to jot down in a journal.

Once your gaze bore promise pure,
Until its glare did pain procure.

I rip blades of grass from the ground. Will I ever write in my journal again?

"Well, Sion, there's nothing to do but go home and pray with the ring added to our clues we have are enough to solve the riddle. At least we know the deadly sin of envy is what we're missing. That knowledge will have to be enough since we don't have a person or item to connect it to."

Sion's grubbing around finally produces a rock, which he launches at the bird. Lucky for our indignant feathered visitor, he misses. The volley does succeed in sending the blackbird into the sky.

"Sion, don't take it out on the bird."

The raven-crow circles once and lands in exactly the same place. It starts scolding us again.

Sion shouts at it. "So help me, I'll stuff you in a cookpot."

"Maybe it'll shut up if it thinks you appreciate it instead of wanting to scald it to death." I shrug. "After all, The Beatles thought it was worthy imagery for a song." I start humming their ode to the blackbird and Sion joins in with the lyrics.

Our duet redraws my jagged lines into gentle arcs. Sion's voice has its magical calming effect on me. I push to my feet. "Looks like Alfie gets the night off. Go ahead and call the Veil." I almost wish we'd driven the couple of hours to get here instead of traveling. Sometimes the drone of a car engine is the perfect way to make the mind a clean slate.

"You're sure?"

I don't know if Sion's asking if I'm sure we should leave or if he should be the one to call the Veil. He's still feeling a little tentative about his restored magic and rightly so after the shit Robber Bright put him through. Taking his hand, I rest my head on his shoulder. "Yes."

As the glassy walls of the Veil settle around us, the blackbird spreads its wings and screeches to wake the dead. In the same instant, there's the slightest crack in the cloud cover. A sliver of moonglow breaks through, dipping each of the bird's ruffled feathers in a sapphire sheen.

"Stop," I holler, nearly wrenching Sion's shoulder out of its socket.

The walls of the Veil fall into spectral puddles at our feet.

I point at the bird. "Look. The crow. The raven. The blackbird. Whatever it is. It's the clue."

Sion's openly gawking at the bird.

I rush toward the tree until I'm directly beneath the animal. "Where do you want us to go?" I shout at it. As if the crow is going to answer me. I whirl to face Sion. "What folktales do you know with crows, ravens —blackbirds?"

He scratches his curls as he thinks. The only damn associations in my head besides the song are Edgar Allan Poe's poem where the repeated word *nevermore* doesn't inspire much hope and Aesop's fable about the crow who dropped the cheese to the fox after succumbing to flattery.

There's a handy fox and crow right here to dramatize the tale, but we lack a morsel to envy.

"There's the one where a father turns his seven sons into crows."

My adrenaline fires up. "*Seven* sons?" Our magic number. "Does it name a place we can travel to? Names? Clues?"

He shakes his head. "Sorry to disappoint, love, I haven't told that tale in a donkey's years, and I don't remember much detail except it wasn't one folks requested." Suddenly, there's a sparkle to his green glass eyes. "Emmm…but there is one about *Cóemgen*, Saint Kevin the monk to you, and a blackbird that people loved to hear."

I squeal. "Yes, yes. I know it." I imitate the holy man's pose from the story. "He held out his hand and stood as still as a statue until a blackbird came and built her nest in his palm."

"Aye," Sion buzzes with excitement. "The man is said not to have moved until the eggs hatched and the chicks flew off." He grabs my hand and spins me in a circle. "We've got a place and person to head off to. *Cóemgen* and Glendalough."

The Veil reignites around us with Alfie just inside. Instead of pausing to enjoy the journey, Sion starts rummaging through our clothing sacks.

I'm charmed and relieved by the return of the old Sion Loho *barrel forward* confidence. A memory comes to me from the early days of our partnership. "You promised to take me to Glendalough some day and show me the round tower. Remember?"

He tosses me a wadded-up bundle of clothes. "A promise from another life, but one I'm pleased to be keeping."

Another life that was less than a few weeks past. How many lifetimes do we live as we traipse through this world?

Sion's thoughtful for a beat. "Although, if it's Saint Kevin in his time we're off to call on, I'm afraid there'll be not much but the man himself to see."

"Then you'll have to take me back when this is all behind us."

He winks. "Consider it done."

Moonlight frosts the lake before Sion and me, one of two *loughs* giving Glendalough its name that means valley of the two lakes. Placid elegance settles over the place. It's so quiet, I hear the easy lapping of water against the shore. Trees grow freely all around us, unhampered by the monastic settlement of stone buildings and graves this will one day become. The air is warm but charged with the similar energy of the very first Veil forest Sion lured me into as a fox. Scuffling creatures supply gentle night music. My Veil sprites whir with a delicate thrum, clearly pleased with our destination.

"Where do you think he is?" I whisper because talking at a normal volume would blast through the serene night like a shout.

Sion leans close, sensing the same need for quietude. "As his story goes, Saint Kevin had a wee cave he used as his bed on the shores of the *lough*."

With tacit agreement, we stroll along the water's edge. Around the next curve of the lake, a barely audible voice breaks the silence—a man at prayer.

As we listen to the pious resonance of Saint Kevin's chat with God, we do not speak or even move. When the monk reaches his conclusion, out of habit from our Catholic upbringings, Sion and I both make the sign of the cross. Both night and saint remain still and undisturbed.

There's a rustle in the underbrush that the monk doesn't acknowledge. Sion and I glance at each other silently questioning how to gain Kevin's attention without altering history by scaring the holy man to death. When Sionnach clears his throat a bit louder than necessary, Saint Kevin turns toward us with a patient smile.

"Ah, pilgrims," says the man with shoulder length silver-gray hair that reminds me a little too much of Finnbheara's. An unchecked beard covers his face. He's dressed in humble homespun robes. Kevin fans an arm across the forest and lake. "There are many places in which to find peace here. I beg you leave me to my solitude." Kevin bows and turns to leave.

"Father *Cóemgen*," says Sion. "Will you grant us but a moment of your time?"

The monk sighs, shoulders bent from whatever spiritual burden he carries. "If I do so, will you allow me to become no more than the tree on the banks of the river or the fish in the *lough*?"

"Aye."

Sion looks at me to continue. I'm kicking myself for not preparing a specific question for the hermit. I expected to arrive while he was in the middle of something the way Cathbad and Mick Ryan were. Immediately being blown off by Saint Kevin was not the plan.

I stumble over words. "I...we...uh...seek your wisdom on the sin of—" I almost say envy or resentment, then land on— "Jealousy."

Kevin seats himself on the flattish top of a low boulder and stares.

And stares.

And stares.

I sense Sion's volatile energy and send up my own prayer he can keep it in check long enough to get something no matter how small or seemingly trivial out of the monk.

Finally, the future saint speaks. "It is of covetousness you speak. You are not the first pilgrims to lay such a mantle upon my shoulders." His eyes drift to the full Veil moon. "And perhaps it is truth. I do covet my simple existence here with only the wind and rhythms of the land as my fellows."

"We do not begrudge you the sanctity of your wilderness, sir," says Sion. "Will you not tell us what it is you seek that seclusion may grant you?"

A renewed sense of awe at the way Sion easily folds into conversation with someone no matter the place or the time washes over me.

Kevin presses his palms together and looks to the stars. "Simply the voice of God, and his guidance as to my purpose under heaven." His gaze settles on us. "That is neither a rapid nor easy gift to receive."

"Thank you for the giving of your truth." To my surprise, Sion kneels, tugging at my hand to do the same. "May we ask a different blessing before we depart—a blessing of marriage?"

Kevin perks up. "You wish such an act from me?"

Sion is brilliant. Our chances of waltzing up to a priest in our time who would marry us on the spot was basically non-existent, considering the hoops one has to jump through for a church wedding.

The monk raises his hand with a weary sigh, but as he stares at us, his eyes fill with wonder. Kevin's voice holds more zip as he says, "I see the splendor of a bond is already upon you, pilgrims. One beyond my earthly comprehension or ability to grant." He raises his eyes to the heavens and whispers. "*Anamchara*."

The Veil sprites within me incandesce in a resounding burst of approval.

"'Tis true," says Sion. "But we would have your sacred blessing as well." He holds his hand out. A glint from Máthair's ring shines in the center of his palm.

There on the tranquil shore of a *lough* in the Wicklow Mountains before a man whose imprint will forever be on these lands, Sionnach Loho and I exchange wedding vows. Our eyes glisten with tears lit by reflections of a Veil moon off the water.

The destiny Sion and I share surpasses the Fae magic that imbued me with life. I'm more than a favor created by Finnbheara for his paramour. I've become the leading lady in my own timeless love story. Eala Duir is a living miracle endowed by fortune's generous touch to welcome eternity with the luminous soul sliding a simple silver band with the words, *find me*, onto her finger.

The monk's next words are prescient confirmation that Sionnach has indeed always been my path to joy, and I his.

"Faith is to believe what we do not see, and the reward of that faith is to see what we believe."

Far away in the Glade of Chimes, I'm certain Máthair's heart sings as Saint Augustine's creed of belief that she taught both Sion and me in separate lifetimes seals our eternal commitment.

Once Saint Kevin says the final words calling us husband and wife, he lays his hands on Sionnach's head to speak a parting blessing. When it's my turn to receive his benediction, I bow. The monk's hand barely touches me before it recoils. He cries in fear, staring at his palm. A slate gray shadow seeps from the crease of his lifeline.

"What are you, child?"

I flash a look at Sion, not sure what to do. Thank goodness when it really counts, he's always ready.

"She is the daughter of two worlds, Father."

Kevin clutches the wrist of his darkening hand. "Not two but three. Three devils I saw." He backs away with terror painting his features. "Your joining has awakened them in the rock." His eyes glaze over as he raises his arms to the sky and wails. "The cave is open, and its beasts flown free."

Sion is already pulling us to our feet and away from the raving monk.

The holy man points a shaky finger. "You have shown evil this place." He begins to advance on us, and I half expect lightning to shoot from under his nails.

This is the second time we've been accused of bringing curses and evil. I recall the distress on Isabel de Clare Marshall's face when Sionnach presented her with the sword from the passage tomb.

While planting himself between Kevin and me, Sion keeps a wary eye on the monk. In a voice calmer than my pounding heart would allow me to speak, he says, "Call the Veil, love."

"Tell your devils to return to hell," roars Saint Kevin. "Close the cursed gate."

His rage rattles me, and I lose my grasp on the Veil.

Sion purrs, his soothing voice a contrast to the unhinged monk. "It's alright, love. Let it come to you."

I squeeze my eyes shut and plead with the Veil. Just as I feel the languid flow of connection, the water of the *lough* explodes in a watery eruption. Icy cold drops as hard as stones pelt our bodies. Black storm clouds gather above, discharging ceaseless bolts that scorch the sky over and over. Enraged winds bend trees until their tops nearly touch the earth. A crack like breaking bones echoes through the wood as trunks cleave in half, their branches ripped away by wanton gusts.

Sion shoves me to the sodden shore, covering my body with his as lightning strikes a line of nearby bushes, rocking the ground beneath us. Fire blazes along the tree line as the maniacal tempest showers violence over Glendalough.

Within the shell of Sion's body, I'm finally able to summon the Veil. Still in our huddle, it plucks us from the violence. We're only afforded a breath of relief before the tunnel of the Veil telescopes down. Its walls cloak us in a tight capsule as the battering continues outside our sanctuary.

Sion and I cling to one another. The shrill whine of the wind replaces any strain of violin or bell that usually fills the Veil. I yell to be heard above it. "What's happening?"

Through the sheer walls, I see we're still suspended over Glendalough. Destruction consumes the land beneath us. I pray Saint Kevin has made it to his cave instead of being swallowed into the gullet of the storm.

Sion's head whips wildly from side to side, trying to make sense of what he sees. "Steer us home, Eala."

"I'm trying." I whisper, "Home. Home. Loho land. The cottage," but we continue to be held captive by chaos.

"Try somewhere else," shouts Sion.

I'm as frightened as my six-year-old self, huddling in our rooftop apartment above Times Square in New York with Máthair when a hurricane off the Atlantic made landfall. It shook the building so badly, I was certain it would fall over, and we'd end up splattered across Central Park.

For the first time since I learned who Máthair truly was and the deal she'd made with Finnbheara to give me life, I wish with all my heart her comforting arms were around both Sion and me as we endure this nightmare.

As soon as the thought runs through my mind, the Veil cracks like a bullwhip and heaves us into the middle of the Glade of Chimes. Still captives in our ruthless bubble, we hover above once shimmering clover now dulled by the lessening light. I recognize the teal lake with its diamond surface and the door in the tree where the spirit of my grandmother dwells.

Unfortunately, we bring the storm with us. Forked blades of lightning attack the lake, shattering its glass to glittering dust. The torrent strikes the semi-circle of sacred trees, felling them one by one. The silver tubes adorning their branches that held the notes of soulsongs yet to be sung melt in the scalding heat pouring from the clouds. Even the crystal sun falls away, bathing the glade in shadow.

If it's one thing my studies of Celtic storytelling told me, it's that devils take many forms. What the foul fiends have in common, both modern and mythic, are dark forces which destroy with weapons of nature and fear. Is the wildness roiling around us truly a devil's doing? Or is it the ire of an angry god or goddess? Three devils are in play if Saint Kevin is to be believed, but which devils, whose demons? Or could this be no more than a vision conjured by the furor of a Fae king because the swan and the fox are close to solving his riddle?

Sion and I both scream for Máthair as her tree snaps in half. He digs into the walls of the Veil, trying to free himself to get into the Glade of Chimes, but they don't yield. I search along tattered clover to the polished rocks now gouged and scratched at the edge of the lake, but don't find signs of my grandmother anywhere.

The Veil begins to spin, throwing us topsy-turvy around the constricted chamber. Its pinch tightens as if trying to protect us from the unpredictable turbulence clawing to get inside and tear us apart. The Glade of Chimes fades from view, replaced in an instant by a smoky green sea.

Waves peaked with steel-colored caps break against our shield. I hold Sion so tightly, I nearly strangle him as we're dunked underneath the boiling sea. Thankfully, we bob up again only to be thrown together so hard, I fear our bones will splinter. Ocean currents treat us like a plaything, rolling our shelter increasingly closer to an enormous crag of rock jutting into the water from the headland. There is a giant split in the middle of the massive formation. Great deep lines carved in the protruding cliff face delineate blocky puzzle pieces of blue-gray and brown rock. It looks like a derelict castle shod of turrets and battlements. The entire natural edifice is coated with black char as if the surface has been burned by an evil flame.

Again, we're tumbled. My cheek collides with Sion's hipbone as we flail, straining to maintain any semblance of an upright position. I catch a glimpse of a lighthouse on the mainland, then a Martello tower on a nearby island. They flicker in and out as our casing rotates with each new punch from the storm.

Sion keeps calling out, "Who," as he maneuvers our bodies until we face one another.

"I don't know who is doing this," I cry back at him.

"Not who, *Howth*," he manages, yelling straight into my ear. Gaining momentary control of his limbs in our freefall, he gesticulates toward the island. "And there…that's called Ireland's Eye."

The Veil folds as if on a hinge, thrusting us forward and down. I'm afraid I'm going to be sick.

Sion is still shouting. "Gar-land. The Garland of Howth."

As soon as he speaks the words, the Veil stalls into a moment of equilibrium, positioning us to stare at the split in the rock. My blood is ice as I prepare to face Saint Kevin's devils. Shadows slither and writhe over the stony surface like serpents of fog until they coalesce into the shape of a head. Features begin to form: a long straight nose, cruel eyes, and harsh cheekbones. There before us, Finnbheara hunts for his target through a steaming sea.

I hide against Sion. He guides my chin up, trying to be gentle, but our wild movements make that impossible. There's a stab of pain near the top of my spine as he turns my head to face the rock. "Look, Eala."

The image has begun to spiral, erasing the king's countenance. When it settles again, Robber Bright's sneer pierces the storm, only to be replaced in an instant by someone with gaunt features and blackish eyes alight with crimson flame. A face I hoped to never look upon again, Aodh.

A sharp rattling noise rises, then quickly shifts into a growing roar. The Veil shudders, then begins to spin faster, picking up momentum until it feels as if my skull is crumbling. I hear the throaty scream of a crow. Images of the bird on the hawthorn tree, Saint Kevin on the verge of madness, and the visages of three devils pulse through my mind, then break into the matrices of a kaleidoscope just before a curtain of black falls over the world.

CHAPTER 24
THE HOUR OF PROMISES

The noise of an incessant drip pulls back a corner of my luxurious state of drifting through dreams. The beat of my swan wings keep time with the monotonous *drip drip drip* as I soar over a winding river. When I try to ignore it and continue through sweet oblivion, a throbbing pain across my cheek ruins that chance. Shivers wrack my body, setting off sharp aches in my shoulders and along my spine. A nearby grunt hauls me the rest of the way into reluctant consciousness.

Water runs off my hair, forming a small puddle next to me on the gravel path where I lie. It explains the *drip* that yanked me from painless fantasy to bald reality. I lift a weary limb to brush away wet strands from my eyes. My fingertips come away covered in a thin layer of iridescent film the consistency of oil.

What is this colorful smear coating my skin?

Its rainbow sheen is so like the Veil, but the cornflower sky above tells me I've left the familiar passageway.

Why have I left the Veil?

A rush of sadness infuses my weakened body. Jeremy Olk scarred the Veil with his evil purple-blue flames. Cathbad's mission to restore additional damaged portions suggests other evils have sought to compromise the Veil. Has our search for sins caused it further harm to the point where it can no longer carry us or worse—its destruction?

Sion once said the Veil knows me. I know it as well. It is the true guide in my search for the truth of what I'm meant to be. The Veil is my conduit for myth and magic…for my fate. It may be within the purview of the Fae, but it is also one of the greatest gifts and mysteries of the world.

My wandering thoughts gather. The scent of lavender, pungent herbs, and grasses revived by a spring shower fills the air around me. When I turn my head toward the sound of an animal rooting for food, sharp pain sizzles across my ribs.

"Ow."

"Eala…" Sion wearily drags himself across the ground toward me, every movement punctuated with a grunt of pain. The purple bruise around his left eye brings me back to the moment when our hellish twist inside the Veil sent my knuckles up to meet his face.

Flashes of Saint Kevin, the decimated Glade of Chimes, and devils in the rock catapult me fully into the present.

I attempt to roll and face Sion, but dizziness prevents me from even the smallest movement. He manages the last few feet to my side and plops his head on my stomach. I lift my hand to his hair and am treated to a new highway of pain. My fingers tremble instead of stroke. The limp palm settled across my knuckles suggests he's as wrecked as me.

His speech slurs. "He…?"

Out of the corner of my eye, I see the whitewashed walls of the cottage nearly close enough to touch, but it may as well be a hundred miles away.

Sion tries to lift his head but fails. Straining, he forces out a single breathy croak. "Heal?"

I feel suspended in syrup. Even my thoughts are sluggish. "Sleep," I mumble, not certain I've actually spoken aloud.

"Heal," he repeats, the word clipped short by a painful groan.

Yes, we need to heal. All I want to do is return to sweet sleep where nothing hurts. When I start to drift off, Sion gives my hand a weak squeeze.

"Heal…us," he moans.

He's right. We don't dare sleep and risk Finnbheara stealing the last of our time to solve the riddle.

Swimming through the soup in my mind is a vision of Veil sprites and a fox curled in my lap.

Heal

The Fae abilities awakened within me still feel foreign, borrowed. First, I must try to restore my own strength. Is that even possible in this state where I'm as weak as a hatchling fallen from the nest?

Calling my scant supply of energy, I sink into my breathing. In and out. With each inhale, I imagine nudging the tiny incandescent beings inside me to wake. Like twinkle lights on a single strand popping to life one by one, the Veil sprites glow faintly. As they become aware of my drained battery, my companions quiver, then brighten. They zip frantically inside me as if searching for the source of my distress. The pinpoints of light expand, growing hotter and hotter until my entire body is coated in a blanket of heat both soothing and painful.

I moan and sob from the agony of their ministrations. If this is healing, I'd rather they leave my body here on Loho land and carry my spirit to Tír na nÓg.

"Ea…" Sion tries my name but can't summon the effort to move his mouth enough to finish it.

This is a fitting place to die. Husband and wife on the doorstep of a family home that might have been ours.

Ever so slowly, the heat subsides. Welcome coolness ushers in stronger awareness. I can think. I'm sore, but not ruined.

Sion lies like a sack of grain across me. I can't tell if he's breathing or not. Allowing my Fae essence to take the lead, I pass through skin and bone until I'm at the very core of Sionnach's being.

With the guidance of my Veil sprites, I cover him in the same healing wave they used on me. His body spasms. I'm deathly afraid his human frame can't withstand another dose of Fae interference, but I have nothing else to offer him.

"Hold on, Sionnach. Hold on."

I search for restraint. Instead of a flood, I let my Fae magic become a tender touch to the battered places inside him. I sense the moment his spirit opens to me. We drift together through the intangible place where our souls are bound together.

Sion's breathing finally syncs to mine, and I allow myself to let go.

The next thing I'm aware of is Sion lifting me into his arms. I open my eyes. Our gazes lock, but we do not speak. We do not need to. Love, passion, devotion, every vow we've made to each other lives in our eyes.

He carries me inside. With every step forward, I feel stronger. Once the door shuts behind us, I find my voice. "You're okay?"

In answer, shaky lips brush mine before he sets me down in front of the kitchen table. I drop into a chair while he opens the cupboard. After producing two glasses and what looks to be expensive whiskey based on the fancy bottle, he pours.

Sion sits next to me and raises his glass. "To my wife."

I clink with him. "To my husband."

We drink, share a whiskey spiced kiss, then grin like fools. We are two people no matter what destiny intended, who fell in love, and, against ridiculous odds, married. Whatever happens at the eclipse tonight, no one can take that away from us. If this is our last day, it'll be wrapped in joy.

We sip and relish the silence for a few moments. The hourglass holding the sand of our eternity isn't just running low, it's been blasted apart.

Blasted apart.

My hand snakes out to grab Sion's wrist. "Máthair? Was that real—the Glade of Chimes being destroyed?"

The whiskey flush fades from his cheeks. Eyes that moments ago shone with happiness, now pinch at the edges. Sion runs his free hand through curls. "I have no goddamned idea."

I unclamp my fingers from his wrist before his hand turns white from loss of blood flow and grab my phone off the table. First, I search Glendalough, then Howth. "The Glendalough website makes no mention of Father Kevin threatened by any tempests. The cliffs of Howth are still intact."

Setting the phone down, I slide my fingers between Sion's. "What we saw must have been a vision, not truth. Maybe it's a message like your dream about the silver ship." My voice catches. "Máthair has to be safe."

"To show us such a gut-ripping scene when we've no means to know the truth of it..." Sion drops his forehead onto our entwined hands. "Fucking Faeries."

I stroke his hair for a few moments, then lift his chin. After licking whiskey off my lips, I attempt a reassuring smile. "Once we're back in Tír na nÓg, we'll insist on an explanation from Finnbheara."

He looks stricken. "If only it were a feast day, we could try to travel to the glade before the eclipse."

I slowly trickle a finger through the stubble on his cheek, enjoying the rugged path. "No matter what comes next, at least it's the last day of breaking our brains trying to solve this cursed riddle."

"I'd appreciate it if we banish the term *last day* from the discussion." Sion downs the rest of his whiskey and pours himself more.

Leaning an arm on the table, I pillow my head against it. "I'm so tired, Sionnach. Not sleepy—drained."

"Amen to that, love." He wraps fingers around his whiskey. "I'm weary of questions, riddles, and a future with a pointy-eared bastard driving the bus."

I lay my hand over his glass. I'm as strung out as Sionnach looks, and now we've got Máthair's safety on our plate as well. If Finnbheara's strategy was to wear us down to the bone on his damn quest—mission accomplished. I'd like nothing more than to polish off a bottle of whiskey with my husband, but one of us has to show restraint. "Agreed, but how about we save the next round until after we take a final stab at the riddle?"

Sion rests his chin on the table and peers up at me. "Heads might be clearer once shored up with a bit more *uisce beatha*."

I kiss his cold nose. "If you make a fire, I'll consider joining you for one more drink."

He moves to the hearth as I switch into *understand this hellish mess* mode.

I play with the chain of my star necklace, and then pull it out for examination. In our wild Veil ride, the pendant dug a trail of scratches across my chest. Sure enough, the top point of the last sideways triangle is as sharp as a blackbird's beak.

"Seven points," I tell Sion. "We did it. Technically, we should have what we need to solve the riddle."

Sion huffs. His negativity is understandable. He's had exponentially more time to build resentment toward Fae dealings than I have. I decide to bypass a pep talk and get down to business before the Faerie eclipse outruns us.

"Saint Kevin made it pretty clear he's our candidate for envy with the covetousness talk about pilgrims envying his selfish solitude." I write a note with his name and then one that says *blackbird*.

I lean my elbow on the table, covering my mouth with my hand as I strain to piece together our evidence.

Seven sins. Seven names. Seven objects.

Seven, a number complete.

Finished with fire duty, Sion comes up behind me and sets hands on my shoulders. "Where are you going to put our wee peek at Howth, love?"

My heart gives a hard thump.

Howth.

Faces on the rocks.

Finnbheara.

Robber Bright.

The fire-eyed man.

I drop my head. "I have no idea."

Sion *humphs*. "Howth." His gaze darts around the cottage as if he'll find missing pieces scribbled on the walls.

His clicking fizzy noises of consideration tell me he's on to something. I should give him space, but I'm too keyed up for patience. "History, stories, what Howth lore do you know to help us?"

He points two fingers at me. "Lore's the word shaking a story loose, my brilliant swan." Sion scratches his chin. "So the story goes, a man threw a holy book to knock the devil away. It hit the rock at Howth Head, splitting it. Since then, many claimed to see the face of *fear dubh*, a right devil, in those stones. Luck or curse, we saw three devils, not just one."

I grab Sion's hand. "Devils. That's it." Thoughts tumble through my head. Could the answer be so simple? "The devil is the face of the seven deadly sins." I jab a finger at the question in Finnbheara's riddle.

> *This ultimate conclusion:*
> *What's all and each the selfsame piece,*
> *Plain truth and no illusion?*

The well stream of surety sends me to my feet. I face Sion. "Do you see it? The devil embodies all the sins. That's the selfsame piece. Seven deadly sins—one piece. The devil may use illusion to tempt, but he can't hide the plain truth of what he is." My bubble pops from the skeptical look on Sion's face. "You don't agree?"

His lips press into a tight white line. "The crack in your reckoning is Finnbheara doesn't believe in our version of the devil."

Fissures crawl through the tower of my confidence, but I stop them from spreading. "But he does acknowledge Aodh, an underworld god." I grab Sion's sleeve. "There's Finnbheara's devil. The answer is Aodh." A chill runs along my spine. "I believe he was the face in the rock with burning eyes. What did Robber call him...the vindictive bearer of the crimson flame? Aodh is associated with fire."

Fire.

Like the flame emblem on Robber Bright's new armor. My suspicion about Robber's shift in loyalty solidifies into surety. I have a sudden urge to reexamine every second of my so-called lessons under this new lens, but the riddle and the eclipse are more pressing matters. My distrust of Robber Bright and his insinuations that our connection isn't finished must come after our showdown with Finnbheara.

Sion scratches his stubble. "It's not same. Finn...Aodh, they're both *Daoine Sidhe* rulers of their worlds. Not one good and one bad, just different perspectives...ways of doing."

The hierarchy of myth and legend scramble in my head. Sion's right. I'm imposing a human system on a world that operates with completely different rules.

I punch the top of the couch cushions. "I—hate—feeling—stupid."

Sion catches my wrist and spins me to face him. "Eala, think on this. Could our devil be Robber Bright?"

I stare at him, trying to herd my escaping logic back into focus. He beckons me to the table and sets hands on my hips, leaning over my shoulder. "Let's fit the bastard to the sins." Sion points to the top note. "Gluttony?"

"It's not like I've ever sat down to a meal with the guy." I shrug. "Don't know."

"Lust and pride go without saying for anything Fae," he says. "Wrath?"

We look at one another and nod. "He showed me a scar Finnbheara gave him, and intimated he holds a grudge against the king so that tracks, and…" I've never admitted Robber's attempt to seduce me to Sion. "Greed. He, ah, tried to talk me into going with him instead of sticking with Finnbheara. Stealing me."

Sion clamps fingers around my upper arm, his voice lethal. "Going with him?"

I wiggle out of the hold before adding any more bruises to my current collection from the week's exploits. "Not now, Sion, okay, please? I'll explain everything later."

He's pissed. Ignoring my previous request, he downs the whiskey and smacks the glass on the table. "If Robber Bright is trying to take you from Finn, that would tick the box on envy as well."

"That leaves sloth," I say, drawing a blank. "Robber's never shown me any evidence of sloth."

Sion grumbles under his breath. The rising tide of defeat laps at me again. It must be contagious because he reaches for the whiskey bottle. I don't blame him. I'm ready to swig straight from it.

Sion stops mid pour and sets the bottle back on the table. The gold ring around his irises flickers. He starts speaking as if in a daze.

"A table set for the king,
Be it sweet, meat, or fine wine,
Welcomes both stranger and friend
To feast without sated end."

"What is that?"

He looks me straight in the eye. "It's part of an old poem Ma used to tell called *Finnbheara's Banquet*."

She never shared that with me. I flick a mental hand at my own flash of envy. "Do you suppose she was still thinking about the king even after she chose your father?"

Sion purses his lips. "It would seem so, but that's not why I thought of it." He blows out a breath. "A *feast without sated end* rings the gluttony bell for ole Finn."

My stare lands on the list of sins. "Pride. Finnbheara meant to give us an impossible riddle because he can't stand the thought of being bested by a mortal. Not any mortal, you, the living reminder your mother chose your father over him."

He nods. "Envy for my da."

Heat rushes to my cheeks. "Lust—his history with luring Máthair and other mortals to be royal lovers or wives." I swallow hard. "As much as it nauseates me, being Finnbheara's *treasure* does connect to the line in the riddle about the crown. That leans into his greed to acquire me. If our efforts end in the sorrow and rift from the poem, it means you and I will be separated because of Finnbheara and his crown."

Sion narrows his eyes. "That'd bring down my wrath to be sure."

"Finnbheara's, too, since he sees you as competition to take me away from him. History repeating itself." Every breath hurts. "Bested by the *Spawn of Loho*."

Sion's hurried breaths sound like a runner with the finish line in sight. "We're left with sloth. What part of Finn proves he can be a lazy bugger?"

I chew on my thumb as I pace in front of the fireplace. "Soldiers doing his work for him?" I shake my head. "No, there are stories of the king fighting in battles." I drop my head back to stare at the ceiling, straining for anything to paint Finnbheara with slothful strokes. "Servants? Does that make him slothful or just entitled?"

We're so close, but the answer feels like trying to hold water cupped in the palm of my hand with a desert to cross.

Sion lets out a loud *hmmm*. "Robber Bright was a servant of the king.

One Finnbheara sent to teach you about being Fae because his majesty couldn't be bothered to."

I rush over to him and grab the hem of his T-shirt. "That or the fact he's too damn lazy and prideful to offer up any challenge where the answer is anything but himself."

The day outside wanes with approaching dusk. Fire is our only light. I wrap my arms around Sion's waist. "What's all and each the selfsame piece?"

He finishes. "Plain truth and no illusion."

"Finnbheara," I say.

"Aye. The king makes no illusion of what he is." The color on Sion's face rises from a cotton candy pink through increasingly darker shades of red until it settles on a deep russet. "The fucker sent us running through time after dribs and drabs we didn't need to solve his cursed riddle. As Faeries do." He shakes fists clenched tightly enough to bleach his knuckles. "All the while, his royal arse sits on that precious throne, altering moons and laughing as we try to gnaw ourselves out of his trap."

I fold my hands over his fists and pry them open. "We suspected the sins were key, but we didn't know for certain until we analyzed everything that we've collected and decided if they were genuine clues or red herrings. We couldn't rule anything out."

Sion's chest ratchets in and out with heavy breaths.

I curl into him and press an ear against his chest to listen to his thundering heart. "We're done, my love."

He rests his chin on the top of my head, tremors of anger still coursing through him.

I wrap my arms around him. "Right or wrong, my darling fox, we've reached the end."

As is the case with so many Faerie riddles, the answer has been teasing us from the moment we figured out the seven deadly sins were the frame to be filled in.

Until the faces in the rock at Howth, would we have considered Finnbheara as the answer? The question remains, who sent the Veil to Howth or the blue moonshine to the blackbird? Robber Bright, who's made no secret he wants me under his influence? Or did Aodh himself strike at his adversary, Finnbheara, by giving us the last piece we needed to solve the king's cryptic riddle?

No matter how we got here or who helped or hindered us, we have an answer. I pray it's *the* answer.

A settled Sion releases me and pats my bottom. "Grab your coat, Swan. I've just the place to say goodbye to the moon."

Eala successfully copies the magic she'd seen Robber Bright perform to peel away our mortal moon and reveal the full Faerie moon lording over the Atlantic.

I've brought my love to *An Branán Mór*, the great sea stack off the Cliffs of Moher near Galway. We huddle together under a thick wool blanket in the O'Dwyer Irish tartan pattern to honor Ma's family. It seems a fitting cocoon as we prepare for what's to come. Our cozy perch is inside an ample niche near the top of the rocky tower that sprouts over sixty meters above the sea like a great fortress. We've agitated the razorbills and kittiwakes who don't appreciate a couple of *fánaí* invading their territory.

I called the Veil to bring us here. It's a miracle our hellacious spin and the devilish faces in the rock didn't destroy our trusted passageway. I'd be lying if I didn't admit to being terrified that might be so.

I wonder if we'll ever wander through the Veil's colorful glory again. Our fate doesn't belong to us, but rather a Faerie king who'd rather see my bones ground into a meal for Fae beasts instead of grudgingly granting me a place in his realm.

Eala's gaze is fixed on the horizon. "What do you imagine will happen?"

She snuggles closer as I muse. "Finnbheara will steal us for some boot licking when the eclipse runs its course." I stare over the abstract pattern of whitecaps stippling the surface of the sea. "I'd prefer to ride through the gates of Tír na nÓg on your *péist síoda*."

Eala guides my face to hers. "We will someday. I dream of introducing you to Cara." She exhales, sending a wisp of fog from her lips. "If she's still mine. Finnbheara seems to enjoy taking back his gifts."

I appreciate her attempt at certainty when I know her guts are in as big a slosh as mine.

"Here's my scenario," she says and kisses the tender spots around my black eye. "If you're still in my arms when the Fae moon returns, we'll know our answer to the riddle is correct."

"And if we're not?"

She slides her hands up the sides of my face, softly caressing my skin with her thumbs. "We've been here before, my dearest fox. Our spirits will never stop fighting to be together. We'll defy Faerie kings and fire gods, searching every realm under the stars until our souls join again. That is my promise to you, Sionnach Loho, friend, husband, soulmate, my hundred thousand heartbeats."

"And I promise you, my beloved swan, Eala *bán* Duir Loho, the very same."

Eala keeps hold of my face as she brings her lips to mine. I open for her. Our tongues twine to seal the bargain. The fear, hope, and desperation seeded in our breasts deepen the kiss. Hot mouths and delving tongues consume each other's oaths.

"Up you come, love." I pull Eala over my lap, tucking her against the cave wall and arrange the blanket upon the rocks. "I also promised to make love to you any chance I had. This is no mattress of lady's bedstraw, but it'll have to do." I pat the wool. "Shall we only expose what we must to manage our pleasures?"

"No," she says. Eala crawls over me to plant her wonderful round Amerrrrican bottom on the blanket. With tantalizing purpose, she locks her gaze to mine as my love sheds all her upper wrappings and then those lower down. She settles back, laying herself bare to me, only keeping socks on her feet.

I throw everything off but my socks as well, giving a shiver when the wind darts in to greet us. We stuff our discarded clothes into a corner of our shallow cave to prevent knocking them into the sea.

Eala holds her arms out to me. I take her hands and set them on either side of her pleasantly pebbled body. As she tries to capture me with her legs, I tease her hard peaks with gentle scratches of my nails the way she likes, lowering myself inch by inch until I lie atop her. When her hums of pleasure set hips rocking into mine, I round my back to take her primed nipples one at a time into my desperate mouth.

I want nothing more than to spend the entire night methodically pleasing my wife, but that is not our reality. Finnbheara's eclipse and our destiny will not grant us such luxury. Sliding a hand from the soft skin of Eala's ankle up to her thigh, I hook her leg over my shoulder, opening her brilliant, pouty rose-colored delights to me.

For a moment, I take in the beauty of Eala's body, skin paler than mine dabbled with her golden freckles. I cup her sex, trembling at the feel of wet heat pulsing against my palm. We're curled close, bodies bending around one another.

"Someday, my swan, I'll lay you on a bed of wild grass and love you under a summer sky while the birds sing your name." Leaning over, I kiss her with as much passion as my sorry self has to give. From her lips, I leave a trail down her throat, between her breasts, then brush my nose lower to take in the sweet scent of her readiness.

With a featherlight touch, she traces the thin scar on my side from the siege at Kilkenny, a moment in time we had no right to disturb. She continues lower until determined fingers dance across my cock. "Your body…" she rasps. "Is so strong, so beautiful." Eala's grip travels purposefully along my length, emphasizing her admiration with well-placed squeezes. "You are a beautiful soul, Sionnach Loho."

It takes every bit of willpower to give the pace over to her. The urgency of the limited time we have, coupled with my need to be inside her before cruel fortune separates us, nearly strikes me blind. Despite the frigid air, sweat breaks out across my skin. Eala will forever be my fire to defy any cold.

We shift in our rocky retreat until she brushes my cock against the entrance to her perfect depths. When her fevered dew drizzles over my tip, there's no holding back. I run my thumbs over her hips, and then appreciate every moment as I sheath myself inside her.

Our kisses change key from ravenous need to the tenderness of love we refuse to surrender. We move with the rhythm we've taught one another. Each of us touches the other in those precious places that send us soaring as high as the star trail in the sky above our joining. The power of our lovemaking becomes an act of defiance to those who would tear us apart.

After we've both fallen, then returned, Eala weeps, pressing palms to my slick chest. "This can't be the last time," she sobs.

We cling to one another as long as we dare. I help her dress before pulling my own clothes back on. Gathering her close, I replace the blanket around our shoulders. We're two small people in a too big world that controls our fate.

I rest my head against hers. "Ours is too great a love to have an end. There will be no last for us."

With my *anamchara* in my arms, we watch the moon disappear.

CHAPTER 25
THE DECEIT

The birds around our private niche in the sea stack squawk their concern at Sion and me, blaming us that the celestial lantern of their night has gone out. Seems our avian audience is privy to Finn's sky. Sharing shallow breaths, we watch the Fae moon's glow strain to break free from behind earth's shadow.

After what feels like a cessation of time itself, the Faerie moon begins to retake its place among waiting stars. Sion and I look at one another, questioning.

Have we triumphed? Through his connection to me, can Finnbheara sense we've discovered the correct answer to his crafty question?

As the final thread of shadow clears the moon, our cave fills with fog so thick, I'm blinded. It doesn't prevent me from knowing the instant Sion is ripped from my arms. The blanket we share drops without his body to hold up half of it.

"Sionnach," I cry.

There's no answer apart from the flutters and chirps of seabirds settling back on their nests. An icy slap of wind stings my face. The gust steals both fog and the wool blanket, tossing them into the sky above the Cliffs of Moher, and I'm alone.

Not for long.

The ocean at the base of the sea stack begins to churn, building a foamy top as it spins faster and faster around the rocky tower. From the turbulence, a watery whirlwind rises the two hundred feet to my niche and expands until it covers the night with a silvery curtain.

The distant figure of a man appears in the mist, approaching with arrogant strides. My heart skips, thinking it's Sionnach. Hope dies quickly as the form before me proves to be of a greater height and wears the body of a marble statue rather than a solid frame built from honest work. The glass crown of twining branches adorning his flowing silver hair confirms the identity of my summoner.

Finnbheara, King of the Connacht Fae, has come for me.

He bows and extends a hand.

I want to slap it away. I want to gouge out his eyes with my bare hands as brutally as the climax of a Greek tragedy. I want to curse him. I want to wrap the Veil around his throat until it's choked the life from him.

Since I can do none of those things, I take the king's hand.

He gently leads me through the curtain of sea spray.

The familiar misty transition into the same antechamber of Tír na nÓg where this journey began drifts through the air around me. Faint music of strings and merry bells surround us.

Finnbheara touches his lips to the back of my hand, then turns it over to press a lingering kiss to the inside of my wrist. My traitorous pulse meets his lips as if returning the amorous attention. This close, I see barely perceptible gold flickers inside the glass of his crown as vibrant as the current gilded color of his eyes.

I pull my hand away, and he chuckles.

"Such a pleasure to see you as well, Eala Duir."

I raise my chin. "It's Eala Loho now."

His expression remains noncommittal, but his eyes darken to the turbid blue gray of a restless sea. A moment later, he flicks his wrist. "Mortal bonds do not concern me." The king narrows his gaze. "As they should not signify to you either."

Standing in the Fae realm before its ruler in my jeans and puffer jacket should feel out of place. Instead, they become the armor of my own humanity. "What have you done with Sionnach?"

"My business is not with the fox." He clasps his hands behind his back and circles me in an unnervingly predatory way that I'm sure is as natural as breathing to him. "A bargain was struck between we two: a king and his subject."

That statement makes it clear there's no gray area as to who has the advantage. The Faerie's eyes settle into the look of cut glass splitting white light into its requisite colors. Is this Finnbheara's subtle message the Veil belongs to him? As if anything about this Faerie is subtle.

I will my voice to stay strong. "True, and I have brought the solution to your question that Sionnach and I uncovered together."

His brows lift as a low rumble escapes him. I can't tell what mood or reaction the noise presages.

Finnbheara stops stalking and stands before me with arms crossed. Muscles bulge against the two wide metallic bands clamped around his forearms. I stifle a gasp when I recognize them. These bands bear the same gold etched with waves and flowers as the captain's ring Robber Bright sent to us. The one he claims is my key to his door, but where does that door lead?

The Fae king doesn't grant me the courtesy of ignoring the hiccup in my composure. "Are you not certain of your solution?"

I collect myself. "I'm quite sure."

He takes a step closer. "Speak."

I counter his advance with a step back. "You asked, what's all and each the selfsame piece, plain truth and no illusion?"

The only acknowledgement the king has even heard me is a slight twitch in his royal jaw.

Summoning the strength I need to finish this, I continue. "Your riddle led us to seek proof of seven deadly sins from the world of human history and tales. I believe you set us on that path to mislead us. The answer to your question is not from the mortal world at all."

Despite his power stance and stillness, Finnbheara's chest stretches his dark silver tunic with every heavy breath.

I give a little curtsy. No harm in showing respect when I'm about to drop a bombshell. "Your majesty…" I meet his stare. "*You* are the answer. These mortal sins are all woven into the tapestry of your nature."

I manage not to drop my gaze as the king's glare cuts through me. His eye color shifts to the loamy brown of a shaded forest floor. Is he pissed we clawed our way through his trickery? Or are we wrong? Is he disappointed that the woman he created when he brought me to life with his *beads of being* was unable to tap into her Faerie wiles to solve his riddle? Have I proven myself unworthy of whatever portion of me is bound to his kingdom?

If only Sion were here. My bravery is incomplete without him.

Finnbheara finally breaks his imitation of a painted portrait. He strokes his sharp chin, settling it atop knuckles while the other fist presses into his hip. With slitted eyes, he speaks. "Am I not also concocted of those traits you hail as virtues? The very ones you aided the fox, a Veil guide, to restore to those in the soulfall?" He raises his arms. "I can be a generous and benevolent king when it is deserved."

My Veil sprites spin like hundreds of tiny windmills. It's no sting of warning, but rather appreciation for their king's logic.

"Eternity is balance, my treasure. Your journey through soulfall then riddle allowed you to experience this credo of my rule. How does one measure virtue without sin?"

The king's defense of his dichotomous nature is confirmation. We were right. Finnbheara himself is indeed the answer to his question. The riddle is the looking glass in which he cherishes his own image.

He offers no clear validation. Instead, those changing eyes scrutinize me nearly as hard as I do him. Finnbheara waves a hand over my head. "Creature of swan and oak, I acknowledge your ability to glean a correct answer to my query. The evanescence of your human spirit has indeed made way for the Faerie gifts of intellect and cleverness that I have bestowed upon you to flower."

A smile breaks across the king's face. For a moment, I'm breathless. He truly is strikingly handsome, a pure white rose, no, a silver rose in the full brilliance of bloom.

Hands grasp my hips, and he draws my body to his. "Yes, my treasure indeed, worthy of your king's attention."

Finnbheara's lips meet mine. It's no quick tap of congratulations for a job well done. Instead, his mouth covers mine, tongue sweeping in like the spin of a waltz. His arms are a prison. The hardness of his body against mine, a threat.

I force my hands between us and try to push him away. "What are you doing?"

My resistance doesn't faze him. Finnbheara laughs heartily and claps his hands twice. "Celebrating."

The mist thins, and with a theatrical reveal, presents a long banquet table laden with goblets, gold plates, and piles of sparkling fare from every Faerie story ever told. Glassy jewel-tone bubbles like the ones in the Gem Kissed Forest dance through the air. The silver green grass shifts into a plush carpet of the same hues. Beyond the table is a line of thin glass trunks bearing leaves made of emeralds and opals.

It's magnificent, a breathtaking aesthetic in a realm wearing a hidden heart filled with danger and cruelty beneath its loveliness.

"Come, my good fellows and ladies. Let us rejoice in the triumph of Finnbheara's Treasure."

As they did before, Faeries materialized where there was nothing but mist and air. These are not soldiers, but Folk wearing silken gowns and tunics of vivid hues. Off to the side, a quartet of Fae strum lyres. Dancers twirl in each other's arms without their feet touching the ground.

Insta-party.

I frantically search for Sion among the revelers, but I only see graceful Fae streaming around the table.

Finnbheara tucks my arm through his elbow. "Welcome to Tír na nÓg. Together, we shall carve an existence of great import here."

The initial shock from his kiss and the transformation of this place shears away. I pull free of the king. "You promised two souls may enter your kingdom if we solved the riddle. Where is my husband?"

He looks amused. "So hasty to collect your prize." The king scans the crowd. "I call the king's man. I wish to reward Robálaí Geal's fine work in guiding my treasure along the path to return to her rightful realm."

I create more distance between Finnbheara and me. Something is unsettling beyond the fluctuating focus of the king. He's completely blowing off our bargain by ignoring my request to see Sion. I'm missing something vital here.

Everything my studies taught me about the Fae suggests their sense of time differs from human perception. Did I overlook a crucial element in the bargain I made? Can Finnbheara let a hundred years pass before he allows Sion and me to be reunited? We spoke of no timeline for the souls entering his kingdom. Does that mean I've doomed my *anamchara* to the mercy of this king's fluid sense of being?

My gaze falls to a line of Finnbheara's guards in their white-gold breastplates with the leaf emblems. The soldiers whisper amongst themselves until the poor Faerie who drew the short straw approaches the king. She bows, then drops to a knee.

"Your Great Majesty. Robálaí Geal and his Host of A Thousand Wings never returned from the hunt."

I'm still close enough to see Finnbheara's muscles go rigid. I'm afraid he's going to kick the poor soldier or summon a bolt of lightning from midair to skewer her.

Her throat bobs as she swallows. "My king, it seems the host's dwellings in the Gem Kissed Forest have been abandoned."

Finnbheara becomes the personification of the wrathful being we pegged him as. His roar resounds throughout the clearing. The royal outcry over Robber Bright's exodus weaves stinging rays of power through the air. Finnbheara doubles in size, flexing superhuman biceps. Flames erupt inside every glass tree trunk, the scorch more akin to the fires of hell than a Faerie glade. The banquet table disappears along with its bounty and all the frolicking Folk.

When the king bellows, "Robálaí Geal," a second time, his mighty voice rocks the ground beneath me.

The moment the name of my renegade tutor leaves Finnbheara's lips, my skull feels as if it splits in two. I drop to my knees, clutching the sides of my head, screaming. Instead of white mist, I'm surrounded with gritty gray fog broken only by long blackened branches fired within from a blood-red glow. I've seen these before on the night the chainmail carried Sion and me to the siege of Kilkenny Castle.

The earth tilts, and I'm propelled forward toward a great black maw rising inside this fetid cloud. Instead of swallowing me into its depths, a great thunder gathers. Shapes break around me, scraping my flesh like bundles of needles. Sounds of snapping jaws and the cries of *péist síoda* are deafening in my ears. I'm helpless to evade the onslaught. Finally, the bulk of the hoard passes me, descending into the black abyss as jagged shadows. A figure at its trailing end halts, poised on the edge of the great pit.

The gloom thins enough for me to comprehend the sight before me. Robber Bright sits astride his silk dragon, Aillil. When he turns, I see the triple flamed breastplate he last wore. It's not the symbol of his betrayal that stops my heart. It's the woman in the saddle before him.

Colleen.

I try to run to her, calling her name, but I cannot move.

Robber Bright calls out, "*Oweynagat,*" then flashes me a final triumphant sneer before plunging into a realm of pitch and fire.

My body, soul, and spirit are as cold as death.

Oweynagat.

I know the place. It is also called The Cave of Cats, and legend decries it as one of the gates of hell.

Truth buries itself like a dagger in my breast. Robber Bright does not hide his destination from me. He issues an invitation.

As darkness closes behind them, a mighty flame explodes, setting the rocks mimicking great decaying teeth around the cave's mouth ablaze with black blood fire as my dearest friend is drawn into the jaws of the underworld.

Not long ago, I imagined Colleen to be a magical being as she danced with abandon in the glow of an early Beltane bonfire in the circle of standing stones where our university tour group celebrated.

Before a fox led me into the woods.

Before my bargain with a Faerie king.

Before I fell in love.

Now she's been swallowed into one of the dark realms in the mystical world that shattered my reality, and I'm the one to blame.

I open my eyes to find Finnbheara, returned to human size and standing over me, his expression contorted with fury. "Why is the shadow of Robálaí Geal within you?"

I'm flat on my back. No one offers help.

"My traitorous kin dares to pollute your essence with his filth, and you did nothing to stop him?" The king grabs my upper arms and pulls me roughly to my feet. "Speak." He shakes me as if he intends to snap every bone in my body.

My head continues to pound. The fear coursing through me doesn't help my ability to answer him. "I…I thought it was one of the lessons you sent him to teach me. He showed me how to heal, how to give Fae gifts by flowing through another's spirit. How was I to know it was blatant deceit?"

He shoves me, and I nearly fall again. "No permission did I grant him to insinuate his power into yours. That is a kingly gift he does not possess the right to wield." The force of the king's breath blows my hair back. "Spiteful, spiteful act to sully my prize. And still more treachery to pledge his host, *my* host, to another."

Robber's power into mine?

My blood chills at the king's revelation that Robber Bright forced something into me. Does it go beyond him sending me vision messages like the one he just sent of *Oweynagat* or the dream of the silver ship he forced on Sion?

The king's glare is relentless. His irises turn the color of a blood moon. "Robálaí Geal knew I would have taken you as my queen…" Finnbheara smashes a fist against his palm. The force of which causes the ground to tremble again. "…now a traitor's shadow has spoiled your spirit."

Even in the turmoil and potential danger of the moment, relief buds inside me. Finnbheara no longer sees me as queen material. The feeling is swiftly overshadowed by the knowledge that in my ignorance, I've given Robber Bright the ability to meddle in my Faerie essence.

Fae dealings walk a much more crooked path than I ever imagined.

I meet Finnbheara's glare with a look of what I hope comes off as subservience to a king. "Can it be undone?"

His eyes narrow to slits. "You permitted him passage. There are countless cracks that must be sealed in your lingering humanity before you are once again pure and free of his influence."

To my surprise, a sheen of tears momentarily softens the king's eyes. Are they born of rage, frustration, or something else? Surely, I'm not detecting sorrow from this ruthless dictator. Our gazes meet and for half a heartbeat, I see the true depth of the cut Robber Bright's defection cost this man.

Finnbheara flips a dismissive hand at me. "This is not our priority." He thumps a fist to his chest.

The king turns away from me and starts barking orders at his soldiers that have multiplied tenfold into a lethal-looking unit. He doesn't speak the name of the one he suspects Robber Bright's allegiance has shifted to, but *Oweynagat* points to one culprit.

Aodh, prince of the underworld, master of the triple red flame.

Aodh, whose crimson glow around the chainmail came so close to defeating our quest before we'd begun.

Aodh, whose passage of burnt branches stole Sion and me away from the hawthorn tree.

Aodh, the only rival Finnbheara has spoken of by name.

Aodh, the dark force behind the corrupted priest embodied as Jeremy Olk who wrought destruction in the Veil.

Aodh, ruler of the shadow realm where Robber Bright took Colleen.

Aodh—the enemy. My enemy.

Finnbheara's ire and accusations sicken me. Am I indeed tainted by something foul from Robber Bright's incursion through my spirit? But if the Fae had never shown me the art of one spirit communing with another, how could I have healed Sion or returned the Fae gifts Finnbheara stripped from him, and…

My chest constricts.

…How would I know except through my connection to Robber Bright that Colleen is in danger? The king gives the illusion of speaking in black and white absolutes, but if I've learned anything about the Fae it's that they truly exist in the dimension of gray tones.

The loyalty Finnbheara expects of me dictates I should share the vision of Robber Bright escaping into The Cave of Cats, but all I can think about is Colleen. Is she to be a pawn in the scalding strife between a god of the underworld and a Faerie king? If she wasn't my friend, danger would never have entered her life. I need to think, to sort this out away from the presence of a raging king.

I need Sionnach.

I may be a tarnished treasure, but I am still Finnbheara's creation, and we have a bargain. I'm sure it isn't the best time, but I'm afraid if I don't push my case through now, the chance might be lost to me. Sion might be lost to me.

Finnbheara has discarded his crown. He rakes fingers through his silver hair, pacing like a big cat trapped in too small a cage.

This is righteously unfair. I've returned to Tír na nÓg in triumph and been denied my due. I hoped to meet with a king who honored his promises. There's so much more I need from him. Sion first and foremost, but also to learn if the Glade of Chimes is truly destroyed. If so, what became of those who tend to the souls searching for their soulsongs—to Máthair?

Finnbheara finally stills, gazing into the mist that once again covers our surroundings. The changeability of his moods is legendary. I must take a chance he's reachable in this moment of pause.

I cautiously approach and drop to my knee. "Great king, given there are events of greater importance to demand your time, may we resolve our bargain so my current tainted status may no longer tax your mind?"

Preparing for another potential eruption, I dig my fingers into the silvery green grass to hold steady.

He stares at me, not speaking or moving. The only sign he's even heard me is the shifting of his eye color through so many hues, I can't grasp the name of a single one. When his irises finally settle, they wear the smear of the Veil's vibrancy.

The unreadable king clasps hands behind his back. The catalogue of his fluid personalities switches as swiftly and thoroughly as a bee seeking nectar in a flourishing garden.

The gaze of those tumultuous eyes targets me. His tone is a blend of curt and cunning. "If it's resolution you seek, then let us attend to it. Our bargain granted two souls permission to dwell in my kingdom." With a wave of his hand, a guard with short bronze hair and eyes to match, drags Sionnach into Finnbheara's presence, then shoves my love to the ground.

To my great relief, Sion doesn't look any more beat up than he was from our ungodly Veil ride. I rush to his side, but Finnbheara catches me around the waist. Malice strains the king's features.

"Peace, Eala Duir. For this man may not be that resolution."

Sion and I stare at one another as if it will keep Finnbheara from whatever menace he seems prepared to unleash. For a gut clenching second, I'm scared the king is going to revisit the unsavory topic of a Queen Eala. As to that, where the hell is Queen Nuala? Was she one of the Folk at our brief banquet? How many wives does a Fae ruler collect?

I tear myself away from the king, and he has the audacity to laugh at my distress. His smile lacks everything but trouble. "You may well be pleased that the bargain between us ripened unexpected fruit."

Finnbheara nods at the bank of mist blocking the depths of Tír na nÓg from sight. A shadow grows, then the abstract silhouette begins to assume the shape of a person. I detect the flow of a gown in its movement, a woman then. Is Nuala finally making her entrance to punish me for tempting her husband?

Fantastic. All I need is another Faerie who has issues with me.

Subtle golden light bleeds into the mist surrounding the woman. She carries herself with elegance and a confident stride. The next detail to emerge is reddish mahogany hair strewn with strands of shining pearls piled atop her head in intricate, twisted strands. Now, a skirt made of layer upon layer of minty green silk sways into view, followed by a bodice wearing the pattern of white-gold leaves and branches like the tunic Finnbheara wore when we first entered his kingdom. Her face is still a blank slate, except for the delicate glass circlet drawn across her forehead.

A queen to be sure.

Brushstrokes from the pale pink rose of youth bloom across skin the color of blanched honey. As the hazy shroud hiding her features recedes, I bend my knees to curtsy to the queen.

Recognition stops me cold.

Standing before us is no mythical queen. It's Máthair, my grandmother. Not the spirit from the Glade of Chimes, but the woman, a young woman, a beautiful woman. This is the woman who, for a time, won the heart of a Faerie king. The woman who struck her own bargain with Finnbheara to save her only child.

The enchanted, eternally young incarnation of Martha O'Dwyer Loho opens her arms. Sionnach, her son, and I, Finnbheara's gift to her, fly into her embrace. My anger and feelings of betrayal don't matter anymore. This is Máthair and love is all that's between us now. Tears, kisses, and cries of joy spill in equal measure from the three of us.

We don't have a chance for questions or lucid words before Finnbheara releases a long note of exasperation. "Touching, but irrelevant."

Sion's body goes rigid and violence flashes in his eyes. The two women who know him best each thread an arm through his, promising to restrain any intention he has of acting on his rage. I pray we can hold him back from inciting an unfixable tragedy.

"Stay with us, Sionnach," I hiss.

A corner of Finnbheara's lip rises. The bastard relishes the murderous mania building inside Sionnach which, of course, makes my soulmate's heat index rival the intensity of the *Oweynagat* hellmouth I witnessed moments ago.

The king exaggerates a pout and taps his lower lip. "Such a conundrum. You—" He points to me. "My creation *bested*—" He chuckles. "Yes, I am not ashamed to use the word since it must be those aspects of me contained in you, Eala Duir, that allowed you to claim victory in our bargain."

When he pauses, I wonder if he's capable of maintaining a consistent line of thought.

Finnbheara gestures at Máthair, Sion, and me with a rapid back-and-forth motion of his hands, signaling we should stand apart. Reluctantly, we mostly follow orders. Sion and I keep our pinkie fingers crooked around one another.

The king glares at our hands, maintaining silence until we release one another.

"Now," he continues, "our bargain allows two souls to enter Tír na nÓg and dwell in my glorious lands."

At his words, fog dissipates behind us, and the mighty gates of the Fae Kingdom gleam with their otherworldly radiance. They open soundlessly, like the outstretched wings of a swan taking flight.

Is a Fae ceremony required? Do we have to officially walk through the gates to greet our king and recite a Faerie oath? Sion's wound so tight, I hear rumblings in his chest. I pray he can keep it together long enough for us to fulfill the king's whims and finally be left to a real reunion with Máthair.

Here on the brink of entering eternity, I'm filled with awe at the workings of fate and embrace the miracle there truly is life after the life I know. The only thing souring this momentous step is the feeling of being toyed with by the Faerie king, so I speak up. "Yes, Sionnach and I are grateful to have earned our places in your kingdom."

Malice gleams in Finnbheara's now silver eyes. Shadows fall across his face, turning his cheekbones and chin as sharp as any archer's arrow.

"Ah." The king tilts his head. "So, the soul you choose to join you for this honor is indeed the fox?"

I'll say it as many times as the king needs to hear it. "Yes, Sionnach Loho, my *anamchara* will be at my side for all eternity."

Finnbheara nods. "So be it." He turns to the line of armored Fae as he aims a finger at Máthair. "Expel my former lover through the gates of my kingdom to the mercilessness void of consequence."

In a flash, two guards are at Máthair's side, dragging her toward the open gates.

With no forethought, I pull off an end run with Sion at my heel to block their way. "Wait. What are you doing?"

The king shrugs, not one worry line mars his handsome face. "We bargained for two souls. You have chosen."

"But Máthair, Martha O'Dwyer, already lives in the realm of the Fae. She's not part of our agreement."

Finnbheara extends a hand to the youthful version of my grandmother, as if granting her leave to speak.

Máthair turns and gently cups my chin. "I've dwelt in the king's lands first as a lover by choice and then as payment for the bargain…" She takes Sionnach's chin in her other hand. "…to save my son's soul." Her lips touch his forehead and then mine. "Never have I been granted the ultimate honor of calling Tír na nÓg my eternity."

I stare over her shoulder at the self-serving son of a bitch who doesn't attempt to temper his gloating triumph. Finnbheara said I'd bested him when the whole time; he knew it was all a lie. Treasure, my ass. I am his plaything.

Máthair strokes my feathery strands and Sion's fiery curls. "You are my hearts. I could wish for nothing more than to see your destinies intertwined."

I grab her hand. "Do you have a soulsong? Can you go to heaven?"

Sion breaks in. "Where is Da?"

"When I pleaded with Tim's spirit at our last parting to play his soulsong, he did so. Sionnach, know your father is finally at peace."

Máthair lowers her arm until we're holding hands.

Her evasion doesn't deter me. "Do you know what is beyond Finnbheara's gates?"

My grandmother's smile is too forced. She's afraid. "Nothing you need to worry about, *a stór,* only the consequences of what I bring with me."

It's as if the gates of Tír na nÓg are a sentient being. They've closed in on us and are open just wide enough for a single person to fit through.

Máthair draws Sion into a hug. "It's with peace I'll be leaving too, *mac,* knowing your light will shine all the brighter with Eala by your side."

She turns to me. "You've been more to me than the dearest of dreams, my beautiful girl. I regret no part of the bargain that brought you into my life. As my final gift, I give you and Sionnach to one another." Máthair places my hand into Sion's. Her smile is the light.

Máthair shores herself up to enter a destiny that, without meaning to, I have forced her to accept. She dips her head to Finnbheara. "I loved you once, and I love you again for the gift of Eala and my son's redemption." Then, ferocity every bit as frightening as the Faerie king's darkest glare, flashes in her eyes. "But now I curse you for choosing your own satisfaction over the kindness I've seen in that silver heart."

To my surprise, Finnbheara looks genuinely shaken. What I assumed had been nothing more than the king's lust and Martha O'Dwyer's folly between the two, now plays a deeper chord. Despite his cruelty and toxic narcissism, the King of the Connacht Fae cares for her.

Which means…

"Enough," commands Finnbheara. "Martha O'Dwyer, the choice is made. I expel you from the Kingdom of Tír na nÓg."

…I am a creation of the king. This realm, and not Máthair or Sionnach's world, is mine. My soul holds an inherent claim to the land of eternal youth, theirs does not. Finnbheara's kingdom is open to them only by invitation or guile. The success of my bargain with the king falls into the latter and affords the pair what they do not come by naturally.

There's no time to pick apart my decision for flaws. "Trust me, love." Grabbing Sion's shirt, I crush my mouth for a quick yet searing kiss, then repeat the oath he swore to me when the moon disappeared. "There will be no last for us."

A Faerie wind blows Máthair toward the open gate. Sion gapes at me, panic in his eyes as I sweep behind my grandmother and hurl her into her son's arms.

I stretch my hands toward the two people dearest to my heart—my life. "I choose Martha and Sionnach Loho to enter your realm." Turning my back on Tír na nÓg and my *anamchara*, I dive out the gates of Finnbheara's kingdom.

Through the receding mist of the Fae realm, Sionnach howls my name. As the merciless arms of my consequences reach for my soul, I do the only thing left to me.

I call the Veil.

Thank you for reading! Did you enjoy? Please add your review because nothing helps an author more and encourages readers to take a chance on a book than a review.

And don't miss the next book of the *Fae Destiny* series, A KINGDOM OF WITCHES AND WANDERERS available now. Turn the page for a sneak peek!

Also be sure to sign up for the City Owl Press newsletter to receive notice of all book releases!

SNEAK PEEK OF A KINGDOM OF WITCHES AND WANDERERS

EALA

Inside the Veil, Sionnach's cries of despair surround me like the decaying notes of a lament. I cling to the music of his voice as it deteriorates into a faraway echo…until it's gone.

The Veil is silent, no soothing notes of violin or gentle chime of bells.

I'm alone.

The poetic notion of a heart hardening to stone feels frighteningly real as I claw at my chest.

Sionnach, my soulmate, my *anamchara*, my fox, the deepest love I've ever known has been ripped away. The very situation we fought with our hearts, bodies, and souls to prevent is now a reality—and it's my fault.

If I'm entitled to breathe, I *must breathe.*

The Veil wavers, then pauses in an uncharacteristic stasis around me. Its scent of lemongrass and spearmint is faint. It waits for my intention to define the place I wish to be whisked off to. My spirit bleeds to be at Sionnach's side, but the Veil doesn't move.

Finnbheara, the very real King of the Connacht Fae lived up to his cruel and callous reputation. Only moments ago, he attempted to expel Máthair, my beloved grandmother, out of Tír na nÓg and into what he named the merciless void of consequence. Naïve me. I thought she'd already been gifted an eternal home in the Faerie kingdom. I was wrong.

Per our bargain, I earned the right for two people to live forever among the Faeries by solving Finnbheara's impossible riddle. My spontaneous choice to leave Tír na nÓg, granted those slots to Sionnach and Máthair. In the heat of the moment, I convinced myself my ties to the king afforded me the best shot at finding a way back into the Fae realm.

On this side of that impulsive rationale, the decision feels as absurd as my never-changing wish on birthday candles that my mysterious birth parents would suddenly appear. I swore the Faeries stole me away from them. Of course, I blamed Faeries for my abandonment after listening to a lifetime of my grandmother's Irish folktales.

I puff a bitter gust from my lips. I'd been right all along. Faeries, Finnbheara in particular, have always been the source of my troubles. Thanks to the Fae king and his magical *beads of being*, my origin story is reduced to a Faerie science experiment.

I shake off the self-deprecating definition. My soulmate's love proves I am a real person.

Here in the motionless Veil, the people I love most are literally a world away.

"Sion-nach…Sion-nach…Sion-nach," I whimper, thumping a fist to my breast with each heartbeat. A wave of unbearable pain hits. Both my Fae and human essences dwindle into an inky pool of regret and defeat. My Veil sprites, the luminous beings coursing through my Faerie spirit, are drowned from any attempt at overcoming the darkness. My muscles groan and bones quiver, threatening to transform into powder.

How can I survive this loss?

I'm a being devoid of form or spirit, but one made of agony alone. Where have I gone? Where is Sionnach's Eala *bán*, the white swan who banished the shadow from the land?

Now, I'm the shadow.

For two hundred years, Sion didn't give up on the soulfall. In two hundred heartbeats, I'm on the verge of defeat.

I failed him by leaving him behind. He would never let our separation stand if the reverse were true. He'd fight his way back to me.

I owe him my strength.

I push through the pain. Sion's Eala *bán* would not accept this as the end of our story. I must find her. I must be her.

"I'm coming for you, Sionnach." I close my eyes and will my swan wings to unfurl.

Beat.

Beat.

Beat.

With each stroke, my swan's confident spirit surges through me as I change from flesh to feather. We rise above the greedy darkness grasping for my soul. The Veil sprites rekindle and incandesce within me. I command the Veil to take us back to Tír na nÓg.

A silent breeze propels me through this mystical passage. My wingtips sketch ripples through the prismatic walls surrounding me. Up ahead, a circle of blazing brilliance marks the entrance to Finnbheara's front door. I'll demand to be admitted back into the Faerie kingdom and refute his hot-headed, royal edict of banishment.

I pray my abrupt exit shocked the king enough that he will accept he acted like an unfair bastard. Impulsive choices do not have to be endings.

My wingbeats falter from the weight of what I must overcome. Sion, Máthair, and I aren't the only victims of the Fae catastrophe. My lifelong friend, my sister of the heart, Colleen, has also been swept into this morass. To strike at me, Robber Bright, Fae thief and villain, enchanted Colleen and stole her away into the Oweynagat hellmouth. I shudder at the thought of her in Aodh's underworld kingdom, a hellscape so often painted with flaming pits and agonized wails of the dead.

Colleen is in danger and needs my help as much as my soulmate and my grandmother.

A fresh wave of panic wrecks the rhythm of my flight. I rebound off the shimmery Veil wall. Pausing in midair, I right my swan body and gather my thoughts.

As mercurial as Finnbheara is, I'm hoping I still have some value as *Finnbheara's Treasure,* the fraught and oppressive title he foisted on me. Even though admitting it sours my stomach, the king and I are irrevocably connected. I am one of his Connacht Fae. I've balked at fully accepting that truth too many times because my human life is precious to me. But going full Fae may be my last hope to rejoin my soulmate.

With a mighty stroke of my wings, I'm off again toward the gleaming circle. As I close in on my target, the burning white light intensifies. Its edges pulse with a golden corona made of dozens of fiery whips tipped in emerald barbs. They stretch then recoil with sizzling snaps.

My retinas throb. It's as if the sun itself leapt inside the Veil to block my way into Tír na nÓg.

"Finnbheara," I scream at the blaze. "Let me in."

The sparking tendrils shoot out to wrap around my wings in hot, thorny vines. They squeeze, mashing my feathers, threatening to snap my hollow bones beneath. Unaware of how damage to my swan translates to my human body, I transform. If I can't protect myself, how can I save the people I love? Fierce Faerie whips snake around my arms, torso, and waist. The cursed bindings threaten to singe whatever skin they touch.

With a teeth-cracking jolt, I'm yanked toward the inferno. Is Finnbheara dragging me back into Tír na nÓg or killing me? Raging heat burns my throat and lungs. Suddenly, like a boulder flung from a catapult, my body rockets away from the scorching light until I crash onto the Veil's forgiving floor. My arms are covered in thin, stinging, bright green welts. An electric shock crackles through my body then dissipates.

Is this yet another of Finnbheara's tests? Do I need to prove I will not be deterred from smashing my fist against the gates of Tír na nÓg? I stumble to my feet and run in the direction of the villainous light.

Before I've gone more than a few steps, the roiling blaze implodes with a deafening roar, knocking me backward and leaving only the wall of the Veil behind.

"Finnbheara, I'm coming in," I shout, pressing forward again. My hands reach for a door, a gate, an opening in the portal that isn't there.

My mind screams. *Take me to Tír na nÓg.*

The Veil walls shudder then still.

I repeat the command aloud. "Take me to Tír na nÓg."

Breaking the Veil's silence, three melancholy notes of a violin repeat over and over without ceasing. Is the Veil singing to me?

A more crushing thought takes hold. I lay both hands over my heart.

"Sion, is that you?"

Is my soulmate singing his soulsong to me as a farewell? There are three notes in a soulsong, the melody a soul plays in the Glade of Chimes to open the path to their chosen eternity.

"No, Sionnach. No." Tears finally destroy the barrier of my strength and fall in a ceaseless trail. They drip onto the Veil floor then rise as spectral haze. As each misty teardrop touches the silky elegance of the Veil wall, the bead solidifies, changing into a crystal that floats around me. Every gem shines with the multitude of hues born inside a rainbow.

As I weep, supplying more chromatic droplets, the Veil transforms around me into a shimmering chamber. It gathers my tears, reflecting them to me with a vibrancy that validates my sorrow.

These are worthy tears.

The Veil is home. We are kindred spirits.

Home.

The Veil may be my ethereal home, but Sion is my true home.

A swirling transparent circle appears in the Veil's wall. Beyond it, I see the Loho cottage with its whitewashed walls, thatched roof, red trimmed windows, and a door to match.

Home.

I burst out of the magic portal and run to the door. When my heart cried out for Sion and home, the Veil brought me here. This is where I belong.

Where we belong.

I pound on the red-painted wood. "Sionnach."

There's no answer. With a shaky hand, I retrieve the key hidden among flowers in the window box and let myself in.

I face an empty room. A minute ago, I belonged in the kingdom of Tír na nÓg. A minute ago, I had a *péist síoda*, a silk dragon. A minute ago, my soulmate was by my side for eternity.

What do I have now?

Sunlight bullies its way past swatches of gray clouds to shine through the rain-spotted windows of the cottage. The path of golden light encourages me to leave the refuge of the doorway and take a tentative step inside. Entering the home Sion and I shared ever so briefly without him feels like a betrayal.

The fragrance of the lady's bedstraw that fills the mattress of the king-sized bed in a nook off to the right makes my breath hitch. I stare at the place Sion and I made love first as soulmates then as husband and wife.

I see him in the two empty whiskey glasses we toasted our marriage with, in the stack of books next to his desk, in the landline phone on the kitchen counter he used to keep in the cupboard.

He's everywhere and nowhere.

It feels as if I've been away from the cottage for months. I expect a layer of dust to cover the simple wooden table then shake my head. It's only been one night…possibly. I need to see the phase of the moon to tell how much time has passed in the mortal world while we were in Tír na nÓg.

The passage of time used to be a steady barometer in my life. Not anymore. How much time will drip away before I see my beloved *anamchara* again? Will Finnbheara delight in robbing us of days or years this time?

Struggling to pluck a coherent thought from the chaos in my mind, I breathe in and close my eyes, calling on my Fae essence to awaken. It's healed Sion and me before. I hope it'll reset me now.

The sparkling energy flows through me, lightening my heart and clearing my head. I allow it to bathe my emotional bruises as well as heal the emerald stings on my skin from Finnbheara's strike. After a few more peaceful moments, I open my eyes and refocus on a single thought.

Get Sion out of Tír na nÓg.

Almost as soon as the thought becomes my beacon, rings of doubt hover around it. How in the deepest hell am I going to do that alone? I tried to return to Tír na nÓg, and Finnbheara attacked me then locked his gates. The Veil can't take me there. If I'm blocked from getting to Sion, how can I free him?

And Máthair?

"Oh, shit, Colleen."

The enormity of it all dizzies me again. I take wobbly steps to a chair at the kitchen table. Right where Sion and I left them are the scribbled notes we used to solve Finnbheara's narcissistic riddle. The one falsely promising to grant us an eternity together.

Atop the table, in the center of a splash of sunlight, glowing like the grin of an evil cat, is a gold ring.

Robber Bright's ring.

A key to unlock one pathway back to the Fae.

Don't stop now. Keep reading with your copy of A KINGDOM OF
WITCHES AND WANDERERS

And find more from Leslie O'Sullivan at
www.leslieosullivanwrites.com

Don't miss book three in the *Fae Destiny* series, A KINGDOM OF WITCHES AND WANDERERS, available now, and find more from Leslie O'Sullivan at www.leslieosullivanwrites.com

Betrayed and broken, Eala Duir has sworn vengeance against the Faeries who destroyed her life.

Once a promising folklore scholar in the human realm, her destiny with the Fae kingdom of Tír na nÓg, has cost Eala everything—her academic career, her position, her best friend Colleen, and most painfully, her soulmate, Sionnach. Torn from him by the treacherous Faerie king, Finnbheara, Eala will stop at nothing to reclaim what was stolen from her.

With her untamed Fae powers still unpredictable, Eala embarks on a desperate quest to rescue Sionnach and Colleen. Using the mysterious Veil, she journeys through time and place, gathering a team of legendary Irish women, including a witch and a pirate, to aid her against the Faerie king. But even their combined might and magic may not be enough to defeat Finnbheara's cruelty.

In a dangerous gamble, Eala is forced to seek out the Faerie, Robber Bright—the very villain who abducted her best friend. Desperate for his help, Eala risks her soul to strike a perilous bargain. But can she trust the one who has already betrayed her? The price of this risky alliance could cost her not just her loved ones, but her freedom as well.

A thrilling blend of fantasy and romance, this epic tale weaves together magic, betrayal, and a love that defies all odds.

Please sign up for the City Owl Press newsletter for chances to win special subscriber-only contests and giveaways as well as receiving information on upcoming releases and special excerpts.

All reviews are **welcome** and **appreciated**. Please consider leaving one on your favorite social media and book buying sites.

For books in the world of romance and speculative fiction that embody Innovation, Creativity, and Affordability, check out City Owl Press at www.cityowlpress.com.

ACKNOWLEDGMENTS

I am humbled and massively appreciative for the support and enthusiasm I received for Eala and Sion's story in *A Kingdom of Souls and Shadows*, Book 1 of this *Fae Destiny* series. A heartfelt thank you to all the readers, book bloggers, sweet people I've met at book events, and podcasters who reached out to share their warmth for the story in person, in reviews and on social media. I love hearing from you and hope this next part of our *anamchara* journey gives you everything you've waited for.

This series is a labor of love and means the world to me. It has provided opportunity and purpose to explore my Irish roots that I never had the chance to learn about from family. No matter how far they stretch or how thin they've become over the generations, those connections to the rich history, culture, and stories of Ireland are dear to my heart.

My belief that magic does exist in the world was confirmed when I listened to the amazing performance by Felicity Munroe on the audiobook of *A Kingdom of Souls and Shadows*. She truly brought the story off the page. I can't wait to experience the rest of Eala and Sion's journey with her. Thank you as well to John Keating who kept the authenticity of Irish language pronunciation on point.

Stories don't make it out into the world without people who believe in them; otherwise, writers would hide alone in their writing caves, drinking too much coffee. City Owl Press gifted this book with the perfect, nurturing home. Endless gratitude to Lisa, editor and cheerleader, who championed this Faerie story of mine until it became a book. Tina, Yelena, and the amazing team at City Owl, your creativity, guidance, generosity, and answers to my thousand and one questions make every step of the process a joy. Jenny your eagle eye copy editing is much appreciated. MiblArt your cover...Wow.

Shout out to my incredible beta readers, Lynn, Melissa, and Sarah, who didn't hold back and helped make the story so-much-better. Hugs all around to my intrepid ARC team, A Company of Readers – Go Team! Laura, my wonderful assistant, I owe my sanity to you. I raise a glass of expensive Irish whiskey to everyone who invested their valuable time reading, reviewing, and creating gorgeous visuals in The Nerd Fam campaign, and MTMC book tour for *A Kingdom of Souls and Shadows*. I can't wait to hear your thoughts on *A Kingdom of Deceit and Desire*, and to see your beautiful, artful posts.

Dearest family and friends, thank you never feels like enough. Your love and support are the brightest lights in my life.

To thirty plus years of my students whose love of story confirm that words are gifts to be treasured. I adored every moment of reading to you and with you. Thank you for putting up with all my voices and terrible accents.

To the wonderful Irish Fae, I promise to never cut down a hawthorn tree and vow to visit as often as I can. I do and always will believe in Faeries.

Let's connect: https://linktr.ee/LeslieOSullivanWrites

ABOUT THE AUTHOR

LESLIE O'SULLIVAN is the award-winning author of *Fae Destiny*, a romantasy series that explores the collision between the real world and the Irish Faerie realm. Her *Rockin' Fairy Tales* romantasy stories shine a new spotlight on favorite fairy tales set against the backdrop of a fictional Hollywood music scene. The completed *Behind the Scenes* contemporary romcom series peeks into the off-camera sizzle of a wildly popular Irish television drama. She's a UCLA Bruin with a BA and MFA from their Department of Theater where she also taught for years on the design faculty. Her tenure in the world of television was mainly as the assistant art director on "It's Garry Shandling's Show." Leslie is a voracious reader who loves to connect with other book lovers and indulge her fangirl side at cons.

www.leslieosullivanwrites.com

facebook.com/leslie.osullivanauthor
instagram.com/leslieosullivanwrites
tiktok.com/@leslieosullivanwrites

About the Publisher

City Owl Press is a cutting edge indie publishing company, bringing the world of romance and speculative fiction to discerning readers.

Escape Your World. Get Lost in Ours!

www.cityowlpress.com

facebook.com/YourCityOwlPress
x.com/cityowlpress
instagram.com/cityowlbooks
pinterest.com/cityowlpress

www.ingramcontent.com/pod-product-compliance
Lightning Source LLC
Chambersburg PA
CBHW072313020726
47501CB00002B/492